BOOK TWO

KINGDOM OF CHAOS

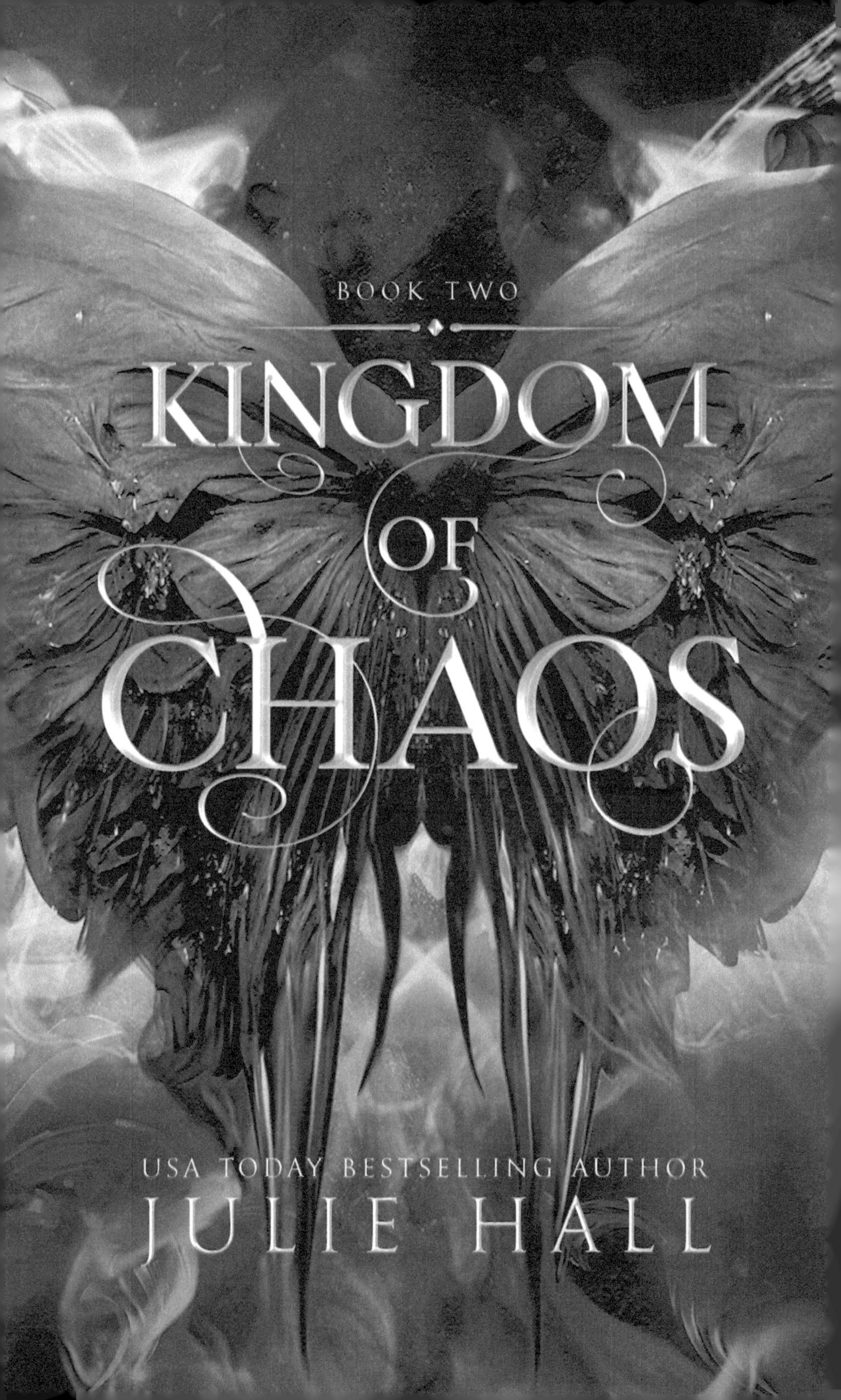
BOOK TWO
KINGDOM OF CHAOS
USA TODAY BESTSELLING AUTHOR
JULIE HALL

Kingdom of Chaos (Book 2)

Published by Julie Hall LLC

www.JulieHallAuthor.com

Editing by Lee Burton. Proofreading by Janelle Leonard and Priscila Perales. Cover Designs by Maria Spada and Damián Sanchez. Cover Typography by Lucas Hall. Interior artwork by Sasha Lee Coleman, Irene Barboni, Vivxor, Gracerstudios, Maya A., Damián Sanchez, & Koti Komori.

ISBN (paperback): 978-1-954510-25-8

ISBN (hardcover): 978-1-954510-24-1

ISBN (signed deluxe hardcover): 978-1-954510-23-4

Books by Julie Hall

JULIEHALLAUTHOR.COM/BOOKS

FALLEN LEGACIES SERIES

Stealing Embers

Forging Darkness

Unleashing Fire

Supernova

LIFE AFTER SERIES

Huntress

Warfare

Dominion

Logan

CURSED FAE SERIES

Cold Hearted

Faint Hearted

Broken Hearted

Black Hearted

SHADOW ANGEL SERIES

Book One

Book Two

Book Three

AUDIOBOOKS

Audio.JulieHallAuthor.com

Awards

JULIE HALL

Winner, Fantasy, YA, & Cover Design / *Creatures of Chaos*
2025 CIPA EVVY™ Awards

1st Place Winner / *Creatures of Chaos*
2025 Herb Tabak CIPA Choice Award

Winner, Fantasy & YA Fiction / *Creatures of Chaos*
19th Annual National Indie Excellence® Awards

Gold Medal Winner YA Fantasy / *Creatures of Chaos*
2025 IPPY Awards

Gold Medal Winner / *Creatures of Chaos*
2025 Illumination Awards

Finalist, Paranormal & Supernatural / *Forging Darkness*
2022 Realm Awards

Audiobook Finalist / *Stealing Embers*
2022 Realm Awards

Winner, Speculative Fiction / *Stealing Embers*
2021 ACFW Carol Awards

Gold Medal Winner / *Stealing Embers*
2021 Illumination Awards

Finalist, Paranormal & Supernatural / *Stealing Embers*
2021 Realm Awards

Finalist, Young Adult / *Stealing Embers*
2021 Realm Awards

Finalist, Readers' Choice / *Stealing Embers*
2021 Realm Awards

Parable Award Finalist / *Huntress*
2021 Realm Awards

Young Adult Finalist / *Stealing Embers*
2020 The Wishing Shelf Book Awards

Finalist, Speculative Fiction / *Huntress*
2018 ACFW Carol Awards

Young Adult Book of the Year / *Huntress*
2018 Christian Indie Awards

Gold Medal Winner / *Huntress*
2018 Illumination Awards

First Place Winner, Religion / *Huntress*
2018 IndieReader Discovery Awards

Christian Fiction Finalist / *Huntress*
2018 Next Generation Indie Book Awards

Alliance Award (Reader's Choice) / *Warfare*
2018 Realm Makers Awards

Parable Award Finalist / *Logan*
2018 Realm Makers Awards

Gold Medal Winner / *Huntress*
2017 The Wishing Shelf Book Awards

Best Debut Author / *Julie Hall*
2017 Ozarks Indie Book Festival

Best Inspirational Novel / *Huntress*
2017 Ozarks Indie Book Festival

Second Place Winner / *Huntress*
2017 ReadFree.ly Indie Book of the Year

First Place Winner / *Huntress*
2012 Women of Faith Writing Contest

***USA TODAY* Bestselling Author**
August 17, 2017 & June 21, 2018

To those who carry it all, the unseen.
You are beautiful, not broken.
You are worthy of love, of another.
Better together, to the end.

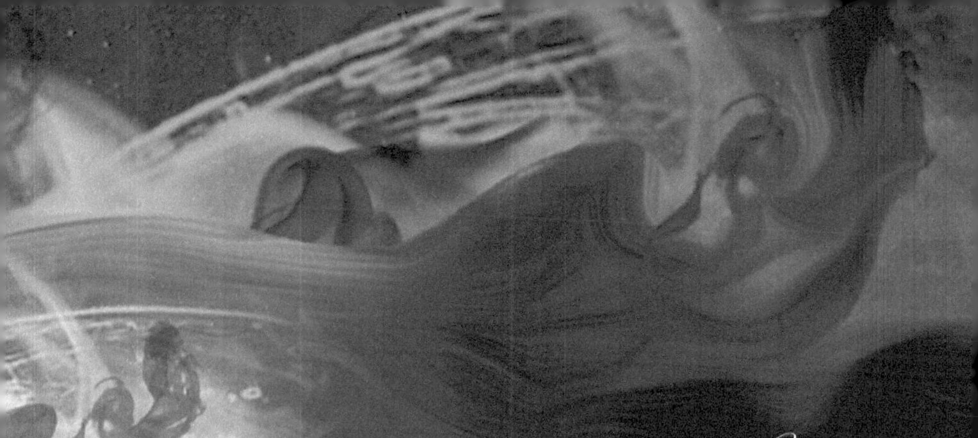

One

NUMB.

That's the only word to describe how I feel since watching Shadow Striker punch through Becks' chest right before the portal slammed shut in front of me. Since realizing everything I believed about myself was a lie.

I'm not a creature.

I'm *human*.

A being from an entirely different world.

Which means the creatures who raised me, the pair sitting across from me right now, waiting for me to say something, anything, probably aren't my parents at all.

We're gathered around the kitchen table, the three of us, like nothing's changed. Like my entire world didn't just implode. A blanket is draped over my shoulders. I can't remember who put it there. My hands are curled around a steaming mug of tea I haven't touched. Concern is etched into every line of my parents' faces as they watch me silently, helplessly.

I haven't said more than two words since they picked me up from the ruins.

The police called them in the middle of the night. I was too shell-shocked to even protest when they arrived. They haven't shown anger or disappointment yet, but I know it's coming.

Maybe I would've cared before. But now? I'm not sure I have anything left to give.

The longer I sit here, the harder it is to look at them. Because whether they knew I was human or not, one thing is undeniable. They knew I wasn't their biological child. They knew I didn't belong, and they kept that truth from me for almost eighteen years.

Regardless of blood, my mom and dad are, and will always be, my parents. But in this moment, they feel like strangers to me. As the repercussions of what went down last night start to break through the shock that's kept my mind hazy, they're not the ones I want to process this trauma with.

The sun is just starting to crest the horizon, its first rays slipping through the thin paisley curtains. Another day, but nothing like the last, and all I know is that I don't want to be here, sitting—doing nothing. I want to find Talon and make a plan to get Becks back. It's my fault he's trapped in another world, and I won't give up until I bring him home.

"Honey," my mom finally says.

She reaches forward to touch my hand, but I flinch away. I don't look up to see the hurt splashed across her face. I already know it's there.

A squeak of wood breaks the silence, and out of the corner of my eye I see my dad put his arm around her and pull her closer.

"Locklyn," he starts, but I push back from the table before he can get any more words out.

I know they're owed an explanation, even if I feel betrayed right now, but I just can't sit here calmly and give it to them.

Not when Becks is still out there. Injured. Trapped in a completely unfamiliar world.

Not when I need to talk to Talon and make a plan.

Not when I've barely had two seconds with Ensley to talk about what happened to her brother.

I don't have time to sit down and unpack our issues, let alone Chaos, right now.

"Where do you think you're going?" my dad barks as I start to walk away.

"To get cleaned up," I mumble, eyes fixed on the door.

"Sit back down," he orders, his voice carrying just enough flint and steel to make me pause in the doorway.

I glance over my shoulder to find my dad standing beside his chair. My mom is still seated, clutching one of his hands, her watery gaze flicking back and forth between the two of us.

"I don't have time—"

"You're not going anywhere until you explain yourself to your mother and me." His voice is steady, laced with firm command. "We've been pretty understanding about all of this so far. But you can't expect to walk out of this room without saying anything after we were woken up by a call from the police in the middle of the night telling us our daughter has been part of some dangerous underground competition for weeks."

I press my lips together, reading the resolve etched into my dad's face. He's not going to let this go. *Understandable.*

The magical noise-dampening barrier around the ruins wasn't the only thing to vanish the moment Kerrim and Becks disappeared through the portal. The magical gag order that kept anyone from speaking about Chaos to those who hadn't been there opening night disintegrated with it. By the time the police found Talon and me beneath the cathedral ruins, they already knew about the competition.

My parents, along with who knows how many others, now know the truth. Or at least fragments of it. More of those details are sure to surface in the coming days.

There was a time I wished for this. Wished I could confide in my parents, tell them everything. But things have changed.

"I can't do this right now," I tell them honestly, my voice low. "I'm sorry, but I'm just too tired. And there are other things I need to do."

Because while they may deserve answers, right now I need to focus on saving the person who took a blade for me. The one I left behind.

"It doesn't matter if—"

"Garrett," my mom says, tugging gently on his arm to stop him.

My dad looks down at her, his jaw tight.

"She's been through a lot tonight," she continues softly. "We can have this conversation after she's had a shower and some sleep. Let her be."

He frowns, clearly not thrilled with the idea. But I know from experience that while my dad may be big and burly, he's putty in my mom's delicate hands. He can deny her nothing.

Despite the swirl of emotions crashing through me, despite the distance I feel from them both right now, I can't help but marvel at the quiet love they have for each other. And not for the first time, my heart aches to have even a piece of that for myself.

But is it too late for that? Was Becks my one chance at a love like that, and now it's gone forever because he is?

I give a small shake of my head, forcing the thought away. I can't allow myself to think like that or I'll crack into a million pieces. Too many to ever put back together again.

Becks is okay. *And I will find him*, I say to myself, trying to cement those thoughts in my mind.

As expected, my dad glances back at me and gives me a tight nod. Without another word, I take the out I've been given, and flee.

I SLAM my fist against the solid wood door as hard as I can. It's quiet behind the imposing double doors, but I know someone's inside. I saw the curtain in one of the upstairs rooms shift, like someone dropped it the moment I looked up.

I pause for ten seconds, tops, before pounding again. I don't care if I'm being rude. That's the least of my concerns right now. What matters is that Talon's ignoring my messages.

My mind won't stop spinning with worst-case scenarios. Becks bleeding out. Becks being taken captive by Kerrim. Kerrim using Shadow Striker to finish Becks off.

The only thing keeping me even partially grounded is the hope that Talon might have some answers. I don't know how I'm going to reach Becks, but if there's a way, Talon is it. But he's not answering his phone. He hasn't responded to a single message. After everything that's happened, after everything we've been through, he owes me more than silence.

Maybe there's a reasonable explanation. It hasn't even been a full day since Chaos imploded. But rising urgency in my gut says I can't afford to wait. Time's running out for Becks.

If Talon won't come to me, I'll find him myself and get the answers I need.

I lift my hand to pound on the door again when it suddenly swings open. Drake Brayden's imposing form fills the doorway, a lowball glass of amber liquid in his hand. His hair is uncharacteristically disheveled, and his eyes are bloodshot. He smells like a distillery as he frowns down at me, his black brows a harsh slash above a hostile stare.

I'm not overly surprised to see Talon's uncle. This is his house, after all, and he answered the door the last time I came here, but I am surprised to see him in such a state.

"What are you doing here?" he barks, and despite myself I take an involuntary step back.

Drake is an intimidating dragon shifter. Standing over six and a half feet tall and powerful enough to hold a seat on the dragon council, he exudes authority. Despite my earlier bravado, it takes a second to gather my courage. What helps is remembering the role he played in tearing Becks and me apart. How he used Becks' freedom to blackmail me into not only ending things, but staging the scene with Talon to make it look like I'd moved on. Some of the blame for Becks believing I betrayed him lies squarely at Drake's feet, and that thought turns my apprehension into anger.

"I'm here to see Talon," I say, proud that my voice comes out strong and clear.

He narrows his eyes at me, then starts to close the door without a word.

"Wait!" I shout, jamming my foot between the door and the frame, stopping it just in time. He reopens it, just enough for me to see half his face and body.

"Where is he?"

"Talon's not here," he says flatly, and tries to close the door again, but I slap a hand against the wood, holding it firm.

"When will he be back?"

Drake shakes his head and lets out a humorless laugh. Without bothering to try closing the door again, he turns and walks away. I shove the door fully open and watch as he strides around the large black dragon sculpture in the center of the foyer, disappearing into a room beneath the curving double staircase.

I take a tentative step into the house.

Drake might be intimidating, but I've stood up to him once before, and I'm ready to do it again. I'm not leaving until I find Talon.

Striding forward, I move through the foyer, skirting the ugly dragon sculpture, and follow into the room where he disappeared. It's dimly lit, with dark wood trim and burgundy walls. Thick red curtains are drawn tight, blocking out any natural light. Wall sconces glow with muted faelight, and a fire crackles on the far side of the room, casting flickering shadows that leave parts of the space shrouded in darkness.

Drake is seated in a wingback chair in front of the fireplace, his gaze fixed on the burning logs as he slowly swirls the liquid in his glass.

I stop beside him, liking that I'm now taller than him. "Where's Talon?"

"I already told you, he's not here."

"But when is he—?"

"He's not coming back," Drake says, still staring into the flames. "He's gone."

Gone?

My stomach drops, and nausea prickles at the back of my throat. Talon can't be gone. He owes me. Owes me answers. Owes me his help.

"But . . . I need Talon to find Becks," I say quietly, mostly to myself.

Drake scoffs, a sneer tugging at his mouth. "Haven't you heard? The dragon heir is dead."

My insides twist painfully, like a lemon being wrung dry. "You know as well as I do that that's not true."

"Do I?" he says, his eyes locking with mine.

The leading theories about Becks are that he was either taken by the mysterious game master, who they believe intends to use him for ransom, or killed by the unhinged creature who orchestrated the nefarious games. The police now believe the entire point of Chaos was to trap the dragon heir.

Neither Talon nor I told them that Kerrim was the game master. What would have been the point? He was long gone, and it's not like they were going to find him. At least not in this world. Our official story was that we were knocked out when the floor caved in and only regained consciousness shortly before the police arrived.

But Talon must have told his uncle what really happened Friday night, which, admittedly, doesn't look good for Becks. Even as I've come to accept that Becks is gone, I refuse to believe he's dead.

"Becks is the strongest creature I know. He survived. But he doesn't understand where he is, and he won't know how to return," I say.

In his own way, Drake cares about Becks, even if it's only because he's the dragon heir. He might want to control Becks, but I know he doesn't want him dead. If there's a chance to get Becks back, I believe that would still be in Drake's best interest.

"Haven't you done enough?" Drake's tone is hollow and emotionless, but I still flinch as if he delivered a physical blow. As much as he blames me for what happened to Becks, I blame myself more.

"You care about Becks, or at least about your precious dragon heir," I say. "No one's looking for him because they all think he's dead. But I'm going to figure out a way to find him and bring him back. I need Talon to do that. So you need to tell me where he went."

Drake finally looks away from the fire, eyeing me as he swirls the liquid in his lowball glass. "They'll just pick a new heir. Everyone is replaceable."

My chest tightens. That's not true. Becks isn't replaceable. And anyone who thinks he is can go to hell.

"Tell me where he is, or I'll . . . I'll . . ."

I'll *what*? What leverage do I have to make Drake tell me anything?

Drake arches a brow. "Or you'll what?" he asks, echoing my thoughts.

I clench my fists, anger and frustration churning inside, threatening to boil over. Once again, I'm powerless against a powerful creature.

The frustration sharpens into fury. Before I even know what I'm doing, I slap the whiskey glass out of his hand. It sails through the air, shattering against one of the burning logs in the fireplace and sending a small burst of flame and embers into the air.

I step in front of him, forcing his full attention. A rough, guttural noise rumbles low in my throat, half growl, half warning, one I've never made before.

Drake's eyes widen as he stares at me, shock clear on his face.

"Where. Is. He?" I bite out.

Then something strange happens. As I stand there, struggling to rein in my emotions, the shadows in the room shift. Just slightly. So faintly I might have imagined it. They ripple across the floor and along the walls. The dim light from the sconces flickers, and for a heartbeat the room feels heavier, like the air itself is holding its breath. Out of the corner of my eye, I think I see dark ribbons curling at the edges of the room, as if stirred by some unseen force.

I blink hard and take a step back, shaking my head. When I look again, everything appears exactly as it was.

Calm. Normal.

Maybe it was Drake subtly asserting his dominance, or maybe just the exhaustion catching up with me. I haven't slept, and the last few days have pushed me past every limit. My mind must be playing tricks on me.

I take a steadying breath and glance back at Drake, who's now assessing me with a calculated gleam in his eye after my outburst. I don't like the look. I don't trust it.

"Talon's returned home," he says, surprising me with a straightforward answer.

"And where exactly is that?" I ask, crossing my arms to hide the slight tremor in my hand. Even though I know the shadows in the room weren't really moving, that it was just a product of exhaustion, I'm still a little shaken at the reminder of the powers creatures have that I lack.

A ghost of a smile touches Drake's lips, but it does nothing to put me at ease. If anything, it makes me more suspicious. He reaches over to the end table beside his chair, pulls open a small drawer, and retrieves a pocket-sized notepad and pen. He scribbles something down, chuckling darkly. "I can't wait to see what the Arcane Society does with you."

Does with me? What does that mean?

He rips the paper from the pad and hands it to me. "Either way, you won't be my problem anymore."

That might have been offensive if I cared one bit about Drake Brayden's opinion of me.

I glance down at the paper, my eyebrows lifting when I see where he's sending me: Grimbrooke. I've heard of the town, but I don't know much about it, only that it's on the coast and at least a half-day's drive away.

Folding the note, I shove it into my pocket with a sigh. I hadn't anticipated it would be this hard to track Talon down. He and I are going to have words once we're face-to-face. Words, or maybe a fist in his gut. I haven't decided yet.

"What's the Arcane Society?" I ask, stepping back as Drake rises and then goes over to a bar tray sitting atop a dark cherry wood cabinet. Lifting a decanter, he pours himself a new drink, downing the whole thing before pouring another.

"You'll find out soon enough." With a full new glass, he sits in his wingback chair, focusing on the crackling fire, effectively dismissing me without words.

I mumble a thanks, though I'm not sure why I bother. I don't truly have anything to thank Drake for. If anything, he owed me this address. After everything he and the meddling dragon council have done, I might never have entered Chaos in the first place. And if that hadn't happened, Becks wouldn't be lost in the human world. But half-drunk, slumped in his chair, alone in his dark, giant house, Drake looks pathetic enough that a small piece of my anger toward him slips away.

I shake my head as I walk away, not exactly wishing Drake well, but wishing that our paths don't cross again. That's the extent of the good will I have for the dark dragon shifter.

His voice rumbles from behind me just as I'm about to cross the threshold into the foyer. "Watch your back. You never know who your real allies are."

I glance over my shoulder and see that Drake has twisted in his seat. Our eyes lock, and a ripple of foreboding crawls down my spine.

I consider asking him what he means, but I don't trust him not to say something cryptic just to mess with me.

So instead I say, "I always have," and walk out of his house without looking back.

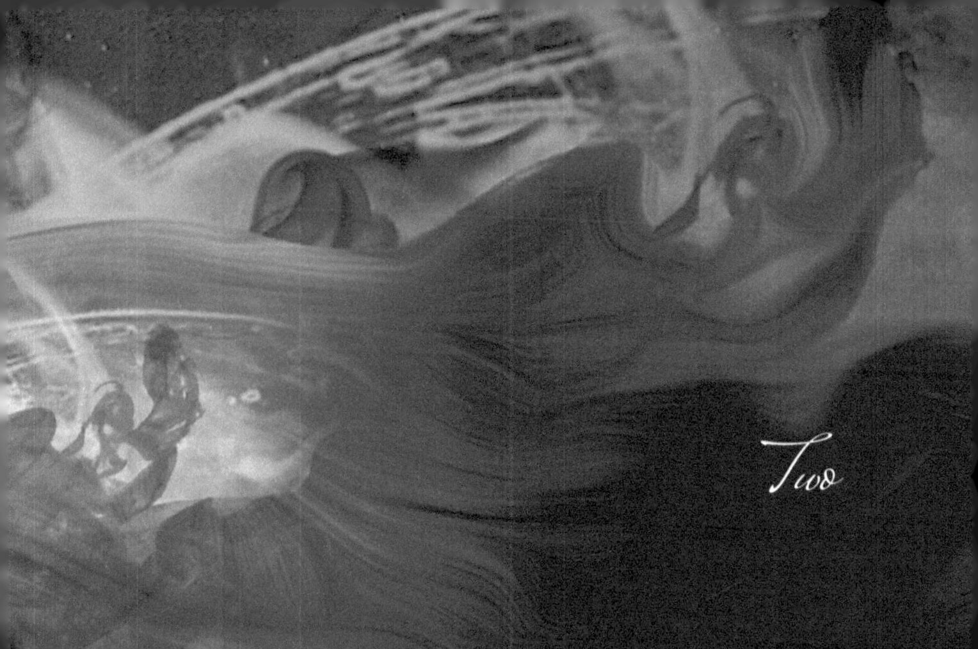

Two

I'M THROWING extra clothes into a duffel when my mom finds me.

"What are you doing?" she asks.

I freeze with a T-shirt clenched in my hand. When I look over, she's standing in the doorway in a pair of jeans and an off-the-shoulder sweater, scanning the mess I've made in my room and the bag I'm packing. Her long red hair is piled into a messy bun on top of her head, and from the smudge of dirt on her cheekbone I can tell she's been cleaning the dusty corners of the store downstairs. Her gaze is full of worried confusion.

I was hoping to make it out of the house without having to explain where I was going.

We haven't talked since this morning, and then I snuck out of the apartment to look for Talon. Between what the police told them and the few details I've shared, they only know the bare minimum about Chaos and everything that's happened over the last couple of months.

They know I entered and competed in Chaos, and that there was a magical gag that prevented me from telling them about it. They figured out on their own that I injured my hand during one of the trials, but that's pretty much it. I haven't told them about Kerrim, or his claim that I'm a human. They don't know what happened to Becks, and they certainly don't know that I'm planning to track down Talon and force him to help me get to the human world to look for Becks.

And I wasn't going to tell them either.

It's cowardly, but I had planned to sneak out and leave them a note explaining everything. I was going to tell them about Becks and that I was going to find him. About Kerrim and the claim that I'm human. About everything. But now that my mom is standing in front of me, a frown on her face as she wrings her hands, I know this isn't going to go the way I'd hoped.

Dropping the T-shirt into the open duffel, I straighten. "I'm going to find Becks."

Compassion softens my mom's features. "Oh, honey," she says and moves into the room, reaching for me like she's going to hug me, but I sidestep and she drops her arms. The hurt look that crosses her face spears me straight through the chest.

"You need to let the authorities look for Becks," she says, wrapping her arms around herself. "There's nothing you can do to help him right now."

I shake my head. My mom has no idea. No one is going to find Becks because they have no idea where to look. "I have to do this, Mom. You don't understand."

I go back to packing.

"Locklyn, stop." My mom lays a hand over mine, staying my movements. "This isn't the right way—"

"What do you know about the right anything?" I snap, my voice sharp enough to make my mom take a step back in surprise. I instantly regret both my tone and my words, but before I can apologize, my dad appears.

"What's going on in here?" he asks, his large frame filling my bedroom doorway. His dark eyes dart between my mom and me, quickly assessing the situation, his expression darkening when he sees the tears welling in her eyes.

My dad is normally a gentle guy, but not when it comes to his wife. I can already see him puffing up, ready to come to her defense.

I can't take the tension and animosity between me and my parents anymore. It's been building for longer than just last night. But ever since Kerrim dropped the bomb that I'm human, not a creature, a heaviness has settled in my chest, making it hard to breathe.

Seeing the confusion and disappointment in my parents' eyes breaks the dam I'd been holding back, and like a cork shooting from a bottle, the words burst from my mouth.

"Am I really your daughter?"

Both my mom and dad go still, their eyes widening. A buzzing sensation, like electricity running beneath my skin, prickles along my arms, and I rub them, trying to chase the feeling away.

My dad starts. "Locklyn, I'm not sure what you—"

"I know," I cut in.

"Know what?" he asks gently, stepping into the room, his presence filling the space.

"I know that I'm human."

A beat passes. He glances at my mom, exchanging a look that's not understanding—but confusion.

"Honey," my mom says, reaching out to touch me before hesitating. "We don't know what you're talking about."

I look back and forth between them, and a rush of relief surges through me. They don't know what the word "human" means. Just like I didn't when Kerrim first said it. And if they don't know, maybe it's not true. Maybe I'm *not* human. And if that's not true, then maybe what Kerrim said about them not being my biological parents isn't true either.

I sit on the edge of the bed, staring blankly ahead. My mom takes a seat beside me and slips her hand into mine. My head is pounding, whether from smashing it against the cave wall or from the weight of everything I've been trying to sort through, I'm not sure.

I can't make sense of this alone. So I open my mouth, and I tell them.

I tell them everything.

I tell them everything about Chaos, including the reason I entered it in the first place. I tell them about Shadow Striker and Talon. I explain the deal I made with Drake to free Becks from the dragon council's control. I walk them through every trial, reveal that Kerrim was the game master, and recount what happened in the ruins—with Becks, the portal, the other world. Finally, I tell them what Kerrim said about me being human. It pours out of me like a waterfall, unstoppable. And when the last detail has slipped from my lips, I look to my parents, silently begging them to tell me that Kerrim was wrong, that it was just a fluke, an accident that a portal to the human world opened when I touched the dagger. That I'm not this mysterious "*human*" he claimed I was, but truly their daughter in every sense of the word.

Because even though, deep down, I've always known I was different, the thought of not being theirs is too much to bear.

Silence blankets the room.

They let me speak without interruption, but now that I've spilled everything, every secret I've kept over the past two months, I think I might've broken them. My mom's hand feels cold in mine. Then I glance between her and my dad, and it's clear there's some silent communication happening between them.

Finally, my dad exhales a heavy sigh and scrubs a hand down his face. He looks at my mom and says, "It's time, Zia."

Her chin wobbles before she presses her lips together, resignation forming in the creases at the corners of her mouth and eyes. She shifts toward me.

I look into her bright green eyes, a sheen of tears gathering there. One glance tells me I'm not going to like whatever she's about to say.

"You need to know that we love you," she says gently, "and there is nothing, *nothing*, that could ever change that. You know that, right?"

I nod slowly, already dreading where this is going.

My dad steps forward and places a comforting hand on my mom's shoulder, whether for her or for himself, I'm not sure. Maybe both.

"What your mom is trying to say," he begins, "is that blood doesn't make us family. And there's no way we could love you any more than we do now, even if you were our own by birth."

No.

I jump up, taking a few quick steps back until my butt bumps into my desk, stopping me. I shake my head, not wanting to hear any more.

"So he was telling the truth. You aren't my parents," I say, my voice sounding hollow even to my own ears. "I'm not your real daughter."

My heart twists inside my chest, and tears spring to my eyes. Part of me knew it was true. I just didn't want to believe it.

My mom starts shaking her head and pushes to her feet, stepping toward me. "No, Locklyn, that's not true. You are our daughter. Our *real* daughter in every way that counts."

"She's right," my dad adds, his voice steady. "We've raised you since you were an infant. We've never seen you as anything but ours. You are our daughter, and we love you more than any creatures ever could."

"Then why didn't you ever tell me?" I ask, looking at them through a veil of tears, one finally slipping down my cheek.

"Oh, honey," my mom says as she pulls me into a tight hug. Even though I'm an inch taller than her, I feel like a small child in her embrace.

"Maybe we should have. But we didn't want you to ever feel like you weren't completely loved and cherished."

The scent of roses and daylilies fills my nose. My mom's natural scent. I always thought my auburn hair came from a mix of hers and my dad's, but now I know it didn't. It came from faceless creatures. Or rather, faceless humans.

I cling to her, feeling like she's the only thing keeping me from shattering. I used to secretly hope I'd one day take after her and develop fae magic, or gain strength from my dad's bear shifter powers. I dreamed of sharing those traits with them, of feeling more connected.

Now I know that day will never come.

It's like I've lost something, even though I never really had it to begin with, and somehow, that feels worse.

My dad's large hand lands on my back, rubbing slow, comforting circles. "We planned to tell you once your powers emerged," he says, pausing to clear his throat. "But when your magic never manifested, we didn't want you to feel even more different than we knew you already did."

Tears fall, from me, from my mom, even from my dad. They stay silent, letting me process, letting me absorb this truth.

When my eyes finally feel dry and my chest a little lighter, I step back. My mom lets me go. Her face is blotchy, probably like mine, and even my dad's eyes look a bit puffy. But despite everything, I feel somehow steadier.

Sometimes you have to fall apart before you can piece yourself back together.

"I love you guys," I say softly. "I'm glad you're my parents."

My mom lifts her hands to her face, covering her nose and mouth as silent tears stream down her cheeks. My dad pulls her into his embrace, a watery smile on his face.

"We love you too, Locklyn. More than anything."

I believe them.

It's only then that I realize how terrifying this must have been for them. They've known the truth all along but never knew how I would react. I wonder if that fear alone is what kept them from having this difficult conversation sooner.

Even though I now know for certain that I'm not theirs biologically, I still haven't unraveled all of Kerrim's claims.

"I need to know," I say. "Do you know who my birth parents are? Could what Mr. Brone, Kerrim, said be true? That I'm a human instead of a creature?"

My mom sniffs and wipes her eyes with the back of her hand. "Let's go sit down in the living room. We have a lot to talk about." She looks over at my dad. "Can you get it?"

He nods and leaves the room, and I follow my mom into the living room. The shelves littered with books and potted plants, my favorite parts of this space, offer a small sense of comfort as I sink into the worn leather couch near the window. My mom sits beside me, and my dad joins us a moment later, carrying a small wooden box clasped between his large hands. He sets it gently on the coffee table and takes a seat in the armchair across from us.

"Your mom and I tried for years to have a baby," he begins, the pain of that time still visible in his expression. My mom gives him an encouraging smile, and he continues. "This was back when we lived farther west, near your grandmother. One night, we were contacted by someone who said they knew we were trying to start a family and asked if we would be interested in adopting a baby girl."

"It all happened so suddenly," my mom adds. "It was a private adoption. We were told the baby needed a home right away, and the paperwork had already been drawn up if we were willing. We said yes, and it felt like almost the next moment someone was at our door with a bundle in their arms. We didn't even have a crib for you that first night."

Her face brightens with the memory. "But that didn't matter. The moment we laid eyes on you, we fell so completely in love, we didn't want to let you go. We took turns holding you all night. Just cuddling you and counting your perfect, tiny fingers and toes. You were a miracle. Our miracle." Her eyes shine with unshed tears, but her smile is radiant.

My dad smiles, tears gathering in his eyes for the second time today. "You were the most perfect little chubby baby. When you grabbed my finger, your tiny hand could only wrap around half of it. We knew in that moment that you were meant to be ours, and we were meant to be yours. We never questioned that."

My mom reaches up and wipes a tear from my cheek, and that's when I realize I'm crying, too.

"Who brought me to you?" I ask, my voice soft. "What did they tell you about me?"

My parents exchange a somber look.

"We don't know," my dad admits.

"How is that possible?" I ask, confused.

"A fae woman brought you to us. We'd never met her before. She said you'd been abandoned and needed a home. After the papers were signed, she left you with us. We never saw her again."

"What?" I don't know much about adoption, but I know that's not how it's supposed to work. "Did you try to find her?"

My mom nods. "Yes. We tried. But we didn't have much to go on, and we were afraid that if we made too much noise, someone would take you from us."

I lean back into the sofa, my mind spinning. "What about the paperwork? All the legalities?"

"She had everything prepared. Including a birth certificate with our names on it. Legally, you were already ours," she says.

"But, what if I'd been kidnapped or something? What if I had a birth family out there looking for me? Without any history, how do you know I wasn't brought to you by nefarious means?"

My mom chews her bottom lip and glances at my dad.

"We should have considered all of that," he admits. "We probably should've done a lot of things differently. But to be honest, everything felt so right in here"—he taps his chest—"that we didn't really think about the consequences. We moved to Everton shortly after you arrived, and because of the blend of red and brown in your hair, everyone just assumed you were our biological child. And we never corrected them."

"Wait. What about Grandma? Does she know?"

"Yes, your grandmother knows," my mom says. "You don't have any aunts or uncles, and your other grandparents have passed. We made new friends when we moved and opened the business."

"The birth certificate we were given has our names on it as well," my dad adds. "No one knows about your adoption except your grandmother and us."

"And Kerrim," I add, unable to even think of him as Mr. Brone anymore.

Taking a deep breath, I force myself to readjust my reality. "So then, it's possible what he said is true. I'm not a creature."

"Hold on," my dad says. "We don't know that."

"Don't we?" I ask, arching a brow. "I never developed creature powers like I should have. No doctor has ever picked up so much as a speck of magic in me. And on top of that, I saw the portal open with my own two eyes when I grabbed Shadow Striker. I saw Becks and Mr. Brone go through it, and I saw it close behind them. That's real. And right now, everything points to Kerrim's claims being real too."

My mother clasps my hand. "I'm so sorry for what you went through. Chaos was diabolical. I'm here—" She glances at my dad when he clears his throat. "I mean *we're* here if you want to talk about anything. And I understand if you can't right away, but I hope someday you can forgive us for what we did."

Forgive them? For loving me? Raising me? Being responsible parents who only wanted the best for me?

Finding out I was adopted is certainly a shock, and I'm not happy I found out from someone else, but I'm also mature enough to understand where they're coming from.

"Maybe I don't agree that you didn't tell me sooner, but it

doesn't mean I love you any less," I assure them, and I can tell right away that they're relieved.

They're not going to like what I have to say next, so I might as well rip the bandage off. I stand, and both of my parents raise their eyebrows.

"Thank you for telling me all this and being honest with me. It means a lot, and I'm glad we finally talked about it, even if it was hard. I meant what I said. You are my parents, no matter what. And I know you both want me to stay safe, but I have to leave."

"Leave?" my dad asks, a furrow forming between his brows.

"I have to find Talon and convince him to help me get Becks back. He's the only person who might know another way to reach that other world."

My parents exchange conflicted looks.

"You can't just pick up and leave," my mom says, wringing her hands. "What you're talking about doing is dangerous."

"Mom," I say, locking eyes with her, "I can't give up on Becks. You've known him for years. He's stood by me when almost no one else would, never caring that I was different. If the situation were reversed, you know he'd go to the ends of the world, and beyond, for me."

"But what about school?" she asks. "You're only weeks from graduation."

I almost laugh at that. *School.* Who cares about that at a time like this?

"I can go to summer school to graduate," I say, the words tasting as gross as they sound, but for Becks I'll endure.

"You want us to just sit back and let you go?" my dad asks.

I square my shoulders. "Yes, I do. I'm not saying it's going to be easy for you, but I'll technically be an adult in a few weeks. I have to do this, and you can't keep me here. I'd prefer to leave with your blessing, but I'll go without it if I have to."

"But how are you even—?" my mom starts, and to my surprise, it's my dad who stops her with a hand this time.

"Will you promise to keep us updated as much as possible? If there's a way to get in touch with us and let us know you're safe, I want your word that you'll reach out."

My dad's gaze bores into me, and I swallow past the lump in my throat. "I promise."

He nods, his face a stone mask, but I can see the concern shining in his eyes. This isn't easy for him, but he knows it's something I have to do.

I'm about to turn to leave when my gaze snags on the wooden box my dad brought in at the start of our conversation. I cock my head and point to it. "Is that anything important?"

"Right." My dad grabs it and turns it over in his hands. "This is yours. You were wearing it the night you came to us."

"We got a new chain for it," my mom says with a wobbly smile. "We were planning to give it to you at graduation, but now feels like the right time."

My dad holds out the box for me, and after sitting again, I take it. Even though it's small, it looks large in my hands compared to his. It's a clamshell box, so I crack the top open. Nestled in velvet is a pendant necklace.

Grasping the thin gold chain, I lift it, letting the purple stone pendant dangle in front of my face for a closer look. Light reflects off the teardrop-shaped gem, sending red rays dancing from its angles. I've never seen anything like it before.

"What kind of stone is it?" I ask.

"We don't know, actually," my mom says.

"We took it to a couple of jewelers when you were an infant, but they didn't know either," my dad adds. "One wanted to send it away to get tested, but parting with it didn't feel right."

The pendant's design is simple. The teardrop stone is held in place by a plain gold mount through which the chain is threaded. The stone itself is the true standout. The deep purples are unlike anything I've ever seen.

Maybe it's just because it feels like a small clue to where I'm from, but even though it isn't ornate or elaborate, I instantly feel connected to it.

"I love it."

I don't realize I'm smiling until I glance at my parents.

"We're glad," Dad says. "I just wish we had more answers for you."

I take a deep breath. I don't need any more answers right now. Becks is the priority. But there's a part of me that clings to the hope that I might find some answers about myself along the way.

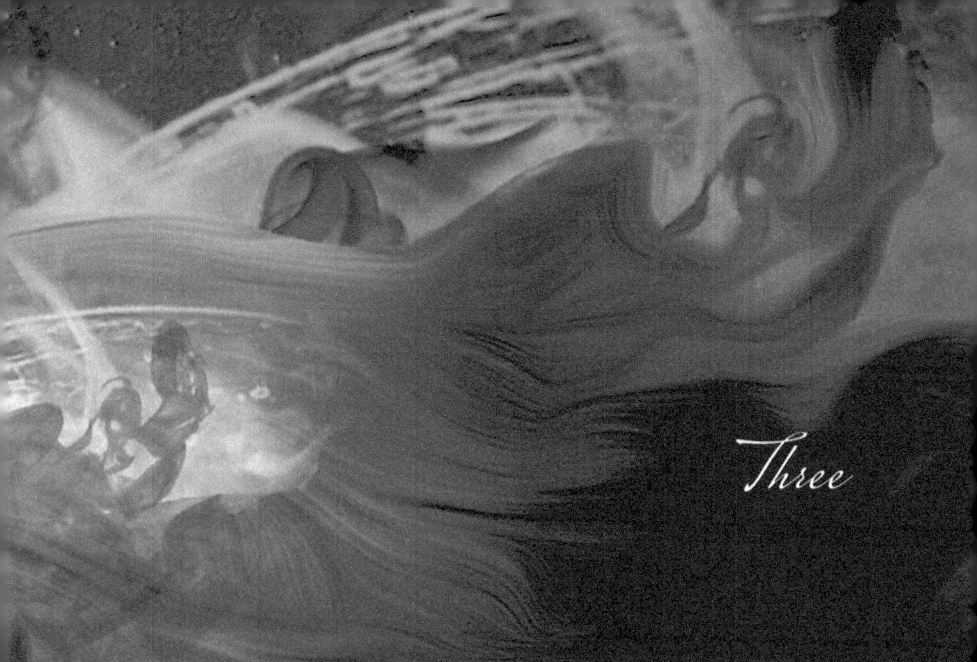

Three

THE FASTEST WAY TO get to Grimbrooke is by car. I could take a bus or a train, but there's no direct route from Everton to Grimbrooke, and I'd rather not waste any more time. The problem is that my parents don't have a spare car, but I know someone who does.

After a tearful parting with my parents, during which they make me promise at least three more times that I'll keep them updated whenever I can, I hop on the local bus with my small duffel and backpack and soon find myself standing on Ensley and Becks' doorstep. I probably should have given Ensley a heads-up that I was coming over, but I want to explain in person why I need to borrow her brother's car. I owe her at least that much.

I stow the duffel and backpack off to the side. Ensley's going to ask about them right away, and I might want to work up to the part where I ask for Becks' truck. I rap my knuckles against the door. I'm barely finished knocking when it swings open.

Mr. Ashford, Becks and Ensley's dad, stands there with a hopeful look on his face. When he sees that it's me, he deflates, taking the light out of his green eyes—eyes that are so much like Becks it makes my heart squeeze to look at them.

"Is it Captain Griffin?" I hear from behind him, just before

Mrs. Ashford pokes her head around her husband. Like him, a little of the light dims from her eyes when she sees me. "Oh, Locklyn. It's just you."

I'm not put off by the hint of disappointment in her voice or the way both their shoulders seem to sag a little as they step back to let me in. They're worried. They don't know what's happened to their son, and they're wrecked over it. Although they appear to be working with the police to find information about Becks' whereabouts, I know they're not going to be able to uncover anything.

"Umm, is Ensley here?" I ask, glancing between them.

Mr. and Mrs. Ashford are usually so pristine and put-together; it's a little jarring to see them like this. Dark smudges sit beneath their eyes, and their clothes are rumpled. As co-owners of a lucrative beauty company, I'm used to seeing them dressed in designer outfits, with perfect hair and glowing complexions.

Mr. Ashford's chestnut hair is disheveled, almost like he's been repeatedly running his fingers through it. With her hair blonde like her children's, and her flawless honey-toned skin, Mrs. Ashford is beautiful regardless, but it doesn't even look like she's wearing any makeup. I honestly can't remember ever seeing her with a fresh face before. In some ways, it makes her appear even younger, and certainly more vulnerable.

Mr. Ashford is equally dressed down in joggers and a T-shirt, which is also a look I've never seen on him before. He works on the development side of B&E Beauty, using a blend of chemistry and magic to imbue products with fae glamour, while Mrs. Ashford is the business mind of the operation, acting as CEO.

Even though they work a lot and Becks and Ensley see less of their parents than I see of mine, I've never doubted that they love and care for their children. The evidence of just how much Becks means to them is written all over their faces and in their disheveled appearance.

"Ensley?" Mrs. Ashford repeats, seeming almost confused for a moment before she shakes her head. "Yes, yes. Of course. I'm so sorry. I haven't slept much."

Mr. Ashford wraps an arm around his wife's waist and pulls her close, placing a kiss on the top of her head. "It's all right, dearest. We're all a little discombobulated right now."

My heart aches for them, but seeing them like this only hardens my resolve.

"Ensley's up in her room, I think," Mr. Ashford says.

I nod and take a step in that direction, then pause. "I'm so sorry. I really believe Becks is going to be okay," I say, trying to tell them without actually saying that I'm going to bring their son home.

The small smiles they muster let me know they aren't convinced.

"Thank you, Locklyn. We know how close you are with both our children. I know you must want him home almost as much as we do."

That comment sits in my stomach like a rock. It couldn't be clearer that Becks never told them how things had changed between us. I can see it in their eyes. They have no idea what Becks really means to me. What we mean to each other. And maybe it shouldn't, but it bothers me.

I tell myself he was probably waiting until things settled down. His parents weren't exactly against his arranged life-mating, and it's probably not super common for guys to talk to their parents about their love life anyway. There are plenty of perfectly reasonable explanations for why he didn't say anything, so I shouldn't be surprised that, to them, I'm still just Becks' good friend.

But I am.

I smile politely and mumble my agreement, all the while wondering if that sick feeling in my stomach isn't surprise at all, but rather an ugly mix of sadness and disappointment that I'm too emotionally overloaded to fully recognize.

The body will go to extreme measures to protect itself, and

surprise is a simple emotion, one easy to brush aside and move on from. But my feelings for Becks, and the complexity of our undefined relationship, are neither simple nor easy.

I head toward Ensley's room on autopilot, finding myself in front of her door without even remembering the steps to get there. I'm about to knock and ask if I can come in when the rumble of voices from inside makes me pause. I recognize Ensley's familiar tone right away, then I hear the low timbre of a male voice and my body locks up.

Becks?

My heartbeat stumbles as I scramble for the door handle and shove it open, my gaze darting wildly around the room. Ensley's sitting on the edge of her bed, her eyes puffy and rimmed with red. And beside her, carefully holding her hand, is . . . not Becks.

Titus?

I blink, stunned to see the tattooed, white-haired fae in her bedroom. *Since when are these two close?*

Tearing my eyes away from Titus, I glance back at Ensley. Her face mirrors my shock, but she quickly slides her hand out of his and stands up. She tucks a strand of her blonde-and-blue-streaked hair behind her ear. Sometimes she uses her fae glamour to match her hair to her mood. Blue seems intentional today.

"Do you have any news?" she asks eagerly, padding over to me with eyes full of hope.

I wince, instantly regretting that I didn't warn her I was coming. When I shake my head, her face crumples and her shoulders slump.

It feels like I've been sucker punched in the gut.

This is all my fault.

"But I have a plan," I say.

Ensley doesn't perk up like I'd hoped. She nods, her eyes taking on a faraway look.

Titus comes up behind her, and although he doesn't touch

her, the move feels protective, like he wants her to know he has her back. I don't know why, but it makes me bristle a little.

I trust Titus. Kinda. Sorta. But the vibe between the two of them is throwing me off. He's only met Ensley once. What's he doing chilling in her room and holding her hand? After discovering the mountain of secrets Talon kept, and how deeply Kerrim deceived me and my family, saying I have trust issues would be an understatement.

"Hey, Titus. I didn't expect to see you here." My tone isn't exactly hostile, but it's not warm either. Ensley isn't paying enough attention to notice, but Titus' eyebrows rise.

"I figured there weren't a lot of creatures for her to confide in right now, considering the circumstances around Chaos and that cursed dagger."

Oh shoot. That was surprisingly thoughtful.

Whatever guard I'd put up slips. Besides Talon and me, Titus is the only other creature who knows the truth, or at least a good portion of it. Ensley can't even speak openly to her parents. They don't know about Shadow Striker. They don't know I'm human. They don't know I accidentally opened a portal to another world. And they definitely don't know their son is trapped there.

He's right. Ensley needs someone right now. Someone besides me. And as much as I want to protect her, shutting him out would only leave her more alone. Denying her that support would be cruel.

I nod toward Ensley, who's wandered off and is staring out the window like she doesn't even realize we're here. "Thanks for being there for her."

"No problem," he says, his gaze drifting over to her, and I swear his face softens a little. Clearing his throat, he looks back at me. "How are you doing?"

I shrug. "I'm fine."

"You seem . . . different."

"Different how?"

He hesitates. "You remember I'm a truth reader, right?"

I nod slowly.

"I can usually sense truth without fully activating my magic. But with you? It's always been blank. Until now."

My brow furrows. "What do you mean?"

He shrugs, a little too casually. "Just that for the first time I picked something up. A flicker. It's never happened before. Thought that was interesting."

"What's your plan?" Ensley asks and I start, not even realizing she's walked back to join us.

"My plan?"

"You said you had a plan," she prompts. "I'm assuming it has to do with Becks?"

"Right," I say, pushing Titus' small revelation about me to the back of my mind. "Well, first I need to find Talon."

Ensley tenses, her expression darkening at the mention of Talon. Apparently, I'm not the only one a little peeved with the dark-haired creature right now. I wonder if she thinks things might have turned out differently if he'd been completely honest with us. I know I do. He kept secrets. Right up until the end.

"Why do you need *him*?" she asks, the sharp edge in her voice confirming my suspicion that she wants nothing to do with Talon.

"When he was talking to Kerrim, Talon mentioned gateways between the worlds. He said they'd been closed for hundreds of years. But if they were closed, then maybe they can be reopened."

"You're saying you're going to try to get to that other world? The human one?"

I nod. "I'm going to find Becks and bring him home."

Her eyes widen, and even Titus looks taken aback.

"But I need Talon's help to do it. I don't know the first thing about these gateways. Where they are or how to open them. I think whatever secret group or cult he's involved with was the one who closed them. As much as I hate to admit it, I think he's my best chance at finding Becks and bringing him back."

"Well then, let's go ask him," Ensley says, grabbing her jacket from the back of her desk chair and heading for the door.

I hold up a hand to stop her. "It's not that easy. I already went to his house. He's not there anymore. His uncle said he left."

"He skipped town?" Titus asks, a furrow creasing his brow.

"He did. But I pried the address out of Drake."

Titus barks out a laugh and then looks at me with respect. "I wish I'd been a fly on the wall for that conversation."

The memory of the shadows shifting, pulsing, reaching forward, flickers through my mind. If he only knew.

"Talon lives in Grimbrooke," I say. "And that's why I'm here. I need to borrow Becks' truck to get there."

Ensley shakes her head. "No."

"But, Ens—"

"There's no way I'm letting you go there alone. I'm coming with you." I start to argue, but she holds up a hand to stop me. "You're not the only one who wants answers from Talon."

She has a point. If she wants to confront Talon, she deserves the chance. But with Becks gone, this doesn't feel like the best time for her to leave her parents. I bring it up, but she brushes it off, saying they barely notice she's around right now. I'm skeptical, but it's not my call.

"I'm coming too," Titus says as Ensley starts tossing things into a small overnight bag.

I shoot him a look, and he holds up a hand too. "Talon's the one who dragged me into all this. I'm part of it, whether either of you like it or not."

I don't argue. He's right. And while I don't know him as well as I'd like, having him along might not be a bad thing. The way his eyes keep drifting to Ensley tells me his real reason for coming, but I don't mind. She's in a fragile place. She can use all the support she can get.

Titus takes off to grab his things, and we agree to swing by and pick him up on our way out of town. While Ensley finishes packing, I grab my backpack and duffel from outside her front door and head around to the side of the house to their six-car garage. I don't have to wait long. The garage door lifts, and her red sports car rolls out.

She pops the trunk and I toss in my bags, sliding into the passenger seat. "What did you tell them?"

"The truth," she says as she pulls out of her driveaway and points the car east.

My eyebrows raise. "Seriously?"

She shrugs. "Mostly. I told them I was going to go out of town with you for a couple of days because I needed to get away from everything. They were cool with it. What about your parents?"

I take a deep breath. "They know everything."

"Everything?" Ensley asks, her eyes wide when she takes a peek at me before focusing back on the road.

"Yep. I told them everything. And so did they."

Ensley's brow creases. "What do you mean?"

"Kerrim wasn't lying. I'm not their biological child. The details around my adoption, if that's even what you can call it, are sketchy at best."

Her face falls, guilt flashing in her eyes. "Shoot, Lock, I'm so sorry. I've been so torn up over Becks that I haven't been there for you."

"No, it's okay. Yeah, it was a shock finding out I'm not a creature, learning I was adopted, but it's not the end of the world. My parents are still my parents and I'm still me. Right now, finding Becks matters more than any of that."

She reaches across the console and gives my hand a squeeze. "Yes, finding Becks is important, but this is huge too. I know you have to be feeling *something* about it. You shouldn't feel like you have to bottle it up."

"Honestly, I just don't have the bandwidth to deal with it right now. I hear you, but there'll be time for that later. Once Becks is back and safe, then I'll unpack that whole can of worms."

It's the only way I can function—by pushing it all down. Falling apart isn't an option.

Ensley's gaze is full of concern, but she just nods. We turn off the main road and head down Titus' driveway. His house is on the outskirts of town but still within the Nightlark Academy district.

I wonder why I never met him before Chaos. Maybe he's a year or two older? Still, if he went to Nightlark, we would've crossed paths. Maybe he's new to the area?

The driveway is long, winding through trees and brush, before finally opening up in front of a large stone manor. Green and red ivy climb the walls, and purple wisteria drips from the eaves. The front foliage looks a little wild, but with night fully fallen, it's hard to make out the details. The only light comes from two gas lanterns on either side of the front door, casting a warm glow over a home that looks like it belongs in a fairy tale, ancient and achingly beautiful.

"Titus lives here?" I ask, surprised. I don't know why, but I pictured a more modern place.

"This is the address he gave me."

Before we even have a chance to get out of the car, the front door swings open and Titus comes bounding out with a black bag slung over his shoulder. Ensley pops the trunk and he tosses it in. I step out to let him into the seat behind me, and we quickly realize he's not going to fit back there. With a sigh, I crawl into the back instead. Sometimes, it really sucks to be vertically challenged.

"What did your parents say when you told them you were leaving?" I ask as Ensley turns the car around and heads back toward the main road.

"Nothing," he says.

I give him a look.

"I don't live with my parents."

My jaw drops. "You live out here all alone in that huge house?"

He shrugs. "It's a family house."

I twist around, trying to catch another glimpse of the manor through the rear windshield, but we're already too far away. It's not quite as massive as Ensley's or Drake's, but it's still enormous. Especially for one person.

As we drive out of Everton and toward Grimbrooke, I start peppering Titus with questions.

"How old are you?"

"Nineteen."

"Are you going to college?"

"No."

"Where did you go to school?"

"I had in-home tutors."

"How long have you lived in Everton?"

"Almost a year."

"What brought you here?"

"Family obligations."

And on and on it goes. I may not know much about Titus, but we've got hours ahead of us and I plan to use every one of them to figure him out.

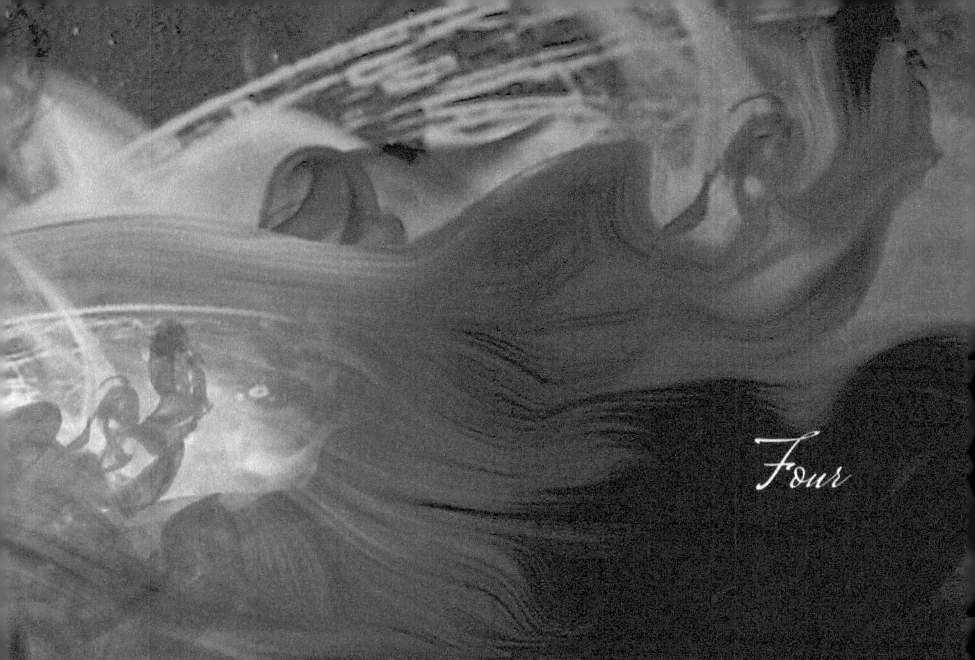

Four

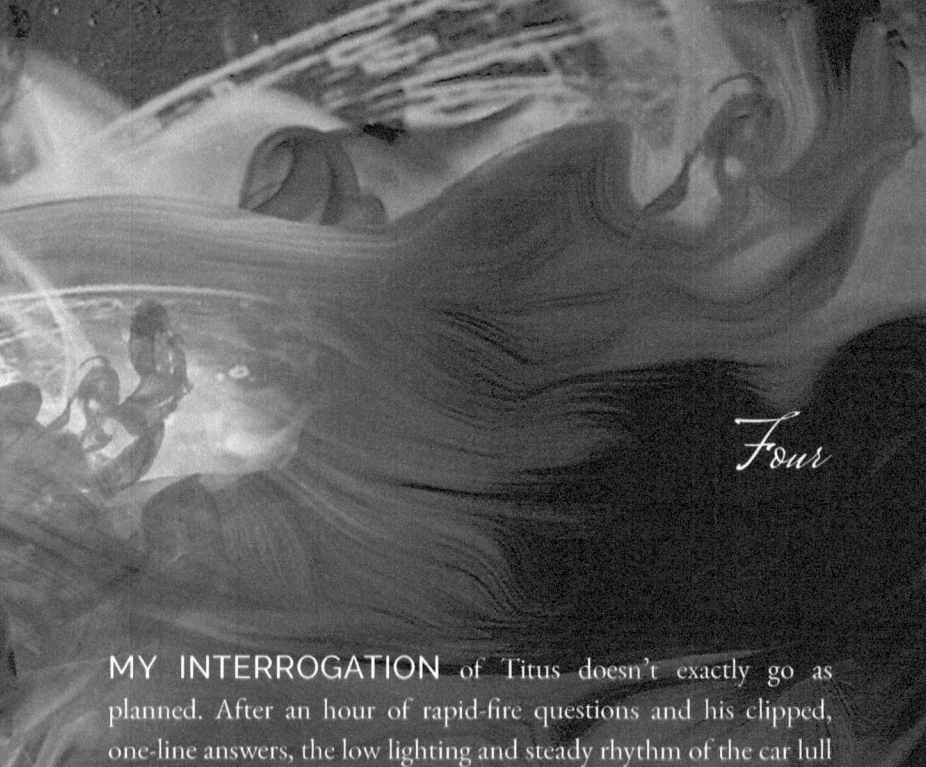

MY INTERROGATION of Titus doesn't exactly go as planned. After an hour of rapid-fire questions and his clipped, one-line answers, the low lighting and steady rhythm of the car lull me to sleep. I drift off with my face pressed against the window, going in and out of sleep for hours.

I wake to the soft murmur of voices. The sky is beginning to lighten, a pale lavender bleeding into the darkness. Titus is driving now, and Ensley is angled toward him, their conversation quiet and low.

So much for being a great interrogator. I slept through a full stop and a driver switch.

I'm about to sit up and ask where we are when Titus says my name and asks what kind of creatures my parents are.

Ensley hesitates. I hold my breath, waiting to see how she'll answer. Not because it's a secret that my parents are a fae and a bear shifter, but because I'm curious if she'll mention the human part. Or at least the *alleged* human part.

"Her mom's a fae, and her dad's a bear shifter," she finally says. "Why do you want to know?"

Yeah, Titus. Why do you want to know?

Titus flicks his gaze to her before focusing back on the road.

"Mostly just curious. It's odd she didn't come into her powers years ago. I've never heard of that happening before."

I tense up, wondering how Ensley is going to respond.

"The doctors think she has. It's just that they are so faint they can't be detected," she says, giving him the general line I've been feeding everyone since I was a kid.

Titus is silent for a minute before saying, "I don't think that's it."

"What do you mean?" she asks.

"I think her powers might be manifesting now."

"What?" Ensley says, her voice just shy of shrill.

Yeah . . . what?

My body locks up as I wait for Titus to go on, wanting to know why he would think that.

He shakes his head. "There's just something different about her now. My truth reading magic usually picks up a trace of magic, some flicker of power, from other creatures, even if it's just a sense of whether or not they're telling the truth. But with her, it used to be like staring into a void. Nothing. Now there's a spark."

"And that makes you think she's manifesting her powers?" Ensley asks carefully, realizing she's in a minefield as Titus doesn't realize I'm a completely different entity altogether—a magicless one by nature.

"Truth reading is tied to magic," he explains. "I can't read kids either, so I didn't think much of it with Locklyn because I'm used to some creatures being harder to read. But I knew right away that she was lying about being fine." He glances at Ensley, his meaning clear.

Ensley scoffs. "It doesn't take magic to realize she was lying about that. Who would be okay considering the circumstances? I'm certainly not *fine* either right now."

Compassion softens his gaze. He reaches out and gives her hand a squeeze before returning it to the stirring wheel.

He shrugs. "Maybe I'm wrong. It's just a theory."

They go on to talk about whether or not we should stop for food, so I feign waking up a few minutes later.

"What time is it?" I ask with a yawn, hoping I'm not laying it on too thick.

Ensley twists in her seat to look at me. "Almost six."

That means we've been driving for nearly twelve hours. We should be there soon.

"We'll be there in just under an hour," she says as if reading my mind. "Should we stop for food first?"

I don't want to stop. Now that we're so close, I'm itching to get there. But showing up at the crack of dawn might not do us any favors. We agree to grab a quick breakfast once we hit Grimbrooke, then keep moving.

Grimbrooke is even older than Everton. Both were early settlements, but Grimbrooke—with its stone buildings and towering spires—*feels* older. Where Nightlark Academy stood apart from Everton's colonial architecture, Grimbrooke embraces its full neogothic roots.

We pull off the main road and park in front of a small café. Ensley's cherry-red car stands out like a flare against the gray stone buildings. After stretching out the stiffness from the back seat, we head inside for coffee and pastries.

The barista, a pretty fae probably in her late twenties or early thirties, with curly red hair and a friendly smile, makes small talk while preparing our drinks. When she asks if we're just passing through or visiting someone, Ensley casually mentions we're here to see a friend named Talon. That's when things shift. The barista's smile falters, just for a second, before she recovers and offers to draw us a quick map to his place, saying that it's easy to get lost on the backroads.

She's polite, helpful even, but there's a shift in her demeanor that suddenly feels guarded. Like we mentioned a topic that's off-limits.

We thank her for the drinks and information and leave without lingering.

As we climb back into the car, Ensley twists in her seat. "Did you see her face when I said we were looking for Talon?"

I nod. "Yeah, that was weird."

"It might be nothing," Titus says. "Maybe she just dated Talon or has some history with him and is curious about two girls visiting him."

I scrunch my nose. "She has to be almost ten years older than him."

Titus shrugs. "Guy's got game."

A bolt of annoyance shoots through me, and I bite my tongue to keep from snapping at Titus, even though I'm not actually mad at him.

"The first time we kiss, Freckles, it won't be to make another guy jealous. It'll be because we can't live another second without tasting each other's lips. I'm a patient creature. I can wait."

Game indeed.

Suddenly my vanilla tea smells sickly sweet; the croissant in my hand might as well be a brick. My appetite's gone.

"Let's just get to Talon's," I say.

Ensley looks over to Titus, who nods in agreement, then starts up her car and we glide out of the center of Grimbrooke.

N
W

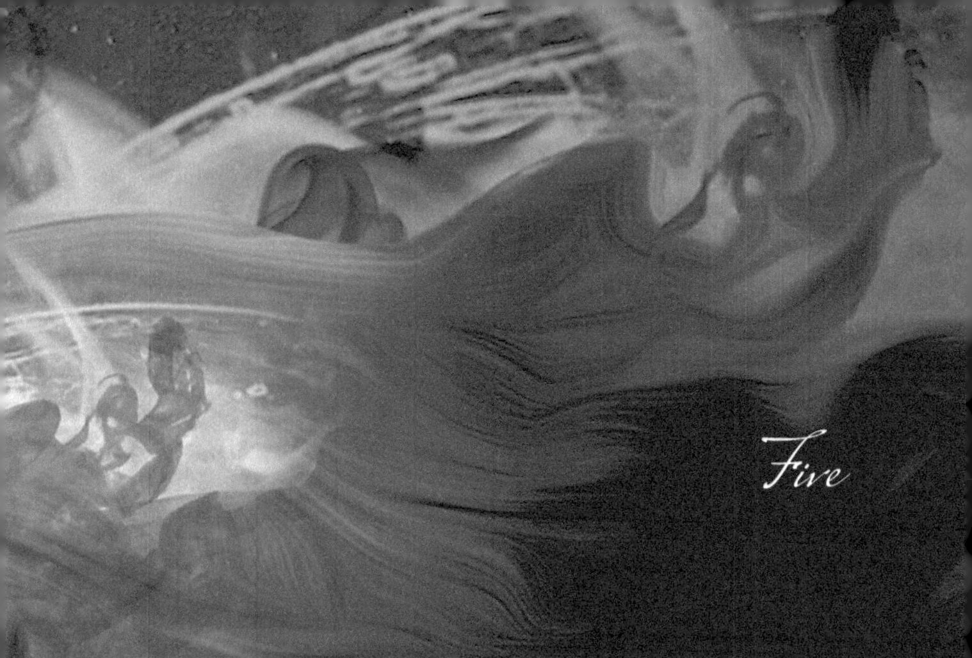

Five

IF WE HADN'T GOTTEN that hand-drawn map from the waitress at the café, we never would've found Talon's house. I vaguely wondered if Drake knew the address he gave me was basically useless and was back in Everton laughing about it right now.

Well, joke's on him. The fae marked out every landmark. After a sharp turn at a massive boulder covered in purple vines, we followed a dirt road barely wider than a footpath, squeezing the car between two drooping willow trees, their branches trailing along the roof. Beyond them, a tree-lined cobblestone drive stretched on endlessly before finally revealing Talon's home.

We spill out of Ensley's sportscar, and I look up. And up. And *up*.

Calling it a house is laughable. It's a full-on stone fortress. Not like Drake's mini-castle either. This one's the real deal. Medieval and creepy in all the right ways, with high gray walls, four cylindrical towers at each corner, and a central courtyard visible through a wide arched opening. The only thing missing is a moat.

"This is wild," Ensley says, staring up at one of the towers. "I didn't think this part of the country was even old enough to have architecture like this."

"Maybe it was just built to look old," I offer.

Titus shakes his head, like he's not so sure.

"Come on," I say, motioning them forward. "Let's see who's home."

The outer walls are surprisingly clean, free of ivy or moss, which tells me someone's been maintaining the place. We step through the arched entry and into the courtyard, the cobblestones echoing underfoot. There's no single front door to knock on, just several smaller stone buildings ringing the yard.

No lights. No voices. No clue where to start.

"Should we split up?" Ensley asks.

Normally, I'd say no. It's smarter to stick together. But I'm too antsy. I *need* to find Talon. We'll cover more ground this way. Besides, this isn't one of the Chaos trials. It's not like we're in danger . . . right?

We each choose a different part of the castle grounds and head off in separate directions. I start toward the southwest tower but get the sudden urge to veer off. A minute later, I find myself in front of a black metal door just to the left of the corner tower. I test the handle, and finding it unlocked, I ease it open.

The thumping of fists pounding a punching bag hits me the second I step inside.

The building is two stories tall but narrow and long, a single open space filled with a chaotic mix of workout equipment: weights, machines, sparring mats, and target dummies. But at the far end of the room, it's not the gear that holds my attention.

It's him.

A jolt runs through me as soon as I spot Talon. He's shirtless, barefoot, wearing only a pair of low-slung joggers. He hammers away at a heavy bag, muscles flexing and gleaming with sweat under the dim lights. Fists, elbows, knees. Blow after blow. Relentless.

Earbuds in and facing away from me, he doesn't hear me. Doesn't know I'm here, and so for a moment, I just stand there. Watching, absorbing, remembering.

I'm not prepared for the sight of him to gut me, but it does.

It all comes rushing back. Kerrim, the portal, the cold spike of panic in my chest when I realized I was holding Shadow Striker and what that meant. That I had basically signed Talon's death sentence. When the magic linked us and began draining his life, I tried to get him through the portal to sever the connection, but everything fell apart when Kerrim threw Becks in first and reached the other side before we could.

That entire night carved itself into my memory like a scar, and now, seeing Talon alive and whole, it doesn't bring the relief I expected. It just hurts. In that raw, quiet way that lingers beneath the surface.

He's here, training like nothing happened. Like it wasn't because of me that he almost died. Like he didn't keep secrets that changed everything. Like he didn't just disappear without a word when I needed him most.

Part of me wants to storm across the room and demand answers. Another part wants to walk back out the door and pretend I never saw him.

And then there's the worst part, the one I don't like to acknowledge, the part of me that's *drawn* to him.

It's infuriating. He makes me angry. He makes me ache. He makes me remember everything I'm trying so hard to bury.

I can't look away, yet I can't walk out either. Like it or not, I need him. And whether he realizes it or not, he's going to help me. He owes me that, at least.

He has no idea I'm there as I move quietly along the stone wall, staying close as I make my way across the room. I'm nearly to the other side when he suddenly stops and, without looking, snatches a dagger off the wall. Before I can react, he spins and the blade flies through the air, end over end, straight toward me.

I barely have time to flinch before it sinks into the mortar between the stones, inches from my head.

Talon yanks out his earbuds, staring at me like he doesn't quite believe what he's seeing.

"Freck—?" he starts, then catches himself. The last time I saw him, I told him not to call me that.

"What are you doing here?" he asks instead.

I glance at the blade, just inches from my face. "I can't believe you just threw that at me. You could have killed me."

Grabbing the hilt, I give it a tug, but the dagger's embedded deeper into the mortar than I expected and doesn't budge. The fine hairs on the back of my neck prickle, and I spin around to find Talon standing there.

Crowding me with his presence, he reaches past my shoulder and grips the dagger's hilt. My breath catches as I look up into his blue-gray eyes and find him staring down at me with an unreadable expression. My heart stutters in my chest, heat rising beneath my skin before I can stop it.

He doesn't move right away. For a second he just stands there, his hand still on the hilt, eyes locked on mine. Something flickers across his face. Regret, maybe, or an emotion I can't name, before he wipes it clean, his expression going flat.

Then he yanks the blade free and steps back, calm as ever.

"How did you find Grimspire Castle?" he asks, completely unfazed by the fact that he almost skewered me.

I give myself a mental shake, irritated by the way my body responded to his nearness.

"Your uncle told me where to find you," I say through clenched teeth, still trying to regain control. I hadn't even known his home had a name—*Grimspire Castle*—and I vaguely wonder if the town was named after it, or the other way around.

"You shouldn't be here," he says.

I thought I was angry at him before, but a fresh wave of fury rises in me. Talon didn't just run from Everton, he ran from me when I needed him most.

"*I* shouldn't be here? *You* shouldn't be here," I snap, letting the anger and frustration bleed into my voice.

He presses his lips together, then grabs a towel from a nearby stool and wipes the sweat from his face and neck before finally answering. "And where do you think I should be, if not here in my home?"

I didn't expect Talon to fall at my feet and apologize for abandoning me, but a touch of remorse would've been nice. Instead, I'm met with indifference laced with just enough hostility to make my hackles rise.

"Back in Everton, helping clean up the mess you made," I say bluntly.

A muscle jumps in his jaw.

Out of the corner of my eye, I catch the shadows pulsing around us, but I don't give him the satisfaction of reacting. I already know he can manipulate them. If he thinks he can intimidate me with his powers, he's going to be disappointed.

His gaze sweeps across the room before settling on me again. His brow pinches, but he smooths it away a moment later.

"I don't know what you expect me to do. Kerrim stole the dagger. It's lost to us now. What more is there to do?"

Is he serious?

I take a step toward him. His eyes flick briefly to my mouth before snapping back to meet mine, his jaw tightening. He shifts back a step, reaching for the dagger he set down and then walking across the room to return it to its place on the wall.

"What I expect you to do is help me get to that other world and find Becks before it's too late," I say, following him.

Talon turns back to me and crosses his arms over his chest. "How exactly do you expect me to get you there? Kerrim took the dagger through the portal with him. There's no way into that world from ours."

I try not to look at the way his arms flex across his bare chest, but it's impossible to ignore. And wildly distracting.

"Could you put a shirt on?" I snap, more sharply than I mean to.

His lips curl into a smirk. "Does it bother you?"

I scowl, refusing to answer even as the heat going to my cheeks gives me away. Instead, I roll my eyes. "There are gates to the human world," I say, getting back on target. "You said so yourself that night."

"Gates that have been sealed for hundreds of years," he counters.

"Then we unseal them."

Talon gives me a look like I've officially lost it. He shakes his head and sighs. "You have less than a month of school left. Go back and graduate, Locklyn. It's what he would have wanted for you."

"You don't get to speak for him," I snap, and Talon winces. "And don't even begin to give me advice you're not even willing to take yourself. If you don't go back to Nightlark, you don't graduate either."

Talon gives me a look I can't decipher.

"What?" I demand, too annoyed to try to puzzle it out.

Talon sighs again. "I'm not in high school. I graduated two years ago."

I blink back at him. "Come again?"

He wipes a hand down his face. "You already know I was only in Everton to look for Shadow Striker. Enrolling in the local high school let me blend in and keep my ear to the ground about the dagger without drawing too much suspicion."

I freeze. It never occurred to me that Talon wasn't a senior. But it should have.

"So that makes you . . . ?"

"Twenty," he says.

It shouldn't matter how old Talon is, but it throws me. Just one more thing I didn't know about him. How many secrets is he still keeping?

"Okay, fine. You don't need to graduate. But I hardly think a high school diploma is more important than Becks' life. I can always go to summer school to finish my degree." I think I just threw up in my mouth a little saying that again, but for Becks I'll endure.

"It's not as simple as that," Talon says. "Even if we *could* unseal one of the gates, which we can't, they were closed for a reason." He looks away, and I get the feeling he can't bring himself to meet my eyes when he adds, "I'm sorry. I truly am."

Talon's words hit like arrows to the chest, each one finding its mark. I shake my head, refusing to believe this is the end.

He moves like he's going to walk away, so I grab his arm to stop him. He could easily pull free, but he freezes, staring down at me with a shuttered gaze.

"Please," I say, feeling my eyes start to sting. I'm not above begging at this point. "I can't just leave him there. There has to be some way to get to the human world."

Talon's gaze bounces over my face. His eyes look haunted as he reaches up, his thumb brushing gently over the curve of my cheek to wipe away a tear that escaped. I quietly catch my breath at the riot of sensations his delicate touch sets off inside me.

"Please don't cry," he whispers, a frown tugging at the corners of his mouth.

More tears gather in my eyes, and a pained look flashes across his face. I shove down the feelings his touch stirred and refocus on Becks.

My best friend who I love. Who I have to save.

"It's my fault this happened to him," I say, trying to keep my voice steady. "I can't live with myself if I don't do everything I can to find him."

Talon starts to speak, but his gaze drops to the hollow of my throat. His expression shifts, pain and sadness replaced by confusion. He lifts the thin gold chain around my neck, eyes fixed on the purple stone pendant my parents gave me the day before.

"Where did you—?"

The exterior door slams open, cutting him off. We jump apart like we've been caught doing something we shouldn't. Heat rushes to my cheeks as I glance over and see Ensley and Titus walking toward us, led by a girl I don't recognize.

She's petite, like me, and wearing only an oversized black graphic T-shirt that hits mid-thigh. Her long black hair is slightly tousled from sleep, and she rubs her eyes like she's still trying to wake up.

"You didn't tell me we were going to have guests," she says grumpily to Talon.

An uncomfortable sensation unfurls in my gut. I want to tell myself this beautiful creature is Talon's sister, but the angle of her eyes and the warm brown hue of her skin make it clear she's of a completely different descent.

She gives him a slow once-over, taking in his sweat and the fact that he's still only wearing joggers. I shift slightly to the side, trying to block part of her view. Her mouth tightens as her gaze cuts right through me.

"You didn't make it back to bed last night," she says—not as a question, but as a statement.

How would she know that unless she'd been waiting for him to return to bed with her?

A flash of jealousy blazes through me, so hot I half expect to look down and see my skin on fire.

Where did that come from?

Curling my shoulders, I step to the side, embarrassed by my reaction and hoping no one noticed. I catch Titus' nose twitching as he sniffs the air, and if I didn't know any better, I'd swear I could smell cinders and taste ash on my tongue.

Talon runs a tired hand through his hair and my traitorous eyes follow the motion, catching the way the lean muscles in his bicep flex.

"I got a little sleep," he says to the girl, but now that I'm looking more closely, I can see the exhaustion written all over his face that I missed before.

Dark smudges curve beneath his eyes; his usually golden skin looks pale and drawn tight over sharp cheekbones. The gauntness should take away from his appeal, but somehow it doesn't. If anything, it only sharpens his already razor-edged features, giving him an almost otherworldly kind of beauty.

I don't know how I missed the subtle changes when I first saw him. Maybe I was too focused on getting him to help me find Becks. Or maybe it was the dagger he threw at my head that threw me off.

I've barely eaten and only gotten broken sleep since Becks and Kerrim disappeared. I haven't spared a single thought for my appearance, so I can't help but wonder if the strain shows on me too.

The black-haired girl crosses her arms over her chest and cocks her head, her body language clear she doesn't believe him.

"Tell that to the bags under your eyes," she challenges.

The stern look he gives her is clearly a warning, but she just rolls her eyes. "Reshelve that glower, cos. Your scary faces don't work on me."

I perk up a little.

Cos? Like in Cousin?

He shakes his head lightly, then shifts his gaze over her shoulder, ignoring her completely. "Ensley, Titus. I see you've met Imogen."

They nod, and Titus and Talon tap fists in greeting.

"Your cousin," Titus says, sliding his gaze briefly to me before looking back at Talon, "has been very hospitable."

Any hackles that were raised when the black-haired beauty showed up immediately go down. That in itself is confusing as well as concerning.

Imogen laughs. "If you call throwing a dagger at his head when he woke me up *hospitable*, then sure."

What's up with this family and throwing daggers?

"Are you the only two here in this castle?" Ensley asks, glancing around the gym-slash-training center.

"We have a big family that comes and goes from Grimspire," Talon says, his tone evasive.

Ensley's eyebrows rise. "But surely your parents are here."

Imogen answers, "Both our parents are out." She glances at Talon before adding, "On business."

"What type of business?" Ensley presses.

"Our own," she replies bluntly.

So it's not just Talon who's secretive. His whole family is too.

"What's the Arcane Society?" I ask, deciding to cut through the nonsense and finally get some answers.

Both Imogen and Talon whip their heads toward me.

"How did you hear that name?" he asks sharply.

"Your uncle mentioned it," I answer truthfully.

See? At least one of us is capable of being forthcoming.

"Uncle Drake?" Imogen asks, and when I nod, she presses her lips into a hard line, clearly angry at the dragon shifter. I couldn't care less if I bring their wrath down on him. Drake deserves it, and more.

"So?" I prompt, looking between the two of them. "What is it?"

Talon starts to answer, and Imogen cuts him off with a harsh, "Don't even think about it."

He sighs, looking even more exhausted than he did a minute ago. "After everything, they deserve to know."

"You're not the one who gets to make that decision. If you want to spill all our secrets, you'd better wait until your parents return. Aunt Jade will have your head if you don't wait for her go-ahead."

Talon crosses his arms over his chest, distracting me all over again, so I look away. "I'm not scared of my mom," he says.

"Well, you should be. I certainly am." A visible shudder runs through Imogen.

Talon turns to the three of us. "You drove straight through the night to get here, right?" When we nod, he continues, "You must be exhausted. I'll show you to the guest rooms so you can rest."

He starts toward the door, but I plant my feet and cross my arms. "You just expect us to sit tight while you decide how much of the truth to share with us?"

Titus and Ensley stay quiet beside me, but their expressions say enough. Ensley even crosses her arms, mirroring my stance.

Talon rubs a hand over his face. When he looks back at us, there's a glint of vulnerability in his gaze. It's a look I don't think I've ever seen from him before.

"Listen, I get it. You guys have no reason to trust me. But even so, I'm still asking you to. Just for a little while," he adds quickly. "There's something I need to check out." His gaze drops to the hollow of my neck before traveling up to my face. "And then I'll explain everything. I promise."

I know he's talking to all of us, but his eyes don't leave mine.

I chew on my bottom lip. I'm not sure how much weight Talon's promises really carry. I don't trust him any more now than I did before I knew half his secrets. Probably less now.

I glance at Ensley. Becks is her brother. She should have a say in this.

When her gaze meets mine, I can see she's torn too. I give her a look that I hope says, *It's your call.*

Resolve sharpens her features. She nods once, then turns to Talon.

"You have one day. I want you to remember that every minute you take is another minute my brother is out there, hurt, alone, and with no idea where he is or how to get home. I'm giving you this time, but I expect it to be worth it. If not, you'll answer to me."

She lifts her hand and creates a glowing orb. The sphere hovers in her palm, growing brighter by the second. When it's so bright I have to squint, Ensley cocks her arm back and hurls it.

The ball flies across the room and slams into a practice dummy, punching straight through the lifelike rubber chest like a hot knife through butter. It leaves a hole clean through the target and scorches a black mark at least three feet wide on the stone wall behind it.

Whoa. I've seen Ensley use her light magic before, but only while goofing off. I didn't know she could do *that*.

Way to go, bestie.

I resist the urge to start a slow clap, keeping my arms firmly crossed as I arch a brow at Talon, daring him to double-cross her.

He tips his head in a gesture that says, *Message received and accepted*.

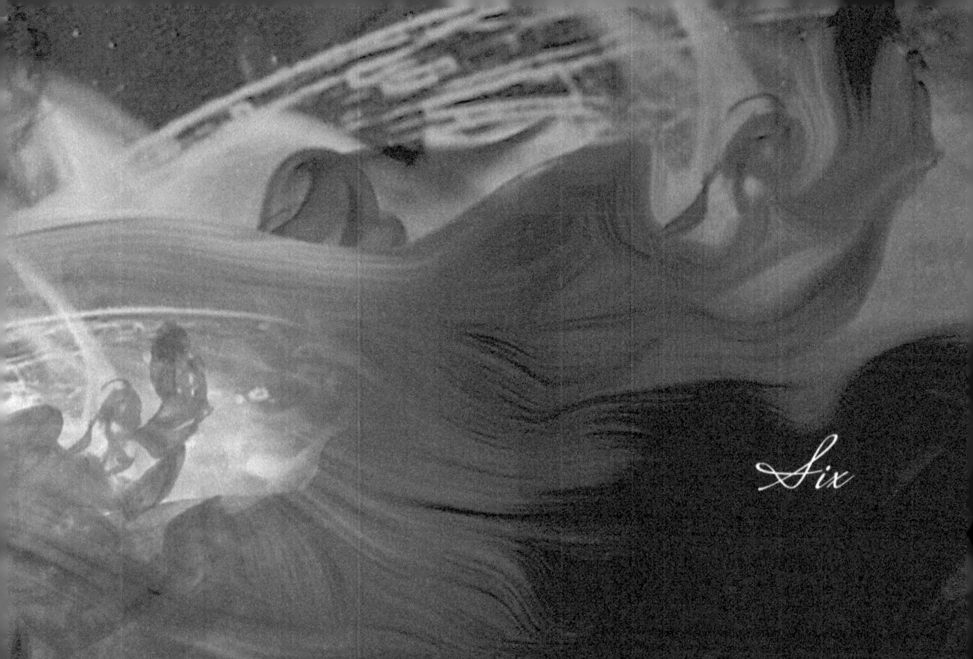

Six

EVEN THOUGH TALON said he'd show us to guest rooms, his cousin convinces him to go shower to "wash the stink off," so it's Imogen who ends up getting us settled. She puts Ensley and me in a room with two giant beds, and Titus in the one across the hall. She gives us directions to the kitchen and main hall and makes it clear those are the *only* areas we're allowed to go without an escort. I resist the urge to roll my eyes when she adds a dramatic, "Or else," before flouncing off, hopefully to put on more clothes.

"This place gives me the creeps," Ensley says, running a hand over the blood-red duvet on one of the four-poster beds.

Besides the beds, the only furniture is a massive mahogany armoire in the corner and a single vanity with a mirror. No nightstands. No lamps. The red-and-black woven rug does nothing to fight off the early morning chill. The castle seems to absorb cold and moisture and trap it. It's definitely colder in here than it was outside. There's a fireplace opposite the beds, but it's unlit and empty.

I have to boost myself up just to sit on the bed. The duvet on mine is black, and when I peek under it, I find matching sheets.

I thought Drake's place was creepy, but Talon's castle takes the cake.

"So, what do you think?" Ensley asks from her spot on the bed across the room.

"I think you're right. This place is crawling with creepy vibes." I glance toward the one window, but the warped, grimy glass makes it almost impossible to see out.

"No, I mean about Talon. Was it the right move to give him this time? Or did we just hand him a chance to string us along?"

I sigh. Who really knew with Talon? If I could read him correctly, we might never have gotten into this mess to begin with.

I spend a few minutes recounting everything from my conversation with him before they arrived. By the time I finish, Ensley looks deflated.

"So we're probably just wasting our time?"

"I don't know," I say, thinking back to the way Talon reacted to my pendant. There was something in that look. "I think part of him wants to help." At least, I *hope* so. "Talon's the only chance we've got right now. I'm not ready to give up on him. Let's wait out the next twenty-four hours and reassess."

Despite insisting she's not tired, Ensley is out cold the moment her head hits the pillow. What sleep I got in the car wasn't exactly quality, but now that I'm lying down, I feel wide awake. After an hour of tossing, turning, and mentally spiraling about how all this with Talon might play out, I finally give up and slide out of bed.

Moving quietly so I don't wake Ensley, I slip on my shoes and tiptoe out of the room.

I have no real plan as I step into the hall. I remember Imogen's directions to the kitchen—down to the left, right at the end of the hallway, left at the end of the next, and then keep going until I get there—but I'm not hungry. Even so, I probably *should* eat, to keep up my strength if nothing else since I've hardly eaten since losing Becks.

Outside the room, I head left, like Imogen said. The long hallway is lined with a red-and-black runner.

I'm sensing a theme here.

When I reach the end of the hall, I'm supposed to turn right, but muffled voices sound from the left, piquing my interest.

It has to be Talon and Imogen. And there's no way I'm passing up the chance to eavesdrop.

Staying tucked against the wall, keeping my footsteps light, I pass several closed doors before reaching one that's slightly ajar. Talon and Imogen's voices are coming clearly from inside, and I take a chance to peek through the opening.

My eyes go wide at the splendor of the two-story space. Lit with buttery faelights, the room is half library, half museum. Floor-to-ceiling shelves line the walls, with glass containers holding relics and artifacts interspersed between rows of thick, leather-bound books. At the far end of the room, a full suit of armor stands encased in glass.

Imogen and Talon are on opposite sides of a long table that stretches nearly the full length of the room. Talon stands with his hands braced on the tabletop, his head bent over a massive tome. From this angle, I can't see what he's reading, but the pages are clearly yellowed with age.

Imogen is sitting atop the table across from him, one foot resting on the tabletop, the other on the chair below. She's finally changed into a long-sleeved, off-the-shoulder shirt and black jeans, wearing a pair of killer black boots Ensley would be drooling over.

But that's hardly the point.

"This is dangerous," she says, her mouth turned down in a frown.

"Don't worry. I'll tell my mom you had nothing to do with it," Talon replies, not looking up from the text in front of him.

"You know it's not Aunt Jade I'm talking about. These are things you shouldn't be messing with."

He glances up at her. "You can go. I never asked for your help."

"This isn't a joke, Talon."

"I know it's not a joke. I'm not acting like it is," he replies, his tone even as he goes back to reading the book in front of him.

But Imogen isn't thwarted. "This is a mistake and you know it," she says. "Those three are trouble. They know about the Arcane Society."

Talon sighs. "Calm down, Imogen. They only know the name because Uncle Drake let it slip. They don't know anything. Not really."

She lets out a loud, frustrated huff, and I can practically feel the heat of her annoyance from my hiding spot outside the room.

When Talon doesn't respond, she slams her palm on the table, but he doesn't flinch.

"You should have sent those three packing the minute they showed up." She cocks her head as if considering something before adding, "Well, the girls for sure. I suppose I could learn to put up with that white-haired fae. He's a snack."

Talon snorts, and Imogen shakes her head like she's trying to clear Titus from her mind.

"No, I take it back. He needs to go too," she says. "If I'd known you were inviting them for a sleepover, I would've kicked them out the second they woke me up."

"Then why didn't you?" Talon asks, flipping a page without looking up. He doesn't sound even mildly curious.

"Because I thought *you* were going to and I didn't want to deal with the fuss they'd make. Honestly, I thought it would be entertaining watching you handle them. I never imagined you'd actually *placate* them. What, have you lost your edge or something?"

Talon glances up from the book and gives his cousin a chilly glare before bending back over the page.

"This whole thing is a horrible idea. I don't know what's gotten into you," Imogen complains. "You're supposed to be the levelheaded one in the family."

Talon lets out a half laugh at that.

"Okay, maybe not *level-headed*," she concedes, "but motivated and loyal to the cause. It's like you've turned into someone else entirely. Is it because of your magic?"

What's wrong with his magic? I wonder, as the muscles in Talon's arm tense. He goes completely still. I swear the temperature drops a few degrees. When he looks up and glares at her again, Imogen lifts her hands like she realizes she's crossed a line.

"Fine, I won't go there. But you're going to be disappointed if you think I'm just going to let you go off and—"

"I found it," he interrupts, still bent over the book.

Imogen leans in, trying to read the page upside down. "What?"

Talon points to a passage in the text and Imogen grabs the book, spinning it around so she can read it properly. Her eyes scan the passage, then lift to meet his, wide and full of fear.

She shakes her head. "No, Talon. You don't even know if that's actually lunacite around her neck."

My hand goes straight to the pendant dangling below the hollow of my throat.

Are they talking about the gem pendant?

I can still see the way Talon's gaze flared when he noticed it. He looked almost spooked, and I'm sure he was about to ask me about it before Imogen and the others interrupted us.

"I'd be willing to bet a great deal that it is," he says. "It's too much of a coincidence to not be. She's a human. If anyone is going to have a lunacite gemstone, it would be her."

"Okay, fine. Let's say it *is* lunacite, even though it probably isn't, because that gem isn't supposed to exist in our world. But let's set that aside and pretend for a second that she really is carrying around some mythical stone from another world capable of opening gates. It's completely insane to even *think* about using it."

I have to put a hand over my mouth to stifle my gasp. Luckily, Imogen's heated words are loud enough to cover the small intake of breath.

Mythical stone from another world capable of opening gates.

I remember what my parents said about the gemstone, how even the jeweler couldn't identify it.

Could that be because it's not from our creature world, but from the human one? The same world Becks is trapped in, the one Kerrim plans to conquer?

What if it's not just from the human world, but *the* item we need to get there, now that we don't have Shadow Striker to open a portal?

It's possible. Someone did leave the pendant for me on purpose. And like Talon said, I'm human. If anyone's going to be carrying something from the human world, it would make sense that it's me.

"Thanks for your opinion," Talon says coldly, "but I'm not asking for your advice, let alone your permission."

Imogen's mouth flattens into a hard line. Even from this distance I can see her nostrils flare.

She's pissed.

It's clear Talon's cousin isn't any more of a pushover than he is, and even though she's trying to talk him out of helping us, I can't help but find some humor in that and respect for her.

"This isn't a joke," she snaps. "Those gates were closed for a reason. We were never meant to mingle with those creatures. Those *humans*."

She says "humans" like it leaves a bad taste in her mouth, and the teaspoon of fondness I had for her evaporates like mist.

"Locklyn is a human," Talon says, his voice just shy of a growl.

"My point exactly," she shoots back. "Look at how you've already lost your head over her. You sacrificed the dagger because of her—"

"That's not what—"

"Don't even try to tell me you wouldn't have gotten it back if it wasn't for her," she says, pointing an accusatory finger at his face. "You're a lot of things, Talon. Ruthless, driven, and not just goal-oriented but goal-obsessed top the list. You fought the hardest out of all of us to win the blade, and every single member of the family or Society will admit it was well fought for and deserved. Having it stolen by that hawk shifter was a fluke. We'd gotten complacent over the years, believing we'd snuffed out all traces of its existence, so we didn't need to be vigilant. We were wrong. But from the moment we learned it was missing, I never doubted you would bring it back. So no, I don't believe for a minute that you wouldn't have recovered Shadow Striker if you hadn't been distracted by her."

My stomach drops to my gut, because she's probably right. If it wasn't for me, Talon may have been able to get the dagger from Kerrim. I didn't put myself at the center of this drama, but that doesn't mean I wasn't there.

"You don't know anything," he says darkly.

Imogen crosses her arms over her chest, a smug look on her face. "I know more than you'd like me to. Even if I only suspected that was the reason before, I saw the way you looked at her this morning. You can stand here and lie to me all you want, but there's only so long you can lie to yourself."

A muscle jumps in Talon's jaw, making me think he's clenching his teeth.

"This conversation is over." He slams the book shut, and the thud echoes throughout the cavernous room. He stares at his cousin like he's daring her to defy him.

It's silent for a moment as they glare at each other. My heart beats wildly, feeling the tension between them as if it's a living thing, ready to open its mouth and consume them both.

Talon picks up the tome, presumably to return it, but when his back is turned, Imogen says, "You open a gate and travel to the other world with her, you might not survive."

What does that mean?

He freezes. His back tenses.

"One way or another, she's going to get you killed," she adds when Talon doesn't respond.

He glances over his shoulder. I can only see his profile, but his jaw is hard, and there's fire in his blue-gray eyes.

"Then so be it."

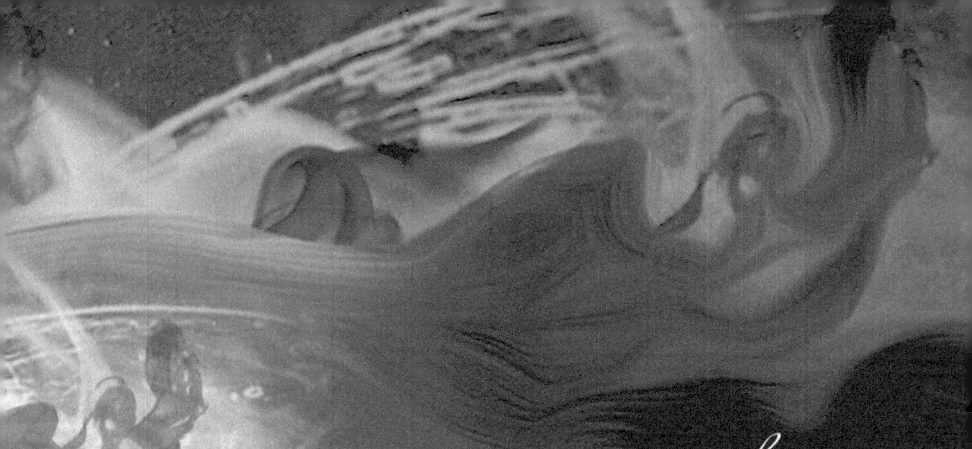

Seven

I FLEE before Talon or Imogen can catch me eavesdropping, my mind whirling with everything I've just learned. As I drift through the halls, heading in the direction I *think* the kitchen is, I sift through it all. Purposefully shelving Imogen's comments about me, I focus on what really matters: my pendant might be the key that unlocks the gates to the human world.

A bubble of hope rises in my chest. For the first time since that portal snapped shut, separating me from Becks, I feel like I can take a full breath.

When I finally pay attention to where I am, I realize I've wandered too far. I must have missed a turn somewhere, because rather than standing in the kitchen, in front of me is a stone staircase leading underground.

I should probably turn around and retrace my steps. Imogen will have a conniption if she finds me roaming when she expressly told us not to. But I don't really care. I heard the prejudice in her voice when she said "*human*." The dark-haired creature's desires aren't on my list of concerns. In fact, I start down the stairs to spite her as much as to appease my curiosity.

The air grows noticeably colder as I descend. Goosebumps rise on my arms, and I rub them, trying to bring some warmth back into my skin.

At the bottom of the stairs, my stomach drops. The tunnel ahead is lit with yellow, flame-like fae torches, reminding me of the underground passages at Nightlark. That alone gives me pause, but I shove the unsavory memories back into the corner of my mind I'd locked them in and keep going.

The tunnel twists and turns, one long corridor snaking back and forth without any doors or split paths. I try to move quietly, but each step echoes off the stone walls, loud and jarring, like I'm stomping through the silence.

At first, I try to track where I might be beneath the castle, but I lose count of the turns. More than once, I consider turning back, but a quiet compulsion urges me on. More than curiosity. It feels like I'm being called forward.

After two sharp turns, a soft rosy glow appears ahead. I quicken my pace, abandoning stealth, and rush toward it. One final curve brings me to a small, stone-walled room, no bigger than an average bedroom. At the far end is a dome of shimmering pink light I instantly recognize as a magical barrier. This one is more opaque than the one Kerrim used to block out sound during the Chaos trials.

I step closer, squinting to make out what the barrier is protecting.

Inside the dome is what looks like a sword stand, but smaller, the kind that holds a blade upright from a U-shaped bracket fixed to a gold pole about two feet tall. The pole is anchored in a base that resembles a large gold nugget, roughly the size of a bowling ball. Etchings spiral around the pole, but the haze of the barrier makes them hard to read.

I take another step and slowly reach forward, my hand lifting toward the veil of magic almost on its own. I want to touch it. I need to know if I can feel anything.

"I wouldn't if I were you."

Yanking my hand back, I whip around with my heart in my throat. Talon is standing with one shoulder propped against the room's entrance. Faelight flickers in the torches behind him, casting shadows across his face and making it impossible to read his expression.

"Why didn't I hear you coming down the tunnel behind me?" I ask, placing a hand over my heart, which is still beating furiously from the shock.

He shrugs. "I'm light on my feet."

"Well, congratulations. If you were trying to scare me, it worked."

He pushes off the wall and takes a few steps into the rose-drenched space. "No, I wasn't trying to scare you. I wanted to see what you were up to."

"I got lost," I say, but the look Talon gives me says he knows how ridiculous that sounds, and my cheeks warm with embarrassment.

"You thought our kitchen was underground?"

I clear my throat and glance back at the magical barrier.

"Why don't you want me touching it?" I ask, changing the subject.

"Well, I assumed you wanted to keep your fingers."

"Excuse me?"

Talon chuckles when he sees the look on my face. "That barrier will burn away whatever passes through it."

"But there's nothing in the stand," I say, my voice rising an octave as I realize how close I was to losing a few fingers, maybe even a whole hand. "It's empty. Why is it even active right now?"

Talon's gaze shifts past me to the empty golden stand within the magical barrier. His face turns haunted. "It's where Shadow Striker used to be kept. Only the dagger's wielder can pass through the barrier. Unless the wielder dies and a new champion has to be chosen. Then it's safe."

"So, you're the only one who can reach in there?"

Talon shoves his hands into his pockets. "Or you. We don't really know anymore. After what happened in that cave with Kerrim, the rules are a little muddy right now."

"Does that mean I might have been able to touch it safely?"

He shrugs. "Maybe. But maybe not. Are you willing to risk it to find out? I'm certainly not."

I shake my head and take another step back.

The shimmering barrier is deceptively beautiful. Even knowing what it can do, part of me still wants to touch it.

I clear my throat and turn away, ignoring the pull in my chest that urges me closer. Facing Talon fully, I study him. I hadn't gotten a good look at him through the cracked door, but it's clear now that a shower and fresh clothes haven't fully erased the signs of exhaustion. Still, the rosy light from the barrier casts a warmer glow on his face, softening the shadows beneath his eyes, making him look a little less worn down than he probably is.

"So, are you finally ready to be real with me?" I ask.

Talon's brows lift. "I've always been as honest with you as I was allowed to be."

I press my lips together, annoyed. That caveat at the end covers a lot of secrets and deceptions.

"You don't believe me," he says, almost looking a little hurt.

I sigh. "Can you blame me?"

He shakes his head. "I don't blame you for anything," he says, his gaze softening.

Considering his cousin basically blames me for everything, those words mean more than I want to admit. I don't know what to say, but Talon keeps going, sparing me the need to answer.

"My family's been part of the Arcane Society for generations. So long we don't even remember a time we weren't involved."

I blink, caught off guard that he brought it up on his own. Is this it? Is he finally coming clean?

"Some members chose to walk away over the years," he says. "But doing so comes at a price. They're excommunicated to protect the Society's secrets. Bound by magic, they can't speak of it again. Their descendants are kept in the dark, and they're even forced to change their last names so they're no longer tied to us."

"That's awful," I say, thinking of families being torn apart just because they didn't want to be part of whatever secret society or cult-like thing Talon's family is tangled up in.

He nods. "It is. But it's also necessary."

"Why are you telling me this?" I ask, confused. He's giving me history, but I don't even know what the Arcane Society is yet.

"So you understand why I couldn't be completely upfront with you before, and so you understand the weight of what I tell you next. Revealing the Society to outsiders breaks one of our oldest and strictest rules."

I swallow hard, unsure if I'm more nervous that he's about to tell me, or that he won't.

"You weren't willing to break that rule before. What's changed?"

Talon's gaze dips to where the chain around my neck disappears beneath my shirt, and I would swear the pendant warms against my skin.

"Where did you get your necklace?" he asks. "I've never seen you wear it before."

If I hadn't overheard him and Imogen, I might think he's changing the subject. But I know better. It's the pendant. Whatever it is, it changed everything.

"My parents gave it to me after they told me the truth. That I'm not biologically their daughter." The words scrape coming out, but I keep going. "They didn't know I'm human. But the way I came to be with them is suspect. They said I was wearing the necklace the night I was given to them. They've had it restrung since. It was supposed to be a graduation gift."

I lift the chain, drawing the pendant out from beneath my shirt. The rosy light from the barrier hits it and the purple gemstone flares to life, catching the light and fracturing it into shimmering waves of violet and magenta that dance across the walls. Talon's eyes flare and he takes a step forward, reaching a hand toward me, stopping just short of touching the gem.

"May I?" he asks, his hand hovering in the air.

I nod, and as he carefully touches the purple gem, he shifts closer, bending his head to examine the necklace.

Tendrils of his dark hair brush the tip of my nose and a delicious scent, part spice, part unmistakably him, wafts over me, sending my pulse into overdrive. Without realizing it, I lean in slightly while he focuses on the pendant, inhaling his scent like I've lost all sense. My eyelids grow heavy, my fingers twitching with the urge to run through the strands of his hair. Just as I start to lift my hand, I snap back to reality.

What is wrong with me?

Becks is in another world, likely injured and alone, probably thinking no one is coming for him and believing I've betrayed him. And here I am acting like Talon's some kind of scratch-and-sniff sticker I can't get enough of.

I lean back and hold my breath until Talon releases the gem and steps away. If he thinks I'm acting strange, he doesn't show it.

I press my lips together, waiting, hoping he'll say something, that he'll confess what he knows about the pendant. But he just stands there, holding my gaze.

Moments pass, the air between us thickening with unspoken tension, and eventually I can't take it anymore.

"Talon," I say, still locked on his blue-gray eyes. "What is the Arcane Society?"

He sighs, then turns without a word and starts back down the tunnel.

Seriously?

"Come on," he calls over his shoulder, his voice echoing off the stone walls. "Let's collect your friends. It's time for that talk."

Eight

THE COLD, windowless room looks more like a converted dungeon than a kitchen, except fully equipped with the latest appliances. Along one wall sits an eight-burner stovetop next to two sets of double ovens large enough for me to fit inside. Across from them are two glass-door fridges, loaded with food, and a long kitchen island stretches through the center of the space.

For the first time in days, the sight of food makes my stomach growl, but I'm too antsy to give in to my hunger. When my stomach growls again, I grab the closest thing I can—a banana, *yuck*—and peel it quickly. Shoving it into my mouth, doing my best to ignore the mushy texture, the goal is to get food in my stomach fast, not to savor a gourmet meal.

"Easy there, tiger," Titus says with a wince as I take another giant bite, nearly finishing the banana in two mouthfuls.

"Where's Imogen?" Ensley asks, sliding into a chair at the island.

Talon snorts a humorless half laugh. "She wants no part of this conversation."

He leans back against the counter, arms crossed, and watches as I settle into a seat beside Ensley. Titus hoists himself up onto the counter a little off to the side. Close enough to be part of the conversation, but just removed enough to say this is mine and Ensley's show, and he's just here for backup.

"So, what's it going to be?" Ensley asks, a frown tugging at her lips, her hair streaked black to match her mood. "Are you going to help us or not?"

I swallow the last bit of my banana, wishing I had some water to wash the taste out of my mouth, but at least my stomach isn't trying to eat itself anymore. Then I lean back in my seat, waiting to see what Talon's going to do.

He looks at me with an unreadable expression, and I arch an eyebrow. He said he wanted us all together to explain. Well, here we are. It's time to see if he's going to be true to his word or not. No more stalling.

"The gates were discovered thousands of years ago," he starts, and hearing mention of the gates gets my attention right away. "We don't know how long they have existed, or how they got there, but they were believed to have been formed by the Creator to be a bridge between his two creations."

I lean forward. Now we're finally getting somewhere.

"Just so I'm clear," Ensley says. "Are we talking about two different planets here? Like is this some sort of gate that takes us from one part of the universe to another?"

Talon shakes his head. "No. It's believed that the worlds are not so much completely separate planets as they are different realities or different realms. It's not understood why or how, but some things in our world affect theirs, and vice versa. So, in a lot of ways their world, their reality, mirrors ours, but with one big difference. The beings in their world, the humans, don't have magic."

He says the last line while he's looking at me.

"How many other worlds, or realities or whatever, are out there?" Ensley asks, her eyes wide.

"Who's to say?" Talon says with a shrug. "As far as we know, there are only two. Theirs and ours. I suppose there could be more, but for some reason it's only our two realities that have been linked."

"Okay, so where are these gates?" Titus asks.

"There are eight, spread across the globe. Some are warded by magic, others hidden in plain sight."

It's an answer. But also not.

"So to find Becks we just need to get to one of these gates?" Ensley asks, practically jumping out of her seat.

"It's not quite that easy," Talon says, his gaze flicking to me before returning to her. "Knowing where the gates are isn't enough. They were sealed two thousand years ago to prevent anyone from crossing between our world and theirs. The gates that aren't hidden are guarded."

Ensley deflates, sagging back in her chair.

"Who sealed and guards the gates?" I ask, my hope still burning faintly thanks to what I overheard in the library.

"Us."

"And by 'us,' you mean . . . ?"

"The Arcane Society."

He pauses, running his tongue along his bottom lip. I can tell he's deciding what to share and what to hold back. It's a look I've come to recognize, and it instantly annoys me, until he starts speaking again.

"Our society was formed during the time right after the first Vampire King. Over the centuries, we've expanded our mission to include protecting the world from dangerous magic no one should access. But our original and most important charge has always been to guard the gateways between worlds and keep them sealed—and to keep Shadow Striker from falling into the wrong hands."

He pauses again, meeting each of our eyes.

"We've already failed with Shadow Striker. If we keep going down this path, we'll fail at protecting the gateways too."

"Why is it so important to keep the gates closed?" I ask, and Talon's gaze shifts to me.

"Nothing good happens when our worlds mix," he says.

I know he's not specifically talking about me, but it still feels like it. If I hadn't entered Chaos, Talon might have recovered Shadow Striker. And even if he hadn't, Kerrim wouldn't have been able to use me as his personal human portal opener. He might never have stolen the dagger in the first place if he hadn't discovered what I am. Any way you cut it, this all still feels like it's my fault, even though I know it's not and that Talon doesn't blame me. Not like his cousin does, at least.

"Do they know anything about us there?" Ensley asks. "The humans, I mean. Do they know our world exists? Do they even know what magic is?"

Talon shrugs. "When the gates were closed, the general population didn't know about us. Only a small number of creatures ever crossed into their world, and vice versa, but stories had started to circulate. About our magic, our powers. Who knows what they believe now? Generations have passed. We might be myths or legends to them, or wiped from history completely."

"If, at some point, the gates were open and creatures and humans traveled back and forth, then why haven't we ever heard about it?" I ask.

"Because we've done our job well," Talon says with a grin that fades a moment later. "One of the Arcane Society's main missions is to keep the existence of the gates, and the world they lead to, a secret. The greater population doesn't even know that world exists, thanks to the efforts of the Society over the years. But one aspect of their world has leaked into ours. Demons."

In the Ancient, Shadow Striker was said to be gifted to the Vampire King by a demon. But demons are nothing more than myths to us, malevolent beings mentioned only in obscure tales. Sure, some believe in them, but that's not the common view. I hadn't thought much about them myself until recently. But considering everything I've learned in the past week, it wouldn't take much to convince me they're real.

"Are you saying demons actually exist?" I ask.

"They're real," Talon says. "They just don't come from our world. They were beings once close to the Creator, but rebelled when he made humans. In the human world, they have limited power. They're not even corporeal, and rely on possession to gain a body. But when they cross through the gates into our world, they can take physical form."

A chill creeps over my skin, and I wrap my arms around myself, trying to shake it off. The idea of something so ancient and full of hate slipping into our world, into *me*, makes my stomach twist.

"They're obsessed with the destruction of the human race," Talon goes on. "It was a demon from the magicless world who created Shadow Striker and brought it into ours, gifting it to the Vampire King. We believe it was that demon's intention for the king to return to the human world and subjugate it. That demon remained at his side throughout the conquest of our world. To this day, we don't know whether it was the demon or the dagger that twisted the king, but we do know the demon who forged Shadow Striker was incredibly powerful."

Talon looks at me, and I hold my breath as he adds, "And there's more to the story you don't know."

My blood hums. The Ancient about the Vampire King and his love feels more than just a fairy tale now. I need to know the full story. From the first time Talon told it, I sensed there was more.

"After the Vampire King was stripped of his power when his love sacrificed herself, the demon tried to manipulate the next wielder into returning to his world and enacting his revenge on the humans. When it didn't work, he took out his rage on the creatures of this world. That's when creatures learned just how powerful and destructive the demons of the other world truly are. If the being wasn't stopped by the dagger's new wielder, who knows what would have become of our world."

"Who wielded Shadow Striker after the Vampire King?" I ask.

"The Vampire King and his love, Isolde, had a son, Lucian.

After the Vampire King was stripped of his power, he was never seen again. Shadow Striker needed a wielder, so the demon showed Lucian how to activate it."

"The Vampire King had a son?" I ask, surprised. "There aren't any stories about that."

"He did have a son. And no, there aren't any stories about it. The Society made sure any mention of Lucian was erased from history."

"What happened to him?" I ask.

"He won the activation trial only to realize what the demon's intentions were. Demons are near indestructible in our world. Lucian figured out that a fatal wound from Shadow Striker wouldn't kill the demon, but it would send its essence back to its own world. So rather than using the dagger as his father had, or as the demon wanted him to, he used Shadow Striker to destroy the demon. Before the demon's body died in our world, it vowed that one day the dagger would find its way back to the human world, which would start a series of events that would lead to not only the subjugation of the humans it despised, but also bring destruction to our world as well."

"The prophecy," I whisper, almost talking to myself.

"Yes. That's where it originated," Talon confirms, his expression grave. "To keep the demon from returning to our world, Lucian, along with a small group of his trusted friends, sealed the gates to keep anyone from being able to bring Shadow Striker to the human world, and so that the demon, or any other, could never return to ours. That's when the Arcane Society was born. A group of protectors vowed to keep anyone from going through the gates to protect both worlds. The mission of the Arcane Society that started with the Vampire King's son has been passed down through the generations ever since."

The kitchen falls silent as we digest everything Talon's told us. It's a lot, and I'm glad we know, but it doesn't do anything to get us any closer to rescuing Becks. It's time to find out how *all-in* Talon really is.

"We can't use Shadow Striker to get to the human world. Is there a way to get through the gates even though they are sealed?" I ask point blank.

I hold his gaze, waiting to see what he does.

"You know there is," he says, surprising me.

"I don't know what—" I start, but Talon tilts his head and shoots me a look. I sigh. "You knew I was listening." It's a statement, not a question.

One corner of his mouth quirks. "From the moment you peeked your pretty brown eyes around the corner to spy on us."

"I wasn't spying. I was eavesdropping. There's a difference." I have no reason to be embarrassed, but heat still creeps into my cheeks.

"If you say so," Talon says, and his deep chuckle makes my stomach flutter.

"What are you talking about?" Ensley interrupts. "What does Locklyn already know?"

Talon tips his head to me. I pull out the necklace, letting the purple pendant dangle for Titus and Ensley to see.

"What kind of gem is that?" she asks, leaning forward to get a better look.

"Lunacite," Titus says before I get a chance to answer.

Talon's head snaps toward him. "You've heard of it before?"

Titus smirks. "You're not the only one with family secrets."

Talon's eyebrows raise.

"Where did you get that?" Ensley asks, and I quickly explain how I was wearing it when I was an infant.

"I always thought they were a myth," Titus says, a bemused look on his face. "They're fabled to be gems that enhance fae elemental magic. As the story goes, one of my ancestors was gifted one by someone referred to only as 'the Wanderer.' Supposedly, my tenth or eleventh great-grandfather saved his life. For generations, the gem was secretly passed down, granting the eldest male amplified powers that helped our family prosper, until about a hundred years ago, when it was lost. Or rather, stolen. It had been mounted in a ring, and my great-great-grandfather was wearing it the night he was murdered. When they found his body, the ring was gone."

"Was he murdered for the ring?" I ask, horrified by the thought.

Titus shrugs. "We don't know for sure. Maybe it was just a random mugging gone wrong. Maybe someone else learned about the gem's power and targeted him. Honestly, I never believed the family stories. I always figured it was just bad luck that dear old Gramps was offed walking home late from the pub. But seeing that stone," he nods toward my pendant, "I'm not so sure the stories weren't true."

"The gem isn't of this world," Talon says. "It was brought by the first humans who traveled here." He turns to Titus. "The stones are incredibly rare in the human world. They may have found more, but at the time the gates were open, there were only a few in existence, and they were highly coveted for not only their rarity, but their ability to amplify powers. Fae were said to be particularly sensitive to them. From stories, we know of three that were brought here, so it's possible your ancestor had a lunacite gemstone. The Society's been looking for them for years, but has never been able to find one."

Titus hops off the counter and walks toward me. "May I?" he asks.

I nod, and the moment he touches the pendant, his eyes flare. With his other hand, he reaches for the small potted plant in the center of the kitchen island. The moment his fingers brush a leaf, a bud begins to grow, then rapidly blooms.

It's a display of earth magic, common among fae, but I've never seen it happen so quickly. Titus lets go of the pendant and steps back.

"That's legit," he says. "I wasn't even really trying." He looks down at his hand like he's never seen it before.

I glance at Talon to see if he's surprised, but his face gives nothing away. I still don't know what kind of creature Talon is, but if he's fae, he must have felt the gem's power too when he touched it.

"So Locklyn has a super special gem from the other world," Ensley says. "Besides being very cool, does that actually mean anything?"

Titus moves to stand behind Ensley, arms crossed, like a silent sentinel ready to protect her at a moment's notice. I can't help but wonder if she even realizes the nonverbal signals he's giving off. She's always been oblivious to things like that.

Talon pushes off the counter and strides forward, stopping just short of where Ensley and I are seated.

"What it means is that we have a way through the gates. Grab your stuff. We leave in an hour."

Nine

SINCE I LEFT ALL my bags in Ensley's car, I don't have anything to pack, so I head to the formal great room to wait for Talon and the others. I try to be patient, but I'm too anxious to sit still. Popping up from my seat, I begin circling the couches and velvet armchairs in the center of the room like a restless shark.

My gaze catches on the painting above the fireplace. It's of a striking young man with shoulder-length dark hair and cloudy blue eyes. He wears a cream tunic beneath a brown leather breastplate, and a swath of red fabric flows behind him from both shoulders. In his hand is a familiar, wavy-bladed dagger.

Shadow Striker.

The painting doesn't look nearly as old as the subject's clothing suggests. His attire seems like it's from another era entirely. Ancient, even. I can't help but wonder if this is an artistic rendering of Lucian, the creature who founded the Arcane Society generations ago.

"Handsome, isn't he?"

I jump, and turn to find Imogen standing behind me, arms crossed, leaning against the back of a red velvet sofa. I can't tell if her expression is openly hostile or just mildly curious. She has that kind of resting face that's hard to read.

"Who is he?" I ask, ignoring her comment.

A hint of a smirk tugs at her lips. "Oh, I think you already know. Our founding father himself."

So I was right. Lucian.

I glance back at the painting, studying it more carefully. Now that I'm looking, I notice a faint dusting of freckles across his nose and cheekbones. It's subtle, but it's there. The detail on the painting is astounding. There's no way it's as old as Lucian himself.

"Was the model one of the later Society members?" I ask, curious to know when it was done.

"Oh no. Lucian himself sat for that portrait."

My eyebrows lift. "The painting can't possibly be that old."

She shrugs like it doesn't matter whether I believe her. "It's amazing what the right wards can preserve."

We've had relics come through my family's shop before, items that were supposedly centuries old, but they were always faded, worn down by time. This painting looks fresh, the colors vivid. If someone told me it was painted last year, I wouldn't doubt them.

"Do you know that Talon's mother, Jade, is our magistra? Essentially the head of the Society?" Imogen asks, abruptly changing the subject.

I tear my gaze from the painting. Her expression is unreadable but not cold. If anything, there's a flicker of calculation in her eyes, like she's weighing my reaction.

When I simply shake my head, she goes on.

"You see, Talon's family has held the reins of the Arcane Society for generations. It's been expected that he'll take over for her someday. Not to say that any of the members are more important than the others, but if they were . . ."

She arches a brow and lets that hang in the air, like she expects me to piece it all together myself.

"I get it. Talon is special."

She pushes off the couch and moves toward me, forcing me to take a step back. "Oh no. I'm afraid you don't get it at all."

Imogen isn't much taller than me, but with her spike-heeled boots she looms nearly half a foot above. I tell myself not to flinch, not to be intimidated, but it's hard. She clearly doesn't like humans, and I know she blames me for Talon failing to retrieve Shadow Striker. The way she looks at me now, it's like I'm the reason everything is falling apart.

"You're about to cost Talon everything. But not if I have anything to say about it."

There's a gleam in Imogen's eye that makes my heartrate spike and an internal alarm start blaring. Years of training and sparring make it second nature to drop into fight mode. I shift into a defensive position with hardly a thought. But Imogen doesn't come at me the way I thought she would. She stays rooted in place, while a familiar inky sensation invades my mind, slipping past my internal barriers and burying claws right into my brain.

Compulsion. She's a vampire.

A bolt of terror shoots through my heart. I only have a split second to react before I'm completely under her thrall, and I defend myself in the only way I know how.

Quick as a viper, I throw a punch, nailing Imogen right in the mouth. Her head snaps back and I feel some of her presence inside my mind retreat. I take off, skirting her and sprinting for the exit.

"Stop!" she shouts, and without permission my feet root to the ground.

She walks into my field of vision, wiping blood from her lip with the back of her hand.

"That wasn't very nice," she says with a sneer.

"Sorry," I spit back. "I didn't realize that compulsion was a sign of affection for Society members."

She chuckles. "You're funny. If the situation were different, I might even like you."

"I can't say the same," I snarl, and she shrugs, not caring in the least.

"Let's be done with this already," she says. The smile slips off her face as she focuses again.

No. No! I can't go through this again.

Pure panic sets in. I do what I can to throw up mental shields against Imogen's invasion, but she shreds them easily. The room darkens as shadows crawl toward us. Not surprising that as a vampire, Imogen has shadow magic as well.

But she's not paying attention as the darkness creeps closer. It's not until they reach her booted feet and start crawling up her legs that she even seems to notice them. When she looks down to see them twisting around her feet and legs, I feel her focus slip and I'm able to move again.

"What are you doing?" comes a booming voice that instantly floods me with relief.

The shadows shatter like glass, then dissipate into the air as if they were never there to begin with.

Imogen's head snaps up, and her gaze collides with her cousin's.

Talon looks furious as he storms into the room. "Did you just try to compel her?" he asks, his voice deceptively calm.

A flash of fear crosses Imogen's face. She squares her shoulders and lifts her chin in defiance. "You're not thinking straight right now. I'm not about to let you throw everything away."

The temperature in the room drops. I'm sure of it this time. And as certain as I am that Talon wouldn't hurt me, I still wouldn't want to be on the receiving end of the icy glare directed at his cousin. But Imogen meets his stare with a fiery one of her own.

I may not like the girl, but I have to hand it to her. She's fearless.

"We've already had this discussion," Talon says, "and you don't get to make those decisions for me."

"Your reasoning—"

"Is my own, and none of your business," he cuts in, his words hitting like a hammer against nails even though he hasn't raised his voice. "It's too late anyway. The die has been cast."

He turns his back to her, facing me. "Are you okay?" he asks, his features softening as his gaze sweeps over me.

Behind him, Imogen shakes her head, her black hair swinging. "No, Talon. It's not too late." She grabs his arm, and he glances over his shoulder. The defiance in her voice shifts to pleading as her eyes well with tears. "Send them away. Please. Aunt Jade and the others never have to know. I won't say anything."

"I can't," he says gently, pulling free of her grip.

"You can," she insists.

"Fine. Then I won't." His tone isn't harsh, but the finality in it silences even her.

I feel like I'm missing something. Sure, Talon agreed to help us, but that can't be the end of the world. At least, it shouldn't be. Yet Imogen is acting like it is.

Talon closes the short distance between us. His hand settles on my bicep, warm and grounding.

"Are you okay?" he asks again.

The heat of his touch begins to chase the chill from my skin.

I swallow and wet my lips as I nod. Talon's gaze follows my tongue as it slides over my top lip, then my bottom. Heat sparks in his blue-gray eyes, and I'd be lying if I said it doesn't make my stomach dip.

A throat clears, snapping us both out of it and reminding us we're not alone. I glance over at Ensley and Titus, and startle when I spot a small group of unfamiliar creatures standing with them.

Ensley's eyes are wide as her gaze bounces between Talon and me. Titus eyes the newcomers warily, and slowly shifts until he's standing between them and Ensley.

For a moment, we all just stare at each other in silence until an attractive middle-aged woman with thick dark hair and tanned skin steps forward. She approaches Talon and pulls him in for a quick hug. "It's so good to finally have you home."

The woman is almost as tall as Talon, and there are too many similarities in their features not to recognize that they're related somehow. His mother, perhaps? Jade.

"I didn't realize we have guests," she says as she pulls back, her gaze sweeping over me. Her eyes aren't hostile, but they aren't warm either. They're assessing.

"They showed up unannounced, Aunt Jade," Imogen cuts in, and Jade glances at her. "You can thank your brother-in-law for that."

Jade's lips press together in unveiled annoyance. "Drake," she mutters under her breath, forcing a smile as she turns to Ensley and Titus, though she keeps me in her peripheral view. "You all must be my son's friends from Everton."

"Something like that," Titus says, side-eyeing the two males who still haven't spoken or identified themselves.

Jade looks back at Talon and a charged silence stretches between them, thick with meaning.

"Well," Jade finally says, "I wish I'd known we were having guests. I would've had a few of the guest rooms prepared, but as it is, we don't have any ready right now."

Lies. We know they have available guest rooms. We've stayed in them.

Jade doesn't want us poking around the compound. And I can understand why. I was here for less than two hours before I stumbled across where they kept Shadow Striker. Not to mention the library-slash-museum packed with rare books and likely magical relics.

"Talon," she says, turning to her son, "why don't you take your friends down to town and get them settled into the Starlight Inn? I'm sure they'll be much more comfortable there than in this drafty old place. Maybe you can show them around. I'll bet they'd find the local museum fascinating."

"With all due respect," Ensley says, stepping forward, her spine straightening like a steel rod, "we don't need a room in town. We just need to get to that gate. We've wasted enough time as it is. My brother's life is at stake, so if the family reunion is over I'd like to leave now."

Jade's eyes widen and fill with dread. Her gaze snaps to her son. "You told them?"

Talon lifts his chin, his expression hard. "I did."

"How much do they know?"

Talon pauses, a muscle in his jaw jumping before he says, "Everything."

The room is silent for a few beats. Jade's chest rises and falls three times before she responds. "You understand what this means. Even as the Society magistra, I can't make an exception for you."

He nods. "I do."

What's going on?

I glance at Ensley, but she just shrugs, looking as clueless as I feel. Imogen, however, has slunk toward the back wall. Short of slipping from the room entirely, she seems to be doing whatever she can to make herself small and unnoticeable.

A muscle in Talon's jaw twitches as he faces off with his mother. His body is rigid, braced for confrontation.

A change comes over Jade. The sadness in her eyes melts away, replaced by cold steel, her face as hard and unreadable as her son's. Her shoulders square, as if she's readying for a battle, and even though she's at least several inches shorter than Talon, she somehow seems to be looking down on him.

"Talon Theron Wintryn. I hereby declare that you are stripped of your membership in the Arcane Society. As such, you will no longer be privy to Society matters, granted access to Society artifacts or relics, or permitted to live within the Society compound. You will also forfeit the name Wintryn, and be magically gagged from speaking of the Arcane Society to anyone who does not already know of its existence."

I gasp, and my eyes swing from his mother to Talon. He hasn't moved an inch or so much as flinched, but though he's holding his façade well, he can't hide the sorrow in his gaze.

"Do you understand that from this day forward you will no longer be a member of the Arcane Society, nor a part of our family?" Jade's face remains stony, but her voice catches on the word *family*, betraying the depth of her true emotions.

Talon nods rather than speaks.

"You'll have one hour to collect your personal belongings and vacate the compound. After that, you are never to set foot on Grimspire grounds again."

"Understood," he says, turning away from his mother and heading toward the exit. He doesn't even look at me, and my heart breaks for him.

As he passes, I reach out and catch his hand. He pauses and glances down at me.

"Talon, I'm so sorry." There may not be tears in his eyes, but there are in mine. "I didn't know. I didn't realize," I stammer.

What comfort can I offer him right now? I probably can't even grasp the full weight of what he's just sacrificed to help us. To help Becks.

But, really, to help me.

He gently pulls his hand from my grasp. "Let's go find your shifter," he says, then strides from the room without another word.

Ten

TALON'S EXPRESSION is locked down as he eyes Ensley's small sportscar. He looks almost bored, but I'm positive that's not what he's feeling right now. I don't know if he even said goodbye to his mother or the two mystery men who arrived with her.

Bending over, he checks out the back seat. When he sees how small it is, he frowns. I don't blame him. Even though I'm petite, it's going to be a tight squeeze for whoever sits back there with me. Talon and Titus are both over six feet tall; even Ensley is tall for a female. We'll just have to deal with it and hope the gate Talon takes us to isn't far away.

He grabs the handle and yanks the door open. After pushing the button to slide the front seat forward, he hunches like he's about to crawl in the back and take one for the team when the roar of an engine and the crunch of tires spitting up gravel makes us all turn.

A hulking machine that's part SUV and part military transport barrels around the corner toward us. I stumble back to get out of its path as it skids to a stop beside Ensley's cherry red sportscar, making it look like a toy someone left out on the battlefield right before the tanks rolled in.

The tinted window rolls down to reveal Imogen in the driver's seat. "Get in," she orders, looking straight at Talon. "Your mom hasn't realized you're about to leave yet, and if you don't get out of here now, she's going to put that magical gag on you."

Talon's face darkens as he locks eyes with his cousin. I can tell he hasn't forgotten or forgiven her for trying to compel me.

Good, because I haven't either.

"Go put the Valkyrie away," he tells her. "You know you can't come with us. The Society would have your hide."

I agree Imogen can't come, but not for the same reasons as Talon. I couldn't care less if she gets in trouble with his mom or the Arcane Society. Honestly, after what she pulled back there, it'd be a little poetic justice. The truth is, I don't trust her. I don't want her with us. I'll be glad to leave her behind.

"It's a half-day's drive to the closest gate, but you know you can't go there because Aunt Jade will have members guarding it now that she knows what you're up to." Her accusatory gaze slides toward Ensley, who blurted out that part of our plan.

Ensley lifts her chin, daring Imogen to call her out, but even so I see a flash of guilt cross her eyes. It's not her fault. How were we supposed to know not to let Talon's mom know that we knew about the gates and were planning on going through one?

"If you want a chance of getting through a gate, you're going to have to go for one of the hidden ones. And the closest one is a heck of a lot farther than a half-day's journey."

Uncertainty creeps onto Talon's face. "We'll just have to fight our way through."

"You're kidding yourself if you think you'll be able to get through trained Society members."

"I've done it before."

Imogen's gaze softens, and the way she looks at Talon now almost borders on pity.

"Yes. But that was before," she says pointedly. "Things are different now."

Talon's jaw tenses as he clamps his lips shut, the muscle ticcing beneath his cheekbone.

Stepping forward, I address Talon. "I'd rather take my chances against other Society members than trust her."

Talon gives a single nod, backing me up, and some of the tightness in my chest eases.

"Let's go," Talon says, and then hunching again starts to fold himself into Ensley's back seat. He only gets one foot into the car before someone shouts his name from the direction of the compound.

Twisting, I see his mother walking briskly toward us. She has something clenched in her hand. It looks like a bottle or large vial. "Wait!"

Talon's face leaches of color.

"Get in!" Imogen yells again. She holds up a black leather-bound book I don't recognize. "I have this too," she says, waving it in the air.

I'm ready to dive into Ensley's car when Talon straightens, his gaze locked on the book in Imogen's hand.

His mom yells his name again and starts jogging toward us. The two other males appear behind her and start sprinting in our direction. They're coming for Talon and we only have moments to escape.

"I get you are angry. But you know this is the best chance you have. Let me help you!" Imogen shouts, her gaze panicked as she watches Jade and the others approaching.

Talon mutters a curse under his breath and then yells for us to get into Imogen's vehicle.

Wait. What? No!

With her backpack slung over one shoulder, Ensley casts a longing glance at her baby before sprinting to Imogen's vehicle and yanking the door open. She climbs into the back seat, and Titus is right behind her.

Talon grabs my arm and hauls me toward the hulking vehicle,

yanking the back door open and practically shoving me inside behind Titus. He dives into the front passenger seat and shouts, "Go!"

Imogen floors it. Gravel and dirt spray everywhere as she spins the SUV around and barrels down the tree-lined drive. Shouts ring out behind us, muffled but angry, and though I hear them, I don't look back.

We don't even make it to the end of the cobblestone before a tree to our left explodes, sending splinters flying.

I cry out as the Valkyrie swerves. My shoulder slams into the door and my head knocks against the window.

"I can't believe Jared just shot at us," Imogen mutters, checking the rearview mirror. "He's definitely off my birthday list."

Talon twists in his seat, eyes sharp. "It was a warning shot. But Atlas is coming."

His voice is low, steady, but I hear the edge in it. Tense. Focused.

"Those shadows sure would come in handy right about now," Imogen says, shooting him a sidelong look.

"Yeah," is all he says.

A bone-rattling screech splits the air, shrill and feral, like an enraged housecat, only louder, deeper, and close. I whip around and spot a cheetah charging after us, disturbingly fast, its eyes gleaming. It's covering ground at an impossible pace, muscles rippling as it dodges debris and launches over potholes with effortless precision.

"Give me your necklace," Titus demands.

I blink at him, startled.

"Quick!" he snaps, already reaching for the ceiling controls.

I yank the chain over my head and shove it into his hand. He grips the pendant, then hits a button on the ceiling. A mechanical whir fills the car as a rectangular glass panel begins sliding open.

Before it fully retracts, Titus is already shoving to his feet, cramming his upper body through the opening.

"Hold on!" Imogen yells as she swerves to dodge a fallen log that wasn't there a second ago. My shoulder slams into the door and I bite back a curse. Loose rocks spit from the tires as she slams the accelerator, the back-end fishtailing before she regains control.

Outside, the cheetah leaps and in a blur of speed lands with a bang on the roof and then scrambles to the hood.

Ensley and I scream.

Imogen jerks the wheel, sending the SUV veering into the underbrush. A branch scrapes across the roof, nails-on-chalkboard loud. The cheetah snarls, its claws digging into the metal, but can't hold on. The force of the turn launches it off the side; it tumbles across the ground in a flurry of limbs and fury as Imogen jerks the Valkyrie back onto the cobblestone drive.

Titus, still half out the roof, grits his teeth and extends one hand toward the trees behind us. The necklace chain dangles from his other fist as he focuses, his jaw clenched and shoulders taut with effort.

The air thickens.

Magic ripples outward in an invisible wave, warping the space around us. I feel it prickle across my skin like static electricity right before a storm.

The ground starts to quake.

Ensley shrieks as the vehicle rocks side to side on the uneven road, and I throw my arm across her to steady both of us. Behind us, a seismic crack ripples through the ground.

"Roots!" I shout, peering out the back window. "They're moving!"

Trees along the drive behind us writhe like they're alive. Branches twist and tangle, slamming down across the road in rapid succession. The cheetah is still giving chase and gaining on us again as thick roots burst from the earth, snaking upward to form an enormous living barricade. Bark splits and groans as the trees fuse into a wall so dense, it swallows the path behind us.

A second later, an impact rocks the barricade. The whole wall shudders, but holds. I don't see the cheetah anymore. I don't even see the castle's outer walls. It's like the forest swallowed everything.

My heart pounds as Titus collapses beside me. Sweat beads on his brow; his face has gone waxy and pale. He looks like he's seconds from passing out. Considering the magic he just unleashed to command those trees, I'm shocked he's still conscious at all.

"Titus?" I say, placing a hand on his arm.

He doesn't respond. His eyes are glassy, unfocused. He's breathing—but barely.

On the other side of him, Ensley grabs his shoulder and gives it a gentle shake, panic washing over her face.

"Keep him upright," Talon orders from the front. "We need him alert in case that wall doesn't hold."

Ensley cradles Titus to keep him from slumping sideways as Imogen barrels forward, the SUV bouncing over roots and stones littering the drive. She doesn't let up, and I don't blame her. Whatever's chasing us might find another way around. And we're not out of the woods yet.

Literally.

We reach the narrow gap at the end of the drive and Imogen slows just enough to squeeze through. I glance out the back window, not spotting any pursuers, and breathe a little easier.

Titus' eyes are half lidded, his skin still pale, but as the Valkyrie steadies on the turn, he shifts and blinks, like he's slowly pulling himself back into the moment. His breathing evens. It's still shallow, but steadier, and he lifts a hand to grip the edge of the seat for balance.

Ensley leans in closer, laying a hand on his bicep. "Are you all right?"

He glances down at her fingers curled around his arm; a faint smile tugs at the corners of his mouth. "Yeah. I'm okay. Just used up a ton of magic. I need a little time to recover, but I'll be fine."

He glances at me, then shifts his gaze to Talon and Imogen up front. Talon is half turned in his seat, eyes flicking between Titus and the back window as if expecting the trees to part and another attack to come charging through. His body is still coiled, alert, even though the danger seems to have passed.

"If there was any doubt that was the real deal before," Titus says with a tired chuckle, "I think that settles it."

In the rearview mirror, I catch Imogen's gaze as she glances at Titus. Her brow is furrowed with concern, but she stays silent.

"Here," Titus murmurs, holding out his hand. The pendant dangles from the chain clenched in his fingers.

I take the necklace and slip it back over my head. Talon's eyes track the motion until it settles against my chest. Then his gaze lifts to meet mine. There's something unreadable in his expression, hollow maybe, but it vanishes as he turns away and faces forward again.

"Okay, Imogen," he says, his voice clipped. "You wormed your way into this, so where are we going?"

I watch her profile as she licks her lips, her fingers tightening on the wheel. "As you know, the nearest gate is down in New Harbor. But we can't go there."

She'd said as much before. Reaching down, she grabs the book she waved at Talon earlier and hands it over. He opens it, flipping through the worn pages.

"The only other gate on the continent we can reach that won't be swarmed is at the Devil's Mouth."

Devil's Mouth?

Talon's head snaps toward Imogen. "You sure about that?" His tone is sharp with surprise, though I don't know exactly what's caught him off guard.

"See for yourself," she says, lifting one hand from the wheel to gesture toward the book.

Silence settles over the car as Talon flips through the pages, his brow furrowed in concentration. After a couple more turns, Imogen weaves the vehicle smoothly back onto the main road that leads out of town, the only sound the steady thrum of tires on asphalt.

The longer he searches, the thicker the tension grows, until finally Talon exhales hard and snaps the book shut.

"Looks like we're headed to the swamps."

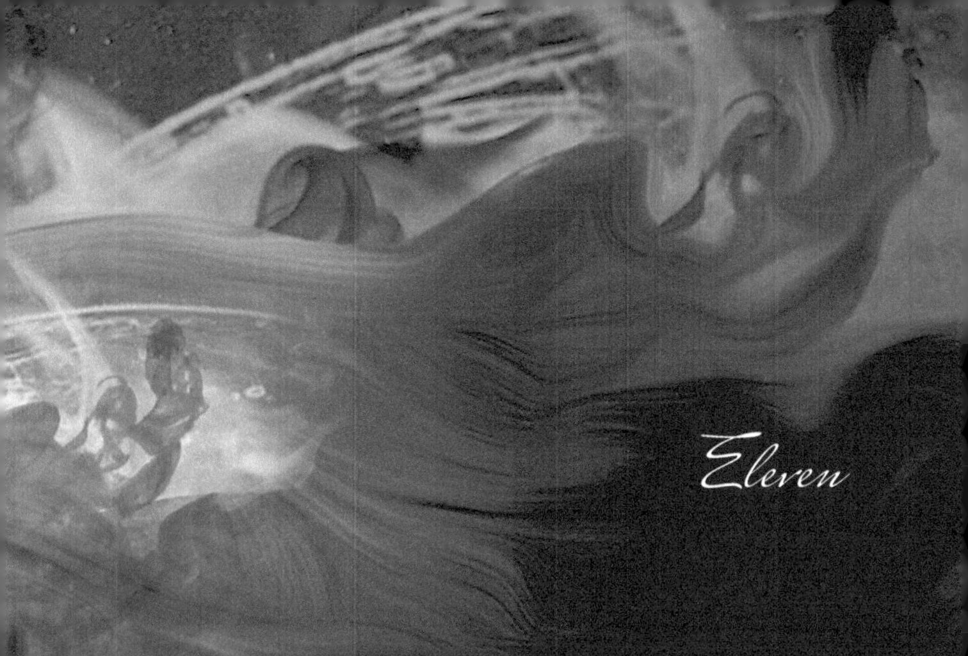

Eleven

WE TAKE TURNS DRIVING, and switch seats often, which is how I end up sandwiched between Imogen and Talon in the middle of the night. Titus is behind the wheel, and he puts on soft music that has Ensley tipping her head against the window and falling asleep within minutes.

A light drizzle taps against the roof; the steady swoosh of the windshield wipers adds to the lull. The combination makes my eyelids heavy, but I force them open, refusing to give in to sleep. Even though I have zero desire to snuggle up to either of my seat-mates—for very different reasons—my head still bobs with exhaustion.

"It's okay if you want to sleep." Talon's voice is low, his lips close enough to my ear that I feel his breath brush the shell, sending a shiver down my spine. "I don't mind if you want to use me as a pillow."

In my sleep-deprived state, the offer sounds far more tempting than it should. My body sways toward him before I catch myself and lean deliberately in the opposite direction, making my thoughts on that suggestion crystal clear.

I bump into Imogen, who immediately elbows me in the ribs and snaps at me to give her some space, even though she's hogging more than her fair share of it. Shooting her a sour look she doesn't even see, since her head is already buried in her makeshift coat pillow, I scoot back toward Talon, leaving the tiniest sliver of space between us.

Talon chuckles and I glare at him, silently hoping he can't see me blushing in the dim light. But as if he can read my mind, his gaze drops to my cheeks, then lifts back to my eyes with a smug look.

It's then I remember he has perfect night vision. I learned that during the first Chaos trial when he found, and basically rescued me, in the cavern tunnels.

What kind of creature are you? I wonder.

I'm no longer sure Talon's a vampire, not after considering all the powers he may have gotten through Shadow Striker. His ability to manipulate shadows might've come from one of the other Arcane Society members rather than being his own. Honestly, any of the powers I saw him use during Chaos could have come from someone else. So I'm just as clueless to what creature he is now as I was the day I met him.

What if, after all this time, it turns out he's a snake shifter?

Ew.

"What's that look for?" Talon asks.

I realize I've pulled my upper lip into a disgusted snarl. Quickly smoothing my expression, I shove the thought of snake shifters from my mind. "Nothing," I mumble.

Talon falls silent, and within five minutes I'm fighting a losing battle to stay awake, and nodding off again. Between the steady movement of the car, the soft rain, the *swish-swish* of the windshield wipers, and the mellow instrumental music playing through the speakers, it's too much.

If I stay quiet, I'm done for. I don't sleep well sitting upright, and if I drift off I'll definitely end up slumped against Talon—or worse, Imogen—whether I intend to or not.

Talon is staring out the window when I say, "How does Shadow Striker tie into the Society's mission?"

I keep my voice low, but loud enough for him to hear.

Talon glances over, one brow raised. "What made you ask that?"

"I've been wondering for a while. But honestly? I just need to talk or I'm going to fall asleep."

He smirks. "Told you you're welcome to."

"Yeah, not happening. So, about Shadow Striker . . . ?"

I can see the indecision in his eyes. Keeping Society secrets is a reflex for him, but what's the harm in talking openly now? The worst has already happened to him.

Because of you, a voice whispers deep inside, and guilt settles heavy in my gut like a brick.

"You already know that Shadow Striker remained in our world to keep the human world safe," Talon says, and I nod, even as I try to bury the guilt over Talon being cut off from not only the Arcane Society but his family as well.

"Well, part of keeping the dagger safe was making sure it was bonded to one of our members at all times, so it couldn't bond to someone else. Over the centuries, champions were chosen through the activation trials. When one Society member passed away, another would rise up to bear the burden of keeping the dagger safe. After Shadow Striker bonded with a new wielder, each of the members of the Society was pricked with the blade, giving the wielder the powers they needed to protect the dangerous relic."

"So Shadow Striker *does* only duplicate powers rather than steal them." I suppose it doesn't matter now either way, but it was certainly heavy on my mind during Chaos.

Honestly, I hope I never lay eyes on Shadow Striker again. I know it's selfish of me to only be going to the human world to get Becks and bring him back, but Kerrim and the cursed weapon are too much for me, or our ragtag group, to handle.

"*Only* when it's given willingly. Otherwise, it does strip the creature of its power," Talon answers gravely.

That gives me pause. A forgotten thought tickles the back of my mind, urging me to remember, but I'm too exhausted. When I reach for the memory, it slips away like mist. All that's left behind is a gnawing sense of unease that makes my stomach churn.

"Up until his death last year, my great uncle Faust was Shadow Striker's wielder. I competed against the other members of the Society in an activation trial and won. I'd only been bonded with the dagger less than a year before it was stolen and this whole nightmare began."

Talon's looking at me but he's not actually seeing me, his gaze glassy, like he's reliving a past memory.

He frowns, and the urge to comfort him hits me hard. I ball my hands in my lap to stop myself from reaching out to smooth the tension from his brow, to trace the rigid line of his jaw, to press my fingers into the knots in his shoulders until the weight he's carrying melts away.

"I'm sorry," I say, my voice small.

Talon gives a slight shake of his head, like he's pulling himself back to the moment. "For what?"

I lift one shoulder in a half shrug. "My life isn't the only one that's been flipped upside down these past few months. It's easy for me to forget that." I fidget with the hem of my shirt. "I guess I'm just sorry I've been so wrapped up in my own stuff that I haven't stopped to consider your point of view."

I glance away, the memory of my parents flashing through my mind. Even with all the changes, I still have my family. I'd texted my mom that morning to let her know we'd arrived safely. She'd replied with a simple *I love you*, and a reminder that she and my dad were proud of me.

When I look up, Talon's gaze has softened, and it does something to my pulse, making it stutter, then race.

"You don't need to be sorry for me, Locklyn," he says, voice quiet as he leans a little closer, close enough that I can feel the warmth of him. "I was born into this life. Trained for it practically since birth. I'm made of pretty tough stuff."

The way he says it isn't boastful, it's matter of fact. Like he's accepted that being unbreakable is the only way he's allowed to exist. That kind of quiet resilience should make him feel untouchable, but instead it makes me want to reach for him. To be the one person who sees the cracks beneath the armor.

I can't keep looking at him. Not with all these soft, tangled feelings rising inside me. I'm afraid I'll do something stupid, like lean in closer or let my hand find his in the dark. So I turn away, and without our conversation to distract me, it doesn't take long before sleep pulls me under.

I COME TO SLOWLY, realizing I'm resting on something kind of soft, yet also kind of hard, but definitely warm. My body is horizontal, and there's a bit of a crick in my neck, like my pillow is just a little too high. I'm swaying gently, the motion making me want to burrow deeper into my bed and drift back to sleep, so I don't bother opening my eyes. Not yet.

I'm on the brink of consciousness when a whisper of a touch ghosts through my hair. Featherlight, but still enough for me to feel the tiny pinpricks on my scalp, as if someone is running their fingers through it. It doesn't hurt. In fact, it feels . . . nice.

I nuzzle into my hard-soft pillow, relishing that delicious in-between where I'm not fully asleep but not fully awake either.

Suddenly, my body rocks forward and someone says, "Pit stop," loudly.

"Finally," comes Imogen's voice, startling me fully awake.

My eyes pop open and I find myself sprawled across the bench seat. And my head isn't on a pillow, it's on—

I jolt upright, scrambling away from Talon's lap just as everyone else piles out of the Valkyrie. At some point in the night, Imogen must have climbed into the cargo area in the back, giving me more room to stretch out. And apparently use Talon's lap as a lumpy pillow.

Kill me now.

My gaze snags on Talon's arm resting on the seatback behind me, nowhere near where my head had been cradled in his lap.

Has it always been there, or did he move it when I woke up? Did I only imagine someone running their fingers through my hair?

I can't decide which would be worse.

"Were you just touching my hair?" I ask, needing to know.

The look he gives me is maddeningly unreadable. Not smug or guilty. Not fake-innocent either. Just . . . blank.

He lifts one brow. "Is that what you were dreaming about?"

Heat prickles at the back of my neck. "Answer the question."

He leans in just slightly, voice low and teasing. "Would it bother you if I said yes?" he asks, his gaze turning curious and making butterflies flutter low in my gut.

I open my mouth, then close it. Heat crawls up my neck. "I—ah . . ."

How am I supposed to answer that?

By saying, "Yes," and telling him not to touch me again. But for some reason I can't force those words out.

"Never mind," I say, brushing imaginary lint off my lap, as if that will distract us both from the heat in my cheeks.

His lips twitch like he's fighting a smile, but then he lets me off the hook.

"You've been asleep for about four hours," he says smoothly. "We've got maybe three left until we reach the swamp. I'm glad you got some rest. You needed it."

Right. So we're just going to ignore the fact that I spent hours passed out on top of him while he may or may not have been petting me like some kind of housecat.

Cool. I'm good with that.

"You need sleep too," I say, rubbing my eyes and then scooting to the other side of the bench seat. "Did you get any?"

"A little," he says, but something tells me he's lying. He tips his head toward the door and then opens it. "Come on. The gate will be there in a few hours. Let's get some food."

Talon slides out of the car, and I climb out the other side. We've stopped at what looks like a truck stop, with a rundown diner sitting across the cracked parking lot. Without a word, Talon starts toward it and I follow, the sky still cloaked in darkness though the faint glow on the horizon hints that dawn isn't far off.

The sign above the diner entrance reads *The Greasy Spoon*. I suppose they get points for keeping it real. A bell jingles as we step inside. It sounds exactly like the one at our antique shop, and a sudden wave of homesickness washes over me. As I follow Talon down the narrow aisle, I pull out my phone and type a quick message to my parents, letting them know I'm still okay.

Titus, Ensley, and Imogen are already settled in a semi-circle corner booth.

"There they are," Titus says with a smirk. "Wasn't sure if you two were going to make it. Talon here refused to wake you up to eat."

My eyes shoot to Talon in surprise, but he won't meet my gaze as he slides into the booth next to his cousin. I slip into the seat across from him beside Ensley, who's glancing between us with a slight frown. Imogen doesn't look thrilled either, though she stays quiet, sipping her black coffee with her head down.

A waitress comes to take our order. I ask for a stack of pancakes, French toast, three eggs, sausage and bacon, hash browns, and a cinnamon roll. I'm so hungry it feels like my stomach's trying to devour itself.

Talon arches a brow after I order, and I catch Ensley trying to hide a smile behind her hand. But in my defense, I haven't had a full meal in days.

"Stop judging," I say once the waitress walks away.

"Yeah, she's a growing girl," Titus jokes.

"So," I say changing the subject, "do we have to worry about fighting through Society members to get to this gate?"

Imogen shakes her head. "They don't know where it is."

"They don't know?" Ensley asks in disbelief. "How is that possible?"

"Some of the gates are hidden," Talon explains. "The Society guards the gates that are visible, the ones in plain sight. Creatures don't know what the gates are or how to use them, but the Society still protects them just in case. But the ones that are magically hidden were deemed safe. Even if a creature stumbled across one, they wouldn't know it was there. So they aren't guarded."

"Okay, but that doesn't mean your mom hasn't dispatched creatures to head us off," I say, just wanting to have a clear picture of what we are going to be facing.

"That's the thing," Imogen says. "Not even Aunt Jade knows where the hidden gates are. Their locations are secret."

I sit back and cross my arms over my chest as questions swirl in my head. "Then how do *we* know where we're going?"

Imogen slaps the table, making me jump. "Finally, someone asked the right question."

Talon cuts his gaze toward his cousin, lips pressed in a thin, irritated line. "The book Imogen stole—"

"Borrowed," Imogen cuts in.

"It has the location of all eight gates, including the four hidden that aren't guarded," Talon explains. "Society members aren't allowed to access the book."

"Then how did you get it?" Titus asks Imogen, looking a little impressed.

A sly smile curves across her lips as she leans in, slow and deliberate, dragging her tongue over her bottom lip. Titus' gaze dips to her mouth for a beat before snapping back up, and he shifts a few inches away from her.

I knew I liked him.

"I have a very particular set of skills," Imogen says, her tone smooth, completely unbothered by the distance he just put between them.

"You mean besides compulsion and general bitchery?" I ask, the words slipping out of my mouth before I think them through.

Imogen shoots me a glare and I smile sweetly in return.

"Aren't you going to get in trouble for this?" Ensley asks.

Imogen shrugs like it's no big deal and leans back in her seat. "Yeah, I'll get a slap on the wrist. Maybe a suspension, but I could use a vacation anyway."

"Wait a second," I say. "So you're telling me you stole one of the Arcane Society's relics with highly classified information and the worst that will happen is a suspension? Talon only told us about the Society's existence and the gates and got thrown out of it. How does that make any sense?"

Imogen narrows her eyes at me and I return the glare. *Yeah, I don't like you either.*

"It's a bit more complicated than that," Talon says.

A bitter laugh escapes Imogen's mouth. "You don't get it," she practically spits at me. "Talon broke our most sacred rule when he brought you into confidence about the Arcane Society. If you hadn't forced—"

"Imogen," Talon barks, cutting his cousin off. She turns the glare that was directed at me to him. He holds her gaze. "Enough. We should be talking about strategies for moving forward, not looking back."

She lets out a low growl and I see the tips of her fangs poke into her bottom lip and a flash of red appear in her eyes.

"What's done is done," he says, almost softly this time. "Let it go."

Shaking her head, she shoves him until he lets her out of the booth. She snatches the keys from where Titus rested them on the table and storms out of the diner.

"Should we go after her?" Titus asks, looking like that's the last thing he wants to do.

Talon shakes his head. "Let her cool off."

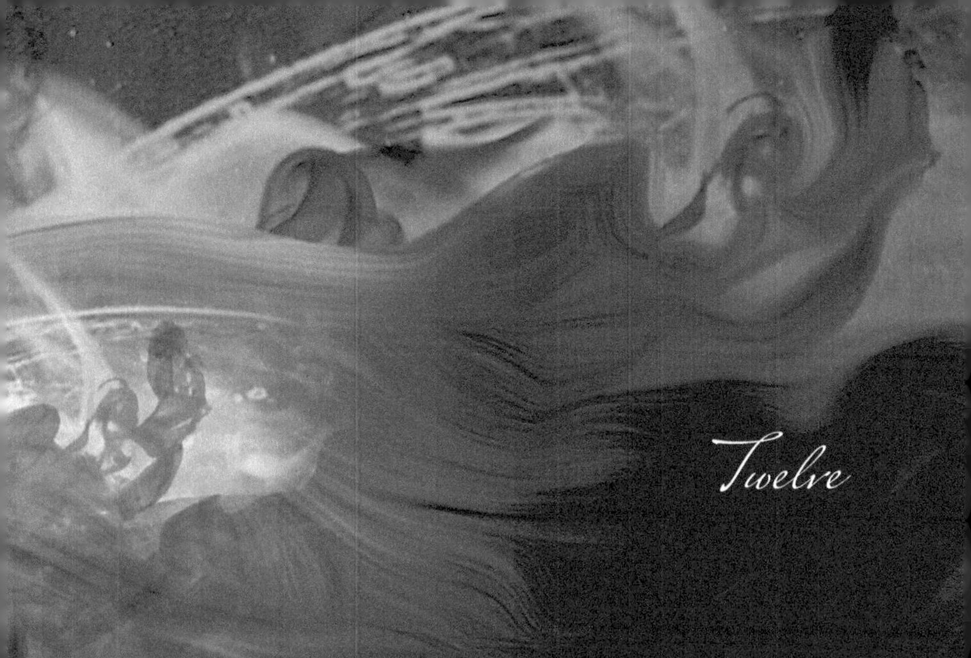

Twelve

THE FOOD ARRIVES, and as we dig in Talon tells us everything he knows about the gates, especially the one we're headed to deep in the swampland. My order takes up a good chunk of the tabletop, and I catch Ensley raising her eyebrows more than once as I demolish everything on my three plates. Even Titus looks like he's trying not to laugh a few times.

I'm on my fifth slice of bacon when I notice something strange. My plate has more food than I remember. I glance at Talon and spot the telltale movement. He's been casually sliding some of his bacon onto my plate when I wasn't looking.

I shoot him a narrow-eyed glare. "Go ahead and make fun of me, but I'm not even mad. If you're dumb enough to surrender your bacon, then I'm obviously the real winner here." I point to my face, triumphant, and bite into the salty strip in my hand.

Talon watches my mouth as I chew, and I pretend not to notice that the room feels a couple degrees warmer than it did a moment before.

"I wasn't making fun of you," he says, his gaze lifting to meet mine.

Oh. Was he just sharing his food with me to be nice? That's . . . unexpected.

"I'm just worried that if we don't keep you fed, you'll start gnawing on my arm to fill that hollow leg of yours. It's really just self-preservation."

A real smile breaks across his face. Genuine, boyish, carefree. It reminds me of the version of him I knew back at Nightlark Academy, before Chaos turned everything upside down.

I chuck the last of my bacon at his face, aiming for his eye, but he snatches it out of the air with his mouth. He grins around the bite as he chews, clearly pleased with himself.

I pout, watching the last piece of bacon disappear. "That was mine."

Talon shrugs, chewing happily. "Call it payment. You used me as a pillow for four hours. I think I earned it."

I blink, heat rushing to my cheeks. "I didn't ask for a pillow."

He leans in, just enough for his voice to brush against my skin. "Didn't hear you complaining."

And just like that, I forget what air tastes like.

Ensley clears her throat and I glance over at her and Titus.

"So, about this gate," she says, staring at Talon with a frown.

He straightens, leaning his forearms on the table. The easy smile fades, and I feel its absence like a weight. But there's no time for that. Ensley is right. *Becks*. Every second we sit here, he's still out there, waiting. That's what's important.

"The gate won't look like an actual gate," Talon says. "At least not obviously so. As you know, the one we are headed toward is in the swamplands, so the gate is going to look natural occurring."

"Natural occurring?" Titus asks.

"Like an arch of vines or maybe branches. You're not going to see a stone archway or anything that obvious. It's going to blend in with the environment. A detail easily missed or dismissed. We know the general area, but not the pinpoint location."

"Okay," I say. "So the plan is we trudge around this swamp until we find the gate, and then what? Do I need to mix a drop of blood with my necklace or perform some kind of ritual to open it?"

Talon shakes his head. "Nothing quite that dramatic. There'll be a place to insert the gem. That will awaken the gate. Then when it's turned, the gate will be activated and should transport us to the human world."

"Should?" Ensley asks.

Talon shrugs. "The gates haven't been used in thousands of years. It's not like anyone alive has ever traveled through one. I only know what was written about them. So yes, it should happen that way, but we should be prepared for anything."

The table is quiet while that sinks in.

"And there's something else," Talon says, looking extremely serious. "There's another reason why the Arcane Society doesn't bother guarding the hidden gates."

My stomach dips and I already know I'm not going to like whatever comes out of his mouth next.

"Each of the hidden gates has a magical protector. A monster created by the first generation of the Arcane Society to guard the gates."

"A monster?" I burst out. Diners around us peek over at us. I sink down in my seat. I didn't mean to be that loud.

"A monster?" I whisper-yell. "And you thought going up against a monster would be preferable to facing off against a few of your Society buddies?" I cut my gaze to Ensley and Titus, expecting them to back me up, but Ensley just shrugs, and Titus leans forward to hear what Talon is going to say next.

"Yes," Talon says. "I do think going up against a single beast is better than a contingent of highly trained Society members."

A brief glint of regret passes through his eyes, and a thought strikes me. Maybe Talon does believe facing a monster is the lesser of two evils, but maybe he's also afraid he couldn't bring himself to fight the Society members who are like family to him.

The idea softens the edges of my anger. Compassion creeps in, dulling the sting of the monster revelation. Instead of arguing, I simply press my lips together and nod.

"So what do we know about this monster, if anything?" Titus asks.

"All the beasts that guard the hidden gates were once regular animals indigenous to the area. Back when the gates were sealed, the members of the Society imbued an animal with magical abilities and long life. So if the gate is in a frozen tundra for example, the guardian might be a polar bear. If it's in a jungle, perhaps it's an anaconda or jaguar, and so on."

I laugh, but there's no real humor in the half-strangled breath that escapes me. "So we're going to be playing chicken with a two-thousand-year-old alligator?"

"It's highly likely," he says with a straight face.

Oh boy.

"Do we actually need to defeat the monster to get through the gate?" Ensley asks, and Talon shakes his head.

"No, we just need to get past it. The beasts sleep until their gate is disturbed. We need to be prepared for it to emerge when we get close to the gate with Locklyn's gemstone. With any luck we can get through the gate quickly without having to engage it."

"Like, they hibernate?" I ask.

"Yes, exactly like that."

I swallow hard. The only thing I remember about hibernating animals is how ravenous they are when they first awake.

"Oh goody," I say flatly. "Sounds like it's going to be a fun time for everyone."

The corner of Talon's mouth quirks. "Depends on what you consider a fun time," he says.

The spark in his eye can't hide that there's a part of him looking forward to this. My first instinct is to think he's crazy, but if I'm honest with myself, there's a restless charge building in my chest and I can't tell if it's anxiety or excitement.

Shoot. Maybe I'm as messed up as Talon.

"Let's get out of here," Talon says as he slides out of the booth.

I nod and push to my feet. Titus and Ensley slide out of the booth after me and we all leave the diner and head back toward the Valkyrie. When we get there, Imogen is leaning against the side. There's a rosy hue to her cheeks that wasn't there earlier, and she has the self-satisfied look of the cat that just ate the canary.

"You seem chipper," I say as I yank open the front passenger's door. I'm the only one who hasn't had a chance in the front seat. I don't care that after Imogen, I'm the smallest. I want the opportunity to ride shotgun too.

"A good meal will do you wonders," she says. "Pro tip: always make sure I'm fed. I'm not pleasant when I'm hangry."

My eyebrows pinch in confusion. "But you left the diner before—"

Oh.

She doesn't mean *food*. At least, not in the sense I do.

I know drinking blood is a natural thing for vampires. They don't usually flaunt it, and in modern times there are plenty of ways to pick up a pint or two without having to tap a vein, but the satisfied look on Imogen's face makes me think she didn't go with the traditional method of buying a blood bag at a pop-up stand.

Seeing my face, she laughs. "Relax. There was a blood stand on the other side of the diner." She rolls her eyes and climbs into the SUV.

I climb into the seat just as Talon slides behind the wheel. He pulls onto the road with smooth precision, merging onto the highway without a word. No one says much. Everyone's wrapped in their own thoughts.

I sneak a glance at Talon. His profile is sharp in the early light, his naturally darker skin tone is unusually pale. Imogen's fresh, glowing face from earlier flashes through my mind. The contrast nags at me.

Is he like her? Does he need blood too?

"What?" Talon says without taking his eyes off the road.

"Huh?"

His gaze shifts to me and he arches an eyebrow before looking forward again.

Busted.

"You're a vampire, right?" I blurt out.

Imogen cackles in the seat behind me. "He wishes."

My jaw drops. "You aren't?"

The hint of a smile curves the corners of Talon's mouth, but besides that, he doesn't respond.

Ensley leans forward from the middle seat, popping her head into the space between Talon and me. "Snake shifter, right? I mean, at first I thought vampire too. But I've come around to Locklyn's train of thought. Definitely snake shifter."

Talon's lips press into a hard line and he shoots Ensley a side-eye, but he still doesn't engage.

"I don't know. I think he might have some fae in him," Titus speaks up from the back seat. I glance back at him and he has a look of mischief in his eyes.

"Fae, no way," Ensley says, wrinkling her nose like the idea that Talon is a fae as well disgusts her.

"You'll never guess. And even if you do, he'll never say," Imogen says in a singsong voice.

"Is that true?" I ask Talon.

"I was taught that revealing your creature was to make yourself vulnerable."

Imogen scoffs. "A super old-school way of thinking that only he and his mom still adhere to."

My brows lift. "Wait, no one knows what your mom is either? Not even your dad?"

I've never heard of someone hiding their species that thoroughly. Sure, asking outright is considered rude, but to keep it a secret from your own family? That feels extreme.

Talon clears his throat and shifts in his seat, clearly uncomfortable. "It's just . . . not something we talk about."

“I have my theories,” Imogen says. “But he won’t even tell me.”

So, vampire isn’t off the table after all. Back to square one on that mystery. It’s starting to feel like it’s going to stay that way. I almost press Talon for more, but it’s obvious he’s done with the conversation, and I don’t see the point in nagging him.

We drive for a couple more hours in heavy silence. My thoughts spiral as they drift to Becks, conjuring up every worst-case scenario.

Did Kerrim leave him behind, wounded and alone? Or did he take him and lock him away somewhere we’ll never find? Has Becks even recovered from his injury? Is he safe? Alive?

He’s never been far from my thoughts since the night they vanished through the portal, but I’ve tried to keep myself from going to that darkest place. The one where we’re already too late. Where Shadow Striker’s blow did more damage than I’ve let myself believe. Where we get to the human world only to find there’s no one left to save.

The what-ifs keep stacking up, and with them comes a creeping dread I can’t shake. I knot my fingers in my lap and stare out the window without really seeing anything. The sky is still clear, but the road around the Valkyrie darkens, as if a shadow is creeping in despite the sun.

Out of the corner of my eye I see Talon shoot me a worried frown, but I ignore him.

“Yo, Talon. Lay off the shadows,” Titus says from the back seat. “One just crawled across my neck.”

I twist around to see shadows swirling on the roof of the Valkyrie. Titus looks annoyed as another one slides over his shoulder. Ensley looks a little freaked, and Imogen just looks confused.

I glance over at Talon and his brow is pinched, a frown pulling down the corners of his mouth.

“Sorry,” he mumbles as the shadows start to dissipate.

Talon must have a lot on his mind to lose control of his powers like that. He is always controlled, especially when it comes to his magic. Back when we competed in Chaos together, I never saw him falter. Every move he made was measured and deliberate. He wasn't showy with his magic like some. He kept a tight lid on his powers, only using them when they were absolutely needed.

Another few hours slip by, and the haunting images in my head only grow more disturbing. Becks isn't just lying wounded in that clearing anymore. Now he's broken and helpless, surrounded by scavengers, his body torn apart while he screams for me to save him.

And I'm nowhere to be found.

"How close are we?" I ask.

"Close," Talon says, and then reaches over and places his hand on my knee to stop it from bobbing up and down.

My muscles lock up as the heat from Talon's hand seeps through my clothes. I wouldn't call his touch comforting exactly, but it does the job of breaking the "Becks is dead" loop playing in my head. As I stare down at my leg, all I can think about is how large his hand is. His tanned fingers wrap around so much of my thigh he could almost circle it completely. I know I need to tell him to move it, but my vocal cords feel frozen. All I manage is a weak throat-clear.

Talon takes the hint and silently removes his hand, but even after it's gone I can still feel the ghost of it pressing into my leg. I rub the spot, trying to erase the lingering sensation, just as Talon turns the Valkyrie into the parking lot of a rundown motel. A flickering neon sign reads "Vacancy."

"What are we doing here?" I ask as he pulls into a parking spot.

After turning off the engine, he twists in his seat to see the others in the back. "Why don't you three get us a couple rooms? Imogen and I have to pick up some stuff."

"Rooms? What do we need rooms for?" Ensley asks.

"It's getting late in the day, and Imogen and I need to collect some supplies, so it's probably best if we crash for the night and hit up the gate in the morning."

Ensley and I exchange a glance. It's at least three hours until sunset. Her pinched features say she doesn't want to wait any more than I do. Titus looks like he's on the fence.

Talon and Imogen have clearly already made up their minds.

I shake my head. "No. We're so close. Let's just go now. If we wait longer, there's a higher chance of your Society friends finding us."

Talon runs a hand through his hair. "I know you're anxious to get your princeling," he says, using that irritating nickname for Becks again like it's some kind of habit he can't break. "But it would be foolish to rush into something like this."

"I don't care if—"

"Listen," Imogen cuts in, "if we don't collect a piece of *tamalite*, then it's only going to be a one-way ticket. Get it?"

I crane my neck to look at Imogen in the seat behind me, and she sneers back at me.

"No, I don't *get it*," I say. "What even is tamalite?"

She sighs. "You know we need lunacite from the human world to travel through the gate. Well, to return, we need tamalite. Without it, we won't be able to get back to *our* world after we find your friend. So, if it's okay with you, *Your Highness*, we'd like to make sure we don't get stuck in a magicless world for the rest of our lives."

I press my lips together to keep from sniping back at her. Talon could have just said so.

"But it's not just the tamalite," Talon adds. "We have to be smart about this. We're going to need weapons, appropriate clothing, food rations."

"Food rations? Is this human world back in the Stone Age or something?" I ask, alarmed even though I know that can't be true. I spotted modern skyscrapers over the tree line through the portal.

"We don't know where we are going to appear in that world or how long it's going to take us to find your princeling."

"*Becks*," I grate out, but Talon keeps going as if I haven't spoken.

"And even when we find this Central Park, he may be long gone from the area. We won't have the local currency or knowledge about the land at all. The information Imogen and I have about the human world is over two thousand years old. Think about how different our civilization is since that time. It's better to be over-prepared than under."

As much as I hate to admit it, Talon has a point. When I look back at Ensley and Titus, I can tell they agree. "Fine. We'll leave tomorrow morning."

Talon nods and Titus, Ensley, and I climb out. We head toward the front desk to ask about rooms, and I glance over my shoulder just as Talon and Imogen back out of the parking space and merge into traffic.

For a wild, irrational second, panic spikes in my chest. What if they don't come back?

I know Imogen's going to try to convince Talon to ditch us. It's probably the only reason she tagged along in the first place. A knot of doubt twists deep in my gut.

But then, in my mind's eye, I picture Talon's face. The steadiness in his gaze. The warmth behind his teasing smile.

He's coming back. I trust him.

I think.

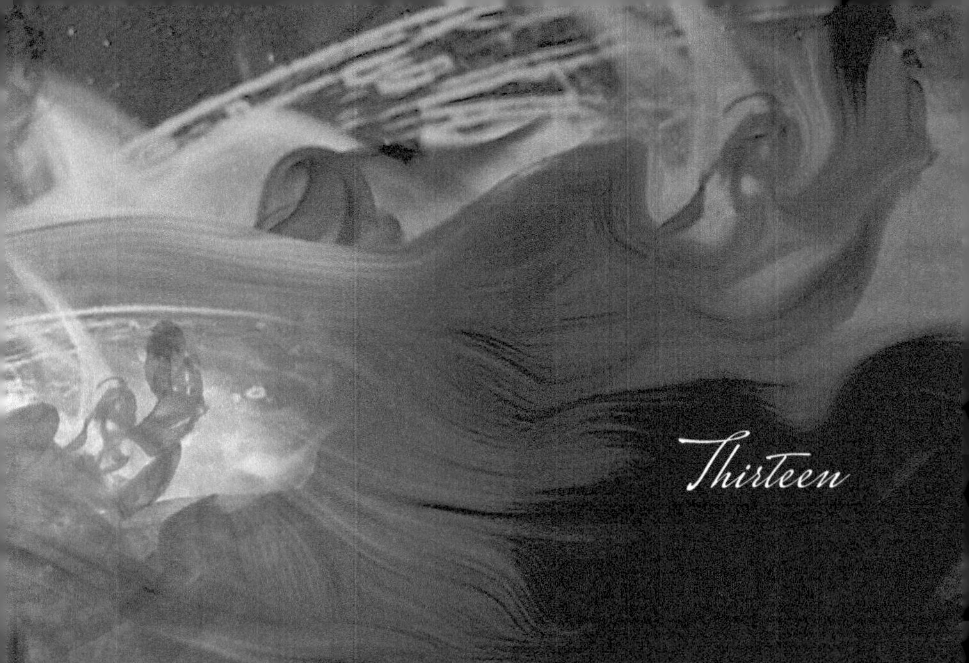

Thirteen

HOURS LATER, the sun's set and Titus, Ensley, and I sit in one of the two shabby rooms munching on lukewarm pizza in relative silence. I tried calling Talon three different times, but I got sent to voicemail every time. As much as I try to reassure myself that there's a perfectly good explanation for why they are taking so long, I'm still nervous.

What if after everything, Imogen convinces Talon to ditch us? There's no way to get to the human world without his help. I'd never see Becks again.

"We should have asked to hold the book for collateral," Ensley says as she drops her half-eaten slice on the napkin she was using as a plate. She eyes the slice with scorn, but it's not the pizza she's upset with. "At least we thought to grab our bags," she grumbles.

"They're going to be back soon," I say with confidence I don't feel.

"Locklyn's right," Titus says as he peers out the window through the curtains. "They just pulled up."

I'm up and crossing the room in an instant. By the time I swing open the door, Imogen and Talon are already out of the Valkyrie. They've moved to the rear hatch to unload whatever they have in the back of the SUV. I jog over to them just as Imogen hefts a couple filled backpacks over her shoulder.

"You're back," I say unnecessarily.

Imogen rolls her eyes. "Wow. Nothing gets by you."

I clench my fist, wanting nothing more than to punch the snark out of her. "What took you so long?"

"What, you missed us?" she asks with a laugh, and then shoves a backpack at me. "Here, bring this inside."

I sling it over one shoulder. It's heavy. "What's inside?"

Imogen pushes past me without answering and disappears into our motel room. I really don't like her.

When I look back, Talon is reaching for something deep in the cargo area of the vehicle. His shirt rides up slightly, revealing a long, angry-looking cut on his side, where blood is slowly trickling down his skin.

Without thinking, I drop the bag and grab the edge of his shirt, hauling it up. Two more slashes cross his ribs. Thin, jagged lines that look almost too evenly spaced to be random. The wounds are red and inflamed, the edges raised and still bleeding in places. They look like claw marks, or maybe the aftermath of barbed wire, messy, but with a strange kind of pattern. Definitely not from a blade.

My stomach knots. "Talon," I whisper. "What did this to you?"

"Whoa," he says, pulling away.

His T-shirt falls back into place, covering the wounds. I try to reach for his shirt again—I want to see how serious an injury it is—but he sidesteps me.

"What happened?"

"It's nothing," he says, ducking his head to avoid my gaze. "We just ran into a little bit of trouble when we were collecting weapons. Nothing Imogen and I couldn't handle."

"Evidently," I say with a raised brow.

He sighs. "Our old suppliers were already alerted by the Society to be on the lookout for us. We had to make sure they didn't report back that they'd spotted us, or come morning the area would be swarming with Society members. Something we definitely want to avoid."

I gape at Talon. "So you killed them?"

The corner of his mouth lifts. "I'm not sure if I should be flattered or offended that you think I'm so bloodthirsty."

"Definitely offended."

His smirk kicks up a notch. "And yet I'm not. But no, we didn't kill them. Not that they wouldn't have deserved it. Underground arms dealers have plenty of blood on their hands. But we did make sure they couldn't reach the Arcane Society. At least for the next day or so. We definitely need to find that gate tomorrow or move on to a different one."

"Where's the next closest?"

Talon winces. "In the drylands."

"The drylands? That's the other side of the country. At least three days' drive from here."

He nods. "And that one is guarded, so we need to make tomorrow count."

I sigh, the weight of the world settling on my shoulders. "About those cuts—"

"They're nothing."

I narrow my eyes. "If they're nothing, then why aren't you healing?"

"I am, just not as quickly as usual. One of the dealers was a Komodo dragon shifter. Some of its venom got into me when he bit me."

"Those are bite marks?" Taking a step forward, I reach for him again, wanting a better look at his injury, but he traps my wrist when I snag the bottom of his shirt, staying my movements.

When I go to pull my hand back, he doesn't let go.

I glance up, and he's watching me. We're standing so close now

I can see the shift in his eyes as his pupils expand, nearly eclipsing the stormy blue-gray.

"Locklyn," he says, his voice dropping, the kind of tone that vibrates more than it sounds. The narrow space between us stretches tight with something electric. "Before we go through the gate, we need to talk."

I lick my lips, suddenly hyperaware of every breath.

"Talk?" I echo, though I'm not sure if I'm asking a question or just stalling.

His gaze drops to my mouth and my stomach hollows. He slowly swipes his thumb over the wrist he's still holding and my heart beats faster.

"There's something I need to tell you about—"

"Yo! What's taking so long?" Imogen yells from the doorway of our motel room.

Talon's grip loosens and I slip out of his grasp, feeling slightly breathless.

Turning my back, I scoop up the backpack Imogen gave me and flee like a coward, speed-walking back to the room without checking to make sure Talon is following. I dump the bag just inside the front door.

"You okay?" Ensley asks, giving me a funny look.

"Yeah. Of course. Why?"

"You look flushed."

Talon enters the room at that exact moment, carrying a large black duffel bag.

"I'm not flushed," I mumble. "It was just cold outside."

Ensley shoots me a confused look. The swamplands are hot and muggy at the best of times, and sweltering during the others.

"I mean hot."

I turn away from Talon and Ensley only to come face to face with Imogen. There's a knowing smirk on her face that I choose to ignore as I sidestep her and take a seat at the small bistro table across the room.

"Did you get everything you needed?" Titus asks.

"We did," Talon says, holding up his hand to reveal a bulky gold ring set with a black stone. "Most importantly, I got our ticket home."

Titus eyes the ring with curiosity. "That's the tamalite?"

Talon nods. "Yeah. Sorry it took so long. Took a little extra convincing to get them to hand it over."

"I tried calling a few times but you didn't pick up," I say, still a little salty about that.

Talon pulls on the back of his neck. "Right. I don't actually have my phone anymore. I left it behind so that I couldn't be tracked. Imogen did the same."

"Oh." I didn't even think of that, but it makes perfect sense.

"What are in these?" Ensley asks as she bends down to look at one of the bags. "They're only half filled."

"We wanted to leave space to bring some clothes and personal items," Talon explains.

"Granola bars, first-aid kit," Ensley says, listing items as she digs through the pack.

"What's that at the bottom?"

"A compact tent."

"We're going to be camping?" she asks, a note of surprise in her voice.

I grimace. I've only been camping once, with my dad when I was nine. He's a nature lover, which is pretty typical for bear shifters. It's basically in their blood. But I learned quickly that it is not in mine. Ensley enjoys glamping, but sleeping in a tent is a stretch for her too.

"We know our worlds influence each other," Talon says. "I think it's safe to assume they have some modern amenities. But we don't know how safe it's going to be for us in the general population. Best to be prepared."

"But we brought our own bags," Ensley says, pointing to her pink backpack in the corner.

Talon nods. "You can keep whatever personal items you need, but these are better suited for traveling light and staying mobile. Just transfer the essentials into the new ones."

Ensley frowns, not looking pleased with her new backpack, but she goes over and starts sorting through her things to figure out what to bring and what to leave.

Bending over, Talon unzips the black duffel he brought in. I can't see what's inside. Titus' eyes widen as he gets a good look. Leaning over, Ensley peeks in the duffel and her mouth drops open.

Titus lets out a low whistle and glances up at Talon. "Are we going to war?"

Talon responds with a grim look. "Take what you're comfortable using."

I get up from my seat and cross the room. Ensley and Titus are already bent over the duffel bag, rifling through the contents.

"Seriously, Talon?" Ensley says, holding up a spiked metal ball attached by a foot long chain to a small rod. "Who's going to use this?"

"That would be mine," Imogen says as she plucks the medieval looking weapon from Ensley's hand.

I peek over Ensley's shoulder and see a cache of various weapons. Some of them I recognize, like knives, daggers, and crossbows, but there are others I don't. Titus grabs a pair of daggers and matching sheaths. He steps away from the bag, not bothering to get anything else.

After a few more minutes, Ensley throws her hands in the air. "I don't know how to use any of these weapons. I'd probably do more harm to myself than someone else if I try to use any of it."

Reaching over, Titus sifts through the weapons and pulls out a small dagger that's safely tucked in a leather sheath and hands it to Ensley. "Here, at least take this. I know you can protect yourself with your powers, but we might not want to reveal ourselves when we are there by using them."

She eyes it with uncertainty, but eventually puts it in her bag and steps back.

I bend over the duffel, gazing at the different options.

I may not have magic, but I've spent years turning my body into a weapon. A glint of gold catches my eye and I reach into the bag, pulling out a pair of brass knuckles. I've never used them before. With the right aim, they can do serious damage, the kind of brutality I've always tried to avoid. But something tells me that's about to change in this new world.

"I thought you might like those," Talon says with a smirk. "Take this too," he says, reaching into the duffel and fishing out a dagger. The blade is wavy and roughly a foot long. I can't help but notice how similar it is to Shadow Striker. I look at Talon as I take the weapon with a question in my eyes.

"You need to learn how to use it."

I balk. "Why?"

Talon shrugs. "Just in case."

I shake my head and try to give Talon the blade back. "No. I never want to touch that cursed dagger again."

He glances down at the wavy-bladed dagger but doesn't take the weapon. "We don't know what's going to happen over there. You should be prepared."

"Prepared to face Kerrim?"

He looks up and his blue-gray gaze is piercing. "Maybe. Shadow Striker is rightfully yours. I think if we find the blade, it will recognize you as its wielder."

I drop the weapon at Talon's feet, shaking my head. "I'd rather die than touch it again."

"You may not have a choice."

Talon and I have a silent faceoff, neither one of us willing to budge. It's only when Imogen interrupts us by reaching over, snatching the blade and saying, "Well, if you don't want it," that I realize just how quiet the room has gotten.

Embarrassed, I turn and grab one of the backpacks, busying

myself with storing the brass knuckles and pretending to look through the contents even though I know all the packs have similar items inside.

The mood turns somber after that. Talon and Imogen finish off the last of the cold pizza, then we all turn in. We've rented adjoining rooms. Talon and Titus take one, and us girls the other. Ensley and I share a double bed. Imogen may be small, but neither of us wants to sleep next to her. I even insist we keep the door between rooms open. I'm not comfortable being in an enclosed space with her. Imogen's just as likely to slit my throat as look at me. That might be extreme, but I don't trust the morally ambiguous vampire who clearly blames me for everything.

It's a long time before sleep takes me, but when it finally does, it pulls me under, sinking its dark claws into my mind and latching on, making me wish I'd never succumbed.

SLOAN'S DINER *is busy as usual, the booths filled with patrons, their chatter a steady hum in the background. The scent of grilled onions and stale coffee hangs in the air as Becks, sitting beside me, cracks a joke that makes me smile. The jukebox in the corner hums with an old rock ballad, and Ensley steals some of Becks' fries when he's not looking and passes one off to Titus.*

I'm happy. My chest full of contentment, like everything is exactly as it should be. I'm with my friends. We're having a good time. We're all safe.

And yet, even as I think it, a slow unease begins to coil in my gut. A sense of wrongness that grows more insistent with each passing moment.

Ensley's laugh is too loud. Becks' smile too bright. And Titus has never come with us to Sloan's. Why is he here now?

My own smile falters as the unease curdles into dread.

The fluorescent bulbs overhead stutter and dim, bathing the diner in a sickly, unnatural hue.

Conversations fade. The warmth seeps from the air.

And when I look up, I see him.

Kerrim.

He's standing in the doorway. Unassuming, with his glasses perched on his nose and salt-and-pepper hair brushed back off his forehead. He looks exactly like I remember him, but every part of me recoils.

His gaze sweeps the restaurant, the once-friendly glint in his eyes sharpening into something cold and shrewd when they land on mine. Then slide to Becks.

"No," I breathe, scrambling to stand. But my limbs don't obey. My legs won't move. My voice barely carries.

Becks doesn't seem to realize anything is wrong. He's still facing me as Kerrim crosses the dining room toward us, each step echoing sharply in the sudden silence. Shadow Striker appears in his hand, black and humming with power.

I try to scream, to warn him, to move, to do anything, but I'm frozen.

Kerrim plunges the blade into Becks' back and the tip punches through his chest. His warm blood sprays across my own, hot and jarring.

Becks' mouth opens in a silent gasp, eyes wide with pain and disbelief as he slips from the booth. Blood spills across the checkered floor, soaking into the seams between tiles as the crimson pool spreads beneath him.

He looks at me like I'm the one who drove the blade into his back, his gaze heavy with hurt and betrayal.

My breath catches. My heart shatters.

And then—

He changes.

Blond hair darkens. His jaw sharpens. It's not Becks lying there anymore.

It's Talon.

His bloodied hand twitches on the floor. He lifts his head just enough for our eyes to meet, and there's nothing but pain in his gaze.

Chilled laughter fills the air as Kerrim stands over him, bloodied dagger still clutched in his fist.

Hate surges through me, burning hot, mixing with the horror already twisting in my soul.

I scream Talon's name—finally able to move, to speak—but the moment I do, the diner crumbles around us like ash in the wind.

And I wake.

Heart pounding.

Sheets tangled.

The echo of Kerrim's laughter still ringing in my ears like a curse.

AMAZINGLY, my thrashing didn't wake Ensley, but I can't fall back asleep. I don't *want* to. Too scared I'll be faced with gruesome scenes of a deranged Kerrim plunging Shadow Striker into the chests of everyone I know and care about.

After tonight, I know one thing for sure: whatever affection I might have once had for the former shop owner was burned away the moment he slammed the dagger through Becks' chest, leaving only hate in my heart for him.

Just after dawn, I drag myself out of bed and into the bathroom, head low as I try to shake off the remnants of the nightmare. Talon's anguish, Kerrim's sadistic glee, and worst of all, Becks' face, twisted with pain and betrayal, won't leave me.

I grab my toothbrush and notice my hand shaking. It wasn't real, but my body doesn't know that. It takes longer than it should to wash my face and brush my teeth, and when I step out of the bathroom, Imogen and Ensley are already in the guys' room. I shove my essentials into my new backpack and get ready to go, but I'm no calmer than when I woke.

Sitting on the edge of the bed, I close my eyes and draw in a deep breath. Three counts in through my nose. Three counts out through my mouth. Again. And again.

I don't know what we're walking into today, but I need my head on straight. If I'm distracted, someone could get hurt. Or worse. I have to shelve the panic clawing at my insides. Becks will have to wait until we're through that gate. Until then, I need to lock down my heart and stay sharp.

"You all right?"

I open my eyes to find Talon standing in front of me, dressed in a fitted black T-shirt and dark jeans, his hands shoved in his pockets as he studies me. The nightmare vision of him lying on the ground, bleeding from the same wound Kerrim inflicted on Becks, flashes through my mind, but I force it away.

"I'm fine," I say, standing and slinging my backpack over my shoulder.

I move to pass him, but he shifts subtly, blocking my path. I glance up, eyebrows raised, hoping he'll take the hint. I don't have the energy to spar with him right now. But he just folds his arms and meets my eyes with quiet determination.

"You don't look fine."

"Thanks," I say tartly, my defenses going up.

Talon's gaze softens. "That wasn't meant as an insult. You just seem off. Upset, maybe. Or spooked. I don't know. You're hard to read."

I raise an eyebrow. "Me? Hard to read?"

He lets out a short laugh. "Yeah. A total enigma. Is it the gate? Are you worried we won't find it?"

I shake my head. "No. I mean, maybe a little. But that's not it. I just had a rough night."

He nods like he gets it, even though I haven't offered any explanation. "He's going to be okay," he says quietly, knowing without me having to say that I'm upset about Becks.

Up until now Talon has always been in the *he probably didn't make it* camp, so hearing him say that is unexpected.

"I didn't think you actually believed Becks was still alive." I get a pang in my chest just suggesting it.

Talon looks away, exhaling a long breath. When his gaze finds mine again, it's shadowed with something unreadable. Not quite sadness, but close. "Your princeling's strong. If anyone could survive that, it's him. And he has you waiting for him. That kind of hope . . . it matters."

He lifts a hand like he's going to touch my cheek, and for a second my heart skitters, but he stops short and lets it drop. "What better motivation is there than that?"

I shake my head, throat tightening. "No. He thinks I betrayed him. That I chose you over him. He probably hates me."

A faint smile tugs at Talon's mouth, but there's no light in it. "Becks could never hate you. Yeah, he was shocked when he saw us together. I won't deny that. But the way he broke through that shield to get to you during the last trial? He knew. Deep down, he had to know you still cared."

I start to protest, but Talon gently cuts me off. "Trust me. He knows."

My eyes sting, tears welling despite every effort to hold them back. "Do you really think so?" I whisper, his words a balm on a wound I've been trying to ignore.

Talon nods. "I do."

A single tear slips free, sliding down my cheek. Talon shifts closer and catches it with the pad of his thumb, gently wiping it away.

"I'm sorry you're hurting," he murmurs. "I'd do anything to take that pain from you."

When I look into his eyes, my breath catches. I see the truth in his gaze. His eyes are telling me that if he could take away my sorrow, he would move heaven and hell to do so.

I don't know how to feel about that. Or maybe I do, but I'm too afraid to admit it.

"Talon," I breathe, barely aware of the word leaving my lips.

I take a small, uncertain step forward, drawn to him by some invisible thread. For one reckless second I just want to let go, to sink into him, let his arms be the place where I can finally collapse, just for a moment, just so I don't have to carry it all alone.

He reads me instantly.

His hands find my arms and gently guide me the rest of the way. I don't resist. I press into him, and his arms encircle me as if they were always meant to. He doesn't speak right away, just draws me in and rests his chin lightly against the top of my head. One hand strokes up and down my back. Soothing, steady.

Softly, he whispers into my hair, "It's going to be all right. You don't have to do this alone."

A quiet sob slips out before I can stop it, and a tear warms my cheek. Talon pulls me tighter, like he's holding the pieces of me together when I can't do it myself.

His fingers trail gently into my hair, and then he tips my face up. His eyes search mine—troubled, intense, unguarded.

"Don't cry," he says, his voice rough. His thumb brushes away the tear. "I can't bear it."

I stare up at him, overwhelmed. My emotions are a tangled, riotous mess, guilt and sorrow crashing against something softer, warmer, I don't want to name. Maybe I'm just tired. Maybe I'm desperate for comfort. Or maybe it's more than that.

I part my lips, unsure what I even mean to say, when Imogen's voice slices through the moment from the adjoining room.

"What's taking so long?"

The spell shatters.

Talon's jaw tightens as he shoots an annoyed glance toward the open doorway. "Just a minute," he calls back, voice clipped.

I slip out of his arms and cross into the next room without looking back.

It's only once I pass the threshold that the strange fluttering low in my stomach starts to fade. I tell myself it meant nothing. That I'm vulnerable. Talon happened to be there when I needed someone. That's all.

But deep down, a quiet voice whispers that I'm running out of ways to lie to myself.

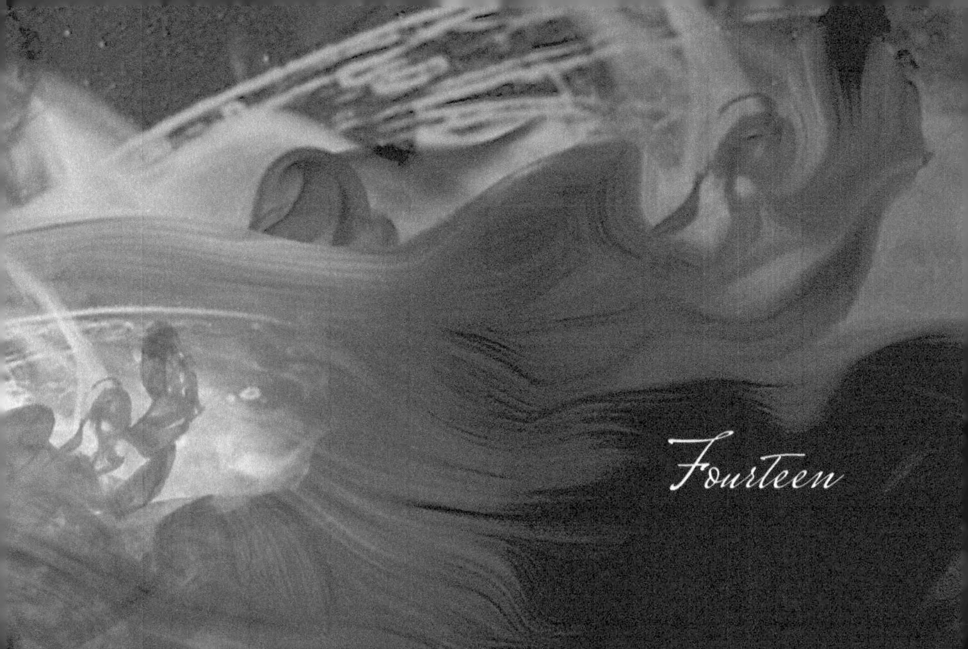

Fourteen

"WHERE'S THE MOTOR?" I ask, tilting my head as I eye the flat-bottomed boat we're about to launch into the swamp. It's a rental that Talon and Imogen secured during their supply run yesterday. Little does the owner know that if we actually find the gate we're looking for, there's a good chance he'll never see this vessel again.

"It's right here," Talon says, tapping the cage that houses a giant fan mounted at the back. The whole setup is welded directly onto the hull.

"I don't get it."

Talon chuckles at my confusion. "Swamps and marshes are too shallow for traditional boats. An airboat doesn't use an in-water motor, it uses that propeller. It forces air behind the boat to push it forward."

I give him a skeptical look, stepping aside as Imogen backs the Valkyrie up to position the trailer. Once the boat is in place, Talon and Titus help ease it into the murky water.

"Have you ever been on one of these?" I ask Ensley as she comes to stand beside me.

"Once," she says. "We vacationed in the swamplands a few years ago and did a half-day fishing trip." She chuckles. "Becks was terrible at fishing. It was hilarious watching him fail at something for once. He got so frustrated he started lobbing fireballs at the fish. Our guide freaked out and cut the trip short. Apparently, swamps are protected areas. Fire? Big no-no."

The guys get the boat in the water successfully, and Imogen drives the trailer to a nearby parking spot.

"I remember these being really loud," Ensley says as Talon and Titus rejoin us.

"They are," Talon confirms. "That's why the rental place gave us noise-canceling earmuffs."

We leave behind any extra baggage and supplies we don't plan to take, including the super-secret book Imogen "borrowed" from the Arcane Society. Talon and Imogen agree that it's only a matter of time, maybe a day at most, before the Society tracks down the Valkyrie and reclaims it. Bringing such a valuable artifact through the gate felt like too big a risk.

Once we've unloaded what we need from the SUV, we climb aboard the airboat. Imogen, Titus, Ensley, and I take the two bench seats in the middle, while Talon settles into the raised seat at the back. From there, he'll be steering with what looks like nothing more than a long stick connected to the massive propeller frame behind him.

"Earmuffs on," Talon instructs, his voice clipped.

We slip them over our ears, and the world immediately falls silent. A moment later, the propeller roars to life.

Dang, it is loud. Even through the earmuffs.

Talon eases the boat into the water, navigating smoothly through the swamp's maze of twisting rivers and pathways. The gate is supposed to be about five miles from our launch point, and Talon handles the vessel with practiced ease.

Wildlife flanks us at every turn, signs of life thriving in the marsh's murky calm. A massive alligator, at least fifteen feet long, glides silently alongside the boat. A turtle basks on a fallen tree branch ahead, and Talon gently steers us around it. A snowy bird takes flight from a nearby cypress tree, flapping noisily. That makes five bird species I've counted so far.

As the boat slows, Talon signals that we can remove our earmuffs. It's still noisy, but not unbearable. If we talk loudly, we can be heard over the propellor.

"Okay, we're in the area," Talon says, reducing our speed to a near crawl. "Keep your eyes open."

According to Talon and Imogen, the gate will look like part of the environment. It will be a ring or an arch shape, but it'll be disguised, hidden in plain sight. If everything goes according to plan, we'll activate the gate and get through before the monster can fully wake and reach us.

If not, we'll have to fight.

We round a bend and the narrow waterway suddenly opens into a dense wooded area that's too thick for the airboat to pass through.

Talon looks to Imogen, who gives a single nod. That's our path forward.

"All right," Talon says. "We're going by foot from here."

With our packs strapped to our backs, we unload one by one from the boat onto a soggy patch of grass. Cold water immediately seeps into my shoes, but I knew it was inevitable. Searching a swamp for a hidden gate to another world isn't exactly a dry adventure.

When did my life get so weird?

We trudge through the marsh in relative silence, accompanied only by the quiet hum of wildlife and the squelching of our footsteps. We try to stick to raised patches of ground, but more than once we're forced into the water. Before long, I'm soaked up to my calves. I really hope the human world has showers, because the minute we get there, I'm going to need one.

The vegetation grows thicker until we're completely surrounded by tangled trees and underbrush. Titus takes the lead, hacking through the dense foliage with a machete or pushing it aside with subtle waves of fae magic. I pass my necklace up to him to make his job a little easier.

We're passing through a particularly tight spot when a sharp hiss makes me freeze. I glance to the side just in time to come face-to-face with a black snake coiled around a branch at eye level. Its belly is a vivid, angry red.

I yelp and jerk back, slamming straight into Talon, who's bringing up the rear. His arm wraps firmly around my waist, steadying both of us and pulling me flush against his chest.

"Easy," he says, his voice low and calm. I can feel the vibration of the words where our bodies touch. "Just a swamp snake. They're not dangerous."

I glance back just as the snake slithers down the tree and disappears into the murky water. A shiver runs through me. Dangerous or not, snakes seriously creep me out.

I silently renew my hope that Talon isn't a snake shapeshifter.

"You really don't like snakes, do you?" Talon chuckles as he lets go of me.

"That's an understatement."

I step forward cautiously, and as we push through a dense patch of brush, my mind drifts to everything *except* what it should. Snakes, Talon, Becks . . . even Imogen and my parents. I *should* be scanning for the gate, staying alert. Instead, I'm chewing my lip and letting my thoughts run wild.

Ensley stops abruptly, and because I'm not paying attention, I plow right into her.

"Shoot, sorry—" I begin, but the words die as I glance past her and see what made her freeze.

There's a break in the trees ahead, and beyond lies a wide, glistening lake. Patches of grass and clusters of trees dot the surface, and thick forest surrounds the open water like a natural barrier.

The five of us step closer to the edge for a better look. The water looks deep. Maybe too deep to wade through, and there's no obvious path across. Still, a tug in my gut tells me the gate is out there, somewhere in that clearing, waiting to be found.

"The gate's somewhere in there," Talon says, echoing my thoughts.

Imogen grimaces and casts a mournful look down at her already-waterlogged knee-high boots. With an exaggerated huff, she trudges forward without waiting for the rest of us. The moment she steps into the swamp, she sinks nearly up to her hip in the murky water.

"We should've picked a gate in the tropics," she mutters. "I could've worn a bathing suit while we searched white sand beaches. But no, we had to pick the one in the nastiest, most miserable location possible."

"Do I need to remind you that *you're* the one who found and suggested this gate?" Talon calls after her.

"I don't remember it that way," Imogen tosses back as she reaches the first grassy patch where a few trees rise from the soggy ground but nothing else stands out.

The rest of us share a look, then start wading in ourselves, fanning out to explore different directions.

I keep my eyes locked on the dark, opaque water, scanning for the flash of scales or a ripple too wide to be harmless. The thought of snakes or lizards lurking beneath the surface makes my pulse spike, and I hurry toward the nearest patch of grass.

When I reach a patch of spongy, semi-dry land, I stop to scan the marshy expanse, but nothing stands out. No arch. No circle. No hint of anything magical. My heart sinks. I didn't expect it to be easy, but I'd hoped we might at least catch a glimmer of *something*.

In the distance, I spot Titus jerk back just in time to avoid stepping on what looks like either an alligator or a crocodile. The massive reptile snaps at him before sliding into the water with a splash, a cold reminder of how dangerous these swamps really are.

One bite could kill me. I don't have supernatural healing. Not like the others.

But now I know why. Because I'm human.

Talon sticks nearby as we search. Not so near that it draws attention, but close enough that I know he's watching my back. I want to be annoyed by that, but with all the creepy crawlies lurking in the swamp, I can't bring myself to mind. If anything, Talon seems like living swamp repellent. Every time he approaches, even the most docile animals scatter. I can't help but wonder if they sense the predator in him. I think it's probably just my imagination, until I watch a turtle bolt with surprising speed after Talon shoots it a side-eye.

We comb through the lake area for what feels like forever, slowly making our way from one side of the circular wetland to the other. By the time we reach the far bank, the water has shallowed to knee height between the scattered patches of land.

No one says much anymore. The silence hangs heavy between us, our faces marked with fatigue and frustration.

I really thought this would be it, that the gate was here. But as doubt creeps in, the ground beneath us trembles.

We freeze.

The swamp shudders with a deep, rolling vibration that ripples through the murky water. Birds explode from the trees in a flurry of wings, and small animals dart for cover. A low, splintering crack splits the air, and trees sway violently, their branches snapping like brittle bones, bending under the weight of something massive and unseen.

"Keep looking for the gate!" Talon shouts. "The monster's awakening. It has to be close!"

I stumble forward, my footing unsteady like I'm walking on a water balloon. The earth shudders again, more violently this time, nearly toppling me. Then, suddenly, everything stills.

Silence falls like a blanket, eerie and absolute.

Where moments ago the swamp teemed with croaking frogs,

buzzing insects, and chirping birds, now there's just heavy, unnatural quiet.

Heart hammering, I scan the area. Everyone's still, wide-eyed and motionless, exchanging uneasy glances. We should be searching, or running, but instead we stand frozen, like prey sensing a predator we can't yet see.

Maybe that was it? Maybe the monster guarding the gate decided not to show itself?

A heavy pressure lingers in the air, thick with tension. This is the calm before the storm. I can feel it.

I snap into motion, unwilling to waste another second. Wading back into the swamp waters, I push forward, sloshing through muck that clings to my legs like glue. I'm halfway to another patch of land when the world detonates behind me.

A deafening explosion tears through the swamp.

Dirt. Water. Mud.

All of it rockets skyward as something erupts from the ground. The shockwave hits me like a wall, hurling me forward. I crash into the grassy patch ahead and roll twice before coming to a stop.

Before I can even lift my head, Talon is there.

"Are you all right?" Talon asks, his gaze snapping down my body and back up again.

I push myself upright, about to say I'm fine when I catch movement behind him—the dense trees and vines trembling, swaying.

Once.

Then again.

Like the swamp itself is shuddering under the weight of a colossal force.

Talon turns, muscles bunching as he readies himself, every line of his body taut with tension. Whatever's coming, it's big. And close.

Ensley's voice cuts through the thick air. "I think I found it!"

I twist around and spot her a couple dozen feet away, kneeling on a raised patch of land encircled by trees. She's digging furiously in the damp soil.

Talon and I scramble to our feet and start toward her, but a deep, guttural growl rips through the swamp. It vibrates in my chest like a bass drum, stopping us in our tracks.

I spin back around, bracing myself for whatever monstrous creature is crashing through the undergrowth. A prehistoric alligator? A multi-headed snake spewing acid? A jaguar with scales instead of fur and claws like machetes?

The last row of trees snaps like twigs.

And what steps out is not what I expected.

It's huge, roughly the size of an elephant, with elongated ears, powerful hind legs, and enormous brown eyes. Its body is covered in downy brown fur that stirs gently in the breeze. It blinks slowly, watching us.

My brain stalls.

Because while it looks oddly familiar, like an enchanted creature out of a children's storybook, there's something deeply unsettling about seeing it here, towering over us in the middle of the swamp, so wildly out of place. But then my thoughts scatter because—

It. Is. So. Cute.

Standing less than a bus length in front of me is the largest, most adorable, absurdly fluffy bunny I've ever seen. I have to lock my knees to stop myself from running over and giving it a cuddle.

I fall in love instantly. I want to name it, take it home, make it my pet.

"What *is* that?" Imogen asks, her face a mix of horror and awe as she stares up at the oversized bunny.

"I think it's a marsh rabbit," Titus says slowly, as if trying to convince himself as much as the rest of us.

"You guys, this is it!" Ensley calls. "I really found the gate!"

I ignore her. All I can think about is whether that fur is as soft as it looks. I take a step toward the giant floof, one hand outstretched.

Monster? Please. This creature couldn't be more adorable. With its twitching nose and wide, innocent eyes, it's clearly not here to eat us.

It just wants love. It just wants cuddles.

And lucky for it, I happen to be an expert in floofy-animal snuggles.

All my fear and trepidation melt away. There's no rush now. We can take our time finding the gate. I'll just distract the "monster" with belly rubs and baby talk.

"I'm going to call you Fluffy," I say, taking another step forward, fully intending to ask if it wants to be my pet-slash-best friend.

The giant rabbit might be a little big for our apartment, but maybe I can convince Ensley and Becks' parents to let me keep it in the stables behind their house. It pays to have rich friends. Then I could visit every day and take care of it. I didn't know I had a bunny-shaped hole in my heart until this exact moment, and only this adorable nugget can fill it.

Before I can take another step, Talon grabs my arm and yanks me back against his chest. "No, Locklyn!" he snaps.

I glance over my shoulder at him, chuckling as I shrug out of his grip. "What are you so afraid of? It's just a—"

A roar splits the air, so loud I have to slap my hands over my ears. The deafening cry fades, leaving only a high-pitched ringing, but when I turn back to my new best friend, the horror hits.

Its mouth is open wide, wider than should be possible. Parts of its muzzle curl back, revealing long, dagger-like fangs—two on top, two on the bottom—flanked by rows of serrated shark-like teeth. A second later, jagged spikes erupt through its downy fur, forming a grotesque mohawk of barbs down its spine.

It lifts one massive front paw, each of its five toes tipped with blood-red talons, and slams it into the marshy ground. The earth quakes beneath us. "Fluffy, no," I whisper, heart dropping as the monster's gaze locks on me. In an instant, my adorable new best friend becomes a nightmare beast.

Its once-soft brown eyes glow a demonic red, and fear slices through me, sharpening everything. I stumble backward as it lumbers forward, the ground trembling with each step.

Oh crap.

Its jaw stretches impossibly wide, like a snake preparing to devour its prey whole. At the back of its throat, a spark flares.

That's the only warning I get before a column of fire blasts straight toward me.

Talon shouts my name, and a second later a body slams into me, knocking us into the shallow swamp water. The fire tears overhead, lighting up the murk around us with flickering orange light.

I fight toward the surface, desperate for air, but arms wrap around me and hold me down. I thrash, panic exploding through my chest. I can't move. I can't breathe.

Swamp water surges into my nose. I choke and instinctively inhale, sucking in more sludge. My lungs burn. I gag, vision spinning and darkening at the edges.

Then the fire fades.

The arms wrapped around me shift, dragging me upward. We break the surface and I gasp for air, collapsing into a violent coughing fit, spitting out swamp water. Talon hauls me to my feet, both of us dripping and slick with black sludge.

"Come on!" he yells, urgency in every line of his body.

I stumble after him, still wheezing. "You didn't have to hold me under so long," I rasp, coughing again.

His eyes cut to me, intense. "I was trying to keep you from getting roasted."

"I know," I mutter, my voice softer this time. "Just, maybe next time give me a warning?"

He huffs, half a laugh and half exasperation. "I think what you mean to say is, 'Thank you for saving my life.'"

Despite everything, a reluctant smile tugs at my lips as he all but drags me toward where Ensley, and now Imogen, are standing.

Another roar splits the air. I glance over my shoulder as we stumble-run toward the gate and spot Titus locked in battle with Fluffy. Thank the Creator he still has my pendant, as he's using his magic to bind the monster with vines, dodging fireballs as he goes.

When we reach Ensley and Imogen, I whip back toward the fight just in time to see Titus misjudge one of the beast's attacks. A fireball slams into his shoulder, sending him cartwheeling through the air. He crashes into a tree and collapses into the water with a splash.

The monster bellows in rage and thrashes, tearing at the vines holding it down.

"Help him!" Ensley cries. Her face is pale with terror as Titus struggles to rise.

"Stay here and be ready," Talon says, sprinting toward him.

He reaches the white-haired fae just as the monster breaks free. With a screech, it lunges and swipes. Talon and Titus barely dodge the claws, and break into a sprint, racing toward us and the gate.

It's like a nightmare unfolding in slow motion. The rabbit's mouth opens, fangs glinting as it lunges again. This time, it strikes. Talon jerks mid-stride, his body jolting from the impact. His face twists in pain, and he stumbles, one hand flying back—

But there's no blood.

The beast's claws tears through his backpack, shredding fabric and supplies; the gear taking the worst of it. He staggers, and falls to one knee.

The monster coils to pounce again, and Titus throws a wild burst of magic. Vines erupt from the ground, snaring its legs and yanking it backward. It howls, thrashing against the hold, buying them precious seconds to escape.

Titus reaches down for Talon, but he waves him off and staggers upright, shouting at him to get the lunacite pendant to us.

Titus hesitates for only a heartbeat before sprinting toward the knoll.

He reaches us, and he, Ensley, and Imogen fumble to find the right spot to insert the lunacite to awaken the gate. But I can't help. I can't tear my gaze away from Talon.

He's still too far. And the monster is free again, barreling toward him.

A sudden flare of white light erupts around the four of us, shooting straight up into the sky as the gate comes to life.

The beast screeches, furious, seeing its chance slipping away.

Talon's not running straight for us, he's zigzagging, dodging through muck and brush to keep the monster occupied. It's right on his heels.

Our eyes meet through the shimmering wall of light, and something shifts in his expression. Something that looks a lot like grim resignation. My stomach drops.

He's not going to make it.

He knows it. And he's planning to hold the beast off so we can get away.

"No," I whisper.

The monster rears back, its jaw splitting wide as fire flickers in the depths of its throat.

Fluffy is about to roast him alive.

"No!" I scream, and bolt from the circle of light.

My heart pounds like a war drum as I race toward him, fear clawing up my throat. Talon turns to the beast and throws out a hand. A faint spark of magic ignites at his fingertips, but it fizzles, weak and unfocused. He tries again, but maybe because he's injured and exhausted, he isn't strong enough to stop the monster closing in.

He's going to die. And I'm going to have to watch.

But then the shadows come.

A wave of darkness rolls out from every direction, sweeping across the swamp like a living tide. In an instant, they swallow the beast. Tendrils of inky black wrap around its limbs, its face, its twitching nose. Within seconds, the monstrous bunny is blanketed in swirling shadows and mist, vanishing beneath the onslaught.

With the beast momentarily contained, Talon spins toward us.

"Run!" I scream.

He doesn't need to be told twice.

He sprints the last few yards and grabs me, hauling us both into the glowing circle with the others. I stumble in after him, breath ragged, heart still lodged in my throat.

But I can't stop staring.

Outside the protective light, the rabbit-monster thrashes and roars, its fury muted beneath the shroud of darkness. The shadows twist and pulse, holding it back.

"Now!" Talon yells.

Titus, or maybe one of the others, must activate the gate, because in the next heartbeat the world erupts in blinding light.

It's so bright I squeeze my eyes shut, but the brilliance cuts straight through my eyelids, stabbing into my skull like hot needles. I drop to my knees and slap my hands over my face. It's like the light is burrowing into my brain, expanding, until it feels like my head might shatter.

Is this supposed to happen? Or has something gone horribly wrong?

Just as panic claws its way up my throat, arms wrap around me. I'm pulled against a cool, solid chest, and I know without looking it's Talon.

"Just hang on!" he shouts, pressing my face into his shirt, shielding me from the worst of it.

The wind hits next, rising in a howling vortex. It tears at my clothes and yanks my hair in all directions. The roar drowns out everything until all I can feel are Talon's arms, his heartbeat hammering against my cheek.

And then . . . everything goes still and there's nothing more.

Fifteen

A SHARP PROD jabs me in the ribs and I jolt awake to find myself sprawled across an unconscious Talon. To my left, Titus and Ensley lie in a crumpled heap, both still out cold. A groan rises from my right, and I glance over to see Imogen beginning to stir.

I roll off of Talon and gasp when I see a guy and a purple-haired girl standing over us. The girl is holding a stick that I think she just used to nudge me awake.

"I'm telling you, they came through the gate," the purple-haired girl says.

"There's no way," the guy next to her replies, eyeing us suspiciously. He's tall and broad, built like Becks. He has shaggy brown hair and caramel-colored skin.

I'm wary of the pair, but I need to know if it worked. I need to know if we made it to the human world.

"Where are we?" I rasp, my voice rough and scratchy, more croak than words.

I sense Talon shifting next to me, but I don't take my gaze off the pair.

"Where do you think you are?" the brown-haired guy asks, his eyes narrowing.

"The swamplands," I answer.

He and the girl exchange a look.

"You mean the Everglades?" the purple-haired girl asks. When I just stare at her blankly, she adds, "In Florida."

"Flur-e-da," I say, testing the word in my mouth.

Never heard of it. That's a good sign though.

"Are you human?" I tentatively ask, my hopes rising.

The girl's eyes widen. "I knew it." She's practically vibrating with excitement. "See, Noah?" she says to the shaggy-haired guy. "I told you."

With effort, I push to my feet and take a wobbly step forward. Noah hastily backs away, like he's afraid to get too close. When the purple-haired girl doesn't move, he grabs her arm and pulls her back with him.

"Is Central Park close?" I ask, taking another step forward.

Alarm flashes across Noah's face. He reaches behind him and pulls out some kind of device, pointing it directly at me. I've never seen anything like it. It's shaped like an L; he grips the short end while the longer end is aimed at me. The longer piece looks hollow, and something about the way he holds it, tense, steady, screams weapon. I instinctively take a step back.

Then he pulls on a part near the top. It jerks back with a sharp metallic click, then snaps forward again.

"If you want to leave this swamp with all your appendages still attached, you'll put that down." Talon's voice is icy, and when I glance over my shoulder he's standing right behind me.

I give him a once-over, making sure he's unharmed. As far as I can tell, he is, and relief makes my muscles a little weak.

Off to the side, Imogen shoves to her feet with a scowl, and Titus and Ensley are slowly waking as well.

Noah's nervous gaze swivels from one of us to the other, but he keeps the weapon pointed at me.

"You don't want to push me right now," Talon says. "It's been a crap day and my patience is worn pretty thin." Suddenly, the air chills several degrees as Talon flexes some of his power.

Noah's and the girl's mouths drop open and twin puffs of white condensation float in the air in front of them. The purple-haired girl recovers the fastest, pushing down Noah's arm so he isn't aiming the weapon at us anymore. She raises her hands, palms out, in a universal gesture of peace.

"Let's all just bring it down a notch," she says, but the temperature doesn't warm. "I'm Violet," she says, and then points to Noah and introduces us to him as well.

The difference between the pair couldn't be clearer. Violet looks like she's trying to hold back a million questions, whereas Noah looks downright spooked. Especially when Ensley and Titus lumber to their feet to join us, making it five to two.

"That was trippy," Ensley says as she comes to stand next to me, rubbing her eyes. Titus isn't far behind her, but his teal gaze scans the area cautiously.

From a quick look around, it doesn't seem like we traveled to a new world. The sun has almost set, so there's not as much natural light, but it looks like we're all on the same round patch of grass. There's a swampy lake around us, and marshlands beyond that. But, thankfully, no murder-bunny in sight.

Aside from Noah's strange weapon and the name of this unfamiliar place, everything else feels normal. But if we want answers, they're the only ones who can give them, and it's obvious they need a little time to warm up to us.

"I'm Locklyn," I say, then introduce the others one by one.

Imogen and Talon both glare as I say their names, but Talon at least reins in his magic, letting the air thaw a few degrees. Ensley and Titus make an effort to appear open, even friendly.

Violet's gaze skims over the group, then snags on Titus. She inhales sharply when she sees his pointed ears. I'm guessing humans all have rounded ones like mine. His could be a problem. Ensley's are smaller and hidden by her hair, but she might be able to use glamour to hide them and Titus' as well once we get out of this swamp.

"You mentioned a gate," I prod, trying to prompt Violet to talk.

She takes a deep breath and glances over at Noah. His lips are smashed into a straight line, but he gives her a curt nod.

"You're not from around here, are you?" she asks, and Talon snorts a laugh.

"If you mean Florida, then no," I answer for all of us.

"That's not what I meant." Excitement sparks in Violet's eyes, but I get the impression she's trying to contain it. She takes a step closer to us. Noah tries to pull her back again, but she swats him away. "You're from there, aren't you? The other world."

Ensley and I exchange a look. She shrugs, and so I nod. They already know our world exists, so why hide it?

Violet squeals, startling me. "I knew it! They always said the gates were sealed, but there had to be a reason we kept patrolling them. I can't believe this is actually happening. What kind of creature are you?" she asks me directly.

"Well, actually—"

"Violet," Noah snaps, a scowl pulling down his features. "We don't even know if this is true. They could be messing with us. What if—?"

"Didn't you feel the temperature drop? Have you looked at his ears?" she says, pointing to Titus, and Noah smashes his lips together. "We both saw the flash of light, that's what brought us over here," Violet goes on. "What more proof do you want?"

"Oh, I'm happy to give you some proof," Imogen says, stepping forward with a wicked smile. It's the first thing she's said, and honestly, I'm shocked she's stayed quiet this long.

"Imogen," Talon warns, shooting his cousin a look that says "behave."

"What?" she says, smirking impishly. "With a little push of my magic I can make him cluck like a chicken while jumping on one foot. It's been a long day. I could use the laugh."

"Don't," is all he says.

Imogen rolls her eyes and mumbles that he's no fun.

Light flares next to me, and when I look over a buttery soft ball of faelight hovers over Ensley's palms. She holds her hands in front of her for Violet and Noah to see.

"How's this for proof?" she asks.

Noah's mouth drops open, but then he snaps it shut again. His gaze moves from the ball of faelight up to Ensley's face. His eyes go wide with awe, or fear. I can't exactly tell which.

"How is this possible?" he asks.

Ensley extinguishes her faelight and shrugs.

Talon crosses his arms. "We'll answer your questions if you tell us how you know about the gates and our world."

Violet straightens, her voice steady. "We're part of a group called the Silent Order. We're not a huge group, but we are widespread. Most of us were born into it. We have units all over the world, keeping an eye on the gates. We're the only humans on Earth who know the truth, that there's another world out there and that the supernatural exists, and we've done what we can to keep it that way."

"A secret society," I say thoughtfully, looking up at Talon, who glances back at me with an arched brow.

I'm sure he's thinking the same thing I am. A secret group who protects the gates and the world from knowing about creatures and our world. Sounds an awful lot like the Arcane Society to me.

"For two thousand years, members of the Order have been watching and waiting for this day," Violet says, her voice filled with awe.

"You mean dreading it," Noah cuts in with a frown.

"Dreading?" I ask, my gaze bouncing between the two of them as I try to pick up any silent communication passing between them.

"Just a prophecy warning the worlds will be destroyed if they ever mix," Noah says, shooting us a pointed look.

Another prophecy. Maybe it ties into the one Talon

mentioned, but I don't bring it up. Talon and Imogen stay silent, faces unreadable. I file it away to ask later.

"The prophecy is vague, at best," Violet says. "But the general warning is clear, that our worlds should remain separate."

"Agreed," Talon says with a nod.

"If you agree, then what are you doing here?" Noah asks with a frown.

"We had to come," Ensley says. "My brother is trapped here. We need to find him and then we can all go home. Can you help?"

"Your brother is here?" Violet asks with a scrunched brow. "How? We have surveillance on all eight gates. None of the units have reported any activity."

"He didn't come through a gate," I say, and I feel Talon stiffen next to me.

Being as secretive as he is, I'm sure Talon doesn't want to give these two any more information than is absolutely necessary, but we have to tell them some things to get them to trust us.

"Not long ago, we accidently opened a portal to your world. Ensley's brother, Becks, was shoved through it. He was injured and couldn't get back through before it closed." I take a step toward Violet, appealing to her because she's been the most reasonable out of the two of them. "He doesn't know anything about this world. Creatures on our side don't know you exist any more than humans know about the creature world. His injury was . . . bad." I have to take a moment to swallow over the lump in my throat before forcing the next words from my mouth. "He's injured and could be dying for all we know. We have to find him, and fast. We really need your help."

Noah crosses his arms over his chest and shoots Violet a somber look. "The disturbance in New York."

"They weren't sure that was anything," Violet says, wringing her hands.

He arches an eyebrow. "How much you wanna bet that's what

it was? And that chapter is particularly secretive. We don't really know what they found."

"Is this 'New York' anywhere near Central Park?" I cut in to ask.

"Central Park is *in* New York City," Violet says, and my heart skips a beat. "How do you know about it?"

"Because I read it on a sign before the portal closed. That's where Becks went through."

Noah looks smug, but Violet just seems concerned.

"Come on," she says. "Let's get out of the swamp before it gets too late. The gators in the area are used to us, but I don't feel like getting munched on tonight. The head of our unit will know what to do."

We trail Noah and Violet to the far edge of the swamp lake, where a boat waits just beyond the tree line. It looks almost identical to the airboat we used back in our world. I know we're not there anymore, but everything feels so familiar it's hard to wrap my head around it.

Noah steers the airboat like someone who knows these swamps well. As the light fades, he flips on a headlamp to guide us through the winding rivers until we reach a small dock. Once the boat's secured, we pile onto the rickety planks, which groan under our weight. Violet and Noah lead us up a muddy embankment to a waiting vehicle.

I freeze when I see it. The brand logo is unfamiliar, and the body shape is slightly off, but otherwise it looks like a regular truck. The paint's a faded, muddy green, and dents line the side, but it's close enough to ours that it stops me in my tracks.

"What?" Violet asks when she notices I've stopped walking.

"Our trucks look really similar," I say.

She glances at the vehicle and then back at me. "Really?" she asks as Noah piles in the front seat and cranks it.

"Yeah. I mean, I don't know what car company that is or anything," I say. "But all the essential parts look the same."

She shrugs. "I guess that makes sense. We've always been told our worlds, even though they are separate, somehow affect each other. I wouldn't be surprised to know our industrial and technological advances are similar. Maybe we even fought similar wars throughout history. It would be fascinating to sit down and compare notes."

She's not wrong, it would be interesting, but that's not what we were here to do. "I just want to find my friend and bring him home."

Pressing her lips together, she nods. "You all must care a great deal for Becks to have gone to such lengths to bring him home."

"Yeah, we do." *Some of us more than others.*

Noah rolls down his window and calls for Violet to get in. She jumps in the passenger seat. Titus and Talon share a quick look and then both jump in the truck's bed without having to be asked. Miraculously, we all still have our backpacks, Talon's mostly shredded pack included, and so after tossing them in the back with Titus and Talon, Imogen, Ensley, and I cram into the cab's second row behind Violet and Noah.

The air in Florida is just as muggy as it was back in our world. Noah rolls all the windows down and yells back to Titus and Talon to stay out of sight, saying it's illegal to drive with anyone in the bed, before he takes off.

The air conditioning in the truck must not be working, because he never rolls up the windows, which makes it hard to converse, so I don't even try. I spend the drive looking out the windows at the human world. I catch subtle differences, but so far it's still a lot like ours, which in a way makes it even more shocking. It's almost like we haven't traveled to a different world at all.

After only about fifteen minutes, Noah pulls the truck off of the main road and onto a gravel drive. We bump along a dirt-and-sand road for probably less than a mile before he pulls to a stop in front of a boxy two-story house that's perched up on stilts.

Teal with white shutters and trim, the house is loud. Not in sound, but visually. It's a large dwelling, rivaling the size of Becks and Ensley's home, with a full wraparound porch. If I had to guess I'd say it has seven or eight bedrooms.

We pile out of the cab at the same time Talon and Titus jump out of the back bed. They're chuckling about something, and their hair is windblown. When Talon's gaze connects with mine there's a lightness in his eyes I haven't seen in a while.

Not since that night.

It draws me in. *He* draws me in.

I turn away before I start thinking about that too deeply.

Following Violet and Noah, we ascend the front steps to the porch, the wood groaning beneath our feet with every step. The house may be large, but up close it's clear it's in need of upkeep. The teal siding is cracked and peeling. The wood on the stair handrail is rotted in places. Many of the white shutters sit askew on the side of the house, and the screen that encases the wraparound porch has multiple holes.

Violet reaches for the front door just as it swings open in front of her. Standing in the entranceway is a brown-haired middle-aged male wearing a short-sleeved button-up shirt and cargo shorts. His gaze darts past Violet and Noah and skims over our group. I don't miss the hint of calculation in his eyes before the hard lines of his face smooth over and he smiles.

"Come on in," he says in a friendly tone, and then steps back to grant us entrance.

His smile slips a little and he gives Violet and Noah a meaningful look as they pass, but then it ratchets back up as our small group filters single-file through the doorway into an open living space.

The inside of the stilt house is rustic and a bit rundown, like the exterior. The walls are mostly white-washed shiplap. There's a smattering of furniture in the large room to the left of the entrance: a couple of couches that have seen better days, an overstuffed armchair, two end tables and a coffee table. The kitchen is open concept at the back of the room, with a round eat-in table that would fit at least eight places, maybe more. But the house's interior isn't of as much interest to me as the human who greeted us.

When I glance back at the male, he's studying our group again, and the intensity of his gaze puts me on edge. Instinctively, I tense and shift my stance, ready to run or fight if I have to.

"Tobias," Violet says almost tentatively. "This is the group I messaged you about. The ones we found near the gate."

Tobias shakes his head. "Right, right," he says, and then motions that we should all move into the room off the foyer and take a seat.

Ensley sits next to me on the long couch, Titus next to her. Imogen and Talon stubbornly refuse to sit, and I notice that Talon hasn't turned his back on Tobias since we entered. His gaze is shrewd as he takes everything in, and I can't decide if he's being overly cautious, or just smart. I also don't miss the small nod he gives Imogen, directing her to stand on the other side of the room. The way they've positioned themselves, no one could sneak up on our group. Between the two of them, they're covering every window and door.

Violet plops down in the overstuffed chair with Noah on a small couch across from Ensley, Titus, and me. Tobias remains standing, just like Imogen and Talon.

"I'm sorry, I don't mean to stare," Tobias says. "It's just I don't think I ever actually thought I'd see the day." He lets out a self-deprecating laugh. "You can be trained your whole life for a moment, but I suppose until it arrives, you'll never really know how you're going to react. I'm Tobias, the head of the Southern United States branch of the Silent Order."

United States? Never heard of it. Just like I hadn't heard of Florida either. In the creature world, our country is called the Unified Colonies of Eldora. UC for short. A couple hundred years back it used to be split into smaller provinces and kingdoms that came together to form one nation. We don't recognize the old boundaries anymore, but the swamplands are part of what used to be Suska.

"Welcome to our home and unit headquarters," Tobias says with a tight smile. "What can we do to help you?"

I glance at Talon, but he keeps his lips shut, seemingly content to let someone else be the mouthpiece for the group.

"We're looking for our friend," I say, and then explain about Becks like we did to Violet and Noah.

Tobias' brow pinches as he listens. "New York is a ways away. And there's no guarantee he's still there," he says when I finish.

"We know," I say. "But it's a place to start."

He nods. "I agree. And your plan is to return to your world after you've found your friend?"

"Yes. The only reason we're here in the first place is to find him. After that, we just want to go home."

But that isn't truly where you belong, is it? a voice whispers in my head, but I shove it down. I may not be a creature, but that world is still my home and I plan to return to it when this is all said and done.

I might be imagining it, but he seems to relax a little at that. I can't really blame him. Creatures have powers, humans don't. I know that better than anyone. It's only natural he'd see us as a threat.

Tobias rubs at his mouth as he digests everything. "Okay. So you need to get up to New York," he says, almost as if talking to himself.

"Can you help us?" I ask.

Our eyes lock, and despite having no real reason to doubt him, unease prickles at the back of my mind. Still, what other option do we have?

"Of course," he says easily. "It's getting late. Let's get everyone fed. We have enough room that you all can stay here if you don't mind sleeping on couches and blow-up mattresses."

When I glance over at Talon, he's looking back at me, his expression unreadable. I don't know what he's thinking, but mine says, *What other choice do we have?* After a beat, he lets out a small sigh and gives a nod. That's all the confirmation I need, and I accept on behalf of all of us.

"You must be hungry. Let's see what we can cook up for you," Tobias says with a smile. He then gestures for Noah to follow him into the kitchen.

I get to my feet, far too antsy to stay seated. To keep my mind occupied, I wander around the room, letting my gaze trail over various objects until it lands on a globe in the corner. Curious, I walk over to inspect it, surprised to see that the land masses look identical to our own, even though the names of the countries and some of the boundaries are a little different.

I sense someone come up behind me and glance over my shoulder to find Violet standing behind me looking uncertain.

"Our world is the same," I say, running my fingers over the curved surface.

"Really?" she asks, coming closer.

I nod, and point out different land masses and what they're called on our world. Their Europe is our Eshya, Australia is Osmain, and their United States is the same as our Unified Colonies of Eldora.

"It's so odd. Our technology seems to mirror one another, we live on the same land masses, we even speak the same language."

Violet's gaze drifts from the globe up to me. "I always thought of our worlds as two different places, but perhaps that's not exactly right. It's more like different realities or dimensions on the same world."

I nod, telling her that's what I was thinking as well. I ask Violet to show me where we are and where New York City is, relieved to see they're both on the same coastline.

"Your home seems large," I say. "Is it just the three of you in your unit?"

"Oh no. There are fifteen members total that live here in our headquarters. They're going to be really excited. Well . . ." She pauses, then gives a small, nervous laugh. "Maybe not *excited* to meet you, but it'll definitely be a moment they won't forget."

I open my mouth to ask what she means, but Tobias' voice cuts in from the next room.

"Dinner's ready."

Violet flashes me a quick smile, but there's something guarded in her eyes now, something she doesn't say.

I don't press. Not yet. But I make a note not to let my guard down.

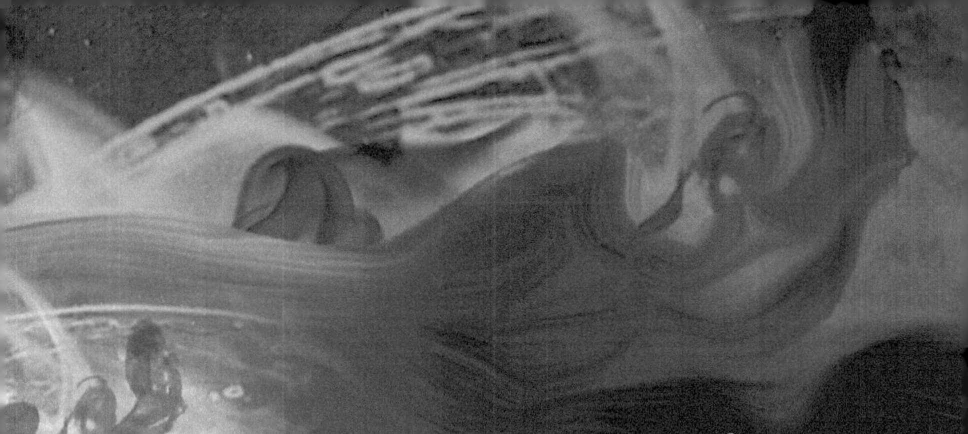

Sixteen

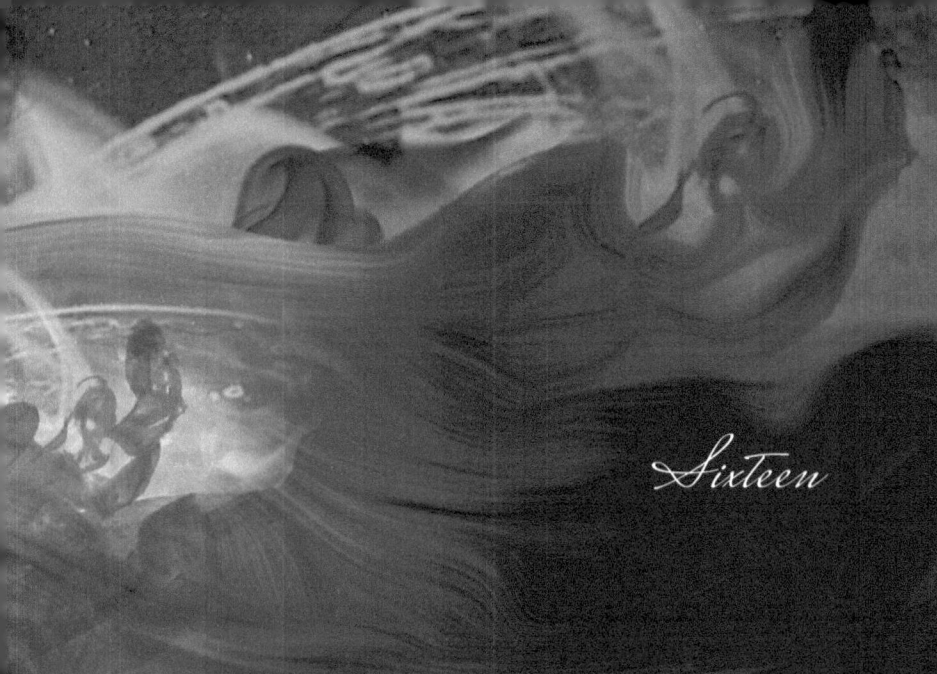

DINNER FEELS ODDLY STRAINED, though I can't tell if it's just me. We trade small talk, careful not to touch on the questions we're all really thinking. Talon and Imogen speak just enough to avoid suspicion, but I catch them sizing up Tobias and the others throughout the meal. I'm not sure if it's warranted or just their natural suspicion kicking in. I *want* to believe they are truly allies, but the way Tobias watches us when he thinks no one's looking makes the fine hairs on the back of my neck rise.

By the end of dinner, my body is flagging. The aches and pains from our fight with the swamp beast are catching up with me. My joints are stiff and my eyelids heavy. It takes more effort than it should to follow the light banter floating around the table. At one point, my eyes drift shut and I pitch forward, nearly faceplanting into my half-eaten burger and fries. I jerk upright so fast my chair screeches across the linoleum floor. Everyone turns to look. Ensley, sitting across from me, barely covers a snort and grin with her hand.

Tobias takes the hint and suggests getting us settled for the night. He assures us he'll contact the New York chapter tonight and that we'll set off in the morning. If I weren't so exhausted, I might argue for a delay, but right now, rest is the only thing I care about.

Before bed, we put on fresh clothes from our packs and clean up in the upstairs bathrooms, which is a welcome relief after spending all day in swamp-soaked gear. When I come back downstairs, air mattresses, blankets, and pillows are waiting for us.

We spread out around the great room, each claiming a spot. I take the couch; it's too short for anyone but me or maybe Imogen, but she snags a twin air mattress near one of the windows. Titus and Ensley set up their beds side by side, and Talon picks a spot close to the front door.

I don't wait for everyone to settle in. The second I lie down on the couch, I'm out, slipping into a heavy, dreamless sleep.

Until I'm ripped awake by a hand clamped over my mouth.

I lash out without even identifying my target, but someone snatches my fist mid-swing.

"Shh. It's just me." Talon's breath tickles my ear and I immediately go limp with relief when I see his face hovering above me. "Follow me," he says, and then removes his hand.

Sitting up, I find the room dark and shadowed. Only a sliver of moonlight streaming in from the open windows provides any light. My human eyes take a second to adjust, and when they do, it's to see Talon slip from the room.

As quietly as possible, I slide off the couch and tiptoe after him. I grab my shoes from where I left them in the foyer, and together we slip out the front door into the thick, humid night. He closes the door carefully behind us, then presses a finger to his lips, signaling me to stay silent, and gestures for me to follow.

My mind is still hazy with sleep, so I don't question anything as I fall into step beside him. The stillness is broken only by the chirps and buzz of swamp insects as we slip past the house. Overhead, the night sky stretches wide and clear, stars scattered across it just like back home.

Talon leads me into a forested area off to the side of the house, away from the main drive and hidden from view. We weave through white-barked trees until the house disappears completely behind us. Only then does he stop and turn to face me.

"What's going on?" I finally ask, the short walk helping me shake off the remnants of sleep.

"We need to talk," he says, and I quirk a brow as if to say "clearly."

Folding my arms overs my chest, I wait for him to go on.

"How do you think I made it to the gate?"

I tilt my head. "I don't understand."

Talon swipes a hand down his face, not in frustration, at least not with me. It feels more like he's searching for the right words.

"How did I get away from that swamp monster?" he asks. "It's bearing down on me. I told you to go without me. And then . . ." He trails off, clearly waiting for me to fill in the blank.

Just thinking about that demonic bunny sends a shiver down my spine. And to think I was going to try to make it a pet.

"You used your magic," I say slowly. "You swallowed it in shadows and made it back to us."

He nods. "Right. Except . . . I didn't."

My stomach tightens. "Didn't what?"

"I didn't use my magic."

"Of course you did. I was standing right there. I saw the whole thing."

But Talon shakes his head at me. "No. I didn't do that. I can't —" he starts and then snaps his mouth shut.

My brows pinch. "What are you saying?"

"I'm saying that I wasn't the one who commanded those shadows to attack the beast. Someone else did that."

"Imogen?" I guess, since shadow powers are typically linked to vampires.

He shakes his head, his gaze intense.

"Well, it wasn't Ensley or Titus. That definitely wasn't fae magic back there. So that just leaves you and Imogen. And I've seen Imogen manipulate shadows back at Grimspire Castle before she used her compulsion on me, so if it wasn't you, it must have been her."

Why is he even pushing this? Who cares if Imogen attacked the swamp monster instead of him?

"It wasn't Imogen," Talon says firmly, and I throw up my hands.

"Of course it was. I don't even understand what we're doing out here arguing about this. We have a long couple of days in front of us, so if you don't mind, I'm going back to get some sleep." Turning on a heel, I start back toward the house when Talon's next words stop me in my tracks.

"It was you."

I slowly look over my shoulder. He can't possibly be saying what I think he is.

Talon strides forward until he's standing in front of me again. He meets my gaze, his expression more serious than I've ever seen it.

"The shadows that saved me from the swamp monster. . . that was you. You commanded them. You saved my life."

I'm shaking my head even as he's talking. "Did you forget I'm magicless? That I'm *human*?"

"I know you're human. But you also won the activation trial and bonded with Shadow Striker. We were separated from the blade before it fully transferred over to you. That's all new territory. So it's not out of the realm of possibility that you might—"

"No," I say, cutting Talon off mid-sentence.

But even as his mouth snaps shut, it's clear this conversation is far from over. A muscle jumps in his jaw, and he exhales sharply through his nose, frustration written all over his face. I can see it in his eyes, in the tense set of his shoulders that he truly believes I controlled those shadows.

But he's wrong.

Right?

"I don't know what she told you, or why she'd lie about it," I say quickly. "But it had to be Imogen."

"It wasn't. Imogen doesn't have that magic."

"That you know of. The Arcane Society is so secret, she doesn't even know what type of creature you are," I say, giving Talon a pointed look. "How would you know if Imogen was hiding part of her magic from you?"

Talon's eyes narrow, his expression hardening as he shifts closer. "Each of the members shared their power with me," he says, his voice low but firm. "I'm the only living person in the Society who knows exactly what powers every one of them possesses." He holds my gaze, unflinching. "And I know, without a shadow of a doubt, that Imogen doesn't have shadow magic."

"So maybe you used it without realizing?" I'm grasping at straws, because nothing seems to be adding up.

Talon flinches and I frown, not understanding that reaction. He heaves a sigh and there's meaning there I can't even start to interpret.

He gazes skyward, clearly warring with himself about something. I wish he would just make up his mind, because it's hot and sticky out here, and frankly, I want to go back to sleep.

"I don't have all my magic anymore," Talon finally says, and I feel the blood drain from my face.

"That's not funny."

"I'm not trying to be. Ever since that last trial—" He shakes his head. "I've started to lose some of the powers I received through Shadow Striker. Shadow magic was the first one to go."

I'm stunned into silence, my mind drifting back to the conversation I overheard between Imogen and Talon at Grimspire. The chilling glare he gave his cousin when she brought up his powers.

Now it made sense.

Emotion flickers across Talon's face, just for a heartbeat, a flash of uncertainty, raw and unguarded. He looks lost. But then, just as quickly, a shield drops back into place and he's unreadable again. He didn't mean for me to see that crack in his armor.

I don't call attention to it. He deserves that much. And honestly, with everything he's been through, losing Shadow Striker, his family, and now his powers, it's no wonder he feels unmoored.

I feel myself softening toward him, and that scares me more than I want to admit. Because part of me knows that if I open the door to Talon, even a little, I may never be able to close it again. And there's no space in my heart for him when Becks is still there.

At least that's the line I repeat in my head while I force myself to keep my guard up.

I look at Talon, unsure what to say. I can't explain what happened in the swamp, but that doesn't mean I suddenly have magic.

"I think you're doing it by accident," he says. "Like, out of instinct when yourself or others are threatened."

"Talon—"

"I'm sure about this, Locklyn. I saw you do it in the training gym, and when I walked in on you and Imogen. And then again when we were driving. All those instances were you."

I want to argue, but his argument settles over me like a weight I don't know how to carry. I remember another instance he doesn't even know about: what happened with Drake in his library, and the calculated gleam in the powerful dragon shifter's eye afterward.

I shoved that moment deep into the recesses of my mind, chalking it up to exhaustion and stress. But when I let myself really think about it, I can still see the way the shadows in the room pulsed. And worse, I can still *feel* it. Just for a heartbeat, I was sure I was controlling them.

"I think when you bonded with Shadow Striker and it didn't finish transferring completely, it somehow linked the two of us. Tethered us together, magically. Somehow my magic is transferring to you, and it probably won't stop with just shadow magic." Talon takes a step closer, his voice becoming soothing. "I know this is a lot, but we need to find out what else you can do. You need to be trained so you can protect yourself."

My instinct is to deny it. To shove the truth away like I've done before. But this time, the wall I've built inside me doesn't rise. A small, terrified part of me already knows he's right.

My breathing turns shallow as I look up into Talon's eyes. It's hard to wrap my head around what he's saying. I've finally made peace with the fact that I'll never have powers. I'll never wield magic. I'm human, and that means limits. Boundaries I can't cross.

And now this.

I don't know how I'm supposed to react. What I'm supposed to feel.

"Locklyn?" Talon asks, his voice surprisingly gentle.

I meet his gaze and find an emotion I don't expect. *Understanding*. I'm not sure how this could possibly be a situation he relates to, but there's a softness in his eyes that isn't usually there. It steadies me.

"You've got this," he says, and there's so much quiet conviction in his voice, I almost believe it too.

I take a deep breath. The last couple of months have been a whirlwind. Competing in Chaos and nearly dying, learning my mom and dad aren't my biological parents, finding out I'm human in a world where that makes me the anomaly.

I've uncovered secrets about myself and about entire worlds. So, really, discovering I might have magic shouldn't be the thing that shakes me.

But somehow it is.

I look at Talon and the steady set of his jaw, the quiet certainty in his eyes, gives me the courage I need to take the next step.

He's right. I can do this.

"All right," I say. "Where do we start?"

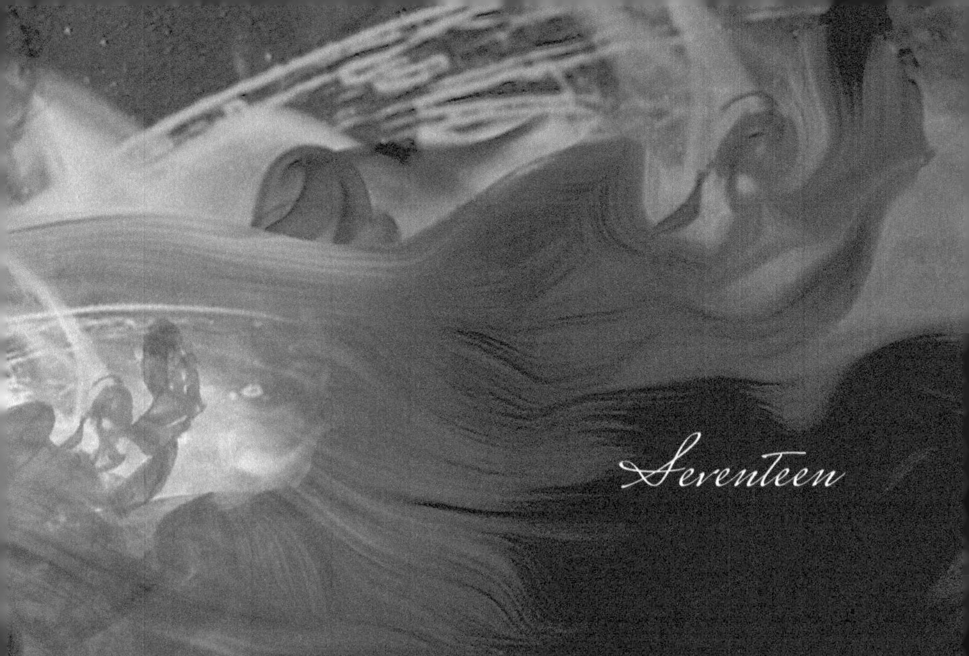

Seventeen

"THIS IS POINTLESS."

We've been trying to tap into my supposed magic for at least an hour, and none of Talon's directions, suggestions, or instructions have worked. He explained different techniques to summon it, describing how to reach for the power inside me, but every time I follow his lead, I don't feel so much as a flicker of magic, and with every passing minute I become more convinced he is wrong about me having powers.

"You're not trying," Talon accuses, and I glare at him.

"That's not true. I've done everything you asked. Nothing's working. I don't feel anything."

"It's because you're not letting yourself feel it," Talon says. "You're scared, so you're standing in your own way."

"I'm not scared!" I snap.

Talon presses his lips into a hard line but doesn't argue. His gaze sharpens, calculating, and the look on his face makes my stomach tighten.

"Close your eyes," he says.

"Why?"

The way he's watching me makes me uneasy, and I take a step back.

"I want to try something," he replies, stepping forward and reclaiming the space between us.

I narrow my eyes at him, suspicion prickling beneath my skin. As much as I want to trust Talon, too many half-truths and buried secrets still hang between us. Some part of me refuses to let my guard down completely.

"Please?" he asks, his voice quiet.

I let out a heavy sigh. "Fine. But if this doesn't work, I'm going back. I might be able to squeeze in another hour or two of sleep before everyone wakes up."

Reluctantly, I close my eyes, just like he asked, and wait for whatever it is he plans to do.

Seconds tick by in silence.

He doesn't speak. Doesn't move.

I start to shift, about to ask what's going on, when his deep voice finally washes over me.

"I want you to take it all in," he says, his voice a smooth rumble just to the side of me. Not close enough for me to feel his breath, but near enough that I could reach out and touch him. It makes me feel exposed in a way I don't entirely hate, and that's confusing.

"What do you hear? Feel? Smell?"

I want to roll my eyes and call this stupid, but I tamp down the instinct to push back, and force myself to try.

Drawing in a slow breath of muggy air, I wrinkle my nose at the scent of stagnant swamp water and damp cypress trees. Frogs croak in the distance, and a soft breeze stirs the trees around us.

"Anchor yourself to the ground. Know that it's solid and will support you. Imagine roots growing from the soles of your feet and tunneling into the soil beneath you, securing you in place."

I don't know where he's going with this or how it could possibly be helping, but I obey him and imagine roots.

"Know that you are safe, and strong."

The words strike a tender place inside me.

Safe. Strong.

Two things that I've struggled to feel my whole life.

"Now look inside yourself," Talon says, his voice no louder than a whispered murmur. "Picture that inner strength. Where does it live? What does it look like?"

With my eyes still closed, I imagine diving inside my own body, flowing through the different parts of me, finally funneling to my heart, where there's a pulsating ball of silver and gold threads. It feels like the strands are knotted in a way they shouldn't be, so without any more prompting from Talon, I imagine the threads untangling.

Talon gasps softly beside me, but I'm too focused on the unraveling to fully register it.

"That's it," he says, voice low and encouraging, like he can somehow see what I'm doing.

It takes several long minutes, but eventually the knots come free. The threads flow outward from the center of me, spreading through my body like veins of light. A soft glow radiates from within, head to toe.

It's beautiful. At least in my mind's eye.

Who knew I had such a vivid imagination?

"Open your eyes, Freckles," Talon says, and my heart stutters at the sound of the nickname he hasn't used in days.

I let my lids drift open and my breath catches.

We're wrapped in shadows so dense I can't see the trees or the sky anymore. The world beyond us has vanished, swallowed in darkness. But we're not alone in the void. Threads of silver and gold float around between us, glowing softly, pulsing in time with the beat of my heart.

I follow a few of the strands and realize they're flowing out from me, reaching across the shadows and attaching to Talon, tethering us together.

Just like they did the night of the final Chaos trial.

With a gasp, I step back and swipe my arm through the air between us, trying to sever the threads. The last time we were connected like this, Shadow Striker was transferring its magic from Talon to me, and it nearly killed him. But before I can do anything more, Talon catches my wrist, stopping me.

"It's okay. You're not hurting me," he says.

"What's happening?" I ask, my voice barely above a whisper.

"This is your magic."

I trace a golden strand from my fingertip to Talon's. The glow from the threads between us casts a warm light across him, making his storm-colored eyes look almost silver and softening the bronze of his skin, giving it a luminous, ethereal quality.

The shadows swirl around us like a living current, and I can't help but get lost in the beauty of the moment. In the magic. *My* magic.

"How is this even possible?" I whisper, looking up into his eyes, breathless with awe. "I'm human. This shouldn't be real."

Somehow, we've moved closer without me noticing, like the threads connecting us have drawn us together. We're not touching, but we're close. So close I can see the striations in his eyes, starbursts of deep blue radiating from a metallic-gray center.

"With you," he murmurs, lifting a hand to gently trace the curve of my cheek, "anything is possible."

I catch my breath as Talon's fingers glide beneath my chin, gently tipping my head back. My world narrows to just the two of us as he gently tucks my hair behind my ear. His fingers trail over the curve of it, lingering for a breath, then slide to the back of my head, where his palm settles with quiet intent.

The magic churning around and through me silences everything, stealing away any thought beyond this moment.

His other hand brushes against my hip before sliding to the small of my back. His touch is steady, grounding, and when he draws me closer, I go without resistance.

The shadows respond to the shift in us. They swirl faster, circling in an unseen breeze that lifts strands of our hair and makes them dance around us. I'm only dimly aware of it, the edges of the world blurring, because all I can focus on is the warmth of Talon's body and the way the space between us disappears.

When he lowers his head, a rush of emotion, sharp and consuming, stirs in me. It's not the same as what I feel for Becks, but it's just as powerful. In some ways, it's more intense.

More immediate.

More dangerous.

More—

Becks.

Cold dread shoots through me, and with Talon's mouth only inches from mine, I shove against him.

My gaze snaps to Talon's eyes and I see confusion there a second before his features go blank and his arm disappears from around me. I stumble back. The shadows that isolated us dissipate, scattering into the dark night as the threads of magic that connected us shatter and then dissolve like mist.

The space between us is all at once too wide and not wide enough.

Adrenaline rushes through me, leaving my body trembling. What I'd almost given in to—what I'd almost *done*—would have been unforgivable.

I love Becks. I always have. And he deserves better than this.

But I can't pretend what just happened with Talon didn't mean something. That it didn't shake me.

I open my mouth, fumbling for an explanation I haven't even formed yet, but Talon lifts a hand to stop me.

"It's late. Dawn's coming. We should get back before anyone notices we're gone."

I search his face, hoping to read something, anything, but as usual his expression is carefully composed, so neutral it makes me question if the last few minutes even happened at all.

Then, just before he looks away, a trace of emotion slips through.

And I know he felt it too.

He didn't mean for me to see it, I'm sure of that. But it was there. As skilled as Talon is at hiding his emotions, I caught a glimpse of his truth for the briefest moment. Longing and pain, tangled together.

And I have no idea what to do with it.

I nod, not knowing what else to say, and we start back toward the house, moving silently through the sparse trees and over soggy ground. The quiet between us isn't easy. It hangs heavy, thick and suffocating like the humid air pressing in around us.

I want to break the tension, but the words won't come. So instead, I shove thoughts of Talon and Becks into the back of my mind and force myself to focus on the one thing I can't ignore.

What I learned tonight.

I have magic.

It may be borrowed. Or technically *stolen*? I don't really know. But it's real. And it's mine. At least for now.

Now that I know it's there, I can feel it, buried beneath my rib cage, right where I imagined the raveled ball of silver and gold threads.

I start to experiment reaching for it when Talon stops, going stock still. His head is tilted in a way that makes me think he's listening for something. There's a frown on his face and his brows are pinched.

"Talon, what—?"

When he looks at me, he's alarmed. He puts a finger up to his lips, gesturing for me to be quiet. Seconds pass and he doesn't move. He just stands there. Listening. It starts to freak me out.

I'm a heartbeat away from breaking the silence when a low, muffled rumble of an engine reaches my ears. I tilt my head, straining to catch more. This place is isolated, and the house is at least a mile from the main road. It's too far for us to be hearing just a passing car. The engine cuts off abruptly, followed by the unmistakable *thunk* of car doors opening and then slamming shut.

Without warning, Talon takes off sprinting in the direction of the house. I chase after him, pumping my arms and legs as fast as I can, but Talon is impossibly fast and I can't keep up. He's almost to the front steps by the time I break through the trees to get a clear view of the house. Spotting an unfamiliar vehicle parked off to the side, my stomach jumps into my throat.

Talon takes the stairs up to the porch two at a time, stopping before going through the front door. Instead, he presses against the side of the house, and leans over to peek in the living room window. I can just barely see the outline of dark forms moving in the living room where our friends are sleeping. I can't make out any of their features, but I can tell from their builds that at least three of the four figures are large males.

The drumming of my own heartbeat fills my ears as I reach the house and carefully ascend the stairs, plastering myself against the exterior of the house next to Talon. I look over at him, my gaze asking him what we should do.

Taking my hand, he tugs me down and we crawl under the windows and around the porch to the kitchen entrance on the other side of the house. The kitchen door is actually already cracked open, possibly because this was the way the intruders got in the house.

"Stay here," Talon whispers. "I'm going to go in and assess the situation."

I shake my head. No way am I just sitting out here and waiting. Ensley is my best friend, and Titus has had my back more than once. I won't go as far to say that Imogen has grown on me, but I can reluctantly admit I don't want her to get hurt either.

Talon scowls at me, but then in the silence we hear a familiar mechanical click, just like the sharp snap of the weapon that Noah pointed at us. That seemingly innocuous click causes my heart to jump into my throat. I don't know what kind of damage that human weapon can cause, but I certainly don't want to find out tonight.

Abandoning trying to convince me to stay put, Talon silently opens the kitchen door wide enough for the both of us to squeeze through. We stay crouched low as we move through the kitchen, keeping our steps light as we rush to get behind the island for cover.

When I peek out from behind the cabinet, I make out the silhouettes and hazy features of six figures, two more than I thought there were. Four male, and two female. I recognize Noah and Tobias right away, but I don't see Violet. The other four are unfamiliar, but they all have similar looking weapons to the one Noah pointed at me in their hands.

At least one of the humans stands over each of the three sleeping members of our group, pointing their weapons at them. Tobias is nearest to where Talon and I are hiding, his profile clearly visible.

"Two of them are missing," he whisper-hisses to the large male beside him. "Take Noah and look for them outside. If you find them, neutralize them."

Neutralize them? What does *that* mean?

Nothing good, that's for sure.

The male nods, then gestures for Noah to follow him. I hold my breath as the two of them pass within feet of where Talon and I are crouched behind the kitchen island. It's a miracle they don't see us. Our only cover is the slight overhang of the counter.

But after they slip out through the kitchen door, I notice that without meaning to, I've shrouded us in deeper shadows, concealing us from view.

I turn to Talon, eyes wide, a little shaken by how easily I just used my powers.

He takes my hand, gives it a quick squeeze, and mouths, "Good job." He doesn't speak. Tobias and the three remaining humans are too close, but he starts gesturing with his hands. I think he's trying to tell me he's going after Tobias and that I should stay hidden.

This isn't the moment to argue, so I give him a short nod to show I understand.

At least, I hope I do.

"Take out the male first," Tobias says in a low voice. "Then we'll question the females. I don't want—"

Dropping the shadows I've inadvertently called, Talon springs from our hidden position. Moving like a striking snake, he twists Tobias' wrist. I hear a snap and Tobias cries out in pain. The weapon drops from his grip, and then Talon puts him in a chokehold, using Tobias as a shield. It all happens so fast that the three remaining humans don't even realize what's happened until their leader is already incapacitated.

"Drop the weapon or I'll break his neck," Talon says in a voice so deadly it even gives me chills.

I peek around the island to find the humans all pointing their weapons at Talon, and fear spikes through me. But what I realize that the humans don't because their focus is on Talon is that Titus, Ensley, and Imogen are all awake.

Imogen's gaze locks on the female human standing above her and the girl's jaw goes slack just before she drops her weapon.

The thud of it hitting the ground startles the other two, but it's already too late.

Titus has leapt to his feet and is grappling with the meaty human in front of him.

Ensley begins forming a ball of faelight, but before she can throw it, the female closest to her swings her weapon toward my friend.

She takes aim—

Then a sharp, percussive crack splits the air, making me flinch.

Ensley jerks, her eyes going wide in shock as she falls back onto her air mattress. I pop out from my hiding spot and rush toward her as the female who discharged her weapon runs toward Talon to help save Tobias.

Shadows swirl in the air around us as all hell breaks loose.

Still in Talon's chokehold, Tobias forces out an order to his group to take us out.

Faelight explodes, lighting up the room, and the male battling Titus screams and doubles over, holding his face.

The female who had been standing above Imogen is now crumpled on the ground and twitching. Imogen grabs a handful of her hair and yanks her head back, raising her other hand to punch her in the face.

I've almost reached Ensley when a series of loud whip cracks ring out, hot and sudden, cutting through the chaos like a blade through the night. The explosive bursts remind me of fireworks on steroids, and I instinctually duck, throwing myself over my best friend to protect her. I brace for some sort of impact, but after a few seconds and nothing explodes, I move off of her to check for injuries.

Ensley's unconscious, but I can't find an injury anywhere. I try to shake her awake, but nothing happens. Her chest is moving up and down, so at least she's still alive.

She needs help. We need to get her out of here.

I look up just as Titus knees the male he's been fighting with in the jaw. The large human goes down, hitting the ground hard. Titus stands over him, panting as he wipes blood from his lip with the back of his hand.

I yell for him and his head snaps up, his gaze passing over me to connect with Ensley. He's over to us in an instant.

"Get her out of here," I tell him, and he immediately scoops her up and starts for the door right as Noah and the other human who Tobias sent to look for Talon and me burst through the front door.

Pointing a hand at them, Titus sends a ball of faelight in their direction and they both dive out of the way, clearing the path for him to rush out the front door with Ensley.

The shadows in the room go berserk, racing erratically back

and forth, making the chaotic situation worse. I know I'm doing it, but I don't know how to control them.

I try to focus like Talon instructed, but I can't quiet my mind enough to feel the power flowing through me like I should.

Oh, screw it. I've managed without magic my whole life. I'm not defenseless without it.

Noah is just getting to his feet when I catch him by surprise with a jump punch square to the middle of his face. He reels backward, blood spraying from his nose.

His hands fly up to cover his face, but I don't give him time to recover. I deliver a roundhouse kick to his gut, knocking the air from his lungs.

I'm about to finish him off with a punch to the temple when someone grabs my hair and yanks me back. Hard. My footing slips, and I crash to the ground.

Before I can roll and get back up, the huge male who left with Noah drops on top of me, slamming his forearm across my throat and cutting off my air.

I claw at his arm, panic setting in, but he doesn't budge. He's an immovable force.

"You filthy creatures all had to do this the hard way, didn't you?" he spits in my face.

I try to buck him off by twisting and lifting my body, but he's too heavy and he actually laughs in my face.

I can't breathe and my vision starts to go blotchy, sending a bolt of panic through me. A tornado of shadows swirls around us, and beefy guy looks up, fear widening his eyes.

All of a sudden, his face goes slack and his forearm disappears from my neck.

I cough as the male slides off me, collapsing face down on the floor, twitching. The swirling shadows dissolve, revealing Imogen standing above me, her intense gaze still locked on the male who had been choking me.

"Thanks," I croak, pushing to my feet.

I barely have time to survey the room before Talon lands a brutal punch to Tobias' jaw, dropping him unconscious and then turning toward us, panting, one hand pressed to his side.

The attackers are all down. He starts making his way over.

Imogen steps closer, fury burning in her eyes as she glares at the human still caught in her compulsion. Under different circumstances, I might feel bad for him, but I can still feel the phantom pressure of his forearm crushing my windpipe.

I swallow and wince at the soreness. Talon catches the movement. When he reaches me, he lowers his head to inspect my throat. His brows draw together in concern as he lifts a hand, brushing his fingers lightly over the bruised skin. His touch is featherlight, and despite everything, a shiver runs through me.

Suddenly, the man at our feet begins shouting, startling me. I jerk back from Talon and glance down. The human thrashes wildly, batting at the air and at himself, tears streaming down his face as he screams for help.

"Imogen, stop that," Talon orders.

There's a wicked gleam in Imogen's eye that makes my skin crawl.

"Imogen!" Talon snaps at his cousin when she doesn't listen, and she sighs.

She tilts her head and the male slumps to the floor, unmoving. Unconscious, I think.

"You are no fun," she says, turning to Talon with her hands on her hips.

Talon shakes his head in annoyance. "Let's just get—"

"Nobody move!"

My muscles lock and I look over to see Noah standing in the shadows, his face and the upper part of his chest covered in blood from his broken nose. He points his weapon in our direction. "If I see anyone so much as twitch a muscle, I'll pump you full of lead."

Lead?

"Put your hands where I can see them," Noah orders.

I'm in the process of putting my hands up when Imogen mutters, "I've had enough of this," and takes a step toward him.

"Stop!" he shouts.

Imogen smirks. "No, I don't think I will."

I know the exact moment she reaches out with her compulsion and touches Noah's mind, because he twitches, and then fear transforms his face.

"Imogen, don't!" Talon yells and starts for his cousin, but it's too late because Noah squeezes his weapon and a loud bang comes from it.

Eighteen

IMOGEN JERKS and then cries out in pain a moment before Talon reaches her.

With a gasp, I start for them when a muffled pop, fast and startling rings through the air. Twisting back, I watch Noah take an unsteady step before crumpling to the ground. Violet stands behind him on the stairs in a sleep tank and shorts, her eyes wide and wild. One of the weapons is grasped in her hands and pointing at where Noah stood the moment before.

"I'm bleeding," Imogen screeches, and I snap my gaze over to her to see Talon holding her arm.

Blood seeps from a wound on Imogen's bicep. She yanks her arm free and takes a menacing step toward Violet, murder burning in her eyes. But before she can get any closer, Talon steps in front of her, his stormy gaze fixed on Violet as he both stops and shields his cousin.

Violet scrambles back, tripping on a step and falling onto the stairs. "Wait! Please!" she says, dropping the weapon and then holding her hands up in front of her to show us she's unarmed. "I didn't know what they were planning. I was asleep upstairs until I heard all the noise. I wasn't part of all this," she says, sweeping her hand in front of her to indicate the carnage from our short battle. "I can help you. I promise."

Talon's gaze narrows, but something in my gut tells me she's telling the truth. She did also just take Noah out for us.

"How can you help?" I ask, and Violet's shoulders sag in relief.

"I can help you get to New York to look for your friend," she says, and then pushes to her feet.

Talon lets out a low warning rumble that's almost a growl, and Violet freezes mid-step.

"What did you do to him?" he asks, jutting his chin toward Noah.

"Oh. Tranquilizer gun," she says. "He'll be out for hours."

"Gun?" I say, testing the unfamiliar word.

Violet's eyes widen. "You don't know what a gun is?"

I shake my head. "We don't have them where we come from."

"You're probably better for it. Tranq guns aren't so bad, but the real ones . . ." Her voice tapers off as her gaze shifts to Imogen glowering at her from behind Talon. She clears her throat. "Well, let's just say you were lucky," she says to Imogen, who scoffs. "If someone points one at you again, be very careful. Bullets are no joke. Someone could put a hole right through your skull by only squeezing the trigger."

Nausea bubbles in my stomach. It sounds like an awful weapon, and I'm glad we don't have them on our world.

Keeping a wary eye on Talon, Violet slowly descends the stairs with her hands raised. She grabs a set of keys off a hook by the door and says, "Come on," before leading us outside.

We're all on edge, keeping an eye on the wooded area around the house, looking for potential threats. Just as we reach the bottom of the stairs, Titus rounds the side of the house. Ensley's arm is draped around him, and although her eyes are open, he's basically dragging her forward.

With a gasp I run to them. Getting on the other side of Ensley,

I put her other arm around me to help support her weight. When she looks over at me, her eyes are only slits.

"Locklyn?" she says, her voice slurred.

"I'm here. We're going to get out of here," I tell her.

She moves her head up and down in a sloppy nod.

"I found this stuck in her shoulder," Titus says, holding up what looks like a cross between a dart and a needle, a couple inches long.

She must have been hit with a tranquilizer dart. I'm just glad it wasn't one of the real weapons. The kind that puts holes through you.

"I think she's going to be fine," he says, but his "I think" sounds a lot like, "I hope" to me.

"She will be," I assure him, and then explain what Violet told us.

"Makes sense," he says. "I used my powers to try to heal her. I was able to fight off some of the medication in her system, but not all."

I'd forgotten Titus had that type of magic. He'd been able to heal Talon of the shade ivy poisoning after one of the Chaos trials. Whatever was in Ensley's system must be stronger, or perhaps it's just so foreign to Titus he didn't know how to heal her completely. But at least she is awake. Kinda.

Talon is chucking our backpacks into the truck when we reach them. One of them must have gone back into the house for them. When Violet comes around the truck, Titus comes up short. He lifts a hand in the air in front of him like he's ready to blast her with faelight if she comes any closer. Spotting him immediately, she throws her hands up in surrender.

"I'm not trying to hurt you," she says. "I want to help you get out of here."

"Why would you help us?" Titus asks, his voice thick with suspicion.

Violet's eyes dart to the teal house and then return to us.

"Because I believe you," she says. "I think you're just here to save your friend."

Titus stares at her, and I can tell he's weighing her words. But the facts are that she hasn't tried to hurt us like the others, and we need her right now. I don't see another option but to trust her.

Titus scoops Ensley up into his arms. "I'll get her into the truck," he says, and then walks around Violet without a backward glance.

Coming up to me, Violet hands me the keys. "Take the truck, but ditch it as soon as you can find another method of transportation."

Opening the passenger side door, she reaches into the glovebox, pulls out a couple folded pieces of paper, and then goes around to the front of the vehicle and spreads one out on the truck's hood. It's a map.

"This is where we are," she says, pointing to a spot in the lower right portion. "And this is New York City," she says pointing to another spot higher. "You can take I-95 almost the entire way. There's a map of the city as well. I'll mark the location of the Order's chapter in New York, but I'm not sure if you'll get the same 'welcome' there as you did here. We don't have much interaction with them. Even though we're all part of the Order, the chapters act pretty independent from each other. But to be safe, I'd advise staying away from them."

"You don't say," Imogen says sarcastically with a pointed look at her injured arm.

"I'm sorry," Violet says. "It never should have come to this."

"Why did your group attack us?" I ask, wanting to understand what happened.

Violet's brows pinch. "We were always taught that the pathways between our worlds were closed down to keep us safe. That if creatures make it into our world, it could mean the end of it as we know it. I'm not saying what they did to you was okay, but I believe they thought they were doing the right thing."

It was hard not to scoff, but fear can lead someone to make rash decisions. World domination isn't on any of our checklists. We truly just want to get Becks and go home. If only Tobias had believed us when we told him why we'd come here, this night never would have happened.

Violet casts a worried glance at the house. "Are they . . . dead?"

I catch Talon's eye over the hood of the truck. He gives me a sharp shake of his head to say they aren't. I don't know why, but I'm relieved to hear it.

"Just knocked out and injured," I tell Violet, who immediately looks relieved.

"We're not bad people," she says. "We've dedicated our lives to protecting humans. That's what they thought they were doing."

"Let's go," Talon barks, his hard gaze on Violet.

Titus has already gotten into the back seat with Ensley. He has her on his lap with her head resting against his chest.

I turn to get in the truck, but then pause, looking over my shoulder at Violet. "You promise she's going to be okay?"

She nods. "It's just a sedative. A strong one, but it will eventually wear off. She just needs to sleep it off."

She'd better be telling the truth or I'll figure out a way to make her and the others pay.

Imogen gets in the back next to Titus and Ensley, her hand putting pressure on her bloody wound, and I jump into the passenger seat next to Talon. He casts me a look out of the side of his eye that I can't interpret and then cranks the engine.

Violet backs up to get out of our way, and within seconds Talon has the car turned around and we are heading away from her. The sky has already started to lighten, and when we reach the end of the driveway and turn onto the road, the first ray of light peeks over the horizon.

I take a deep breath, my body heavy as it starts to come down from the adrenaline high.

That was close. *Too close.*

"Why didn't you use your powers?" Imogen snaps at her cousin from the back seat.

He glances at her in the rearview mirror with a hard look. "I wasn't trying to kill them."

Her mouth drops open. "Why the heck not? They were trying to kill us."

"We don't know that," he says, and Imogen gestures to the makeshift bandage wrapped around her bicep.

Talon winces, but doesn't comment. It's then I notice he has his hand pressed against his side again, and in the dim morning light I can now see that his dark T-shirt is wet under his palm. I lean over, getting a better look, and then gasp when I realize there's blood on his hand.

"Talon, you're bleeding!"

Imogen leans between the seats

"What happened?" she asks.

"It's nothing. I'm fine," Talon says, brushing it off. But when I look closer, I see the tightness in his expression and the way the color has drained from his face.

I twist in my seat, looking back at Titus. "Can you heal him?"

Titus shakes his head. "My healing power doesn't work like that. It's fae magic, so I can help cleanse the body so that it runs better. That's why I could help him during the trials and also lessen some of the sedative effects in Ensley. But I can't knit wounds back together."

I turn back to Talon and I can tell he's annoyed. What did he expect? That we'd just let him bleed out?

"Pull over so I can look at the wound."

Talon shakes his head.

"Talon. I said pull over," I say, trying to take a tone that leaves no room for argument.

By now, we're on the expressway heading north. Talon flicks one of his incisors with his tongue, the gesture sharp with irritation, before letting out a sigh and taking the next exit. He pulls over about half a mile off the expressway, the truck rolling to a stop on the shoulder of a quiet rural road. There isn't another vehicle in sight.

Opening his door, Talon gets out and heads around back toward the bed, where all our bags are. Everyone else stays put as I scramble out and meet up with him. I find him digging through his backpack. The bag is ripped from the monster attack in the swamp, but amazingly the zipper still works and a lot of the items inside are still intact.

The sun is fully up now, and my stomach clenches when I see how much of his T-shirt is soaked through. After grabbing a few supplies from his pack, he reaches down and pulls the shirt over his head with a pained grunt.

I gasp when I see his injury. There's a hole leaking blood on the left side of his torso right above his hip. It's on the opposite side of his body as the slashed bitemarks he got from the Komodo dragon shifter the night before—or was that two nights ago? It feels like both an eternity and the blink of an eye since we landed in the human world.

The gashes from the Komodo dragon still haven't fully healed. The skin around them is red and inflamed, raw and tender-looking. A knot tightens in my chest. Wounds like that should be healing faster.

I try to tamp down my concern, reminding myself that Talon said the poison in the bite was slowing his ability to recover. Even so, it's the gunshot wound that draws my focus. Blood still leaks steadily from it. It's clearly far worse.

Talon twists, craning his neck to see behind him, and I realize there's a matching wound on the other side of him. I look up at him sharply, alarm shooting through me.

"It must have gone through me. What did she call it? A bullet," he says calmly.

"Talon, you have a hole in your abdomen. We have to get you help. Do you think they have hospitals here?"

"It's my lower abdomen at least. That's good."

"How is that good?" My voice comes out high and tight with panic. Even as I watch, blood leaks in a steady flow from the twin wounds.

He shrugs. "Less important stuff down there. There's a better chance an organ didn't get hit."

I drag my gaze from his wounds back to his face, certain the panic on mine is impossible to miss.

"Do you think it hit an organ? Could you be bleeding internally?"

I take him in from head-to-toe and back up again. Is he paler than he was a few minutes ago?

Another shrug. "Maybe."

Pulling a water bottle out of his bag, he splashes water on the wound and then tries to mop up the blood the best he can with a piece of cloth. Then he reaches over, grabs a roll of heavy-duty silver tape, pulls out a strip, and tears it off with his teeth.

"How are you not freaking out right now?" I ask, as he pinches the torn skin together and presses a strip of duct tape over it like it's no big deal. "You could be *slowly dying*!"

Talon chuckles and shakes his head like I said something funny. This is *not* funny. He has holes in him, and all he has to help fix them is a roll of tape and a piece of cloth.

This is serious.

He twists to the side, trying to reach the exit wound, but he's clearly struggling to get the right angle. I reach forward, snatch the rag from his hand, and step behind him.

The hole on his back is a little larger than the one in front. I'm relieved he can't see how badly my hands are shaking as I do my best to clean away the blood so the tape will stick.

Still, he doesn't need to see my face to know what I'm feeling. He reads the silence like I've spoken my fears out loud.

"It's okay, Freckles," he says, and despite the gruesome sight in front of me, a trickle of warmth runs down my spine at the use of my nickname. "I'm pretty hard to kill."

I want to believe him, but there's a lot of blood.

"Just ask Imogen," he says with a chuckle. "She tried to take me out at least twice when we were growing up."

Even though his tone is light, I can't tell if he's actually joking. The thought of that infuriating vampire hurting him makes my fists clench with anger. I force myself to breathe, to focus, and finish cleaning the wound as best I can.

I hold out my hand, waiting for Talon to pass me the silver tape.

"If it was really bad, I'd already be dead," he says quietly, all traces of humor gone.

I sigh. "You could be half dead and still tell me you're all right."

It was the truth, and that scared me to my core. Talon was reckless at the best of times, and never admitted when he needed help. I didn't know if that was pride, or something else.

After pouring water on the wound and cleaning the blood away, I do my best to pinch the skin together before taping over the hole, but it's immediately clear the wound is too big for that.

"Do you have anything I can pack this with before I tape it?"

He rummages in his pack again, pulls out some sterile gauze and hands it to me. I gesture for him to turn back around, but he lifts a hand toward my face, and for a second I think he's going to cup my cheek. Then he realizes his hands are covered with blood and drops it again.

"Are you okay? You look a little pale," he asks, his brow pinched with concern.

"I'm fine," I mumble, not sure if I actually am. "Turn around."

This time he obeys, and after packing some of the sterile gauze in the wound, I put several long strips of tape over it, praying that it will be good enough until his natural healing kicks in.

We clean our hands as best we can with the remaining water,

then Talon throws on a clean T-shirt. Both this one and the old one are dark enough to hide bloodstains.

When we go back to the truck I offer to drive, because Talon is definitely paler now. He doesn't put up a fight.

Inside the cab, Ensley is seemingly sleeping peacefully against Titus.

Imogen stares at her cousin with a scrunched nose. "I need to stop for food soon, because even you are starting to smell tasty right now."

Ew.

"You'll live," Talon shoots back at her.

"If you don't, do I have permission to drain your corpse?" she asks with a grin.

Double ew.

Talon rolls his eyes. "Sure. I wouldn't want to go to waste."

I give them both a look like they are crazy, and Imogen purses her lips at me.

"Oh, get over yourself," she snaps.

"Imogen," Talon warns.

She shakes her head and rolls her eyes. "I don't know what you even see in her," she says, gesturing to me. "She's so uptight."

Talon opens his mouth to respond, but I beat him to it.

"It's not uptight to think it's gross that you want to eat one of your relatives."

Imogen leans forward, baring her teeth, even the pointy ones. "It's a joke. Have you ever heard of one before?"

I really don't like her, but I tell myself she's not worth the energy and crank the truck. My eyes connect with Titus' in the rearview mirror just before I pull back onto the road.

"She's going to be okay. She just needs to sleep it off," he says, easily reading the question in my eyes.

I nod even though I know the worry gnawing at my gut won't disappear until I see it for myself.

"It's going to take an entire day to get up to New York," Talon says.

He has the map that Violet gave him out on his lap and he's tracing the path between Florida and New York. I'm hit with another wave of how strange it is that our worlds are so similar. The coastline looks so similar to ours, maybe even identical.

"My best guess is about eighteen or nineteen hours," Talon says, lifting his head. "Maybe more, depending on what traffic is like here, but at least it's a pretty straight shot up the coast. If we drive straight through, we can make it there in the early morning hours."

"Is that wise?" I ask, thinking of how pale he looks, and Ensley passed out in the back seat. Even Imogen looks worn out.

I want to get there quickly, but after what we've all been through, I worry about everyone. Myself included.

"There are enough of us to trade out driving, but if it feels like we're pushing it, we can stop and rest. Let's just see how it goes," Talon suggests.

I nod, and ease the truck back onto the road. I'm nervous to drive but I try not to show it. If Ensley were awake, she'd probably be nervous too. She's been in a car when I was driving before.

At least most of the way is on the expressway. I just need to get us back to the main road and focus on keeping the truck in the lane.

Easy-peasy, I tell myself to settle my nerves.

I maneuver us back in the right direction, but I only drive for about thirty minutes before Imogen orders me to pull over so she can take the wheel, grumbling about my turtle pace as we switch seats. I'd be offended, but that half hour was so stressful I'm just relieved to be done. My fingers ache from how hard I was gripping the steering wheel.

When I slide into the back to take her place, I immediately check on Ensley, still curled up against Titus. Her color looks good, and if I didn't know better, I'd think she was just napping.

The wave of relief that washes over me is immediate and powerful. For the first time since Talon and I found the members of the Silent Order standing over our sleeping friends, I finally start to relax.

The adrenaline crash hits minutes later, heavy and sudden. My eyelids grow impossibly heavy, and I drift off to sleep to the rhythm of the truck's gentle swaying as we speed down the expressway, racing toward Becks.

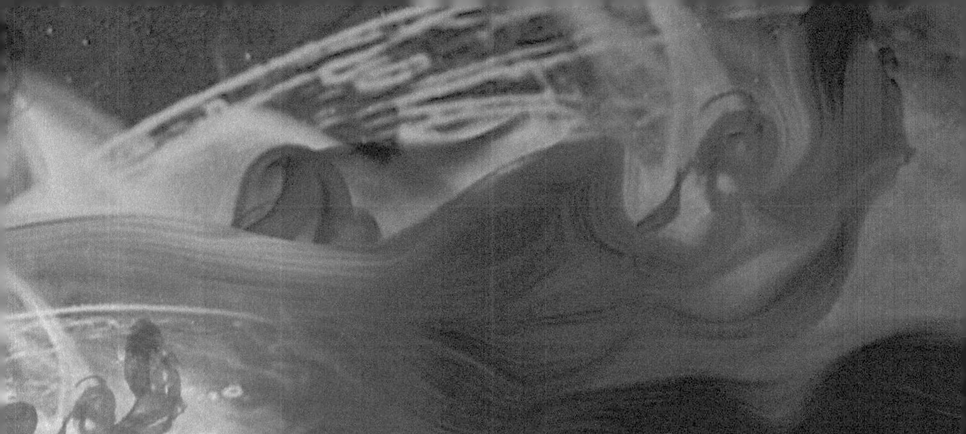

Nineteen

"FRECKLES, TIME TO WAKE UP."

I open my eyes to find myself cuddled up against Talon in the back seat of the truck.

Again.

We'd switched drivers a few times over the hours and the last thing I remember is being squished between Talon and Imogen. At some point I must have fallen asleep, because my cheek is pressed against Talon's chest and he has an arm thrown over my shoulders, his hand lazily brushing over my exposed arm as he holds me in place, a trail of goosebumps following the path of his fingers.

I wiggle out from under his arm, trying to make sense of what is going on. The truck is empty and it's just the two of us. Again. I never realized what a deep sleeper I must be.

"Sorry," I say, my voice husky and low with drowsiness. I rub my eyes, silently praying to the Creator I didn't just drool on him. "I don't mean to make a habit of passing out on you."

Talon chuckles lightly, and the soft laugh sends a flutter through my chest I would die before admitting.

"I wouldn't mind if you did," he says, his gaze sweeping over me with slow intensity that sends a flush of heat across my skin.

I clear my throat and drop my eyes, trying to ignore the sudden warmth rising in me, until I notice a dark spot on his already dark T-shirt.

"Talon," I gasp. "You're bleeding."

He looks down with a frown and lifts the bottom of his shirt to reveal a slow leak coming from between the seams of the duct tape covering where the bullet tore through him.

Sighing, he runs a hand through his hair in frustration. "I guess it needs to be rebandaged."

"Agreed. Let's get that taken care of," I say, and then look out the window to find we're parked in the parking lot of a restaurant. "Where is everyone else?"

"The others are inside ordering food," he says as he opens the door and climbs out of the truck. "Ensley said she'd know what to get you."

As I shift to jump down after him, Talon offers his hand. The truck's high clearance isn't a problem. I can manage on my own. But I take his hand anyway, moved by the small, unexpected gesture.

Going around to the tailgate, Talon grabs his backpack and jerks his head toward the restaurant. "Let's get inside so we don't have to do this out in the open."

I nod in agreement. The area looks rundown and a little sketchy, so I'd rather be inside. A small group of what appear to be the homeless sit on the grass near the edge of the parking lot, two of them arguing loudly. The restaurant itself looks like it's seen better days. The neon sign above the entrance reads *Mom's Homemade Kitchen*, flickering with age, and the glass on the front door is cracked, held together by only a couple strips of tape.

But as we get closer, I catch a glimpse through the window. The inside looks clean and cozy, which makes me feel a little better.

The restrooms are immediately to the right and down a hall when you enter, so Talon and I go there first. They're single stalls with locks on the doors, which makes it easier for us to have privacy while I re-dress his wounds. When we get inside, Talon goes to lock the door behind him, but asks if I'm comfortable with that before turning the deadbolt.

I give a little laugh and say, "If I don't trust you by now, we're all in trouble."

He glances over his shoulder at me, a hint of vulnerability in his eyes when he asks, "You trust me?"

I realize that, to him, trust is no small thing. So I take a moment to really think about it, to search my heart. And I'm a bit surprised to find that yes, somewhere along the way, I *have* learned to trust Talon, despite everything.

Yes, he lied to me when we first met, and at the time it nearly destroyed any faith I had in him. But now that I know more, I understand why he did it. Especially after meeting his mother, who was willing to coldly excommunicate him, not just from the Arcane Society but from his family and everything he'd ever known, simply for revealing their secret to us.

Moving forward, I reach around him, my gaze locked with his as I turn the deadbolt, making it clear that I do, in fact, trust him.

The crooked grin that lifts the corners of his mouth makes him look lighter than he did a moment before. Without another word, he reaches for the bottom of his shirt and I step back as he pulls it right off his head.

I've seen Talon shirtless more than once now, but the last few times were in high-stress situations when my concern overpowered everything else.

This time feels different.

Seeing his bare chest now makes my stomach drop. Even with the three healing slashes across his ribs and a bleeding bullet wound in his side, his body is still a work of art.

My mouth goes dry and I can't peel my gaze from his abs.

So. Many. Ridges.

So. *Hard*.

By the Creator, I need to stop staring. If I don't, Talon is going to look up and see me wiping drool from the corner of my mouth.

Gosh, Lock. Thirsty much?

With an embarrassing amount of effort, I turn away and busy myself by fishing the gauze and heavy-duty tape from his bag. When I find it and straighten, Talon is leaned up against the sink, a knowing smirk on his face that I pretend not to see.

Clearing my throat, I ask him to turn so I can look at the exit wound first, using that as an excuse to get his eyes off me while I compose myself. I'm irritated to find his back just as appealing as his front, but the prickle of annoyance helps clear the lust from my brain, so I lean into that emotion and get to work.

I'm relieved to find that the exit wound that I packed with gauze is looking better. The bleeding has stopped and it's already starting to heal. I carefully remove the gauze, then cover the area with a fresh layer and secure it with tape.

When I tell him to turn around so I can check the entry wound, I've mostly regained control of myself. Still, I keep my eyes firmly on the injury and away from his annoyingly perfect stack of abs, just to be safe.

As I peel back the tape, I'm surprised to see it's not as bad as I expected. There's a little blood, but it's just a slow ooze; the wound is beginning to close. I don't want his body to heal over anything left inside, so instead of packing it, I place a thick layer of gauze over the surface and tape it securely in place.

When I'm done, I finally glance up at Talon. "I think you'll live."

He cocks an eyebrow. "The look on your face makes me think you're on the fence about whether that's a good thing or not."

I roll my eyes, unwilling to say anything that might inflate his ego more than it already is. I'm about to turn away and tuck the supplies back into his bag when my gaze catches on the slashes across his ribs.

A frown pulls at my lips. I checked them this morning, and they look exactly the same. No change. No improvement. At least that I can tell. I'm no expert in creature healing, but I'd expect some progress by now. The wounds have scarred over, but the skin is still raw and uneven, the flesh ridged and angry-looking.

Something about it doesn't sit right.

Without thinking, I reach forward and run my finger over one of the newly formed scars, and Talon jerks a little.

"Oh, shoot. That probably hurt. I'm sorry," I say as I try to snatch my hand back, but he catches it, and lays it flat against his ribs, right over the trio of scar tissue.

My breath catches and I glance up at him, finding his blue-gray gaze.

"You didn't hurt me," he says, his voice soft, and far more alluring than it should be.

I nod, because I'm not capable of doing anything else.

My mind has turned to complete mush. The only thing I seem capable of processing is the coolness of the skin beneath my palm and its contrast to the jagged scars.

Lifting a hand to my face, he brushes his thumb first over my cheekbone, and then trails it down my throat only to gently wrap his fingers around the back of my neck, lightly holding me in place.

He releases a sigh, quiet and laced with sorrow, but I don't know why.

Truth is, I don't know anything right now except that my heart is pounding and my lips are buzzing and nothing seems to exist except this moment and the two of us.

Leaning forward, he lowers his forehead to rest against mine, our breaths mingling, only the barest sliver of space separating us.

I trail my fingers up his ribs to lay my hand against his chest, and his breath catches.

"Oh, Freckles," he whispers, and a delicious shiver runs down my spine.

I hate it when he uses that nickname . . . but I also love it.

He leans back a few inches so he can look me in the eye, and says, "What am I going to do with you?"

The air around us heats. Thoughts are completely gone from

my head, and like a magnet drawn to metal, my gaze slides down to his mouth in a silent plea.

Talon winces; pain tightens his features, and some of the brain fog lifts. It's not the air that's hot, it's me.

Suddenly, small flames burst to life on the tips of each of my fingers. With a yelp, I jump back, waving my hand to try to put myself out.

"I'm on fire!" I yell as I continue to flap my hand up and down.

Spinning, Talon turns on the faucet and grabs my hand, shoving it under the water and putting out the fire.

I look over at him with wide and scared eyes.

"It's okay," he says. "It's just another one of my former powers. We can work on your control of that one too."

"It's *okay*? Talon, I just spontaneously caught on fire." I glance down at his chest and see five angry burn marks, one for each finger, and I gasp. "And I burned you."

"That's okay too. I'll heal fast."

I give him a look, then drop my gaze to the scars on his ribs that still aren't fully healed.

"That's just because of the Komodo dragon venom, remember?"

I nod, but my throat clogs with emotion.

I just hurt him. How could I have done that? And what if I accidentally do it again?

Seeing my eyes start to shine, Talon tries to reassure me again that he's okay and everything is all right, but how could it be? These sudden powers on top of everything else are just too much.

I do my best to rein in my emotions. This isn't the time to fall apart. I can deal with this new magic once we find Becks and bring him home.

Becks.

A wave of guilt slams into me.

I love Becks. I want to be with Becks. Yet I just allowed myself to fall into Talon's arms and almost crossed a line I don't know I could have come back from.

Whatever this thing is that keeps almost happening with Talon, it needs to end. Now.

"The others are probably wondering where we are," I say in a small voice, looking anywhere but at him.

Talon tries to catch my eye, but I keep my gaze lowered.

He sighs. "Yeah, let's get some food."

I grab his bag as he unlocks and opens the door. As we're headed out, he slides his shirt over his head and almost runs straight into a large male in his thirties dressed in biker gear.

Puffing up his chest, the male gives Talon a once-over, a touch of malice in his eyes, before he shifts to the side to let him pass.

Talon shakes his head and scoffs as he passes.

I start to follow behind him when the male steps in my path, blocking me.

His gaze rakes over me in a way that makes me feel gross and somehow violated, before he says, "Hey, honey, since you're finished with him, I'll take the next ride."

It takes a beat for me to realize what he's saying, and by the time I do Talon has already grabbed him by the back of the neck and thrown him against the opposite wall hard enough to crack the drywall.

"Hey, what do you think—?" the guy starts right before Talon's fist smashes into his nose.

The crunch of a broken nose is unmistakable. Blood gushes from his nostrils, and he howls in pain and rage before dropping a shoulder and rushing Talon.

I know that move, and I'm shouting a warning at Talon when, lightning-fast, Talon shifts to the side and hammers his fist into the male's temple, putting him down.

It all happened so fast, I'm still standing in the restroom door when Talon reaches under the unconscious human's armpits and hefts him up. I scramble out of the way as Talon drags the human into the bathroom and drops him on the floor with a look of disgust on his face.

He turns to me, his features softening. "Are you all right?"

"Yeah. Is he . . . ?"

"Just knocked out. He'll probably be out for a while, but we should get going in case someone finds him."

"Right."

Talon crouches down and checks the male's jacket pockets. I curl my lip in disgust, a little disappointed he took him out so quickly. I wouldn't have minded landing a punch myself.

Hitting him now, while he's unconscious, would be wrong. Though the thought definitely crosses my mind before I push it aside.

Talon pulls a set of keys from the human's pocket, then straightens and locks the door behind us as we leave, making sure no one accidentally stumbles across him before he wakes.

"Come on," he says, and then takes my hand to guide me down the hallway toward the dining room.

We spot the others right away. It looks like they're finishing their meal, with a couple of to-go boxes already stacked on the table. I immediately notice that both Ensley and Titus have rounded ears now, like the humans around us, and assume she glamoured them to blend in.

Smart.

As we approach, Ensley's gaze drops to Talon's and my clasped hands. She frowns, then lifts her eyes to mine, a silent question clearly written across her face.

As discreetly as possible, I tug from his grasp.

"Where have you two been?" Imogen asks with a smirk and quirked eyebrow.

"I needed to re-dress my wound and then we ran into a little bit of trouble," Talon says. "We should get out of here."

The smile slips off Imogen's mouth. Titus and Ensley trade concerned looks.

"Need help with anything?" Titus asks.

Talon shakes his head. "Nope. I took care of it."

Titus gives a curt nod and then slides out of the booth. Imogen and Ensley follow his lead.

Grabbing the to-go boxes, Ensley hands them to me. "Got you a double cheeseburger, fries, onion rings, and a salad." She glances at Talon. "Imogen said she didn't know what you like, but it's a lot of food, so you guys can share."

Talon waves her off. "I'm good. Locklyn can have it."

"I don't mind," I say, but Talon just says he's not hungry. I can't tell if he's lying or not.

We start to leave and then a thought occurs to me. "Wait, how are we paying?" I ask in a lowered voice. We don't have any human currency. At least as far as I know.

"I've got that covered," Imogen says with a wink.

"How—?" I then realize what she means. She used compulsion to make the waiter think we've paid.

I don't feel good about it, but this whole situation is extenuating circumstances.

"We should switch rides," Talon says, his gaze fixed on a large SUV that's pulling into a parking spot as we exit the restaurant. "Think you can help out with that as well?"

Imogen grins. "I thought you'd never ask."

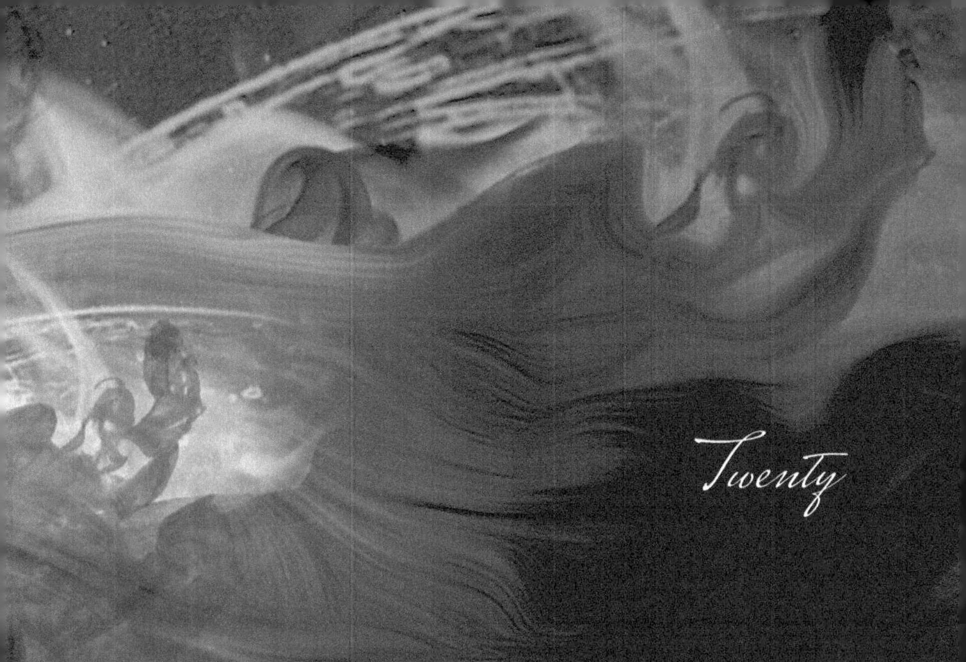

Twenty

FIFTEEN MINUTES LATER, we're back on the road in a black SUV, with Talon trailing behind us on the biker's motorcycle he found parked behind the restaurant. It's larger and clunkier than his usual chrome one, but he still looked completely at home as he swung his leg over the seat.

There was an extra helmet strapped to the bike, and when he caught me eyeing it, he asked if I wanted to ride with him. I turned him down quickly.

I didn't feel an ounce of guilt about taking the motorcycle, but the SUV was another story. The owner had just stepped out of the vehicle when Imogen walked up and compelled him to believe the truck we'd stolen from Tobias was theirs. She handed him the keys, so at least he wouldn't be stranded.

Still, I assume theft is illegal here too, so I can only hope he snaps out of her compulsion before he gets arrested for stealing the thing.

Night begins to fall, and we're still at least nine hours from New York City. We drive for a couple more hours before stopping at a fast-food place for dinner. Imogen compels the staff into thinking we've already paid, and I do my best not to dwell on it.

The car ride has been quiet since lunch. The strain of the last few days is showing on everyone's faces. We agree to push through for a few more hours, then find a hotel to crash for the night, wanting to tackle the city when we're fresh and rested.

By the time we pull into a rundown motel late that night, I'm sore in places I didn't know could be sore, and can barely put one foot in front of the other. Everyone looks worn out, but Imogen looks as bad as I feel. Maybe worse.

After compelling the girl behind the front desk to give us the last remaining room, Imogen sways slightly on her feet. Titus reaches out to steady her but she brushes him off. Even though I don't like the vampire, I feel a twinge of concern.

"What's wrong with her?" I whisper to Talon as we walk to the rented room.

He glances at me with a furrowed brow. "She was injured and has been using a lot of magic. She needs to feed."

He doesn't mean regular food. She needs blood.

Back in the creature world, it's easy for a vampire to find blood. There are even mobile food trucks that sell it, but here she'd either have to steal it from someplace, like a hospital or blood bank, if they even have those here. Or compel someone and take it by force. Both options are risky, and make my stomach turn.

When we reach the room, Imogen uses the keycard to enter. She's only two steps into the room before she collapses to her knees. We rush in after her and find her still conscious, but so drained she can't even summon the strength to stand.

"I'm fine," she snaps, swatting Talon's hands away when he tries to help her up.

Clearly she isn't.

"This is ridiculous," Titus says as he plows a hand through his hair, sending his white strands in all directions. "She can't go on like this."

With an exasperated sigh, he reaches down and pulls Imogen to her feet, slinging one of her arms over his shoulder and wrapping his around her waist. The fact that she doesn't snap at him to let her go shows just how far gone she is.

"What are you doing?" Ensley asks in alarm.

Titus can't meet her gaze. "I'm going to take care of it," is all he says, but it's clear what he means.

He's taking a third option I failed to consider. He's going to let Imogen feed from him.

Ensley takes a step toward them, her gaze filled with worry. "Titus, no. There has to be another way."

"Do you want to find an innocent human for her to feed on instead, probably traumatizing them for the rest of their life?" he asks gruffly.

Ensley seals her lips, concern for the hypothetical human flashing across her face.

Titus finally looks at Ensley, his gaze softening as it connects. "We don't really have any other options right now. It's not that big of a deal."

Ensley chews on her bottom lip, visibly upset. It's clear she doesn't want Imogen feeding from Titus, but she probably doesn't feel like she has a claim on him to stop it from happening.

I exchange a glance with Talon. I can tell we're on the same page. Both of us have kept our mouths closed, knowing this is between the two of them.

"Fine, whatever," Ensley finally says in a small voice, turning away.

Titus looks like he wants to say something to her, but instead he tightens his grip on Imogen. "I'll take her to the SUV for privacy. The windows are tinted."

"Don't let anyone see you," Talon warns. "The humans won't understand."

With a grim look on his face, Titus nods and then all but carries Imogen out of the room.

When the door closes behind them, Ensley gets up and heads to the bathroom and slams the door behind her. A minute later, the shower turns on and I worry that she's trying to cover the sound of her crying.

I get up to check on her but Talon catches my hand. When I look over at him, he shakes his head. "Give her a few minutes. She needs it."

He may be right. Even though Ensley's like a sister to me, she's always been a little secretive with her heart. As much as I want to be there for her, she probably does want to be alone right now.

"You should go to sleep," Talon says when I sit down heavily on one of the mattresses.

I eye the beds. There are two of them, but there's no way more than two of us will fit in each of them. Someone is going to have to sleep on the floor, but I can't muster the strength to care. I'll let the guys flip for it.

Pulling off my shoes, I don't even bother brushing my teeth or changing out of my clothes before peeling back the scratchy sheets and climbing into one of the beds.

"You're not going to wake me in the middle of the night for a magical training session, are you?" I ask Talon as I try to get comfortable on the lumpy pillow, slurring from exhaustion.

I hear rather than see him chuckle because my eyes are already closed.

"Not tonight."

"Good. If I set anything on fire, wake me before I burn to death. That would be an awful way to go."

The bed rocks slightly and I think Talon might have just sat on the edge next to me, but it's too hard to open my eyes to check.

"Oh, Freckles," he says with a gentle sigh. "Haven't you realized by now I'd never let anything happen to you?"

I make an incoherent noise, already half asleep.

"Sweet dreams," he whispers, and then there's a light touch on my temple and I know no more.

I BLINK OPEN MY EYES, feeling more rested than I can remember being in a long time. I slept like the dead and I'm thankful for it. I don't remember anything after I closed my eyes the night before. Not Ensley coming out of the bathroom, or Imogen and Titus returning.

Wanting to check on Ensley, I turn over, expecting to see her lying next to me, but come face-to-face with a sleeping Talon instead.

My stomach dips.

Talon's breaths are slow and even, his features wiped clean of tension, making him appear, not younger, but less burdened. I don't know why he's in bed with me, but when I glance down I see there's a pillow wall between us.

His doing or Ensley's?

The curtains are drawn, but the sunlight beyond seeps through the cracks and around the edges, brightening the room enough for me to see. I should get out of bed, but no one else seems to be awake, and I'm hesitant to break the peace, so letting my gaze travel back to his face, I openly study Talon: the straight line of the bridge of his nose, his unfairly long and dark eyelashes, the rich color of his bronzed skin. Finally, I allow my gaze to drop to his mouth.

His lips are full and far too tempting, and the longer I stare, the more a knot of longing forms in my gut, making me desire things I have no right to.

"You know it's rude to stare," Talon says with his eyes still closed, startling me. His voice is low and quiet and thick with sleep.

"I wasn't staring," I whisper back, my cheeks warming.

The corner of Talon's mouth hitches up. "Sure you weren't," he says, and then lazily blinks open his eyes.

For a split second I think that his pupils are slitted, but he blinks again and they're completely normal, making me think I just imagined it.

"What are you doing here?" I ask.

"I'm so glad you asked. You see, someone asked me to break through the gates between worlds that have been sealed for thousands of years to rescue their boyfriend. At first I didn't want to, but then I thought, 'Meh, why not? I have the week free.'"

I give a dry look. "*Here*, as in, in bed next to me?"

"Ah, well, you see the lovebirds made up last night," Talon whispers, and then cranes his neck toward the bed behind him.

Lifting up, I glance over Talon to find Titus and Ensley sleeping in the opposite bed. They're cuddled together snugly, both still fast asleep.

My eyebrows shoot up. My best friend and I have some catching up to do.

I drop back down on the pillow and Talon says, "It was either me or Imogen. I took a guess that perhaps I was the lesser of two evils."

He guessed correctly.

"And also, Imogen said she'd rather sleep next to the corpse of the Vampire King than share a bed with you. So . . ." He shrugs.

I purse my lips. "Yeah, well, I'm not really a fan of hers either."

Talon chuckles, the bed shaking a little with the movement. "Imogen takes a little while to warm up to others."

"You don't say," I deadpan. "And what about this?" I ask, gesturing to the pillow wall erected between us.

He grins; it makes him look boyishly rogue. It is absolutely not adorably sexy.

"I tried to wake you to ask if you were okay with me sleeping next to you, but you tried to deck me."

"I did not!" I whisper-hiss.

His grin widens. "You absolutely did. You're a violent little thing. I didn't want you setting me on fire this morning, so I put the pillows up to protect your virtue."

I roll my eyes and sit up, trying not to worry about what my hair looks like. "I'm going to get ready," I say, and then slide out of bed.

Grabbing my backpack, I head toward the bathroom without a backward glance at Talon. The last thing I need right now is a picture of him sprawled out in the bed that we've just shared burned into my mind.

After I brush my teeth and take a quick five-minute shower, the others are awake and moving around in the motel room. Apparently, Imogen slept in the back of the SUV last night, preferring to be away from not just me, but everyone.

She pushes past me to get to the bathroom without so much as a, "Good morning," but even so I'm a little relieved to see she looks in far better shape than she did last night. There's color in her cheeks, a sharpness in her gaze, and her movements are quick and purposeful. The gunshot wound on her arm has healed too, which is also a relief.

As Titus packs up his bag, I notice a bandage wrapped around his forearm and assume that's where she fed from him. I avert my gaze quickly, not wanting to get caught staring at it. Instead, I grab Ensley's arm and tug her toward the door.

"We're going to go grab some coffees," I say with Ensley in tow behind me.

"We are?" she asks, and I give Titus a pointed look and then nod.

She gives a nervous chuckle. "Oh right. Coffees."

"Yeah, I noticed a café across the street. We'll bring back drinks for everyone," I say, without bothering to take their orders before dragging Ensley out of the room.

I count out half a dozen footsteps and then order Ensley to spill.

She casts me a nervous glance. "What do you mean?"

"Um, how about what's going on with you and Titus? When I showed up at your house he was there and you both have been very cozy since then."

She clears her throat, visibly uncomfortable. "Yes, well, I'm glad he's here with us. He's a very powerful fae, and has been an asset on this mission."

"Ensley!" I say, stopping in my tracks. "You were snuggling in bed this morning after you were practically in tears last night over him donating his blood to Imogen."

Casting a glance behind us, she pulls me around the side of the motel.

"Okay, fine," she says, throwing up her arms in surrender once we're out of eyeshot of anyone who might come out of our room. "I like him. All right? He's attractive and sweet and attentive, and I hated the thought of him sharing anything with Imogen last night, let alone his blood. Are you satisfied?"

I do my best to cover my smile, but I can tell from the way Ensley is glaring daggers at me that I'm not doing a very good job.

This is big though. Ensley never admits when she likes someone. For all the years we've been friends, I've never once seen her act this way over a guy before. And it's not because she hasn't had interest. She's a beautiful and powerful fae from a wealthy family. There's been plenty of interest. Just not on her part.

"I like Titus," is all I say, and her expression shifts, a small smile tugging at her lips.

"Really?" she asks, vulnerability in her tone.

I nod. "Really. And I think you guys are good together. He obviously cares about you. You should have seen how concerned he was for you when you were hit by that tranquilizer. He wouldn't let you out of his sight or his arms. I think he has it bad for you."

A coy smile spreads over my best friend's face. "You think so?"

"Definitely."

She straightens her shoulders and fluffs her hair. It's streaked pink this morning. "As he should be. I'm a catch."

"That's right you are," I laugh.

She places her hands on her hips. "I spilled. Now it's your turn."

I furrow my brow. "What do you mean?"

"You and Talon. What is going on there?" The look on her face isn't exactly judgmental, but it's not happy either.

"There is *nothing* going on between us," I quickly assure her.

"Seriously, Lock? I may have been a little out of it yesterday, but I have eyes. Something is definitely going on," she says with a frown.

"I'm not lying. There's nothing going on between us," I assure her.

Because I won't allow it.

I think about the powers I've only just begun to understand, and how Talon helped me unlock them the other night. Guilt tugs at me for not telling her everything yet.

"At least not in the way you're thinking," I say.

She crosses her arms over her chest. "Oh yeah, and what am I thinking?"

"That I've forgotten about Becks and how much he means to me."

Her gaze softens. "No, Lock, I'd never think that. I know how much you care about my brother. I know that you love him, even. But sometimes . . ." She sighs and gives me a pitying look rather than going on.

"What?" I ask.

"Sometimes feelings change."

I shake my head, refusing to even entertain the idea that my feelings for Becks have lessened.

Have Talon and I had a moment or two over the last few days? Sure, but that doesn't have to mean anything. It's been Becks for me from the beginning. He's my best friend. We've already been through so much. There's no way I'm giving up on us. Especially not for what I'm sure is just a harmless flirtation and maybe a little trauma bonding.

"He's teaching me how to control my new magic," I confess, needing Ensley to understand.

"New magic?" Ensley asks, her brow creased with confusion. "What are you talking about?"

"Remember I told you that when I touched Shadow Striker I felt the power transfer from Talon to me?"

She nods. "Yes, but you said that cut off when the portal closed."

"It did, but apparently there's still a connection between us, and it seems like some of his magic is transferring to me. First, it was shadow manipulation, and then fire."

Her mouth drops open. "You have shadow and fire magic?"

I nod.

She stares at me, clearly lost for words.

As we head over to the café and order drinks, I tell her about the times I lost control and used my new powers by accident. I also tell her about how Talon was trying to teach me to use them the other night, which is how we caught the members of the Order about to attack while they slept.

By the time I get done, we have drinks for everyone—paid with from money Imogen compelled off of someone the day before—and are headed back to the room.

Ensley shakes her head in awe. "This is everything you always hoped for."

I give a nervous laugh. "Yes and no. I always wanted magic, but not like this."

She cocks her head at me. "What do you mean?"

"This isn't really *my* magic. It's Talon's. Or at least the magic he used to have because of Shadow Striker. It kind of feels like I'm stealing them from him."

"How does Talon feel about this?" she asks.

I take a deep breath. "He doesn't seem concerned. I was worried I was hurting him, but he said I wasn't. But every power I develop, he loses."

A pit of worry churns in my gut. What if I keep taking powers from Talon until he has none left, including his own?

I voice my concerns to Ensley, who then asks, "Are shadow and fire magic even Talon's original powers, or are you just picking up what he obtained through Shadow Striker?"

"I think just the magic he got from Shadow Striker."

"Well, there you have it. You're not actually stealing anything from him, then. Those weren't his powers to begin with."

I chew on my bottom lip. "I suppose you're right, but still—"

"You have enough on your plate right now. It won't do any good worrying about things you can't control. Just take it one day at a time."

I nod, agreeing with her, but the sick feeling churning in my gut doesn't disappear.

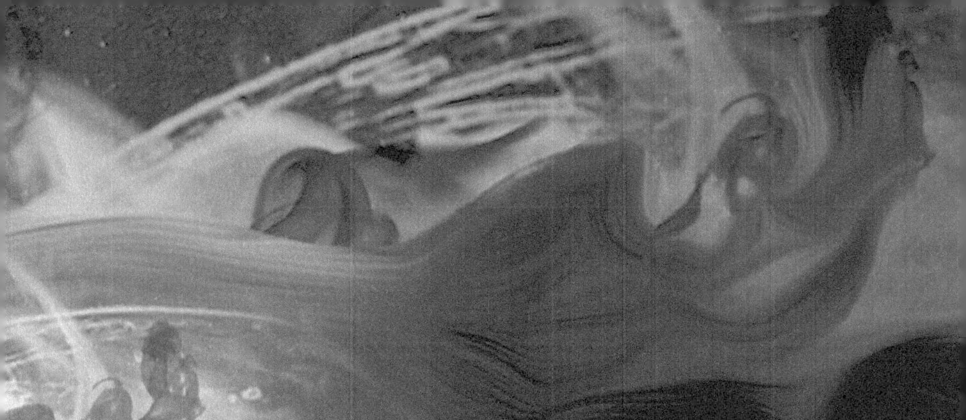

Twenty-One

"IS THIS THE PLACE?" Ensley asks as we walk through one of the entrances to Central Park, the large central green space in the middle of the biggest city I've ever been.

"I think so," I answer. The sign I read said "Central Park," so this has to be it, right?

"But it doesn't look familiar?" she asks, a pleat between her eyebrows.

"Not exactly," I say as I glance around.

"It's a big park," Talon says. "We just have to find the right spot."

"Should we split up?" Titus asks.

Imogen stays quiet, which is weird. I've gotten somewhat used to her quips and barbs over the last several days, but all day she's been strangely subdued. Especially around Titus. She's gone out of her way to avoid him as much as possible, and I wonder if she's embarrassed about how she needed him last night. I guess I'll just have to wonder though, because if I've learned anything about Imogen, it's that she's not a sharer.

Talon is already shaking his head at Titus' question when Imogen steps forward and loops her arm through mine. "That's a great idea," she says brightly. "I'll go with Locklyn. The three of you can search together."

Talon starts to argue, but his cousin snaps back at him. "You do want to find this dragon shifter, right? If we split up, we can cover ground twice as fast."

Talon presses his lips into a hard line. I can tell he's not a fan of dividing the group, but Imogen has a point.

"Only you and Locklyn saw through this portal, right?" she asks and he nods. "So we'll make two groups. I'll go with Locklyn, and you with Titus and Ensley."

Talon doesn't look happy about it, but he nods. "Fine, but everyone meets back here in two hours."

"Sounds great. Let's go," Imogen says, and before I have a chance to argue, she starts dragging me away.

"Wait a minute," I say, but she's a vampire on a mission and her iron grip on my arm is solid.

I regret that I missed the old Imogen for even a second, because over the next two hours I have to listen to her complain and berate me as we search for the field where I last saw Becks. We don't expect to find him here anymore, but the hope is we'll be able to pick up some clue as to where to start looking for him.

I bite my tongue, keeping my mouth shut for most of the two hours, but as time slips by and we don't find the field, my anxiety and fear grow and my patience for Imogen's sharp tongue wanes.

Eventually I snap.

"What is your problem?" I ask, planting my feet as I swing around to glare at her. I've had enough of her. I'm not interested in going another step with her by my side.

"My problem?" she asks, her gaze cooling to ice.

She steps closer, the heels of her boots clicking against the sidewalk, but I hold my ground. I've been dealing with bullies all my life, I know it only makes you look more like prey if you back down.

"My problem," she starts, getting in my face. "Is that you are going to get my cousin killed."

"Talon can take care of himself," I scoff, even as a flicker of guilt tugs at my chest.

"Oh yes, I know he can. But the *problem* is that he's so busy taking care of you he's forgotten to watch his own back. And not only that. It's your fault he's losing—"

"Imogen!" Her name cracks through the air, and when I look over, I see Talon striding toward us with Ensley and Titus close behind.

Imogen rolls her eyes. "What? Are you really just going to let her—?"

"Enough. Now is *not* the time," he says sharply, leaving her no room for argument. Turning to me he says, "We found the field."

A burst of hope flares in my chest, only to be extinguished the moment I see his expression. "You didn't find anything, did you?"

He shakes his head. "I'm sorry. It's been days. Becks and Kerrim are long gone, and we couldn't find anything that might help us figure out what happened to him or where he might be now."

Becks is here in this city somewhere, I know it. But he might as well be on another planet, because without a clue as to where he might be, it would take a lifetime to find him. The city is too vast and unfamiliar. We're only left with one choice now.

"We have to find the Silent Order," I say.

"Is that really our only option?" Titus asks with a frown. "Last time didn't exactly go well." He reaches over to take Ensley's hand, giving it a reassuring squeeze. She offers him a small, grateful smile in return.

"Locklyn's right," Talon says. "But we don't have to go knocking on their front door. Thanks to Violet, we have the location of their headquarters. Let's stake it out before approaching them. See what we can find out about this chapter before we make our presence known."

"Or I could just walk in the front door and compel them all to tell me everything they know," Imogen says as she checks out her nails, seemingly only half-paying attention to this conversation.

"No," Talon says firmly. "Blood is much harder to come by in this world. From now on, you need to use your magic only when it's absolutely necessary."

Imogen scowls back at him, probably not appreciating the reminder about her weakness.

"Let's get a homebase," Ensley suggests. "Then we can plan our next step from there."

We agree, and as we leave the park I tell myself this isn't a dead end, even though it feels like one.

WE GET adjoining rooms in a rundown but mostly clean hotel. Rather than relying on Imogen's compulsion, Titus pickpockets a couple of humans to get cash. Thankfully, the hotel accepts both the local currency and credit cards, a system we also have in the creature world.

It's when we're all sitting around the room, eating burgers while we plan out our strategy for staking out the Order, that Imogen announces she's leaving.

"Where are you going?" Talon asks with a frown as Imogen starts for the door.

"Out," is all she says.

"Imogen," Talon says, getting to his feet. "We could use your help."

She shrugs. "I'm sure you could, but this is all boring me. And I'm not about to act as the third wheel in one of your little love groupings," she says, pointing between Titus and Ensley and then Talon and me. "I'll be back when I'm back. Don't wait up."

When the door closes behind her, I glance over at Titus. "Did something happen when she fed from you last night? She can hardly look at you now."

Titus seems taken aback by the question. "No. She was barely conscious at first. I had to cut my arm myself to get her to drink. When she was done, she barely said two words to me."

Talon is still staring at the door. "Imogen doesn't like to show weakness. She's embarrassed, so she's lashing out. She'll be back. She just needs some time."

That makes sense. Imogen is a proud creature, and needing our help, especially Titus' last night, was probably humbling for her.

Going to his bag, Talon pulls out the map of New York City that Violet gave us with the location of the Silent Order's headquarters marked. He lays it out on the small table in the corner of the room and the rest of us crowd around him.

Over the next half hour, we strategize on the best vantage point and how to spy on the Order undetected. It's decided that Titus and Ensley will go first, then Talon and I will relieve them at nightfall. I hug Ensley tightly before they leave, and tell her to stay safe. She promises she will.

After they go, Talon insists we work on my magic, so we spend the next few hours holed up in the cramped hotel room doing just that. The times I get stuck, he has me close my eyes and center myself, finding that tangled ball of magic inside me, the one with threads that connect to him. It works every time to jumpstart my powers.

I practice my fire magic in the bathroom, keeping close to the sink and shower faucets just in case, which ends up being a good call because I almost set the room on fire twice. Shadow magic is a little easier to summon and control, but neither type comes to me easily, which only adds to my frustration.

"You shouldn't beat yourself up," Talon says after we call it quits for the day. "Most creatures spend years developing their magic, learning how to manipulate and control them. Yours appeared full-force overnight. You didn't get the luxury of training wheels the rest of us had."

"Was it like this for you when you first started accumulating powers through Shadow Striker?"

Talon thinks for a moment. "It was and it wasn't. There was a lot of new magic I had to sift through and learn how to master, but I'd been familiar with my own powers for years, so I had a sense on how to control the new ones. This is all new for you, so it's going to be more challenging than it was for me."

I sigh. I don't want to complain. Having magic is all I've ever wanted. But this is daunting.

"Hey," Talon says, pulling my attention back to him when I become introspective. Getting up from his seat across the room, he comes over to where I'm sitting on the end of the bed and crouches down so we're eye-to-eye. "If anyone can do this, it's you. I believe in you. You have an inner strength that makes you unyielding. You're going to learn to control these powers. You were always a force to be reckoned with, but now you're going to be unstoppable."

My breath catches in my throat. There's no doubt from the intensity in Talon's eyes that he means what he's saying. But I don't understand how he sees me that way. I've never felt strong, at least not in the ways that matter in the creature world. And yet, when Talon looks at me, it's like he sees the version of myself I wish I could be instead of the one I know I am.

"I don't understand how you see me that way," I confess.

His gaze searches my face before locking on mine. "I don't understand how you don't."

I shake my head. "Everyone always treats me like I'm weak."

I don't say it out loud, but even those closest to me have treated me that way. My parents. Ensley and Becks. I never doubted their love or that they care about me, but without magic I'm someone to protect. To shelter. Breakable and vulnerable on my own.

The truth is, even though I know it comes from a place of love, I still resent it.

"I've never seen you as weak. From the first moment I laid eyes on you, I only ever saw this beautiful and strong female. Brave enough to declare I was a snake shifter because I had, and I quote, 'a sketchy slimy vibe.'"

I burst out laughing, remembering that first day he walked into Sloan's with his knit cap, drawing the attention of everyone in the restaurant. "I said that because you were glaring at me."

He lays a hand on his chest. "Me? I wasn't glaring. I couldn't detect your magic and it confused me. I couldn't figure out why. Of course, now it makes sense."

"I guess that explains why you were always staring at me then."

"Does it?" he asks with a grin as he cocks his head.

A lock of dark hair falls over his forehead that I desperately want to brush back in place. I sit on my hands to keep from reaching out.

His gaze dips down to my mouth and the energy in the room changes, becoming charged when it wasn't a moment before.

There's nothing between us. There can never be anything between us, I repeat to myself, remembering my conversation with Ensley about Talon just that morning.

Just then, the lock on the door clicks open. Talon is on his feet a split second before Ensley and Titus step into the room. Ensley's face, lit with excitement and hope, has me rising quickly, my pulse already racing.

"What happened?" I ask, heart pounding.

"I think they have him," she says, her smile wide and bright. "We found him, Lock."

I glance at Titus, who gives a confirming nod.

"Sit down," I say, barely able to contain the rush of anticipation. "Tell us everything."

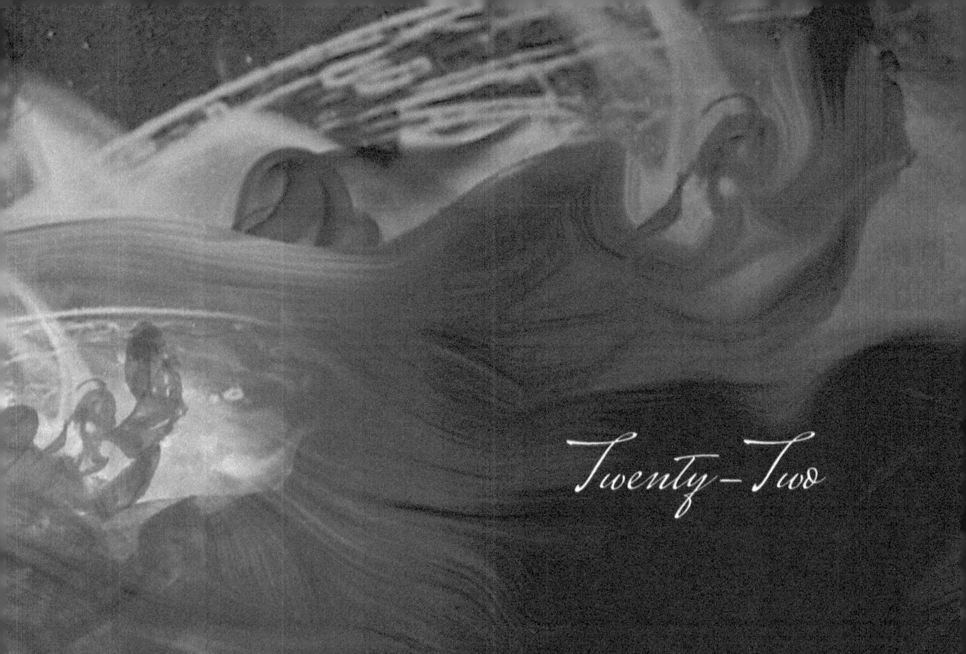

Twenty-Two

"WE'RE NOT GOING IN THERE HALF-COCKED, yelling Becks' name," Talon reminds me unnecessarily.

I shoot him a sideways glance as we weave through the throng of New York City evening commuters, dodging briefcases and coffee cups, as they rush to catch their trains home. He's watching me like he expects me to lose it at any second. Like I'm a ticking bomb.

"Yes, *Dad*, I know."

Talon's lip curls and his nose scrunches in disgust at being called "Dad," and the sight makes me laugh. My heart feels impossibly light, like nothing in the world could bring me down.

Ensley and Titus staked out the café across from the Order's headquarters. They watched two humans exit the three-story building and cross the street to grab coffee. Thanks to their enhanced hearing, they overheard the pair discussing an injured creature brought in earlier that week. The two were arguing about whether their leader, someone named Kade, made the right call by bringing the creature back to headquarters.

There's no doubt in my mind they were talking about Becks. The timing and everything lines up perfectly. Which means he's not only alive, but close.

"I know you want to get your princeling," Talon says, giving me an uneasy look. "But we have to be strategic about this. The members of the last Order chapter were hostile. We need to move forward assuming the same of this group."

"Yes, yes, I know," I say, waving a dismissive hand. "We've been over it already. We're just going to try to find a way into the building. We're not going to engage or stage a prison break . . . yet."

I expect Talon to make a remark about the whole prison break thing, but when he doesn't, I glance over and notice he looks a little worn out. There are faint shadows under his eyes I hadn't seen earlier, and his skin is pale again.

He got plenty of rest last night and hasn't done much physically today. We spent hours working on my magic, but I was the one expending most of the energy.

Is he getting sick? Or are his wounds not healing like they should be?

"Hey," I say, laying a hand on his arm. "Are you okay? How are your wounds? Are they healing?"

He nods. "Yeah, they're fine," he says, but he angles away from me, giving me the impression he doesn't want me checking.

"If you're not up to this, we can go back and see if Ensley or Titus want—"

Suddenly a stabbing pain drills into my temples, forcing me to my knees in the middle of the busy sidewalk. Talon calls my name, but I can't concentrate on him over the red-hot agony. I squeeze my eyes shut, pressing my hands against my head.

Talon scoops me into his arms and starts running, but I don't open my eyes to see where he's taking me. The pain intensifies until I think I may pass out, before it disappears as quickly as it began.

"Freckles, look at me," Talon begs, carefully setting me down on what I hope is clean ground.

I'm scared to open my eyes, but the fear in his voice forces them open. The moment I see Talon crouched in front of me, I gasp and jerk back, only to slam my head into a brick wall.

"Whoa, whoa. Careful." He cradles my head, probing the back where I hit it against the wall. His gaze skims over me, checking for injuries he won't find.

"Talon."

Reaching up, I grab his wrist to get his attention.

"What?" he asks. "Are you okay? What just happened?"

I stare at him with wide eyes, confused as to what I'm seeing. "You're . . . glowing."

His brow furrows as he glances down at himself, then back at me like I've lost my mind. "You hit your head pretty hard. Maybe we should get it checked out at a human hospital."

He tries to get me to my feet, but I swat his hands away and stand on my own.

"No. I mean yeah, I did hit my head, but that's not it. I swear, it's all around you. Like a soft glowing blue and white halo or aura."

As Talon stands before me, a shimmering halo that looks like captured starlight rings him. Its outer edges are soft icy blue and pulse gently like the rhythm of a heartbeat. Closer to him, the glow brightens into a radiant white, almost too pure to look at it directly —like moonlight reflecting on fresh snow. The two colors blend seamlessly, giving the illusion of movement, as if the air around him is alive with energy, bathing him in an ethereal light. Faint wisps of luminescence curl off its edges, trailing like smoke in slow motion.

It might be the most beautiful thing I've ever seen.

And it's really freaking me out.

"An aura?" he asks, freezing.

I nod, and as I do the brightness flickers and then disappears.

"Wait, it just went away." I search for the light, going as far as circling him to make sure it's truly disappeared.

"It's okay. I know what's going on," he says when I finish circling him.

"You do?"

He nods. "You just picked up another one of my powers. The ability to see magical auras."

My mouth drops open. "That's what that was?"

He plows a hand through his hair. "Yeah, that's what that was. You were seeing my magical signature."

"That's fae magic," I say in awe. "*Rare* fae magic."

"It is."

And I just stole it from Talon.

The pit of worry grows in my gut. "I'm so sorry. I don't know how to stop taking your magic."

He shakes his head. "It's not your fault. You're not doing it on purpose."

"I'm not, but still. How do we stop it?"

He shrugs. "I don't know that we can."

"Talon, what if it doesn't stop until I take *all* your magic? Including your own?" I say, voicing a concern that's been bouncing around my head since I told Ensley what's been happening.

He thinks about it for a second and then shakes his head. "I don't think that's going to happen. My best guess is that you're going to keep absorbing the powers I obtained through Shadow Striker, but not my own."

"But you're not sure."

Sighing, he shoves his hands in his pockets. "No. I can't be. This isn't a scenario that's happened before. Unfortunately, we can't be sure of anything when it comes to this."

I worry my bottom lip, and Talon's eyes drop to my mouth.

His pupils dilate before he clears his throat and lifts his gaze. "It's going to be okay. We'll take it one day at a time."

"I just feel so bad. It's like I'm stealing from you."

"You're not. Those powers were never truly mine to begin

with. You're acting like I'm going to be left defenseless if you take them all. I was pretty powerful before I ever laid a finger on Shadow Striker. I can still best your princeling without any of my borrowed magic."

I snort. Becks is the most powerful dragon shifter of his generation. "Sure you can," I say sarcastically.

"Maybe one day I'll prove it to you," he says with a smirk.

"I hope not."

He tilts his head, then steps in closer. "How's your head?"

Before I can answer, his fingers brush lightly against my scalp, searching for the spot I hit. I flinch when he finds it, and he immediately pulls back.

"Sorry," he murmurs. "You're probably going to have a bump."

"Yeah, probably," I say, trying to sound casual. "It's not that bad. I've had worse in sparring matches."

He studies me for a beat longer, then straightens. "Okay. Let's go. We've got a princeling to save."

His smile is there, but it's dim, like a shadow of itself.

"I'M GOING DOWN THERE," I say. I start to stand and Talon grabs my arm and pulls me back down to my stomach.

"Freckles, you promised," he says, giving me a stern look.

"I know, but he could be right there," I say, pointing at the squat, three-story brick building we've been watching for the last several hours from the roof of the neighboring apartment complex.

A few humans came and went earlier, but even with Talon's enhanced hearing we were too far away for him to catch any of their conversations over the constant hum of the city. Now that it's late and nearing midnight, no one has entered or exited the building in over two hours. All this watching and waiting has gotten us nowhere, and it's killing me to think that Becks might be so close, just out of reach, while I sit here. Doing nothing.

I know what I told Talon, but I'm done waiting. It's a risk, but we need to get into that building and look for Becks.

"Look, there's a window on the second floor that's cracked open. If we climb the drainpipe, I think we can get inside."

I'm not even finished before Talon is already shaking his head. "No. It's too risky."

"Well, what else are we supposed to do?" I ask, throwing up my hands. "Sitting up here has gotten us nothing. We have to get inside and start looking for Becks, otherwise what's the point of even being here? It's not like they're going to walk him out the front door. If he's in there, we need to act. It's a risk, but it's one we have to take."

From the look on Talon's face, I can tell he's not convinced, so I try a different approach. If that doesn't work, I'll go in alone. I want his help, but I don't need his permission.

"What are you worried about anyway?" I ask. "They're just humans. They don't have magic, but *we* do. If it comes down to it, we can easily overpower them."

I'm confident I can handle myself physically, but when I talk about magic I really just mean him. I still can't use my new powers reliably.

"What am I worried about?" he asks. He lifts the bottom of the shirt high enough that the edges of the gauze and tape he has covering his gunshot wound are visible. "I'm worried that they'll have guns and they're going to shoot first and ask questions later."

Right. I forgot about that.

Getting to my feet, I twist out of the way when Talon reaches up to grab me again.

"Listen, I came to this world to save Becks, and to do so I need to know if he's in that building or not. If he isn't, then we're wasting time looking for him in the wrong place. I'm going in. You can come with me or stay here. Your choice."

I turn away and head for the fire escape we used to climb onto the roof. Behind me, I hear Talon's frustrated sigh, followed by the crunch of his footsteps as he moves to follow.

"Wait up," he says, and when I peek over my shoulder, he's jogging to catch up with me.

"Glad to see you've come to your senses," I say with a grin, knowing I've won.

He chuckles and rolls his eyes. "You're going to be the death of me, Freckles."

My insides clench, feeling like my breath was stolen from me. I know he meant it as a joke, but Imogen's warning that I'm going to get Talon killed is still fresh in my mind.

"What?" he asks, noticing the change.

I shake my head. "Nothing. Just, don't do anything stupid when we get in there."

His eyebrows shoot up. "Me?"

"Yeah," I say, my mood dipping. The last thing I need is another creature's life on my conscience.

SHORT HAIRS that have escaped my ponytail cling to the sides of my damp face as I haul myself through the window and into the Order's headquarters.

I'm drained, both physically and mentally. Climbing the drainpipe without being spotted by either passersby or any of the security cameras we identified meant I had to keep us hidden in shadow the entire way.

It took nearly half an hour just to summon the shadows, even with Talon's help, and even longer to hold them steady as we climbed. The strain of holding the shadows in place has my limbs trembling and my head throbbing.

I glance up and look around the room I've just dropped into. I think it's a small office. The lights are off, but city glow spills through the window, enough for me to make out two desks pushed against opposite walls of the narrow room. One is immaculate, the other buried under a mess of papers and candy wrappers.

I lean against the wall to catch my breath as I wait for Talon to slip through the open window behind me. The moment he does, I release my hold on the shadows cloaking the alley and let out a quiet sigh of relief.

When he glances over, concern flashes in his eyes, but he doesn't say anything. There's nothing to say. We're in the building now. There's no turning back.

With a quick nod in my direction, Talon steps past me and presses his ear to the door, his brow furrowed in concentration. He listens intently, using his heightened hearing to judge if the coast is clear. After a moment, he gives a short wave, signaling me over.

"I think the hallway is empty," he whispers. "It's quiet out there, but even so, we have to be careful. We need to get in and out without them ever knowing that we were here."

If we find Becks and leave with him, they'll know we were here, but I don't bother saying that out loud. I just nod.

Talon carefully opens the door, peeking out to scan the hallway before slipping through, with me right on his heels. Without any exterior windows, the hall is even darker than the office we just left. I can barely see a thing, but I know Talon can. He saw perfectly in the underground caves during the first Chaos trial.

I place a hand on his back to guide myself. He glances over his shoulder, then reaches back and takes my hand. My heart is pounding, but his cool, steady grip is grounding.

We move quickly, checking each room along the hall. A bathroom, a broom closet, a few more identical offices. Nothing useful. Only one door remains when Talon suddenly stops. I'm about to ask what's wrong when he spins toward me and quickly ushers me back into a small office we've already searched, closing the door behind us without a sound.

"Talon, what the—?" He slips a hand over my mouth and holds a finger up to his lips, telling me to be quiet.

I nod, and he pulls his hand away just as the door next to us creaks open.

My eyes widen. We were nearly caught. I press my ear to the door, heart pounding, and catch the low rumble of a male voice on the other side.

"No, no, everything's been quiet. It was weird though. Cameras five and six seemed to glitch for about ten minutes. There were dark spots in part of the feed."

He's quiet for a bit before saying, "No, it was just the cameras in the side alley. I've never seen a malfunction like that before. They're working fine now, but I want to see if there are any loose wires or faulty connection."

I assume the male is talking about the shadows I pulled around Talon and me while we were climbing the drainpipe to get inside. I glance at Talon and catch his eye. He gives a small nod, letting me know he heard it too.

"I'll call Drew if we need a replacement," the male says. A door slams shut, muffling his voice until it fades away entirely.

Talon and I slip back into the hallway to find that the male left the door to what looks like a security room ajar. Inside, several computers hum softly, and rows of monitors display surveillance footage from around the building, both outside and within.

"We have to be fast," Talon says, keeping one eye trained on the hallway.

I nod, nerves tightening in my chest. We have no idea when the human might come back.

"Let's check the monitors. At the very least, we'll be able to see where the cameras are so we know which areas to avoid."

"Go ahead," Talon says. "I'll keep watch."

I rush into the room, scanning one monitor after another as

they cycle through different camera feeds. Most of them appear to be trained on the building's exterior, but a handful show the inside as well. I spot what's likely the front entrance, then a hallway, and a conference room, each flashing by in seconds. Then one of the feeds shifts and my heart stumbles, pounding violently against my ribs.

I lean forward, holding my breath as I try to make out the grainy image on the screen. It looks like some kind of hospital room, stripped down and sterile, with little more than a narrow bed and an IV stand. But it's not the setting that holds me, it's the blond-haired male pacing away from the camera, his back broad and familiar even with bandages wrapped around his torso.

The slope of his shoulders, the shaggy blond hair, even the way he moves—it all sends a jolt of recognition through me. My breath catches. It *could* be him. I'm still not sure. Until he turns. And then, as if he somehow knows I'm watching, he lifts his face to the camera.

I gasp.

Even through the pixelated screen, I can see his green eyes flashing.

Becks. I've found him.

"What's wrong?" Talon asks, turning from his lookout post to find me standing with a hand over my mouth and watery eyes.

I point to the screen, unable to speak around the lump of emotion in my throat. Talon comes up beside me, his gaze going to the monitor and then widening when he sees Becks.

He smiles down at me, but there's a touch of sadness in his gaze when he says, "You did it, Freckles. You found your princeling."

I start to tell him we need to figure out where that room is when there's a sudden pop, followed by a sharp, stabbing pain in my side. Before I can even draw a breath, electricity rips through me from the point of impact, seizing my muscles and locking my entire body in place. I can't move. I can't scream. I can only stand there, frozen, as the current takes control.

My limbs finally give out and I crash sideways into the desk, pain exploding in my skull as it connects with the edge before I collapse to the floor. Somewhere through the haze, I hear Talon shout my name, followed by a thud of fists and the crash of shattering objects.

I force my eyes open just long enough to see him fall beside me, his face twisted in rage, his body twitching as he fights the same electric paralysis that took me down. Then everything goes dark.

Twenty-Three

MY HEAD POUNDS, my body aches, and someone is shouting my name, making it feel like I'm being stabbed in the skull with an icepick. I want nothing more than to slip into oblivion again, but an errant thought runs through my mind, snapping me back into full awareness.

Becks.

My eyes snap open with a gasp, and I find myself bound to a cold metal chair.

"Thank the Creator," Talon's voice comes from nearby. I turn to see him tied up as well.

Ropes are looped tightly around his chest, his arms secured behind the chair, each ankle lashed to a leg. One cheekbone is bruised, and a trail of dried blood runs from his split lip down his chin. His shirt is torn, and his bloodshot eyes meet mine.

The sight of him beaten and restrained sends a surge of fury through me.

"Are you all right?" Talon asks, his gaze sweeping over me.

"Am *I* all right? You look like you've been trampled in a stampede."

He grimaces. "I look that good, huh?"

"Worse."

"Well, you should see the other guy," he says with a flash of his signature smirk, but it falters when the movement reopens the cut on his lip, sending a fresh trickle of blood down his chin.

"If you look like this, I can't imagine the other guy is still alive," I say, meaning it.

"Unfortunately, he is," Talon says, sounding put out. "But listen, we need to get out of here," he says, casting a glance at the door.

Besides a single unoccupied chair in front of us, the room is completely bare. No windows. No other doors. Just stark concrete block walls and a drain set into the center of the floor. It's obviously an interrogation room, and I shudder to think what the drain is for.

"I can't use my magic," Talon says, and a spike of fear shoots through me. "They put some kind of device on my wrists. A gold cuff that disrupts my powers. But they think you're human, so they didn't bother with you. You'll have to use your fire magic to burn through the ropes."

My stomach drops. I've practiced more with my shadow magic than fire; fire still scares me. I'm afraid of losing control and accidentally hurting someone.

"You can do this, Freckles," Talon says, easily reading the apprehension on my face.

I nod, even as tendrils of doubt put my heart in a chokehold.

"Concentrate like I taught you. Close your eyes and imagine the source of your magic deep inside, and use it to stoke your power."

I'm just about to close my eyes and try when the door swings open. A large, objectively handsome man steps inside. He looks to be in his late twenties or early thirties, with deep brown skin, black eyes, chin-length locs, and muscles stacked on top of muscles.

He's built like a bear shifter, like my dad, but the look of pure disgust he throws Talon tells me he's definitely human.

"You sent three of my men to the ER tonight," he says, his voice deep and laced with authority.

Talon lifts his chin and smirks. "Must have been an off night for me if it was only three."

The male narrows his eyes, and for a moment I brace myself, thinking he's about to strike Talon. But then his gaze shifts to me. There's no open hostility in his expression, but the way he studies me makes my skin crawl. It's like he's trying to peel back my layers, searching for secrets I haven't even admitted to myself. For a wild second, I second-guess my assumption that he's human, worried instead that he's a creature with some kind of truth-sensing magic.

The male grabs the empty metal chair, turns it around, and straddles it, planting his feet wide as he rests his arms across the back. He stares us down, unreadable, and the silence stretches, heavy with tension.

"A creature and a human break into an Order headquarters. I guess we should start with the obvious question. Who sent you?"

Talon and I keep our mouths closed.

"Are you part of the Sinclaire or Murphy clan? Or are you part of the new player's group?"

I have no idea what he's talking about, so I don't say anything.

He leans forward, his arm muscles bulging. "Are you sure this is the way you want to play it?" he asks. "This is me asking nicely, but I can guarantee you're not going to like it when my patience runs out."

"We're not telling you—" Talon begins, but I cut him off. "Where's Becks?"

The male's gaze flicks to me, his eyebrows lifting in surprise.

Sinclaire? Murphy? Someone new? It's clear there's more going on in this world than we understand. But we're not part of any of it.

Talon lets out a low groan, and I know that if his hands were free, he'd be dragging one down his face in frustration. But I'm not in the mood for games.

"We know you have our friend somewhere," I accuse. "We saw him on your monitor. We just want him back and then we'll be on our way. You'll never have to see us again."

"You're here for the dragon shifter?" he asks, his gaze assessing.

I nod. "Yes. He's my, um, friend," I say, stumbling over the words. "He's important to us."

The male stands and circles the chair, then crouches in front of me. The tension in the room spikes, climbing from ten to ten thousand. Talon lets out a quiet rumble of warning beside me, but the male doesn't acknowledge it. Now that he's closer, I can see I was wrong about his eyes. They aren't black after all, just an intense, deep shade of brown.

"You need to back up. Now," Talon warns, his voice low and hard.

The male doesn't even glance his way. His full attention is locked on me.

"I just need to know one thing," he says calmly. "Then we can talk about your dragon shifter." He leans in slightly. "Are you the human who opened the portal to our world?"

"Don't tell him anything," Talon snaps.

I nod, hoping I'm not making a huge mistake confessing, and Talon cusses under his breath. I glance at him out of the corner of my eye, and the glare he's sending the male is nothing short of murderous.

"Well," the male says, a grin spreading over his face. "That changes things."

Someone knocks on the door and the male barks for them to enter.

Straightening, he glances over his shoulder as a brown-haired male smaller in both height and body mass opens the door. The newcomer's green eyes land on me first, then shift to Talon and stay there.

"What is it, Kai?" the dark-skinned male asks, startling the other.

"Right. Sorry, Kade," he replies quickly.

So now we have a name for our interrogator. *Kade.*

"You asked to be updated," Kai continues. "Sam and Ryder were just discharged from the hospital. They're keeping Pete overnight for observation because of the concussion, but they expect to release him in the morning."

Kade nods, and Kai shoots a scowl in Talon's direction.

Talon just stares back, a small smirk playing on his lips, one that clearly gets under Kai's skin when his jaw tightens and his nostrils flare.

"Do me a favor," Kade says, turning to Kai. "Go get Ares."

Kai's head snaps toward him, eyes wide. "Are you serious?"

Kade lets out a dry, self-deprecating chuckle. "Looks like those Floridians might not be as crazy as we thought. But I want to be sure."

My stomach drops into my belly and I exchange a wary glance with Talon.

What did the members of the Florida Silent Order tell the humans about us? Nothing good, I imagine.

"You don't mean . . . ?" Kai gazes at me with wide eyes, looking almost spooked.

"Like I said, I want to be sure. I'll need Ares for that."

Why? I wonder. Is Ares some sort of master torturer?

This situation is going from bad to worse, and as my heart rate spikes, so does my body temperature. Heat prickles beneath my skin, and the familiar tingle of fire magic sparks at my fingertips. Unlike the time I accidentally burned Talon, I don't push it away—I embrace it.

Kai sniffs the air, his nose wrinkling. "What's that smell?"

Kade's head whips in my direction so fast his locs slap him in the face. But it's too late, I'm already burning through the ropes wrapped around my wrists, seconds away from freeing my hands.

"Quick, get a cuff before she burns this place to the ground!" Kade shouts.

Kai bolts from the room, slamming the door shut behind him.

Kade lunges for me, but Talon throws his weight sideways, somehow dragging his chair into the path. He slams into Kade, knocking them both to the ground.

Still bound, Talon shouts, "Free yourself and run!"

Kade struggles beneath him, trying to push up, but I've already burned through the rope at my wrists.

By the time Kade manages to roll halfway upright, I'm on my feet, fire curling over my fingers as I raise my hand and level it at him.

"Move to the corner of the room. Slowly," I order.

Kade's gaze travels from my hand to my face and then back again, before he slowly stands and shuffles toward the corner.

I glance down at Talon, heart still pounding, fire flickering over my hand. "Are you okay?" I ask, unsure how to help him while my fingers are still ablaze.

He nods and then glances at my hand. "Just do it," he says, wanting me to burn through his bindings, but I shake my head.

If I grab the rope with the hand that's on fire, it might catch *him* on fire as well.

"Freckles," he growls. "I can take it."

"I'm not hurting you on purpose."

"Here," Kade says, and to my surprise he pulls a pocket knife out of his boot and slides it across the floor to us.

I blink at him in surprise. Why would he help us?

I reach down with the hand that isn't on fire, grab the knife, and start sawing through the ropes binding Talon while keeping a wary eye on Kade. As soon as I cut through one, Talon twists free and is on his feet in an instant.

"Come on," he says, and grabs my hand.

"Wait," Kade calls. I glance over my shoulder to find him holding both hands up in a gesture of surrender. "You want your dragon shifter back? I'll give him to you. *After* you've cleaned up the mess you made in our world."

"What are you talking about?" I demand, just as the door slams open and Kai bursts in, a shimmering gold cuff clutched in his hand.

My stomach drops. That's what they use to block magic.

Before Kai can take a single step toward me, Talon is already moving. He lunges, slamming into Kai and locking an arm around his throat.

The cuff flies from Kai's hand, skittering across the floor with a metallic clatter. He kicks and claws, trying to break free, but Talon's grip is like iron.

"Go!" Talon shouts, apparently under the mistaken assumption I'd leave without him.

"Everyone, calm down," Kade's voice booms throughout the small room, causing all of us to snap our heads in his direction. He looks straight at me when he says, "Listen, we got off on the wrong foot, but I believe we're on the same side."

Talon releases a dark chuckle. "Is that so?"

Kade's gaze shifts to him and he nods slowly. "Yes. And if you give me a few minutes to explain, I think we can come to an agreement that will benefit all of us."

"You're crazy if you think we're trusting you now," he says, his arm tightening against Kai's throat, making the male claw at his throat, releasing a choked gasp that makes me wince.

I want to tell Talon to let him go, but there's a darkness in his gaze that tells me he's not in a merciful mood.

Kade presses his lips into a straight line, his nostrils flaring. He digs into his pocket and pulls out a small key. "This will unlock the magic blocker on your wrist. With magic like you're packing, you can easily overpower us. I just ask you give me a few minutes to explain, and then if you want to walk out of here on your own, we won't do anything to stop you."

"What about Becks?" I ask. I'm not leaving without him.

Kade's dark gaze shifts back to me. "I'll let you leave, but I'm not giving up all our leverage."

"With my powers back, I can just make you give us the dragon shifter," Talon says.

Kade looks him dead in the eye. "You can try. But I won't promise not to fight back if you do. And if that happens, we may not be the only ones getting hurt."

Kade's gaze drifts to me in a clear warning. Talon makes a noise low in his throat that's as close to an animalistic growl as I've heard from him.

"But it doesn't need to go down like that. We can all sit and have a civilized conversation."

Kade extends his hand, the small key pinched between his thumb and forefinger. I hesitate for a beat before cautiously taking it, then make my way over to Talon. Kai's eyes go wide when I approach, the flames still curling around my fingers.

"How do I turn this off?" I whisper to Talon as I wiggle my flaming fingers.

"Unlock my cuff and I'll take care of it," he says.

The cuff blocking his magic is clamped around the same arm he has pressed to Kai's neck. Talon eases the pressure just enough for me to unlock it, and Kai immediately gulps in air. As soon as the cuff is off, Talon presses his fingers to Kai's temple. His eyes roll back, and his body goes limp in Talon's hold.

Keeping a wary eye on Kade, Talon lowers Kai's body to the ground, and then, before I realize what he's doing, he grabs my burning fingers.

I gasp and try to yank my hand away, but Talon holds firm. A cooling sensation spreads from my fingertips, enveloping my hand and trailing down my arm, raising goosebumps in its wake. When he finally lets go, the flames are gone, replaced by a thin coating of frost.

I look up at him in surprise. That's not a kind of magic I've ever seen him use before. Sure, I'd suspected he'd messed with the temperature a time or two, but this makes me wonder if it's part of his original abilities he's kept hidden, just like Imogen said his family tends to do.

"Thanks," I say, a little breathless.

He gives a single, silent nod.

"Is he okay?" Kade asks, and I flinch, his voice startling me. I'd somehow forgotten we weren't alone.

Talon's sharp gaze tracks to Kade. His face hard and devoid of warmth. "He'll wake up in a couple hours, unscathed."

Kade nods.

Talon takes my hand and tugs me toward the door. "Come on, Freckles. Let's get out of here."

"Wait," I say, and turn back to Kade. "Becks. Where is he?"

Kade crosses his arms, his chin lifting with defiance. "Like I said, we need to talk. Now that you're both free, we can do that as equals."

Talon scoffs, and Kade narrows his eyes. "What? You don't consider humans equals? You one of those creatures who looks down on anyone without powers?"

Talon's not like that. If anyone knows that, it's me.

I'm about to come to his defense, but he sets Kade straight himself.

"No," he says, voice steady. "I don't look down on anyone for not having magic. Powers don't define your worth or prove your strength any more than your guns do."

He glances at me, and the words he once spoke during Chaos echo in my mind.

"What's inside is more powerful than any magic."

"It's not magic that makes the creature powerful, it's the strength of their character and the depth of their soul. And you, Freckles, are the most powerful creature I've ever met."

Just remembering his words warms a hollow place deep inside me. Talon never treated me like I was less-than, even before I had magic. Not for a single moment.

Looking back at Kade, Talon says, "So no, I don't look down on you because you are magicless. I look down on you because you're an ass who didn't even give us a chance to explain before you attacked us, and now you're asking us to give you what you didn't afford us."

Kade's nostril's flare, but to his credit he doesn't snap back at Talon. He nods once and concedes. "That's fair. Like I said, we got off on the wrong foot. In my defense, things have been pretty hostile around here lately. Something is brewing, something dark and evil. It's no longer so clear who's friend or foe. Maybe I don't deserve it, but I'm asking for it anyway. If you don't like what I have to say, we can still part on amicable terms."

That makes me snort a laugh. Does he consider this amicable?

One of his men is lying unconscious at our feet. Three more are in the hospital, and Talon's a bruised and bloody mess.

"If we agree to talk, will you release Becks to us?"

Kade shakes his head and my anger spikes.

"No, but if you want him back eventually, you're going to have to talk to me now."

This guy is driving me nuts. "Fine," I bite out. "We can talk. But not before you bring me to see Becks."

Kade opens his mouth, and I can tell he's about to argue. But I'm done listening.

I round on him, every ounce of fear, frustration, and desperation I've been carrying pouring into my words: "I'm willing to hear you out, but not until I see Becks with my own eyes. You have no idea what I've been through to find him, or how far I'll go to bring him home safely. You say we're on the same side? Then prove it. Because if you don't take me to him, I'll consider you an enemy. And believe me when I say you don't want me for an enemy."

As if summoned by my fury, the shadows in the room stir and darken. I know I'm the one calling them, even if the magic is responding more to my emotions than my command. But that's a problem for another day.

When they slither up the wall, I catch the first flicker of fear on

Kade's face, a crack in the calm, controlled exterior he's worn since the moment we met. He quickly schools his features, but it's too late.

I step closer, tilting my head back to meet his gaze. He's taller, but I don't let that intimidate me.

"Do you understand?"

Kade is silent. His stare is hard and assessing, and for a moment I worry that he's going to refuse, forcing me to raze this building to the ground to find Becks, but then he nods slowly.

"All right," he finally says, and relief runs through me like a healing balm. "But on two conditions. You agree to be cuffed when you see him, and your guard dog stays here," he says, nodding his chin toward Talon.

"No way," Talon says firmly. "We're not separating."

"Talon," I say, turning to him.

Talon frowns at me. "Separating is a bad idea," he warns.

I don't disagree. But the truth is, I'd agree to even harsher terms if it meant I could finally see Becks. To make sure he's truly okay and let him know I'm here for him.

"I'll be all right," I say, trying to sound more confident than I feel.

Talon scowls. "You don't know that. This could be a trap."

I glance over at Kade, remembering how his demeanor changed the instant he found out I opened the portal that let Kerrim into this world.

"This isn't a trap," I say, suddenly certain. "He needs us for something. He's going to play nice until he gets it. Isn't that right?"

Kade quirks a brow, but nods. "You have my word I won't hurt either of you. To be blunt, I want to ensure I keep my leverage." He crosses his arms over his chest, making his biceps bulge. "We have safeguards in place so your dragon shifter doesn't escape, but I'm not taking the chance of sending anyone in there with powerful magic. If you'd like," he says, looking at Talon, "you can be cuffed again and go in with her." He shrugs. "I assumed you'd rather keep your magic though. But it's up to you."

"You're not cuffing me again," Talon growls, his voice hard as ice.

"That's what I figured." Kade shifts his attention to me. "So, what will it be?"

"Fine," I reply. I can practically feel Talon tense beside me. "But the cuff comes off after."

Kade nods. "Agreed." He tries to move forward but Talon blocks him.

"If you hurt even a single hair on her head, I swear you won't live to regret it. You've only gotten a taste of what I'm capable of."

"Oh, my friend," Kade says. "I've seen enough from both of you to know that."

"I'm not your friend," Talon growls, and for the first time since meeting him, Kade smiles, and it takes me aback.

"Not yet."

Twenty-Four

AFTER AGREEING TO HIS TERMS, we follow Kade out of the interrogation room and down the hall to a freight elevator, one of those ones with a large platform and a collapsible metal grate you'd typically see in warehouses or lofts. When we enter the elevator, Kade pushes an unmarked button and it groans, making my stomach bottom out, before starting to move. There aren't any distinctive floors as we descend. The elevator just keeps going down, down, down, until finally jerking to a stop.

Talon watches Kade with a wary eye as he pulls open the scissor gate and we step into a poorly lit hallway of some sublevel underneath the building.

"He's being held at the end of the hall," Kade says, pointing in the direction.

When we get to the door, Kade tells Talon this is where he'll have to wait, and then asks for my wrist to put the magic-blocking cuff on.

I'm suddenly very apprehensive to put on the shiny piece of metal. It has a slight rose gold tint, is roughly two inches wide, and opens and shuts like a manacle.

"What is it?" I ask.

"Manacite," Kade says. "It was discovered to disrupt magical pathways, making it impossible to channel magic. No one knows why, but it works. It's very rare here in the human world."

"It doesn't exist at all in our world," Talon says, glaring at the cuff.

Taking a deep breath, I hold out my arm, reminding myself that Becks is worth it. I'd trade all this new magic to have him back. Gladly. So what's the big deal if I muffle my abilities for a little while?

The moment the cuff snaps shut around my wrist, the magic within me falls quiet. The change is instant, like someone's flipped a switch and shut off a part of me I hadn't even known was fully awake until now.

It's not painful, but it's deeply unsettling. A hollow sensation spreads through my chest, as if a vital connection has been severed. I hadn't realized how quickly I'd gotten used to the thrum of magic beneath my skin, how natural it had started to feel.

Now, its absence leaves me unmoored, empty in a way that feels more emotional than physical.

"Let's go," I say to Kade, doing my best to suppress my anxiety.

Talon catches my hand right before I go through the door.

"I'll be right here the whole time," he promises. "If anything goes wrong, just scream. I'll be through that door in seconds. Nothing will be able to stop me."

I nod, my throat suddenly dry at the thought of seeing Becks.

Becks, who I've been secretly worried was dead because of me since the moment I watched Shadow Striker punch through his chest.

Becks, my oldest and dearest friend who I care so much about and who I have the most jumbled mess of emotions for.

Becks, who thinks I betrayed him by choosing to be with Talon instead of him.

Becks, who I'm suddenly and inexplicably so nervous to see my palms are sweating and I hope Talon doesn't notice.

"Tell your princeling I said 'Hey,'" he says. After giving my hand a quick squeeze, he lets go, his fingers brushing lightly across my palm as he does.

I let out a nervous laugh. "Don't take this the wrong way, but I'm not sure Becks is going to want to hear anything about you."

"Good point," he says.

With a small smile, I step through the door after Kade, casting one last glance over my shoulder just as it begins to close. Talon is watching me, his eyes locked on mine, and there's something in his expression that tugs at my chest. Something I can't unpack right now.

Because Becks. I'm about to see Becks.

The door Kade takes me through leads to a small outer room. He tells me I have thirty minutes with Becks, and that's it, then nods at the only other door in the room.

"Go ahead," he says.

"He's just on the other side of that door?" I ask, a swarm of butterflies flapping like hell-bats in my gut.

"Yep."

I push through my nerves and rush to the door, shoving it open before I can psych myself out. The moment I cross the threshold, I freeze. What the surveillance feed didn't show was that Becks is in a cell. A surprisingly nice one, sure, but it's still a cell, one wall made entirely of metal bars.

Becks sits on the edge of a twin bed, shirtless, wearing only green scrub pants. A large bandage is wrapped across his upper torso, leaving the lower half of his abs exposed. He looks like he might have lost a little weight, and he has a layer of scruff on his face I'm not used to seeing. But his coloring looks good and he's not holding himself like he's in pain.

"Just leave the tray on the ground and go," he snaps, irritation ringing from each word.

I go to say his name, but a sob rips from my throat instead.

Becks lifts his head, his green eyes flashing when he spots me.

Jumping to his feet, he stumble-runs toward the bars in his haste to reach me.

"Locklyn," he says, his voice clogged with emotion.

I press my hand over his where he grips one of the bars, then reach my free arm through the gap to embrace him as best I can with the cold metal between us. I wish I still had access to my fire magic. I'd melt the blasted bars if I could, because touching him like this, knowing with my own hands that he's alive and real, is not enough, Not nearly enough.

Tears slip down my cheeks, and when they dampen his neck, he pulls back just far enough to meet my eyes.

"What are you doing here?" he asks, voice rough. "How did you even get here?"

"In this room, or to this world?" I ask with a shaky laugh, my eyes still filled with tears.

"Either. Both." He reaches out and cups the side of my face, his palm warm and steady.

The tenderness in his gaze, so open and full of love, breaks me all over again. Fresh tears spill down my cheeks.

"Are you real?" he whispers. "Is this really happening? Because every night I dream you're here, but every morning I wake up alone."

I place my hand over his, savoring the warmth of his palm against my cheek. "It's me. I'm here. I came to find you and bring you home. Well, *we* did."

"We?" he asks.

I nod. "Ensley's here too. Not in this building, but back at the hotel. She's going to flip when I tell her I found you."

His brow furrows sharply. "Wait. You and Ensley came here alone?"

I shake my head quickly. "No, not alone. Titus is with us too. And . . . also Talon."

"Talon?" he repeats, the word landing like a blow. His expression darkens instantly. He takes a step back, hands dropping from me. The warmth he'd given a moment ago vanishes and cold tension fills the space between us.

I wrap my hands around the bars, leaning in as close to him as I can. "He was the only one who knew how to get to the human world. Without him, I'd still be stuck in the creature realm, wondering if you were dead or alive, not knowing where you were or how to reach you, maybe never finding you at all."

"Oh yes. Talon is ever so helpful," Becks says, voice dripping with sarcasm. "I'm sure he's not expecting anything in return."

I bristle at the accusation. "It's not like that. Talon gave up everything to get me here."

"Like what, exactly?" he challenges.

I press my lips together, heart pounding. It's not my story to share. "I don't want to talk about Talon right now."

A bitter half laugh rumbles from Becks' chest, an unfamiliar, unsettling sound. "I see. So you don't want to talk about your new boyfriend to your old one."

I flinch, and he notices. His expression shifts, the sharpness in his eyes dulling with regret. He drags a hand through his hair and exhales heavily.

"I'm sorry, Lock. That wasn't fair. If Talon's the reason you're here, then I'm grateful. Truly. It's just . . ." He trails off, shaking his head, and when his gaze finally rises to meet mine, there's no anger, only sadness.

I swore I'd never tell him the truth. But so much has happened since the day I made that bargain with Drake, it doesn't feel like a secret I should keep anymore.

"I need to tell you something," I say, my voice low.

I draw in a steadying breath, bracing myself.

"I tricked you," I confess quietly.

His brow furrows. "What do you mean?"

Where do I even start?

"It's a long story, and I can explain it all to you later, but basically, I'm not with Talon. I never was." Guilt twists in my chest at the admission, but I push the feeling down, unwilling to unpack it now. "I convinced Talon to pretend to be with me so you would let me go. So you would move on."

Confusion darkens Becks' green eyes. "Why would you do that? If you didn't want to be with me anymore, you could have just told me."

"If I had come to you and said that suddenly my feelings had changed, that I didn't want to be with you anymore, would you have believed me? Would you have let me go?"

He steps closer, curling his fingers around the bar just above mine. "So that *was* the truth? You didn't want to be with me, but thought I wouldn't move on unless you were with someone else?"

I flinch, just slightly, but enough that my hands slip from the bars. "That wasn't the truth. But it was what I had to make you believe because . . ."

"Why?" Becks prompts gently when I can't make myself go on.

I take a deep breath, knowing that there's a chance the truth might shatter what we have just as effectively as the lie.

"Because that's the deal I made with Drake Brayden. To break up with you and convince you there would never be any chance for us."

"You made a deal with Talon's uncle?" Confusion is clear on Becks' face and I can understand why.

"Apparently, the dragon council knew about us all along. Kerrim made sure of that to give me motivation to enter Chaos," I say bitterly, my hatred of the hawk shifter swirling in my gut. "The council was worried you'd mate with a magicless creature, which is what spurred them to pick a life mate for you so much earlier than expected. They wanted you settled with a mate of their choice, not yours. I worked out a deal with Drake that if I promised to stay away from you, forever, you'd get to choose your own mate someday."

Becks stares at me, stunned into silence. The air between us is heavy, until suddenly he lets out a laugh. Stepping back from the bars, he turns away, running a hand through his hair and gripping the strands tightly as his laughter grows louder, echoing off the cell walls.

At first, I just blink at him, bewildered.

Did I break him?

What could possibly be funny about this?

But then small embers of anger start to ignite. I went through hell to give him the freedom to live the life he deserved, made impossible choices, and he's laughing?

"What about any of this is funny?" I snap.

Becks pulls himself together and turns to face me again, but there's a lost, hollow look in his eyes that doesn't match the erratic edge in his voice.

"You want to know what's funny?" he says, letting out a breathless laugh. "It's that none of it even matters. Forget the fact that I'm locked in here." He gestures vaguely around the cell. "Ever since I was stabbed and woke up in this place, my magic's been gone. I can't even shift."

I gasp, my hand coming up to cover my mouth as my gaze drops to Becks' wrists to notice only now that he's not wearing a cuff.

In my mind's eye, I see it all over again: Shadow Striker plunging into Becks' chest just before the portal snapped shut. Of course, the dagger didn't just wound him, it stole his magic and gave it to Kerrim.

Becks was never boastful about his powers, but they were a part of him, woven into his identity. Losing them must feel like losing a piece of himself.

Becks shakes his head, his gaze hardening. "They were so concerned about losing control over their heir. Well, in the end they lost me anyway. I'm as weak and powerless as one of these *humans*."

I know he doesn't mean to hurt me, but his comment feels like a blow because it reveals his true thoughts about humans.

About me.

That they're weak. That *I'm* weak.

"I'm sorry," he says, dragging a hand through his hair again. "None of that matters right now. What matters is getting out of here and getting home. You still haven't told me how you got in. Please tell me you're not a prisoner too."

"I'm not," I answer, trying to shake off the yuck from Becks' careless comment. "At least, not yet. They let me see you because they want something from me."

Genuine concern flickers across Becks' face as he steps closer to the bars again. "What do they want from you?"

"I'm not exactly sure," I admit. "But I think it has to do with Kerrim. Kade wanted to talk, but I told him I wasn't saying a word until I saw you. Until I knew you were okay."

Becks grips the bars tightly, his jaw tightening. "You have to stay away from Kerrim. That shifter is unhinged."

"I'm aware, but if I help Kade and the Silent Order, he said they'd release you."

Becks is shaking his head. "Don't do it, Lock. You could get hurt, or worse. With that dagger, you're no match for him."

His words shouldn't sting—he's just looking out for me—but they do. I hold up my cuffed wrist. "I'm not as powerless as you think. At least not anymore."

"What are you talking about?" he asks, eyeing the cuff.

"I have magic now."

His eyes widen in surprise. "You do? But I thought—?"

"That I was weak?" I cut in, sharper than I intended.

"No. Never," he says quickly, shaking his head. "It's just that they told me a human had to have opened the portal, and humans aren't supposed to have magic. So I figured . . ." He falls silent.

Sadness creeps into his eyes. "Lock, you have to know I've never thought you were weak. You're the fiercest creature I've ever met. You're strong, and brave, and so beautiful it hurts just to look at you sometimes. Especially when I can't touch you." He reaches through the bars and gently strokes my cheek.

Some of the fight drains out of me as I look at Becks. My Becks.

Am I letting my own hang-ups trigger me? Maybe. I've spent so much of my life hearing creatures call me weak that even the suggestion of it feels like a slap.

I lean into Becks' touch. "Well, just for the record, I'm not actually a creature. I'm just a human who happens to have magic."

He chuckles. "Truly one of a kind."

His hand slides to the back of my neck, drawing me closer until our foreheads touch. "Thank you for coming for me," he whispers.

"You came for me first," I remind him. "If you hadn't broken through the barrier during that last Chaos trial and fought Kerrim, I don't think I'd even be alive. I'm going to get you out of here. I promise."

He exhales a heavy breath. "I believe you. Just, please be careful."

I lean back just enough to meet his eyes, and the plea in them nearly undoes me.

"I will," I whisper.

"Lock," Becks says, his voice rough as his gaze drops to my mouth. "I thought I'd never see you again. And that—" He swallows hard, emotion tightening his throat.

"I know," I whisper, because I do. Even though I tried not to let my mind go there, there were moments I truly believed I'd never see him again, and the pain of that almost broke me. Just remembering it now makes my eyes sting with unshed tears.

His thumb glides gently across my cheek in a soothing rhythm. "I never want to go through that again," he murmurs.

His hand slips down, tilting my chin up, and he presses the softest, most heart-wrenching kiss to my lips.

It's not like the other kisses we've shared. This one doesn't ignite a spark of passion, it wraps around me like a blanket, warm and steady. Comfort. Safety. The two things Becks has always been to me, and probably always will be. And even though there's a small voice in the back of my mind whispering that things aren't the same anymore, I shove it aside, choosing instead to lose myself in the way this kiss feels like coming home.

When Becks pulls back, there's a hint of turmoil in his expression. A furrow creases his brow, and his eyes sweep across my face like he's trying to find an answer I don't know how to give. He opens his mouth to speak, but before he can, Kade knocks sharply on the door, signaling that my time is up.

My shoulders sag. "I have to go."

Becks nods and steps back.

"Are you really okay?" I ask, gesturing to his wound.

He glances down at the bandages wrapped around his chest. "What, this? It was barely a scratch," he says with a lopsided grin.

A shudder runs through me because I can still clearly see Shadow Striker punch a hole in his chest.

He must see the distress on my face because he says, "Hey, truly. I'm fine. I won't lie, it was touch and go there for a while, but I still have accelerated healing. In a few days I'll be like new. Promise."

I pull in a big breath of air to steady myself. "And they're treating you all right?"

He shrugs. "They're the ones who patched me up, so I can't say they've treated me badly. I don't exactly trust them, but without their med team I might not be standing here." He glances around the cell with a wry smile. "Still not thrilled about being locked up like a criminal, but yeah, they've been decent."

"I'll get you out of here as soon as I can," I promise.

He nods, and I turn toward the door, my heart squeezing tighter with every step I take away from him.

My hand is on the knob when he says, "Tell Talon if you get hurt, I'm holding him responsible."

I glance over my shoulder at him, thinking of how Talon threatened Kade.

These guys . . .

"I'm responsible for myself."

He smiles, but there's sadness behind it. "I know. But still, the thought of beating the ever-loving crap out of him brings me a little comfort."

Despite myself, I laugh. Shaking my head, I turn and step back through the door, where Kade is waiting.

"Content that we haven't hurt your friend?" he asks.

I purse my lips, a pulse of irritation running through me, but also confusion. If what Becks said is true, they saved his life. So why lock him up?

"Why are you keeping him down here?" I ask, crossing my arms.

Kade lets out a slow sigh. "There's a lot you don't know. For thousands of years, we've been preparing for the day a great evil would enter our world. When Becks came through the portal, we had no idea who—or what—he was. We couldn't risk releasing him until we were sure he wasn't the threat, or aiding it."

I throw my hands up. "Well, he's clearly not! So why is he still locked up?"

Kade crosses his arms. "Because now we need him for other reasons."

"As leverage, you mean?"

He dips his head in a subtle nod. "Yes."

"Is what you need me for really that important? Is it really something you and the other members of the Order with all your resources can't take care of yourself?"

"Like I said, there's a lot you don't know."

I rub my temples, feeling a headache brewing as exhaustion weighs down my limbs. "Fine, let's get on with it, then."

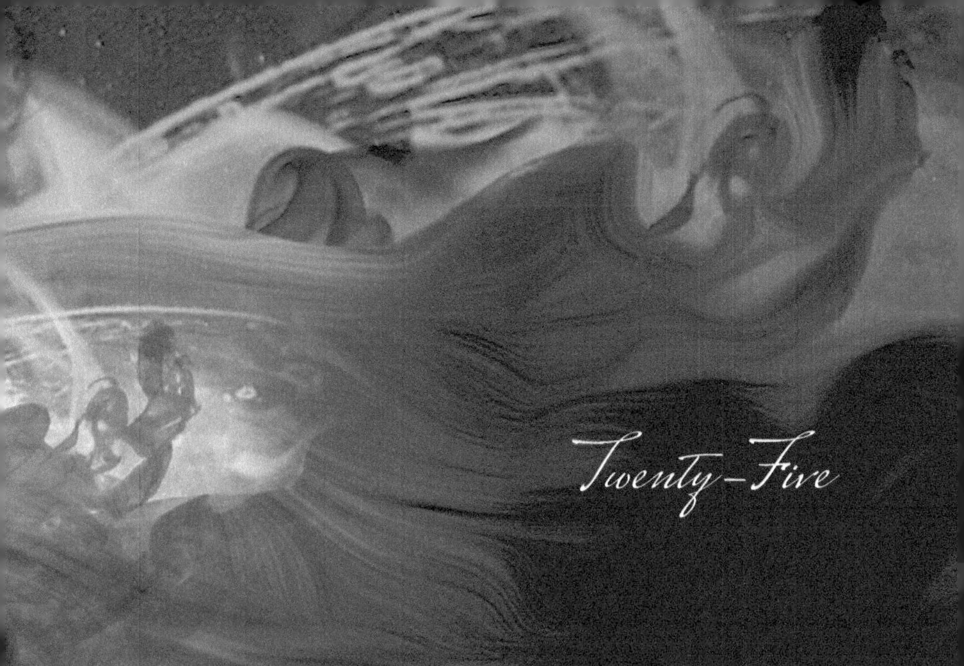

Twenty-Five

TALON IS LEANED up against the wall waiting for me when we leave the room. He takes one look at me and declares that we're leaving and will come back tomorrow for that talk. I try to argue with him, but he reminds me how late it is and that Ensley is probably going out of her mind with worry right now. It would be cruel not to go back and let her know we're okay and that we found her brother. I agree, but we set up a time later in the morning to come back and talk to Kade.

Kade doesn't seem concerned about letting us go, confident that with Becks still here, I'll come back. Before we leave, he even hands over five of their cell phones, each one already programmed with his number. When I stare back at him in confusion, he tells me that whether I believe it or not, we're on the same side. I'm not about to argue with him; having a way to communicate with the group when we're in different locations will be invaluable.

By the time we step outside, it's well past midnight and the city has quieted to a low hum.

We walk in silence except for the whoosh of passing cars and the steady fall of our footsteps against the pavement. It isn't until we're halfway back to the hotel that Talon finally speaks.

"How'd it go with Becks?"

I glance over at him but he doesn't look my way. His eyes stay fixed ahead, scanning the quiet street as if searching for something. Danger, maybe, or just the right words to follow up with.

"It was . . ." I struggle to find the right word. Seeing Becks again was a tangle of emotions. Relief. Heartbreak. Guilt. "Overwhelming."

Talon casts a sidelong glance at me. "Overwhelming?"

I nod slowly. "He's alive and on the mend, which is a huge relief. But he's trapped in that room. And . . ." I'm unsure if I should tell Talon about Becks losing his powers. It feels like Becks' secret to share, not mine.

"And?" Talon asks gently, his voice careful, but curious.

He's going to figure it out sooner or later, if he hasn't already. I feel a little foolish for not questioning it myself sooner. Of course Kerrim stole his powers.

"He's lost his magic," I admit, hoping Becks won't be angry with me for sharing something so personal.

Talon's head snaps toward me, surprise flashing across his features. Looks like he hadn't considered that either. Maybe I'm not the only one who missed such an obvious detail.

"When Kerrim stabbed him with Shadow Striker," I explain. "He says he can't even shift."

Talon's brow furrows. "He can't shift into his dragon?"

I nod. "That's what he told me. Shadow Striker steals abilities—"

"Magical abilities, sure," he interrupts, his tone troubled. "But shifting, that's who he is. It's not just magic, it's in his blood."

He falls quiet for a moment, thinking. "Maybe it has to do with the dagger being here in the human world. It's said to be more powerful on this side."

"Maybe," I agree, and we fall into silence again until Talon quietly asks, "Did you tell him the truth about us?"

My first instinct is to say yes. But the word sticks in my throat.

Did I really tell Becks the truth? Or did I just tell him the version of the truth I was ready to admit? The part that served my purpose, not the whole of it?

"I told him how I asked you to help me trick him into thinking we were together," I say, my voice low.

Talon nods once. "He should know that."

There's a beat of silence before he adds, "So, are you planning to pick up where you left off with him?"

When I glance over, he's still not looking at me. His jaw is tight, his posture guarded.

"We didn't talk about that," I answer honestly.

"But that's what you want."

It's not a question, it's a quiet conclusion he's drawn on his own. And maybe if he *had* asked, I still wouldn't have known how to answer, because suddenly, I'm not so sure.

I stay silent, which only seems to confirm something for him.

Then, softer than before, he asks, "Did you kiss him?"

The question hits like a dart out of nowhere, sharp and unexpected. My breath catches, and for a beat, I can't tell if it's guilt or confusion tightening in my chest.

His profile gives nothing away. I almost ask him why he cares, but there's only so much lying I can do to myself. I *know* why Talon wants to know if I kissed Becks. And now that I've seen Becks, now that I know he's alive and safe, everything I've been trying to deny about what's happening between Talon and me becomes too loud to ignore. It's there, pulsing in every glance, every touch, every word left unsaid.

Something is growing between us. I don't know what it means yet, or if it's stronger than what I have with Becks, but I do know I can't ignore it forever. Sooner or later, I'm going to have to face it.

When I don't respond, Talon glances over and gives a small nod, clearly reading my silence for what it is.

"That's what I thought," he murmurs, and there's a brief twist of pain on his face before he looks away.

Seeing that look on Talon's face is like a dagger to the chest, stealing my breath. We're almost back to the hotel and I panic, feeling the need to make things right. *Somehow.*

Grabbing his arm, I pull him around the corner into a narrow alleyway. The shadows offer a moment of privacy, even if I have no idea what I'm going to say.

Talon glances down the street, then back at me with a confused expression. "The hotel's right there."

"I know. I just . . . before we get back, I need to explain."

His head tilts slightly. "Explain what?"

Yeah, good question.

"I guess, about Becks and me—" I start, and Talon's expression shutters immediately. Whether it's to block me out or to protect himself, I don't know. Maybe both. Either way, it's not what I want.

I shake my head quickly. "No. Forget Becks for a minute. I want to talk about you and me. About us."

His brows lift, a glint of surprise in his eyes. "Is that so?"

I nod, heart hammering.

"Okay, then," he says, leaning back against the brick wall, arms crossed as he waits for me to speak.

Under the weight of his gaze, I hesitate. The storm inside me is a mess of guilt and confusion, but also something deeper. Longing, maybe even hope. So much of what I feel for Talon is tangled up with what I feel for Becks. And vice versa.

I open my mouth to speak. Then close it. Try again. Only a few words make it out each time before I falter. My throat tightens. My thoughts spin. How do I even begin to explain something I'm still trying to understand myself?

Talon finally shakes his head and pushes off the wall. "I thought maybe, after everything we've been through, you'd finally admit . . ." He trails off, scrubbing a hand through his hair. "You're not ready for this. Maybe you never will be. Just forget it," he mutters, turning to walk away.

"Wait, that's not true," I call, my voice soft but urgent.

He stops, glancing back at me, and that's when my vision shifts. His aura flickers to life, swirling blue and white in the shadows, wrapping him in a glow that makes him look almost otherworldly. Ethereal. Dangerous. *Beautiful.*

I suck in a breath, unable to look away. He's breathtakingly handsome and wholly tempting in a visceral way. And in that moment, I just want . . . I just want . . .

His gaze darkens as he watches me. "Freckles," he warns, his voice low and rough, "I suggest you stop looking at me like that."

My tongue darts out to wet my bottom lip, and Talon steps closer, narrowing the space between us until I'm nearly backed into the wall, his presence overwhelming in the best and worst way. My pulse thunders, the blood buzzing fast and hot through my veins.

"Unless," he says, his voice a low caress, "you're finally ready to do something about it."

My stomach flips, and heat blooms across my skin at the thought of what that entails. Crossing that line we've always hovered near, never touching it, but always aware it is there.

I know I should look away, but for the life of me I can't. I'm rooted in place, unable to move toward Talon, unable to pull away, caught in a silent war between desire and reason. The indecision paralyzes me. And then, after a few long, pounding heartbeats, Talon makes the choice for both of us. He turns and walks out of the alley. And Creator help me, because what hits me isn't relief.

It's disappointment.

Twenty-Six

"**DON'T** you *ever* do that to me again!" Ensley cries, yanking me into a hug so tight it knocks the air from my lungs.

Talon and I walked the rest of the block to the hotel and up the stairs in complete silence, only to find a red-eyed Ensley and stoic-faced Titus awake and waiting for us. Ensley was mid-pace across the room to us when we entered, and she immediately swallowed me in the world's tightest hug before I had a chance to get a word out.

"I thought you were dead," she wails, squeezing me harder.

Guilt crashes over me. "So sorry," I wheeze.

She finally releases me and steps back. Her eyes are glassy with tears, and the sight only makes my guilt worse.

"Where were you? What happened?" she asks, her brow furrowed with worry.

"I saw him, Ens. He's alive."

Her hands fly to her mouth as the tears shimmering in her eyes finally spill over. Titus steps in behind her, wrapping his arms around her waist and gently pulling her back against his chest. She leans into him, visibly trying to steady herself.

"Tell me everything," Ensley says, her voice thick with emotion.

I glance at Talon, wondering if he wants to take the lead, but the moment our eyes meet he looks away and crosses the room to sit on the edge of one of the double beds. I wonder what he's thinking, what he's feeling, but I push the thought aside. Now isn't the time. Ensley and Titus have clearly been waiting for hours, likely fearing the worst the entire time. They deserve my full attention.

We spend the next hour telling them what happened at the Order's headquarters. How we decided to sneak in—Talon is quick to give me the "credit" for that—and then got caught. Meeting Kade and how the vibe changed the moment he realized I was the one who opened the portal between the creature and human world.

We also fill Titus in on everything he didn't already know about me, namely, that I'm human and have been accidentally siphoning Talon's powers since the final Chaos trail. He doesn't seem overly upset that we kept him in the dark. If anything, he seems satisfied to finally have an explanation for why he can suddenly read me now when he couldn't before.

And of course, I tell them about seeing Becks.

Just like when I told Talon, I hesitate before telling them that Becks has lost his powers, but ultimately I do. Ensley's eyes fill with sadness, then she straightens her spine and says she's just happy he's alive, we'll find a way to get them back.

By the time we finish recounting everything, the sun has started to rise, and it's only a few hours until we're supposed to meet with Kade again. I apologize and tell them I need to get a few hours of sleep. Ensley understands, and Titus agrees, adding that we all need rest before heading back to the Order. He and Ensley insist on coming with us this time.

"Where's Imogen?" I ask, only now realizing she's not here.

Ensley and Titus exchange a look. "She never came back," Titus says, pressing his mouth into a hard line.

I glance at Talon and he shakes his head. "She'll come back

when she's ready," is all he says, but I don't miss the hint of concern that shadows his gaze.

"If anyone can take care of herself in this city, it's her," I say, mustering what I hope is an encouraging smile.

Talon returns the small smile and nods, but sadness lingers in his eyes. I have to turn away because it breaks my heart.

I BLINK open my eyes and scream. There's a face hovering inches above mine.

Talon and Titus burst into the room, and Ensley tumbles out of the bed beside me in a tangle of blankets.

I lay a hand over my chest, my heart thundering in my chest even though I know I'm not in any danger.

"Imogen!" I snap. "What the heck?"

Her face was so close when I woke up, she nearly scared the soul out of me.

"What? I thought it would be funny," she says as she flops down on the bed next to me.

She is the most annoying creature I've ever had the misfortune to meet.

Annoyed, I fling the covers off me as Ensley moans from the ground. Titus walks over to help her up, scrubbing a hand over his eyes and mumbling about how that wasn't the way he wanted to be woken up.

"Where have you been?" Talon asks his cousin, his voice sharp.

When I glance over at him, I lose my train of thought. His hair is tousled from sleep, his cheeks still flushed, and he's very shirtless, only a few bandages covering his sculpted chest. And those sweats are slung far too low on his hips.

Only Talon could look half asleep and still manage to resemble a character out of a forbidden fantasy. He's the perfect mix of sweet and sinful, and I can't seem to tear my eyes away.

Imogen snorts a laugh, snapping me out of it, and I find her smirking knowingly at me.

"You have a little something right there," she says, miming whipping drool off her face.

I duck my head, warmth blooming across my cheeks as I scramble out of bed and make a quick escape to the bathroom. The only consolation for my flustered state is hearing Talon rip into Imogen as I shut the door behind me.

IMOGEN IS SUSPICIOUSLY chipper as we make our way back to the Order. Whatever funk she was in yesterday after feeding from Titus seems to have evaporated overnight. Her cheeks are flushed, her eyes sparkling. She looks like someone who had a very good night. The kind of "good" I don't want any details about.

Not that she'd offer them anyway.

Even after Talon tore into her, all she gave us was a vague, "I was out learning the city." Which, honestly, is fine by me. What Imogen does in her free time is her business. Still, for Talon's sake, I'm just relieved she made it back to the hotel in one piece.

"So, this is it?" she asks, eyeing the unmarked three-story building tucked between a pawn shop and a pizza parlor otherwise known as the NYC Order's headquarters. Her lip curls in clear distaste. "What is it with humans and their obsession with setting up shop in glorified dumpsters? I'll give it this: it's a step up from that swamp shack, but still, I'm not impressed."

"If you knew what real estate prices were like in Downtown Manhattan, you would be," comes Kade's deep voice from behind us.

I turn to find him standing there with his arms crossed over his chest. Imogen gives him a slow once-over, then runs her tongue along her bottom lip, looking like she'd love nothing more than to take a bite out of the tall human.

Kade doesn't miss the look. Rather than appearing nervous or put off by the way Imogen so blatantly checked him out, he simply arches a brow.

"These must be your friends," he says to Talon and me, holding Imogen's gaze without flinching.

We had texted him on one of the phones he gave us to let him know they'd be coming with us today.

"Ensley and Titus are," I say. Imogen breaks eye contact with Kade to glare at me, so I add with a grin, "That's Imogen, Talon's cousin. She wasn't invited but tagged along anyway."

She sticks her tongue out at me.

Kade greets Ensley and Titus, then acknowledges Talon with a nod. "Let's go inside and we can talk."

We push through the front doors, and the moment we cross the threshold an alarm blares. The shrill so piercing I lift my hands to cover my ears.

Ensley and the others cry out in pain, and all of them, even Talon, drop to the ground. Talon manages to stay upright on one knee, but the others are sprawled on their sides.

What's happening?

I run to Ensley. Tears stream down her face as she clutches her ears, curled into the fetal position. The high-pitched alarm is deafening, but not incapacitating.

Not understanding what's happening, I lift my head to look for Kade, only to see members of the Order flooding into the entryway. They surround our group, guns raised and pointed at us.

"Stand down!" Kade barks, loud enough to be heard over the alarm. "And someone turn that blasted noise off!"

The humans around us exchange unsure looks.

"But, sir," a young blond male starts. Kade cuts him off by yelling "Now!" authority booming in his voice.

Reluctantly, the group surrounding us lowers their weapons and backs off. The man Kade snapped at runs to the far wall and slams a button, cutting off the alarm.

My friends get shakily to their feet. Titus immediately checks on Ensley. Talon slowly, but smoothly, gets to his feet, his gaze icy as he stares at Kade with accusation in his eyes.

"Not cool," Imogen says, brushing imaginary dirt off her pants and glaring at Kade.

I glance at Kade, wanting an explanation to what just happened, when suddenly Titus slams into him, shoving the large male into the wall.

"What was that?" he spits, murder in his eyes. "Locklyn said you wanted to be on our side."

Titus and Kade are evenly matched in height, but Kade has at least thirty pounds of muscle on him. Still, Titus is a powerful fae with some wicked magic, so in my mind he holds the upper hand.

All around us, I hear the cocking of guns again, sending a spike of anxiety through me.

Kade could probably fight back, but instead he holds up his hands in surrender.

Titus has his forearm pressed up against his throat as he holds him in place. He must not be putting too much pressure on him because Kade can still speak.

"I'm sorry," he begins. "That was all just a misunderstanding." He glances over Titus' shoulder at his men. "I told you all to stand down!" he snaps.

When they lower their weapons again, Kade orders them to return to their normal duties. A tense ten seconds pass before the group finally begins to disperse. Once they do, Kade's gaze shifts to Imogen.

"I'm going to guess you're the vampire?"

Her eyes widen in initial shock before she schools her features.

"If you'd like to go somewhere private, I can show you exactly what kind of creature I am," she says. Then, letting her fangs descend, she gives him a sultry smile that's clearly more of a warning than an invitation.

"We're not on the friendliest terms with vampires here in this world," Kade replies. "They're the one creature humans have almost always been at war with. When a vampire enters headquarters, it triggers an alarm that emits a frequency designed to disable most creatures."

Kade looks at Titus, who still has him pinned up against the wall. "I understand why you're angry, but can we move this into a conference room? There's a lot we need to talk about, and despite what just happened, I am still on your side."

Ensley makes a noise next to me, drawing Kade's attention. "If that were true, you'd release my brother."

I kind of agree with her, but I keep my mouth shut.

"Let him go," Talon says. "We've come this far. Let's at least hear him out. I'll let you fry him with faelight later if we don't like what he has to say."

Kade has the sense to look a touch nervous at that comment, which makes Talon smile wickedly.

"Fine," Titus says. "But anything like that happens again and I'm unleashing on you and every one of your human friends here, understood?"

Kade nods as best he can with Titus' arm still pressed against his throat, and Titus finally releases him. Kade cracks his neck, looking like it takes real effort to keep himself in check, then gestures for us to follow.

He leads us down a narrow hallway to a room centered around a long conference table. After what just happened, we're all a little wary as we take our seats around it.

"I'm just going to cut to the chase," Kade says once we're all seated. His gaze shifts to me. "When you opened the portal and let that lunatic into the human world, you might have just kicked off the apocalypse. We need your help to stop it—or more accurately, him."

"Starting the apocalypse. That sounds about right," Imogen mutters under her breath beside me, but I ignore her.

"Him?" I ask, already dreading the answer.

Kade pulls out his phone and after unlocking it and running his fingers over the screen, he lays it flat on the table and then slides it across to me.

I stare at it as if it's poisonous before cautiously reaching out and grabbing it. On the screen is a photograph of a man just before he pushes through a set of double glass doors. The kind you'd see leading into an apartment or office building. He's glancing over his shoulder, his gaze almost connecting with the camera.

Kerrim.

The image of him in the nightmare I had where he stabbed Becks at Sloan's rises unbidden in my mind's eye.

Murderous. Deranged. Off.

My stomach roils, and I feel the blood drain from my cheeks.

"A shifter named Kerrim," Kade replies. "Ring any bells?"

Across from me, Ensley's eyes go wide as I nod slowly, sliding the phone back to him.

I dread whatever Kade is about to say next. Considering the lengths Kerrim went to in order to get to the human world, I seriously doubt he's planning to live out his days as a quiet store owner anymore. Whatever Kade is about to tell us about Kerrim, I already know it's going to be bad.

Putting away his phone, Kade starts to say something else when a sharp knock interrupts him. I glance over to see a red-haired male filling the doorway. Tall and lanky, I'd peg him for mid-twenties. He surveys the room with a keen eye, taking each of us in.

"Ares," Kade says, waving him in. "Just in time."

Ares. Ares. Why does that name—?

Then it hits me. Wasn't that the master torturer they were going to call in the night before?

Panic spikes in my chest, and suddenly my vision winks out and then comes back. When it returns, Ares is coated in a soft, glowing aura. Different than Talon's. Not quite as bright, but also beautiful, it's predominately white with interwoven streaks of vivid green that are crackling with energy, like vines unfurling in fast motion. The aura shimmers with quiet power, ancient and wild, casting him in a wraithlike light.

I gasp softly and the aura disappears.

"You're a creature," I say, and one of Ares' dark red brows quirks.

"But you're not," he replies.

"You work with creatures?" Titus asks, eyeing Ares warily.

Kade nods. "We do. Not all chapters are integrated like ours, but here we have a harmonious relationship with creatures. As long as they don't cross the line. At least a quarter of our members are non-human."

"Wait, back up," I say. "You mentioned there were creatures here in the human world. How many are we talking?"

Since humans are virtually unheard of in the creature world, I assumed the same applied here. The cuffs that cut off magic and the vampire alarm should've been a clue, but I'd chalked them up to human paranoia, not actual experience.

"Quite a few of us, in fact," Ares answers. "Part of the mission of the Silent Order is to keep our existence secret from humanity, but many were trapped here after the gates were sealed. Or part of Lucian's group."

Talon leans forward, and Imogen tenses on the other side of me.

"Lucian's group?" he asks. "What are you talking about?"

Ares and Kade exchange a loaded look.

"We have a lot to fill you in on," Kade says. "Then I'm hoping you can fill us in on some things too."

Kade launches into a brief history of the Silent Order's formation and mission. According to him, Lucian—the Vampire King's son—and a group of loyal creatures, crossed into the human world over two thousand years ago, sealing the gates behind them.

"Lucian is the founder of the Silent Order," Kade says, and when I glance at Talon, I can't tell if he believes him or not.

Then I catch him stealing a glance at Titus, who gives a little nod, and it occurs to me what's going on. Titus is using his truth-telling powers to gauge if Kade is lying or not.

Talon leans back in his seat, crossing his arms. "Lucian is credited with founding the Arcane Society back in the creature world."

"And who's to say he didn't?" Kade says. "But we know for a fact that he traveled to the human world and then lived out the rest of his life here."

Talon cocks his head, assessing. I know that's not what he was taught. "Why would he have done that?"

"Because of the prophecy," Kade says.

"We know the prophecy," Talon challenges. "And I can't think of anything in it that would make Lucian leave his world for this one."

"That's because you don't know the *whole* prophecy." Kade leans forward in his seat, his glance locked with Talon's. "Do you know how the prophecy came into being?"

"It was told to Lucian by the demon before he was vanquished back to the human world," Talon says, which is what he told us back at Grimspire.

Kade nods. "And what do you think the prophecy says?"

Talon glances at Imogen, who just sighs. "You've already spilled most of the Society's secrets and been expelled because of it. Why stop now?"

Even so, Talon hesitates before saying, "That when the dagger was returned to the human world, it would eventually lead to the destruction of their world, and then ours. More or less."

"That's right," Kade confirms. "But there's more to it than

that. The demon told Lucian that one of his direct descendants would be the reason the dagger returned to the human world. To prevent that, Lucian knew he had to leave the creature world, putting distance between himself and the dagger so none of his descendants would have the opportunity to be the cause of its return."

"Well," Imogen laughs, "too bad he went to all that trouble, because our girl Locklyn over here opened the portal to the human world anyway."

"She sure did," Kade says, and then his gaze, along with every other head in the room, turns in my direction.

"What?" I say, blinking as they all stare at me, Kade giving me a pointed look. I can't help but let out a half laugh, unable to believe what he's actually implying. "You can't seriously think I'm a descendant of Lucian? That makes no sense. Lucian was this super-powerful creature, and I'm clearly human."

"A human with the ability to wield magic," Ares says, speaking up. "Do you think an ordinary human could do that?"

My mouth falls open. "Come on, that's because of Shadow Striker. I don't have my own magic."

I glance around the table, expecting someone to back me up, but all I see are mixed expressions of surprise, concern, and even a little envy.

"Still," Ares says, glancing over at Kade. "It's her. I'm positive."

"No way," I say, shaking my head. I refuse to believe this.

"If that's part of the prophecy," Talon finally speaks up, "then why have we never heard about Lucian's descendant?"

"That's a valid question," Kade says. "You haven't heard that part because Lucian hid the full prophecy from the creatures in your world. In fact, from what we've been told, he forbade the original members of your Society from recording any account of his departure, which matches what you know. He didn't want anyone to know that one of his descendants might one day be the cause of catastrophe.

"He feared someone would try to use that descendant to bring about the destruction of the human world. So, he left the creature realm and had every possible means of travel between the worlds sealed and guarded, ensuring his bloodline would remain separated from Shadow Striker.

"The hope was that this day would never come," Kade finishes, his gaze shifting back to me.

"Stop," I say, shaking my head. "I am not Lucian's descendant." I'm starting to sound like a broken record. "I grew up in the creature world, remember? And let's say, for argument's sake, you're right and Lucian did travel to the human world. If that's true, then his descendant would be here, somewhere in your world, not in the creature one."

"That's right. His descendant would have been born here."

Kade slides a manila folder across the table to me. I'd noticed it when we entered the room but hadn't thought much of it.

"What is this?" I ask.

"Open it," he says.

I glance over at Talon, feeling off-balance. Under the table, he places a hand on my knee and gives it a gentle squeeze. I take it as his way of saying he's here for me, no matter what's inside that folder.

Taking a deep breath, I flip it open. Inside is a single sheet of paper: a birth certificate for a girl. There's a small square photo of a baby in the corner. Her features are scrunched like she's about to let out a wail, and she has a full head of hair. According to the document, she was born here in New York a little over eighteen years ago.

"Why are you showing me some random girl's birth certificate? Who is she?" I ask, looking up at Kade.

Kade stares straight into my eyes and says, "That's you."

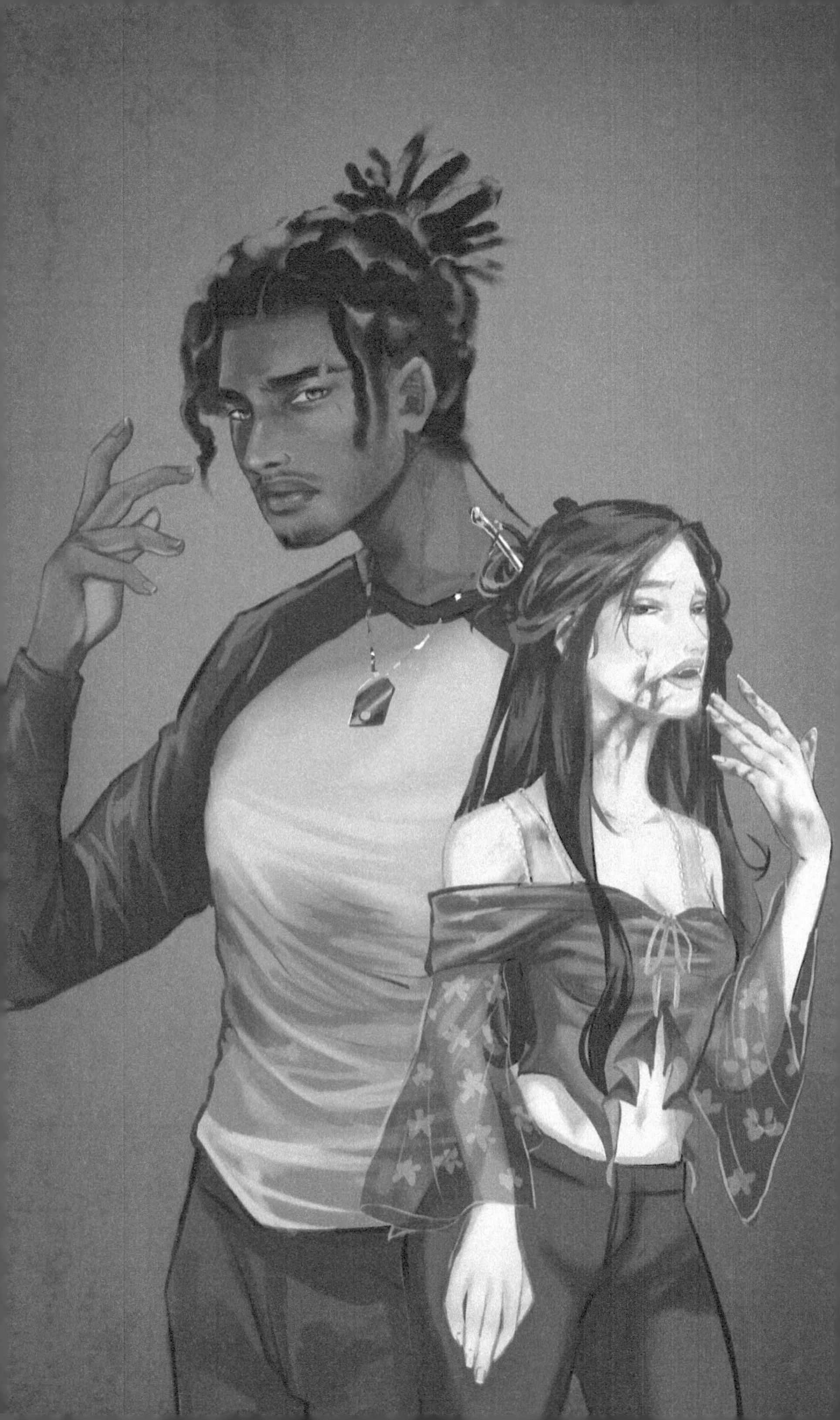

Twenty-Seven

DROPPING THE BIRTH CERTIFICATE, I shove away from the table and stand. My body temperature spikes, and I'm sure flames are about to burst from my fingers.

Before that can happen, Talon jumps up and grabs my hands, cooling them instantly with whatever magic he's using. A moment later, shadows swirl around the room, and Ensley gasps. My vision flickers, and suddenly everyone but Kade has a glowing aura.

I slam my eyes shut, overwhelmed. I want to curl up on the floor and disappear. It's too much. The magic surging through me, this impossible story Kade and Ares expect me to believe. I just can't.

"Everyone, out," Talon barks.

Chairs scrape back from the table, and I think the others are actually listening and leaving until I hear Ensley's tentative voice asking if I'm okay.

I don't even know how to answer her. Am I okay?

Yes. No. Maybe.

All I want is to go back a few months to when I was just a girl without powers, hopelessly in love with her best friend. Life wasn't perfect then, but it was a lot simpler.

"Just give me a second to help her control her magic," Talon says gently. I'm grateful he didn't snap at her.

I hear a sigh, then Ensley says she'll be right outside with the others. As soon as the door clicks shut behind her, Talon releases my hands and places his on my shoulders.

"You can open your eyes now, Freckles."

I shake my head.

"It's okay. You're safe. Just take a few deep breaths like I taught you. Look inside for that core of magic."

I follow his instruction, locating the knotted ball of threads easier than before.

"There you go," he says quietly. "It's your magic. You're in control."

I take another deep breath and open my eyes to find the room dim, cloaked in the shadows I've accidentally summoned. The delicate silver and gold threads are twisted around the two of us again. Talon's aura casts a soft glow across his features as he stares down at me.

"I've got you," he says, and even if it's not true, the words calm me.

I nod at him, believing him, until a sudden rush of unfamiliar magic surges through me, and some of the brightness in Talon's aura dims.

"Did I just take more magic from you?" I ask, horrified.

The shadows around us twist and whip erratically, and heat blooms across my skin.

"Don't worry about any of that right now," Talon says, his hands gliding up and down my arms in a soothing rhythm. "Just focus on breathing, on taking control of your magic and reining it back in."

"Don't you mean *your* magic?" I ask, looking away. I can't hold Talon's gaze, too ashamed that I keep stealing from him.

"Listen to me," he says firmly. "You're not taking anything from me that was mine to begin with. So stop feeling guilty."

I press my lips together, not sure I can do that. No matter what he says, it still feels like I'm stealing a piece of who he is.

A cool hand presses against the side of my face, then his fingers slip beneath my chin, gently tipping my head up and forcing me to meet his gaze.

"If I had the ability to give you this magic," he says softly, "I would anyway."

"You would? But . . . why?"

Talon's blue-gray gaze softens. "How have you not figured it out by now?"

The shadows around us slow to a stop, creating a cocoon around us. Talon's aura and the silver and gold threads cast a glow over the both of us.

"Figure what out?" I ask, my voice barely above a whisper.

"That I would give anything, do anything, for you."

The breath catches in my throat because the truth is there, plain as day. Shining from his eyes. Staring me right in the face.

"You can do this," he says as he brushes the pad of this thumb lightly over my bottom lip, making me shiver. "The magic doesn't control you. You control the magic. Now pull it back into yourself."

I don't break his stare as I find that place inside me where the magic lives, and do as he says, tugging it back inside me. The room starts to lighten as the shadows dissipate. Talon's aura disappears; even the thin threads connecting us fade into nothing.

"Well done," he says with a soft smile, and because for once I'm not thinking about yesterday or tomorrow, I rise up on my toes and press my lips to the very corner of his mouth.

It's not a real kiss, barely more than a brush of contact, and our lips hardly touch before I'm already pulling away. But it rocks me to my core.

"Freckles," Talon starts, but then the conference room door opens behind him and Imogen pokes her head in.

"I drew the short straw to check if it's safe to come back or not? Or are you still having a prepubescent magic meltdown?" she asks. Noticing how close we are, she arches a brow. "Oh, looks like I'm interrupting something very interesting."

Turning her head, she says to everyone waiting in the hall for us. "I think they may need another few minutes to, ah . . . finish."

Imogen!

Pulling away from Talon, I rush to the door and throw it open, finding everyone loitering just outside.

"I'm sorry. I've got control again. You can all come back in."

Ensley gives me a strange look, but I can't hold her gaze. Ducking my head, I retreat into the room and take my seat. Talon resumes his place beside me without a word, but even without looking at him, his presence is suddenly all-consuming.

I do my best to pretend it isn't. I shove down whatever just happened between us, locking it away in the deepest part of myself. It's not something I have the capacity to deal with right now.

Once Kade, Ares, and the others are seated again, I pick up the birth certificate still lying on the table. I study the photo, trying to recognize any part of me in the tiny, scrunched-up face in the corner. But honestly, it's impossible to tell. All babies look so similar when they're born.

Looking up, I catch Kade's eye. "Okay, I'm ready, tell me everything."

"Are you sure?" he asks.

I let out a sharp laugh. "No, but tell me anyway."

He nods. "Fair enough." Leaning forward, he steeples his hands on the table in front of him. "We believe that you're Rose Emilie Velgrave. Daughter of Colin and Sophia Velgrave."

"And why do you believe that?"

"Because Colin was Lucian's last living descendant, which would make Rose one as well."

"Was?" I ask, picking up on Kade's use of the past tense.

"Sadly, after Rose was born, the whole family was attacked.

The bodies were never found, but there was a lot of blood. Up until now, we presumed everyone had been killed."

I give him a doubtful look. "It's a bit of a leap to assume I'm this missing baby. And it still doesn't account for how I ended up in the creature world."

"There is a sector of creatures here in the human world who know about the prophecy," Kade explains. "Over the years, the Order has done their best to hide the identities of Lucian's line because we never wanted anyone to be exploited because of it. But a week before the break-in, a group of creatures managed to get their hands on some computer data that included the true identity of the Velgrave family.

"The leader of the Order at the time was trying to hide the family after the data breach. They were in a safe house when they were attacked. Our theory is that creatures killed your parents and took you. We believe they removed your parents' bodies to make it look like you were killed too, then smuggled you into the creature world so you could fulfill the prophecy."

"Why would they want to fulfill the prophecy?" Ensley asks.

"Not all creatures are happy here in the human world," Kade says. "Some believe they are superior to the human race, and so they see the fulfillment of the prophecy, essentially the end of the human race, as a good thing. They see whoever is coming to take over almost as a savior-figure."

"But that creature is supposed to destroy the creature world too," Talon says.

Kade's gaze shifts to him. "They believe the human world will fall first, and that this figure will lead them back to the creature world, where he'll ultimately rule."

"Well, that's messed up," Imogen mutters in disgust.

"I don't disagree," Kade replies.

Now that the shock has passed, I'm able to think more clearly.

"Okay, so there's a motive," I say. "But how would they have gotten me to the creature world if all the gates were sealed and guarded?"

Kade leans forward, resting his forearms on the table. "About eighteen years ago, a small group of creatures breached one of the gates. Apparently, they had a piece of tamalite that had been passed down through generations, originating from one of the first creatures to travel to the human world."

At the mention of the stone, my gaze flicks to the tamalite ring on Talon's finger before bouncing back to Kade.

"They slaughtered a dozen Order members guarding the gate," Kade continues, his voice grim. "And were never seen again. The assumption was that they went through the gate. We think that's how you ended up in the creature world."

"Okay, then if I'm a descendant of Lucian like you claim, how am I human?"

"That's easily explained," Kade says. "Creatures trapped in the human world have been mating and producing offspring with humans for over two thousand years. Lucian was no different. In fact, his bride was human. As far as we know, his bloodline has continued to mix with humans over generations, gradually diluting the creature magic."

Every question we ask him, he seems to have an answer for. But there are still a million more.

I fall silent, turning it all over in my mind.

"I don't know that I fully buy it," I say at last. "You're making a lot of leaps and assumptions. You're basing everything on the fact that I opened a portal. It feels like you reverse-engineered this theory just to make me fit the prophecy."

"I can see how it would look that way, but there's more evidence than what I've told you," Kade says, glancing over at Ares.

"Right," Ares says, straightening slightly. "I guess that's my cue. I have a very specific type of magic. I can detect bloodlines, specifically in creatures. I can also tell whether someone is human or creature, and if they're a creature, what species they belong to."

Talon shifts in his seat beside me, and Ares' gaze slides over to him.

"Speaking of, you're very rare, my friend."

"You know what kind of creature he is?" Imogen gasps, her wide-eyed gaze bouncing between Talon and Ares.

Talon tenses, and Ares chuckles. "Don't worry, your secret is safe with me." He turns his attention back to me. "As for you, if you have creature genes, I'll admit they're very faint. But I am picking up Lucian's line in your blood."

It's my turn to steal a glance at Titus. He's watching Ares with a look of intense concentration, but as if sensing my gaze, he turns to meet my eyes.

He doesn't smile, just gives me a small nod, letting me know that Ares is telling the truth. Or at least that he believes he is.

I blow out a slow breath, feeling like my entire world is shifting on its axis. Ensley chews on her bottom lip as she watches me, waiting for my reaction. Talon is a silent sentinel next to me, letting me work through this on my own while also being close should I need him.

"Let's say all of this is true," I start. "That I was stolen as a baby and brought to the creature world. I'm a descendant of Lucian, the Vampire King's one and only son. I accidentally fulfilled some ancient prophecy handed down through generations of Order members."

My hands come up in a half shrug, frustration and confusion tangling in my chest. "I've already screwed up and let Shadow Striker into the human world. What could you possibly need me for now?" I lean forward, pinning Kade with a stare. "Because right now, all that really matters to me is getting Becks back. And there's something you want from me before you'll let him go, so I'd like to just get to the point."

Kade leans forward as well, his locs brushing against his cheeks as he does. "We need you to take down Kerrim, because if the prophecy is right, you're the only one who can."

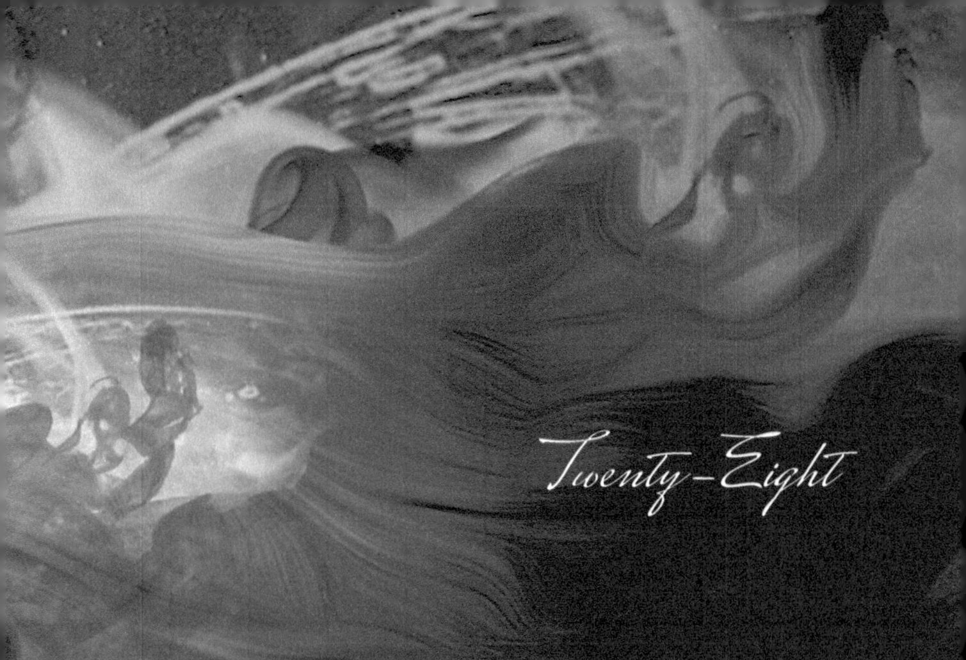

Twenty-Eight

"WHAT IF HE'S LYING? Or not even that," Ensley says, stopping mid-pace.

After Kade dropped his parentage-and-prophecy bomb, we all returned to the hotel room to figure out what to do next. Ensley's been wearing a rut in the carpet ever since.

"What if he's just wrong about this so-called prophecy? It might not be about you at all. Or what if it's not even real? Talon and Imogen both said they've never heard the parts he brought up. It's like a bazillion years old, right?"

"Two thousand," I interject.

"Whatever," she says, waving me off. "The point is, maybe the whole thing is just a complete fabrication."

I shrug, not knowing what to say. She's right. Kade could be lying, though I can't figure out why he would. There's no way for us to know if the prophecy is bogus or not. Only time will tell.

"Lock, if you face off against Kerrim, there's a real chance you could die. Like *dead* die."

"As opposed to living dying?"

"I'm serious," she snaps.

I let out a sigh.

According to Kade, since arriving in the human world, Kerrim has been recruiting creatures into some kind of personal army. With Shadow Striker, he's already powerful, but with the dagger *and* an army at his back, he'll be unstoppable. Potentially capable of bringing the human world to its knees, just as the prophecies from both worlds warn.

And as if the part about Lucian's descendant being the reason for Shadow Striker's return weren't enough, Kade claims Lucian made one final prediction on his deathbed: that his descendant would either become the savior of the human race—or the means by which it is destroyed.

And who do they think that descendant is? Me, of course.

No pressure.

Kade finally laid out his terms. I defeat Kerrim and retrieve Shadow Striker, and in return he'll release Becks and escort all of us to the nearest gate so we can return home.

"Do we really have a choice?" I ask.

If I don't do what Kade wants, he won't hand over Becks.

"Yes," Talon says from his seat across the room.

I twist to face him. He's been quiet and hard to read ever since we left the Order's headquarters.

"What do you mean?" I ask, searching his expression.

"You have two choices. Actually, three."

"Which are?"

"Well, now that we know Becks is alive and relatively unharmed, we could choose to leave without him." He lifts his hand, wiggling his fingers so the black gem catches the light. "We have the tamalite, so we can use the same gate we came through to get back."

I'm already shaking my head before he finishes, but he holds up a hand to stop me.

"But I'm guessing you don't want to leave your princeling behind."

I shoot him a look that clearly says, *What do you think?*

"We're not leaving my brother," Ensley snarls.

Titus, who's also been quiet since we left the Order, comes up behind her and puts a comforting hand on her shoulder. "I don't think he actually thinks we're going to do that."

Talon shakes his head. "I don't. But I wanted to point out that it *is* an option. As is the third, we could attack the Order and take Becks by force."

Imogen perks up from where she's been filing her nails in the corner. "I like that option," she says, no doubt still salty about the Order's anti-vampire bias.

"You don't get a vote," I tell her.

She squints at me. "Says who?"

"Me," I say, giving her a hard look.

She rolls her eyes and goes back to her nails like she doesn't have a care in the world. I suppose she doesn't. She doesn't care one way or another whether or not we bring Becks home.

It makes me wonder, and not for the first time, why she even followed us on this misadventure. Was she just bored?

"Trying to free Becks from the Order might be easier than going up against Kerrim," Titus says thoughtfully.

They have a point. But what if . . . ?

"I don't like that look," Ensley says, reading me like only a best friend can.

I chew on my bottom lip, a million thoughts zipping through my mind. "It's just . . ." I glance at Talon, and for some reason it feels like he knows what I'm going to say. "What if Kade and the Order are right? What if I am Lucian's descendant, and if I don't stop Kerrim, no one will be able to?"

I expect Talon to say something, to give his opinion, but he just crosses his arms over his chest and remains quiet.

"Are you saying you want to go after Kerrim just so you don't feel guilty?" Ensley asks.

"I'm saying breaking into the Order to get Becks might be easier, but that doesn't mean it's the right thing to do."

Ensley drops her head into her hands and groans. "I just want my brother back and to go home."

Titus pulls her into his arms, holding her close, and I'm struck by an unexpected, sharp pang of jealousy. Not over Titus, but over the fact that Ensley has someone to lean on.

There's a part of me that aches for that kind of connection. I used to have it with Becks. But Becks isn't here right now, and even if he were, things feel *off* between us.

"Come on," Talon says, suddenly appearing at my side. "Let's take a break and pick up dinner for everyone."

It's a little early for dinner, but I think he knows I need a mental reset.

"Ugh," Imogen moans. "So now I have to decide which third wheel I want to be? Just shoot me."

"You can come with us," I offer, feeling magnanimous. "You won't be a third-wheel."

Imogen shoves out of her chair. "Whatever. I'm going out again."

Talon steps in front of her before she can breeze out of the room. "Where are you going?" he asks.

"Wouldn't you like to know."

"Yes. That's why I asked."

She purses her lips. "I'm going *out, Dad.*"

With a sigh, he runs his hand through his hair. "At least take one of the phones so we can reach you."

"Fine," she says, snatching the one he pulls from his pocket and slipping it into her jacket.

"And can you please get back at a reasonable time tonight?" Talon asks, folding his arms.

She shrugs, already halfway to the door. "No promises," she tosses over her shoulder, then disappears down the hall.

"So, is she, like, your favorite cousin?" I ask, glancing at him.

Talon laughs, the tension in his shoulders easing. "Actually, she is," he admits.

I arch a brow. "You have a weird family."

"You have no idea," he says with a grin.

After grabbing a coat, I ask Ensley and Titus what they want for dinner and they tell me to just get whatever looks good.

I'm about to follow Talon out when I catch Ensley's eye. "Whatever happens, we're getting your brother back. You believe me, right?"

She nods. "I do. But at what cost? I don't want to bring my brother home just to lose my best friend."

"That won't happen," I say, trying to make myself believe it.

"I hope you're right," she says, and then looks away.

BY CHANCE, we stumble across a place called Chelsea Market not far from our hotel. It's an indoor market inside a warehouse-style building, and we quickly discover it is a veritable food cornucopia. Without Imogen around to use compulsion on the vendors for freebies, we use up what's left of the money Titus pickpocketed for us, buying clam chowder, lobster rolls, tacos, even cookies and the fattest, fudgiest brownies I've ever seen for dessert.

Walking back, arms loaded with food, when I joke to Talon that I'm going to have a delicious last meal, he doesn't laugh. I clear my throat to fill the silence, the awkwardness suddenly heavy between us.

"Are you going to try to stop me?" I ask when the silence becomes unbearable. I don't bother specifying what I mean. He already knows.

To my surprise, he chuckles. "As if I could, even if I tried." He glances at me out of the corner of his eye. "You're a force, Freckles. But even so, this is your decision, not mine. We came all this way for your princeling, and I'm going to see it through with you. One way or the other."

"Do you mean that?" I ask, a little in awe.

"With all my heart."

Tightness forms in my chest. It's not painful, exactly, but it's impossible to ignore.

"You really see me for me, don't you?" I ask, not even sure he'll understand what I mean.

He cocks his head, a half smile tugging at his lips. "You're just now figuring that out?"

"Yeah," I admit softly. "I guess I am."

"About time," he says, and I look away, suddenly feeling shy under his gaze.

"I think I should do it. Take on Kerrim," I say after a moment. "I know it probably sounds insane, but it feels like the right thing. It's my fault he's here. That makes it my responsibility. At least in part."

"It's not your fault," Talon says firmly. "It's not like you willingly opened the portal and invited him through. You're as much of a victim. In fact, probably more so than anyone else caught up in this mess. He manipulated you, used you, to get what he wanted. He planned to bring Shadow Striker to the human world from the beginning."

He searches my face.

"You shouldn't carry guilt for that. You were deceived. I know you feel like all of this is on you—Becks getting hurt, being trapped here, Kerrim taking Shadow Striker—but it's not. You came here to save your princeling, not to face off with Kerrim. He isn't your responsibility."

I didn't realize how much I needed to hear those words until Talon said them. That what happened at the end of the last Chaos trial wasn't my fault.

I know it's true, at least in my head. I've been trying to convince myself of the same thing for days. But the guilt has been like a chain wrapped around me, dragging me down to the bottom of the sea. In a lot of ways, it feels like I've been drowning ever since that day.

"Thank you," I say, and I mean it. "But Kerrim needs to be stopped."

"Agreed. But he doesn't have to be stopped by you. You have nothing to atone for, no matter what Kade or some dusty prophecy says."

I glance at him out of the corner of my eye. "Do you agree with Ensley? That I'm no match for him?"

He blows out a breath of air. "What I think is that it would be easier to break your princeling out of Order headquarters. Kade and his people are organized, I'll give them that, but I'd still rather go up against them than Kerrim. I, more than anyone, know what Shadow Striker is capable of in the creature world. And I've always been told it would be even more powerful here in the human world. I'm not ashamed to admit that scares me."

"You, scared? I have a hard time believing you're afraid of anything," I say with a chuckle.

"You'd be surprised at the things that scare me," he replies.

When I glance over at him, he's staring at me with a look I can't quite read, and suddenly I can't find the words.

I look up and realize we've reached the hotel. We both stop just before going in.

"Ensley's going to put up a fight," I say.

"She is," he agrees. "But it's because she loves you. She'll have your back, though."

I nod, because he's right. Ensley will always have my back. And I'll always have hers.

"All right," I say, drawing in a breath. "I'm going to do this. I'm going to find Kerrim and figure out how to get Shadow Striker back. Without the dagger, he won't have all that power. But if I'm going to do this, there's something I have to do first."

"What's that?" he asks.

"Get Becks back."

Twenty-Nine

THE LOOK KADE gives me is incredulous. "Let me get this straight. You want us to give you the dragon shifter and then just, what? Trust that you're going to take care of Kerrim for us?"

I nod. "Yes. Exactly that."

Kade's eyebrows shoot up. He glances at Ares seated next to him at the round bistro table of the all-night coffee shop where I asked them to meet me—a neutral location away from Order headquarters.

"Well, she has guts, I'll give her that," Ares says.

Kade shakes his head, a look of disappointment on his face. "Contact us when you're serious. We're done here," he says as he pushes to his feet.

I sigh. I didn't actually think they were going to give Becks over just because I asked nicely, but I was hoping they would.

"Actually, we're not," I say firmly. "If you want to stay on friendly terms, like you keep claiming, you'll sit back down."

Kade's nostrils flare. "This isn't a game—"

"Oh, I'm well aware of that. But I want my friend back and that's a non-negotiable for me. If you walk out that door, I promise you I'll still get Becks back by the end of the night, but I won't lift a finger to help you defeat Kerrim."

It's a tense thirty seconds before Kade reluctantly takes his seat again, his gaze sharp as he assesses me.

I have his attention now, and a bit of the knot of anxiety in my chest begins to loosen.

"I'll be honest with you," I say. "I don't like the idea of Kerrim running around your world with unchecked power any more than you do. And even though he deceived and manipulated me, I still feel somewhat responsible for him being here. Even if the part I played was completely unintentional."

I lean forward, meeting both Kade's and Ares' eyes.

"I don't know if I'll be able to get Shadow Striker back from him the way your prophecy claims. But I'll admit this much: I know him better than anyone else here. And with me, you may have a better chance of defeating him."

Kade crosses his arms over his chest, a frown pulling at his mouth. "*We'll* have a better chance of defeating him?"

"That's right," I say. "I'll agree to stay and help you with Kerrim, but I'm not going up against him alone. That would be suicide. If you want my help, you're going to release Becks, and we'll all work together to bring Kerrim down. No more blackmail. No more leverage hanging over my head to strong-arm me into doing what you want. After this, that ends."

Kade starts to say something but I cut him off by holding a hand in the air. "And I'll tell you why you're going to be so accommodating. It's because if you don't agree to these terms, my friends, who I'm sure you've noticed by now are suspiciously missing from this meeting, are going to break Becks out of your headquarters and then destroy it on their way out. We'll leave the human world for good, and Kerrim will only be your problem then, not *ours*."

Kade's face hardens to granite, his eyes boring into me as he tries to determine whether or not I'm lying.

I'm not.

Talon was right. It would be easier to break into the Order's headquarters and free Becks than to go up against Kerrim. But at the same time, Kerrim has to be stopped, and I don't know that I can live with myself if I just leave. I have to at least try to get Shadow Striker away from him, no matter how perilous it might be.

But I don't want to be a sacrificial lamb either. Taking down Kerrim is going to take more than just one human or creature. It's going to take a small army. And that's exactly what the Order is.

But because of the prophecy, Kade believes *I'm* the only one who can defeat Kerrim, so he won't go up against him. Not unless he's forced to. Which means not until I'm either gone . . . or dead.

There are two things I need from Kade that he hasn't been willing to give me: Becks, and backup against Kerrim.

So when Talon and I got back with dinner, we sat down with Ensley and Titus and came up with a plan. While I meet with Kade, the others are already at the Order's headquarters, including Imogen, who was practically vibrating with excitement at the chance for violence when we called to tell her. Their mission is simple: retrieve Becks peacefully if Kade agrees, or break him out if he doesn't.

If we have to take Becks by force, we'll return to the creature world immediately, leaving them to deal with Kerrim on their own. But if Kade agrees to release Becks and stand with us, we'll stay and fight too.

"You're bluffing," Kade says.

"I'm not."

His phone buzzes with a message, and I say, "That'll be someone at your headquarters letting you know the power's been cut. Go ahead and check it."

Imogen and Talon are a strategic force on their own, but once Titus got involved, it took the three of them less than an hour to come up with a plan to cripple the Order and infiltrate the building.

We know exactly where Becks is being held, and with the

combined powers of all four of them, it would take the entire NYC Order to stop them. But we also know the building isn't fully staffed in the middle of the night.

The first phase starts with disabling their electrical systems. Not just to help us get in and move around undetected, but also to show Kade we're serious.

Kade checks his phone like I suggested, then mutters a curse under his breath. Ares leans over to read the message and his eyes go wide.

Kade sets the phone face down on the table and looks up at me. "You're really asking us to give up our leverage and just trust that you're going to put your life on the line?"

"Yes," I answer.

"Why? Because you'll promise? I'm supposed to believe you'll keep your word?"

I meet his stare, seeing the calculation behind his eyes. He's considering it. He'd be smart to, because this is his only real option.

"I can do better than a promise," I say.

His head tilts slightly, interest piqued. "How so?"

"I happen to know a vampire who can facilitate an unbreakable bond. I'll swear that if you let Becks go and join forces with us, I'll stay and fight to take down Kerrim. Once that bond is in place, I won't be able to go back on my word."

"And neither will I," Kade says, and I nod.

Talon was the one I had to convince about this part. He didn't want me entering into an unbreakable bond, which, honestly, surprised me considering he once tricked me into one. It was that very incident that gave me the idea.

I know Kade won't release Becks based on my word alone. He doesn't truly know me, and as he already pointed out during this meeting, there's nothing stopping me from walking away the moment Becks is safe. On the flip side, I need a guarantee that if I stay, my friends and I won't be left to face Kerrim alone.

The unbreakable bond makes sense, for both sides. Eventually, Talon relented, even if it was reluctantly.

Kade rubs a hand over his mouth, thinking.

"You have three more minutes to decide," I say. "If I don't message my friends, they're going in. They'll get Becks out, but some of your people are going to get hurt in the process."

He lets the silence stretch between us, eating up precious seconds, starting a cold sweat prickling across my skin. I knew going into this that I had to be ready to follow through, no matter how Kade responded. But the longer he just stares at me, the more I worry he's not going to agree.

Finally, he extends his hand. I glance down at it, then back up at his face, still a stoic mask.

"I'm just glad you're on our side," he says.

Relief sweeps through me so fast it makes my muscles weak.

"Call your friends off and get Imogen over here to seal the bond. You have a deal. The Order doesn't back down from fights, and this one won't be any different."

I shake his hand, then pull out my phone and type a message to Talon. *He agreed. Stand down.*

His response comes quick and makes me laugh. *Imogen will be disappointed.*

I listen while Kade calls someone at headquarters and explains that Becks is to be prepped to be released to us. As we wait for Imogen to arrive so Kade and I can enter into an unbreakable bond, Ares catches me staring at his pointed ears and grins. "They are quite sexy, aren't they?"

"No!" I blurt. "I mean, that's not what I meant. Or rather . . ."

Ares laughs at my blundering.

"What I mean to say is: you don't glamour your appearance?"

I'd noticed his ears back at their headquarters, but I assumed they were only visible because we were on their turf, where everyone already knew about creatures. So I was surprised to see them uncovered again when he and Kade showed up in such a public setting.

"There's no need," he says with a shrug. "There's a lot of strange fads these days. Humans just assume I'm wearing a prosthetic or had my ears surgically shaped to look like this."

I scrunch my nose. "Some humans do that to themselves?"

He nods. "Fae are *in* right now." Then he lowers his voice and leans in conspiratorially. "If humans knew I was truly a fae, do you know how much action I'd—"

Kade clears his throat and Ares grins over at him, not looking chastised at all.

Crossing his arms over his chest, he says, "Let's just say I'm pretty popular with the human ladies."

Yeah, okay. I didn't need to know that.

When Imogen arrives a few minutes later, she scowls at Kade, but I don't miss the way she takes a moment to check him out as we follow him into the alley behind the coffee shop.

The unbreakable bond only takes a moment to seal, and just like that, both Kade and I are sealed to our word. I try to convince myself that the sensation settling in my gut isn't foreboding, but it certainly feels that way.

Once that's done, we head back to Order headquarters, where the others are waiting, Becks included. I should be ecstatic, but I'm a giant ball of nerves. I can't ignore how things were strained with Becks the last time I saw him. Yes, he was glad to see me, or maybe shocked is a better word, but we're in a weird place right now.

Given the circumstances, that shouldn't matter. But for some reason it does.

When we turn the corner and the front of the Order's headquarters comes into view, my stomach bottoms out. The broad back and blond hair of the guy hugging Ensley are unmistakable.

My steps slow, then stop entirely.

Imogen and the others don't notice, and continue walking until they reach the group. When they join them, Becks looks around, scanning faces, until he spots me a little farther down the block.

Even from this distance, I see his gaze soften. That's all it takes for me to break into a run.

Becks pushes past Kade and Ares, and when I reach him, he scoops me up in his strong arms and lifts me into the air.

"You did it," he says into my ear as he hugs me.

The nerves from before are gone. No matter what happens from here on out, Becks is going to be with me, and that fills me with overwhelming happiness.

Still in his arms, I lean back so I can look into his eyes, my smile so wide it makes my cheeks hurt. His face is clean shaven now, the stubble from the other day gone. There's color high on his cheeks, and rather than hospital scrubs, he's wearing jeans; a T-shirt is stretched across his broad chest.

His chest.

"Becks, your injury. Let me down," I say, squirming in his grasp. I don't want to hurt him.

He laughs at me. "I just got you back. You think I'm going to let you go anytime soon?"

"But—"

"Lock, I'm fine. Better than I've been in a long time. Just give me a moment to really take you in."

Becks' gaze travels over my face like he's trying to memorize it.

"Do you promise?" I ask, and he nods.

"Almost good as new," he says, but then sadness fills his green eyes and I wonder if he's thinking about his magic being gone. I don't know what I could say to make that better for him.

"Okay, Becks!" Ensley shouts over to us. "Put her down. We get it. You're happy to see one another. Now get back over here so we can talk about what to do next."

Becks has his back to the group, and he twists just enough to glance over his shoulder at them. "Just as soon as I get a proper hello from her," he calls back.

A proper hello?

As he looks back at me, there's a sharp glint in his gaze that throws me. It almost looks . . . calculating.

Just as I'm about to ask what he meant by *a proper hello*, he leans forward and captures my mouth. The kiss takes me completely off guard, and I gasp. Becks uses the moment to deepen the kiss.

My mind spins, struggling to catch up as his mouth moves over mine in a way that feels unfamiliar. It still sends a thrill through my nerves and makes my stomach drop, but this kiss feels different. Almost possessive.

That's not the Becks I know.

Kissing him has always made me feel alive, but also safe. Cherished. Becks has always been home to me. But this . . . this feels like I'm kissing a stranger.

I pull back, overwhelmed and confused, cheeks flushed and lips swollen. Instead of the warmth I usually feel, there's only a lingering sense that something isn't right.

And yet, when I look into his eyes, I see the creature I've always known. The one who shielded me from school bullies, who held me during my most vulnerable moments. The friend who always knew what to say to lift my mood, or when to say nothing at all. The guy who nearly died protecting me from Kerrim, and ended up wounded, magicless, and lost in a strange new world because of it.

This is Becks. *My* Becks.

So if something feels off, maybe it's not him. Maybe it's me.

Becks smiles, completely unaware of my inner turmoil, and pulls me closer, burying his face in my hair as he whispers, "I missed you, Lock."

I nod, because I can't seem to find my voice right now.

Then I look up, and over Becks' shoulder I watch Talon turn and walk away.

Thirty

WE DON'T STAY at the Order's headquarters for long. It's late, and Becks doesn't even want to set foot inside the front entrance after being held captive there for so many days. We hang around just long enough to agree that we'll meet the next day to come up with a plan to deal with Kerrim and his ever-growing creature army.

Apparently, even in the short time we've been in the city, Kade's men have reported an unusual number of unfamiliar creatures flooding into New York, more than they've ever tracked before. And to make matters worse, leaders of some of the largest and most influential creature factions have been seen entering and leaving the building where Kerrim is believed to be running his entire operation.

One thing is abundantly clear: If we want any chance of stopping Kerrim, we have to strike sooner rather than later. The more time we give him, the more time he has to gather power and support.

I thought Talon might return to the hotel before us, but when we get back to our rooms he's nowhere to be found. He doesn't answer any of my texts or calls. I keep trying throughout the night, my anxiety growing with each unanswered message. When I wake the next morning, bleary-eyed and nursing a low-level headache from lack of sleep, there's still no sign of him.

We wait for him as long as we can before leaving to meet up with Kade and other key members of the Silent Order. We aren't meeting at headquarters, but at an industrial building in an area called Brooklyn. It is a neutral location, since Becks refuses to set foot inside their headquarters again. I can't say I blame him.

I send Talon a message with the meeting address and hope he shows up. My heart leaps into my throat when we push through the metal doors of the seemingly empty warehouse and see him leaning against the far wall, waiting. As soon as we step inside, he lifts his head, his gaze locking with mine before shifting to Becks' arm draped over my shoulders. He presses his mouth into a hard line as he pushes off the wall and walks toward us.

"You didn't come back last night. Where have you been?" I ask.

"Just scoping out the city, trying to get a lay of the land," he says. "If we're going to go on the offensive with Kerrim, I want to know our battleground."

I have no reason not to believe him, yet . . .

"Besides, I wanted to give you guys some space to reconnect," he says, his gaze shifting to Becks. "Glad you're back," he says with a nod.

Becks mirrors the gesture with a nod of his own, then removes his arm from around my shoulders and extends a hand to Talon. My eyebrows lift in surprise. Becks has never exactly been Talon's biggest fan, but maybe he's ready to put that behind him after everything we've gone through to get him back.

Talon looks a little taken aback. He hesitates for a moment, then reaches out and clasps Becks' outstretched hand.

"I know it cost you, coming here to get me," Becks says. "I also know you didn't have to do it. I appreciate it."

"You're welcome," Talon says, then his gaze slides over to me, "but we both know I didn't do it for you."

A muscle jumps in Becks' jaw, a sign that he's irritated. He drops Talon's hand and purposefully wraps his arm around my waist, tugging me close. "Well, *we're* grateful, then," he says with a smile that's a borderline smirk.

I don't like what's happening, but I feel caught between a rock and a hard place. If I pull away from Becks, it'll hurt him, and he's already endured so much because of me. But I get a yucky feeling inside standing in front of Talon with Becks' arm around me.

Talon glances my way, and for a moment I think he's waiting, hoping, for me to say or do something. But I don't know what the right move is.

So I do nothing.

Talon shakes his head and lets out a dry, humorless chuckle, turning away. "Come on. Kade and his crew are already here."

He heads across the open warehouse toward a metal staircase that leads to a room overlooking the cavernous space. Through the windows, I spot a few figures already waiting inside.

As we follow him, Imogen jogs forward to catch up with her cousin. They exchange a few words, but they're too far away for me to make out. Talon says something else, and Imogen glances back at me over her shoulder, her eyes sharp and unreadable.

No love lost there. Good to see some things have stayed the same.

We climb the stairs into the room to find Kade, Ares, and nearly a dozen other Order members already inside. My eyebrows shoot up when I spot a familiar head of purple hair among them.

"Violet?"

She turns when I say her name, and a tentative smile lifts the corners of her mouth.

"Wait, is that—?" Ensley starts to ask before she's cut off.

"Oh, hell to the no!" Imogen shouts, and with a burst of speed I didn't know she was capable of, she's suddenly across the room and has someone pressed up against the wall with her hand on their throat.

"Nobody move or I'll rip his throat out with my bare hands," she snarls. The tension in the room spikes instantly.

"Who is that?" Becks asks, and I crane my neck, trying to see past Imogen blocking my view. Her reaction makes total sense when I realize who she attacked. *Tobias.* The leader of the Florida chapter of the Silent Order.

"Will one of you stop her?" Kade asks, looking at our group, but none of us move or say a word.

I cross my arms over my chest, content to let Imogen do whatever she wants with the human who tried to kill all of us.

Kade sighs and shakes his head.

"Okay. Everyone calm down," he says, his voice booming.

"Do you know what he tried to do to us?" Imogen snarls.

Kade pushes through the humans in his path until he's standing next to Imogen.

"I know," he says as Tobias struggles in vain to pry her fingers from his throat.

Watching him squirm in her grasp is deeply satisfying, and judging by the looks on Ensley's, Titus', and Talon's faces, they feel the same way.

"I've spoken with Tobias about the misunderstanding when you met," he says.

That is the exact wrong thing to say, because a look of rage comes over Imogen. "*Misunderstanding*?" She tightens her grip and Tobias' face turns an unattractive shade of purple. "You expect us to trust this piece of garbage after he tried to kill us?"

Kade lays a hand on Imogen's wrist. "Nothing like that will happen again. You have my word on it. Tobias knows you're not the enemy, and he's offering to help. That's not an offer we can afford to turn down right now."

Imogen bares her teeth at Kade, her fangs fully extended, but to his credit he doesn't even flinch.

"Come on," he coaxes. "Let him go so we can get down to the business of defeating the real enemy here."

When Imogen still doesn't release Tobias, Kade leans in a little and whispers in her ear. I'm too far away to hear, but it looks like he says, "He's not worth it," to her.

With a huff and a final fang-filled snarl, Imogen releases Tobias. He crumples to the ground, coughing and gasping for air. Even from where I stand, I can see the indents her nails left on his throat.

Without sparing him a second glance, Imogen turns, and wide-eyed humans quickly scramble out of her way as she strides back to Talon's side.

Talon gives her a smirk and a small nod of approval.

I'd already filled Becks in on the Florida incident, so I quickly tell him that Tobias was the leader behind the attack. Around us, everyone grabs chairs and pulls them into a large circle so we can talk.

Once we're settled, Kade stands and begins explaining why we're all here. He includes his theory about me being Lucian's heir, the one mentioned in the prophecy, and it makes me want to melt into the floor. The faces of the Order members around us, who I've learned are mostly heads of different chapters from across the country, show a mix of reactions when they sneak glances at me. I catch everything from awe to fear in their eyes.

After he lays everything out, Kade opens the group for discussion on how to defeat our common enemy, Kerrim. I don't say much as the Order leaders discuss and debate our options. I may consider myself a fighter, but strategy isn't in my wheelhouse. With the exception of Ensley, everyone else in my group takes turns voicing their opinions, with Imogen and Talon being the loudest.

Eventually, everyone agrees that the best course of action is to lure Kerrim to a location of our choosing and try to separate him from the dagger. In a crowded city like New York, there is no perfect battleground, but the Silent Order, whose mission is to keep the existence of creatures hidden from humans, decides that Central Park is the least problematic option. They believe they can establish a perimeter to prevent unsuspecting humans from accidentally stumbling onto the battle, and the park's open layout should make it harder for Kerrim's followers to ambush us. Kade adds that he has a creature ally who can magically seal off part of the park, making any destruction invisible to the human world until the fighting is over. Once that is settled, the discussion turns to how to lure Kerrim where we want him.

Imogen stands up, garnering everyone's attention. "I know exactly how to get Kerrim to Central Park," she says, and then looks at me. "By using her as bait."

Wait. What?

"Me?"

Imogen nods. "He's already looking for you, so all we have to do is let him know where to find you."

Panic sends a spike straight to my heart. "What are you talking about?" Glancing around, the others in my group look just as perplexed as I do.

Imogen tosses her hair over her shoulder. "Where do you think I've been going at night?"

"Ahh . . ." I hesitate, because if I were to wager a guess, I would say that Imogen has been out feeding on unsuspecting humans, and it's not something I really want to think about, let alone announce to this crowd.

She rolls her eyes. "I infiltrated Kerrim's group," she says, and I just stare at her, momentarily stunned.

"You did *what*?" Talon snaps.

Imogen glances at Talon. "You, of all creatures, should have realized I didn't tag along on this misadventure just to watch you make moony-eyes at your pet human. I came because we were trained for one reason and one reason only: to keep Shadow Striker out of the hands of anyone like Kerrim." She crosses her arms over her chest. "You may have abandoned the mission, but I haven't."

I don't appreciate being called Talon's "pet human," but I'm more concerned about the other barbs she just threw at him. Talon tries to hide how her accusation hurts him, but even though his expression remains unreadable, I see the subtle shift. His features tighten and the tension in the room grows heavier, like a storm about to break.

"How does Kerrim even know Locklyn is here?" Becks asks, interrupting their stare-off. "Or maybe more importantly, *why* is he looking for her?"

"Excellent questions, my magicless friend," Imogen says with a cruel smile that makes me want to punch her. "Even though Locklyn doesn't have possession of Shadow Striker, she's still tied to the dagger. The moment she entered the human world, the dagger stopped funneling powers to Kerrim."

I perk up, feeling like this is the first great news we've gotten. Imogen definitely buried the lede. "Are you saying he only has his original magic? That he doesn't have access to any of Shadow Striker's powers?"

Imogen scoffs. "If only. No, Kerrim is plenty strong, but the dagger stopped increasing his magic when you entered the human world, alerting him you'd traveled here. And because he now has a network of creatures on his side, he knows you're in the city."

The thought of that chills me, making me almost numb.

"How do you know all this?" one of the Order leaders asks, and Imogen turns her cold stare on him.

"Listen, you may know a little more of the prophecy than we do, but we've been successfully protecting both worlds from Shadow Striker for hundreds of years. We know more about the dagger than you do, and as long as Locklyn's tied to the dagger, Kerrim can't access its full power. And trust me, he won't be satisfied with what he has. He wants *all* the power Shadow Striker can give him." Imogen points to me. "She's our bait. If you dangle her in front of Kerrim, he won't be able to pass up the opportunity. We place her where we want, when we want, and I guarantee Kerrim will show up."

"The opportunity for what?" Becks asks, speaking up.

Imogen turns to him and gives him a look like he's an idiot. "The opportunity to kill her."

My stomach drops, and before I can even process Imogen's proposal, Becks is already shaking his head. He grabs my hand and pulls me to my feet. "No way. I'm not letting you gamble with her life," he says. "Come on, Lock, we're out of here."

I plant my feet and yank my arm from his grasp. Hurt flashes across his face, but I force myself to stay firm.

"I'm not going anywhere. I knew the dangers when I agreed to all this. Even if I wanted to, I can't just leave. I'm under an unbreakable bond, remember? I have to see this through."

Becks digs his fingers into his hair, gripping the strands tight. "Well, then . . . we'll come up with a different plan. One that isn't so dangerous for you."

A wave of frustration rises in me, tightening my chest.

I know he's just trying to protect me, and if our roles were reversed I might be begging him to run too. But it still scrapes a raw nerve inside me, a part of me that whispers I'm not good enough, not strong enough. Which isn't fair, I know. The threat Kerrim poses is real, and deadly.

"I'll make sure she's ready," Talon says, and Becks' gaze snaps over to him.

"What do you mean?" he asks, his brow bunching.

"She has access to a massive wellspring of magic. Even more than she realizes. Perhaps she's not as powerful as Kerrim, but I believe if she can figure out how to tap into her power, she'll be close. I'll work with her and get her where she needs to be."

Becks gives Talon a skeptical look. "How do you know what magic she has?"

"Because it used to be mine," he answers, and Becks' eyebrows lift slightly.

"When she won the activation trial, Shadow Striker was sealed off in the human world before it had a chance to transfer completely over to her. That's the only reason I'm still alive. The powers I acquired when I was the dagger's wielder have slowly been transferring over to her for days now. I think she has almost all my old powers, so I'm very familiar with each and every one, and can teach her to use them to her advantage."

The room falls into an eerie silence after Talon's confession. We hadn't told Kade the truth before now. He knew I had magic, but not how I'd come by it. I hadn't told Ensley the full story either; the shock on her face makes that obvious. Only Imogen looks unsurprised, like she'd known all along.

"This is set to go down in a couple of weeks. Do you really think that's enough time to train her?"

Talon glances at me. "She's a fighter by nature. I have faith in her. She'll pick it up fast."

Warmth bursts in my chest at Talon's confidence in me, but Becks doesn't look convinced.

"You're still gambling with her life," he says with a frown.

Talon meets Becks' gaze head-on. "I'll do everything in my power to keep her alive."

Becks shakes his head but retakes his seat. "That might have been enough during Chaos, but what if it's not this time?"

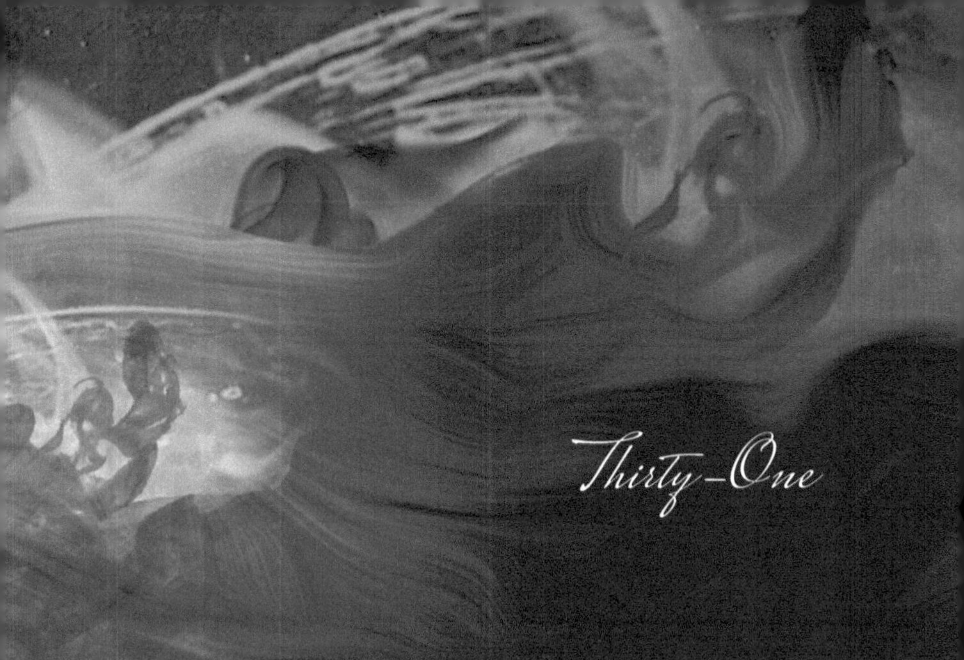

Thirty-One

WE CONCLUDE the meeting with a plan to lure Kerrim to Central Park in two weeks, giving me at least a little time to learn how to better tap into my new powers, and allowing the Order to gather their forces and plan an offensive against Kerrim and his followers. Tobias gives us a wide berth as he leaves, but Violet shyly comes over to tell us she's glad we made it and found our friend. I thank her for her help and introduce her to Becks.

She tucks a piece of lavender hair behind her ear and offers him a small smile, her cheeks going a little pink as she says hello. Becks, ever the charmer, flashes her a warm grin and thanks her for everything she's done. I catch the way her eyes flick to the floor before daring another glance up at him.

I bite back a grin, more amused than anything. Becks has that effect on females.

When the rest of the Order members disperse, most returning to the NYC headquarters to continue preparations, my friends and I stay behind in the empty warehouse to train.

At first, everyone hangs around, but I find the crowd too distracting, so Ensley, Titus, and Imogen trickle out one by one. Becks refuses to go with them. I'm used to him watching me train and spar at the gym, but this feels different. I struggle to access my magic with his eyes on me, and even Talon seems off. Eventually, I convince Becks to meet up with the others and help prepare for the eventual confrontation. He's reluctant to leave and makes a show of giving me a long hug and a kiss on the nose before he goes.

I expect Talon to return to normal once it's just the two of us, but something still isn't syncing between us like it usually does. I'm not sure if it's him or me. Even so, he manages to coax the wind and water magic out of me, and begins teaching me how to make the shadows semi-corporeal—which, incidentally, is what he did the first time we met, when it felt like a snake was sliding up my calf at Sloan's diner.

Progress is slow, and I can't shake the feeling that it should be happening faster. Something is blocking me. Or maybe blocking us. We're six hours into training when I finally have enough.

"What is it?" I ask. "Just tell me."

Talon tilts his head slightly. "What are you talking about?"

"We've been off. The whole day. Honestly, it's a miracle we've made the progress we have. But in two weeks, I have to face arguably the most powerful creature in both this world and ours. So if there's an issue here causing this disconnect between us, just say it. Get it off your chest so we can move past it."

He studies me in silence for a few beats, his lips pressed in a firm line and his arms crossed over his chest. The longer he stares, the harder it is not to shift under the weight of his gaze.

At last, he shakes his head. "It's nothing," he says, turning to retrieve the loose brick we've been using to practice my wind magic.

Frustrated, I stomp over and catch his arm. He pauses, then slowly turns back to me with a sigh.

"It's not worth talking about," he says. "We have more important things to focus on right now."

"Yes, I agree. But this," I say, gesturing between us, "isn't working right now, and it's affecting my ability to train."

"That's all in your head, Locklyn."

Locklyn. Not Freckles.

My eyes narrow. I notice, again, that Talon can't quite meet my gaze.

"Is this about Becks?" I ask, and that finally gets his attention. He looks straight at me for the first time. "You've been acting off ever since we got him back."

He just stares, silent. The longer he doesn't answer, the heavier the silence becomes, until it presses against my chest and I start to babble.

"Because I know we still need to talk about . . . stuff. And things with Becks aren't really clear right now. But then there's also this something that's here," I say, and Talon's eyebrows rise as I continue to word vomit. "And I don't know what to do with it. Or what it even is. Like, are we trauma bonded with sparkly side effects? I don't even know anymore, and it's distracting, and I'm pretty sure I almost set my own pants on fire trying to summon fire magic earlier, so clearly it's affecting me."

Locklyn. Shut up.

I clamp my mouth shut, my cheeks burning as I wish I could shove the words back down my throat.

A small smirk tugs at the corner of Talon's mouth. "Feeling guilty?"

I throw my hands up. "Yes, of course I feel guilty. None of this would've happened to Becks if he hadn't been trying to protect me. In fact, we should *both* feel guilty."

He crosses his arms. "All right, I'll bite. What exactly should I be feeling remorse over?"

"We're both to blame for Becks being stuck in the human world."

Talon arches an eyebrow. "And we've both sacrificed plenty to get him back, so my conscience is clear on that front." He pins me with a knowing look. "But let's be honest, that's not what's really bothering you."

"What are you talking about?"

He steps closer, and the energy between us shifts. Heat prickles across my skin, my pulse skipping in my throat, throwing me off-balance. The space between us feels suddenly too small, so I take a step back, needing the room to breathe.

"This is what I'm talking about," he says, giving me a knowing look. "You think you're betraying Becks because of what's growing between us."

I freeze, caught off guard. I didn't expect Talon to go there. To peel back the layers and expose the one thing I've been too afraid to name, even to myself.

"That's not true," I say, even though it might be.

"Isn't it though?" he challenges.

Flustered, I take a step back, but Talon closes the distance again, reclaiming the space I tried to create. He steps in even closer.

"That's not what this is about," I argue, but he scoffs.

"You can keep telling yourself that if you want, but deep down, you know it's a lie."

Is he right? Maybe. I don't know. Everything feels tangled.

"I love Becks," I say, needing to ground myself in something I still believe is true. And needing him to hear it too.

Instead of hardening like I expect, Talon's face unexpectedly softens, and he sighs. "I don't deny that you do," he says, gently. "But sometimes love changes."

I rear back and hit the brick wall, startled to find I've backpedaled across the entire room. "What is that supposed to mean?"

Talon meets my gaze without flinching. "That Becks was your first love, but not your forever love."

His words hit like a slap, and part of me recoils.

Heat flares in my chest, fueled by a rush of defensiveness. Things with Becks might be complicated right now, as they are with Talon too, but that doesn't mean I'm ready to give up.

Not on him. Not on us. Not after everything we've fought through just to be here.

"Why would you think that?" I ask, warring within myself over whether the anger rising in me is directed at Talon or myself.

Talon exhales slowly. "Becks is a good guy," he says, and the unexpected admission throws me off. "In a different life, I might even like him. Might have wanted to be his friend. But I'm not going to stand by and watch him stifle your potential or diminish your strength in the name of protecting you."

"That's not what Becks is doing," I shoot back, more defensive than I mean to be. Still, Talon's words hit deeper than I want to admit.

"Isn't it though?" he asks, his eyes seeing too much.

"There's nothing wrong with wanting to protect someone."

Talon gives me a sad smile. "There is when it means you don't let them walk on their own two feet. When you refuse to see or acknowledge how strong they are."

I want to snap back at Talon. To defend Becks the way I always do. But too much of what he's saying rings true. Isn't that the very disappointment I've been trying to ignore? Not just in the past day, but all the way back during the Chaos trials?

If I'm honest, the lack of support has been gnawing at me for a while now, like a slow-acting poison, stealing what used to be beautiful between us and turning it into resentment. But I didn't want to admit it. Because it's Becks. My best friend. The guy I've loved for as long as I can remember.

I kept telling myself I could get past it. Or at least bury it. That maybe Becks would change, especially after learning I had powers. But even today, when he tried to drag me out of that meeting, he proved he hasn't. And maybe he never will.

Talon's quiet, but his blue-gray gaze holds me—gentle, steady, and seeing more than I want him to.

"That's not what you need in a partner," he says. "You don't need to be coddled, set on a shelf or a pedestal to be looked at or fawned over. You need to be challenged and treated as an equal, not just a pretty object to be protected. You want someone who understands your strength and stands with you, not someone who's too afraid you'll break to let you learn how to fly."

But I feel like I'm about to break. Not because I was wrong before. Wanting to protect someone isn't a flaw. But Talon's right too. That kind of love isn't enough for me anymore.

I don't need someone to shield me.

I need someone who sees me.

Talon lifts a hand to my face. His thumb brushes gently against my cheek, wiping away a tear I hadn't even realized had fallen.

"I see you," he says as he moves closer, cradling my head between both his hands so my entire view is filled with him and him alone.

"I see someone who's stronger than she knows. Who fights even when she's breaking. I see fire. I see loyalty. I see someone who terrifies me in the best way, because she never backs down. Not from her pain, and not from her power. But I also see the cracks you try to hide. The fear you don't speak out loud. And I still see you as the bravest soul I know."

"Talon," I whisper, overwhelmed. Not just by his presence, but by the weight of his words.

An ache blooms in my chest. I can't tell if I want him to stop talking . . . or never stop.

But he doesn't pause. He keeps going.

"I see someone who deserves to be chosen. I'd choose you, every time. Every version of you—strong, stubborn, scared—I see it all. I. See. *You.*"

The air between us shifts, charged and heavy, as something electric crackles under my skin. My magic stirs within me, and the gold and silver threads that bind us together appear, casting Talon in a soft glow and taking my breath away.

"I know this is difficult for you," he says. "You don't want to hurt anyone, and all of this is messy and confusing." His tongue swipes over his bottom lip, wetting it, and I'm drawn in, helpless against the slow, deliberate motion. "But every time we get close, you push me away, like we don't already know how this ends."

"How does this end?" I ask, mesmerized.

His eyes search mine, not with uncertainty, but with a quiet promise I feel in my bones.

He steps in close, his hand sliding to the back of my neck, holding me like he's afraid I'll run before saying, "Becks was your first, but I'm your forever."

A shiver rolls down my spine, and every part of me tilts toward him like gravity has chosen sides.

"Do you remember what I told you about the first time we kiss?" he asks.

Awareness coils low in my stomach as words that have been impossible for me to forget run through my mind.

"The first time we kiss, Freckles, it won't be to make another guy jealous. It'll be because we can't live another second without tasting each other's lips."

I nod, not able to find my voice, and Talon's gaze drops to my mouth. The look in his eyes makes my breath hitch, and as he inches closer every nerve in my body goes on high alert.

"And are you there?" he asks. "Because I am. I'm tired of waiting."

My heart hammers in my chest as I whisper, "Yeah," my voice barely there. "I think I've been there for a while."

Something shifts in Talon's expression. Relief, maybe. Or a sharper longing, raw and intense, like he's been holding his breath for days and I've finally let him exhale.

He leans in slowly, giving me every chance to pull away. I don't.

"Good. Because I'm done holding back," he murmurs, and then his mouth finds mine.

He tastes like an intoxicating mix of danger and desire. His lips are soft and smooth and I can't seem to get enough of them as they brush up against mine again and again.

The kiss is everything he promised it would be. Not about jealousy. Not about proving anything. Just us. Raw, consuming, inevitable. Deeper and different than anything I'd ever experienced before. More than I could even fathom a kiss being, because at once I'm broken into a million pieces, but then in the same breath, right back together again. It feels like electricity is being passed back and forth between us. This is the most alive I've ever felt in my life.

A moan rises from my throat and slips from my lips when his mouth breaks from mine and trails down my neck. I dive my hands into his hair, holding him close, refusing to let him go.

In one swift motion, Talon reaches down, hooks his hands under my thighs and lifts me. Instinctually, my legs wrap around his waist as he presses me back against the rough brick wall, his mouth never leaving my skin.

He brushes his lips along my throat, slow and deliberate, until he reaches my ear. When he catches the lobe gently between his teeth and bites down, a rush of heat pulses through me like a live wire snapping beneath my skin.

I drag his mouth back to mine, and when his tongue brushes up against mine, my mind goes hazy.

I can't think. I can't stop. I don't exist beyond this bubble.

As his mouth moves over mine again and again, the world doesn't tilt to throw me off balance—it settles, like it's finally fallen into the place it was always meant to be. The thing that's been trying desperately to grow between us finally bursts to life, bright and beautiful, like an all-consuming fire, impossible to contain.

Suddenly, Talon pulls back and we break apart, both struggling for breath as we stare at each other, wide-eyed and stunned.

"Damn, Freckles," he murmurs, his voice rough and low, and I feel it all the way to my toes.

"Wh-what's wrong?" I ask, breathless, confused by the sudden pause.

He lets out a soft laugh, and I feel it rumble in his chest with how close we still are. "Had to stop," he says, eyes dark and steady. "Because if I didn't, I wouldn't have."

Oh. *Oh*.

"Well. That was, um, a lot," I say with a nervous laugh, still tingling from the way his kisses lit every nerve in my body. "Honest, yeah. And kind of wrecking me, just a little."

He brushes a thumb across my cheek, his voice low. "Yeah? That's kind of how I've felt since the day I met you."

A shaky breath escapes me. "I don't even know what to do with that," I whisper. "Except maybe admit that you've been under my skin since day one too."

His brows lift slightly, eyes narrowing. Not with anger, but disbelief.

"Since day one?" he echoes, voice low. "Because the way I remember it you were mooning over a particular dragon heir and treating me like the guy who couldn't annoy you more."

He searches my face like he's trying to find the lie, but all he finds is me.

"Tell me that again," he says, softer this time. "And mean it."

I huff out a laugh, my cheeks warming. "I said you were under my skin, not that I was doodling your name in the margins of my notebook and daydreaming about our wedding." I meet his eyes, trying not to smile. "You were obnoxious. And unfairly hot. It was *very* inconvenient."

His eyes widen comically, like I've shocked him. "You mean to tell me that you weren't composing love sonnets about my jawline?"

I can't help but laugh with him at that. "No!" I pause, then mutter, "Though it is a really good jawline."

He chuckles, and a sudden burst of embarrassment hits me as I realize I'm still latched on to him like a spider monkey.

"You should probably, um, let me go," I say.

He quirks an eyebrow. "Let you go? Never."

Butterflies flutter in my stomach, but once I've untangled my limbs from around him, he lets me slide down the front of him until my feet touch the ground again.

His gaze travels over my face, like he's searching for something, and a moment later I know what when he asks, "Any regrets?"

There's a touch of vulnerability in his gaze I'm not used to seeing.

I draw in a slow breath, eyes dropping for a moment as the question settles between us.

Do I have regrets?

The truth is, I don't know how to untangle one feeling from another right now. What I feel for Becks, what I thought I knew, what I wanted to believe, it's all still there, layered and complicated.

But things with Talon have never been simple either.

"I don't know what this means for everything else," I say finally, meeting his gaze. "But this moment? You?"

I pause, feeling the truth of it settle in my chest like a heartbeat I hadn't noticed until now. "No. I don't regret it."

Talon's smile is equal parts relief and joy, lighting up his entire face. Just as he opens his mouth to respond, the door to the warehouse slams open.

The bang reverberates through the space like a gunshot, and we both jolt. I spin toward the entrance, my pulse still racing from everything that just happened, but now for a very different reason.

Becks stands in the doorway, a takeout bag clutched in one hand, his eyes fixed on us.

He freezes.

The lighthearted expression he wore only a second earlier dies on his face as he takes in the scene: me still flushed with swollen lips and standing far too close to Talon, whose hand hasn't quite dropped from my waist.

"I—" Becks starts, his voice catching. He clears his throat and lifts the bag slightly, like that somehow makes this moment less raw. "I, uh . . . brought dinner. Thought you might still be training."

His gaze darts between us, and emotion shifts behind his eyes. A wound I opened once and somehow tore open again. Hurt. Betrayal. Maybe a feeling he won't let himself name.

He sets the bag down on the nearby folding table with more force than necessary.

Neither Talon nor I say a word. The silence is thick. Heavy.

"I'll give you two some space," Becks says, already backing toward the door. "Clearly, you don't need me here."

Then he's gone before I can figure out what to say. Before I even know what I *want* to say.

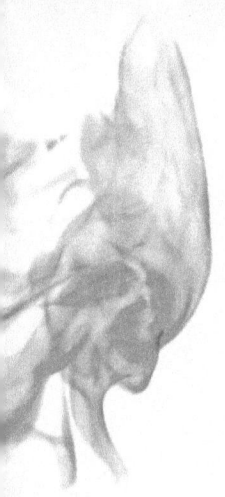

Thirty-Two

THE DOOR BANGS shut behind him, the echo ringing through the warehouse like a warning bell.

For a few heartbeats, I can't move. Frozen. Caught between the intensity of what just happened with Talon and the wreckage Becks left in his wake.

The warmth of Talon's hands still lingers on my skin, but guilt creeps in like a chill.

Talon exhales hard beside me, stepping back just enough to meet my eyes. "That went well," he mutters, voice tight, caught between frustration and regret.

I press a trembling hand to my mouth. "He wasn't supposed to see that. We weren't even—"

"Doing anything?" Talon finishes for me, but there's no accusation in his voice. Only quiet resignation. "Didn't look that way to him."

I step away completely now, needing space to think, to breathe. "I should go after him."

"Should you?" Talon's voice is quiet, but the question lands hard.

"I'm sorry," I say, not even exactly sure what I'm apologizing for as I backpedal away from him.

Talon doesn't stop me. He just watches me go.

I push through the door after Becks, the cold night air crashing into me like a punishment.

I find him just outside the warehouse, pacing like a storm bottled in a human body. He doesn't hear me at first, or pretends not to, until I step off the gravel path.

"Becks."

He stops. Doesn't turn. His fists are clenched at his sides.

"So that's what I left you alone with him for?" His voice is low but sharp. "Training?"

I swallow hard. "It wasn't planned. It just . . . happened."

"Right," he says, finally turning to face me. His jaw is tight, eyes darker than I've ever seen them. "You just accidentally climbed into his arms?"

"It wasn't like that," I say, but even I can hear how weak it sounds.

Becks lets out a hollow laugh. "You know what the worst part is? I knew something was happening between you two. I felt it. And when you lied and told me there was nothing going on, I silenced that voice inside because I didn't want to believe that there was."

"Nothing happened before today," I say quickly. "You have to know that. I didn't mean to hurt you—"

"Yeah, well, you did."

The words land like a slap. He shakes his head, looking away again.

"I thought I mattered to you."

"You do," I say, stepping closer. "You've always mattered to me, Becks. You're—"

"Not enough," he cuts in, the words soft but brutal. "At least not anymore."

We stand there in silence for a few seconds. Me still catching my breath, him trying to hold himself together.

"So . . . what?" he finally asks, quieter now. "Are you choosing him?"

I open my mouth, but no words come out. Because the truth is I don't know yet.

And maybe that silence is all the answer he needs.

He nods slowly, lips pressed in a tight line. "Got it."

Then he turns and walks away. This time, I don't chase him.

AFTER BECKS LEAVES, I can't bring myself to go back to the warehouse and face Talon. What happened between us was amazing, but it also unearthed things I'm not sure I'm ready to deal with, and now I'm completely overwhelmed by the fallout.

So I walk.

Brooklyn buzzes around me as I keep my head down, weaving through streets I barely register until the city starts to quiet and the river comes into view. I follow the path along the edge, the water dark and choppy beside me. It probably isn't smart to be out here alone, not with everything going on, but right now I need space more than safety. I need to breathe.

The wind stings my face. The world feels too loud and too still at the same time.

Then my phone rings.

I pull it from my pocket, expecting a message from Talon—or maybe Becks—but it's neither. It's Titus, and for some reason my stomach twists before I even answer.

"Hello?"

Titus' voice is sharp. Panicked. "Locklyn. It's Ensley. She's gone. Someone took her."

My heart stops.

"What do you mean she's *gone*?" I ask, my voice shrill. "Gone where?" I'm already turning back the way I came, legs moving on instinct.

"We were scoping out the park and we were jumped. We fought, but there were just too many of them."

"Tell me everything. Who took her? When did this happen?"

Not Ensley. Anyone but Ensley.

My pulse pounds in my ears, drowning out everything but the voice on the other end of the line. I can barely keep up as the words pour out. Something about more than a dozen attackers. All creatures. They'd ambushed them. Surrounded them. Titus fought back, but they managed to split him from Ensley. By the time he'd taken down enough of them, she was gone.

"Where are you now?" I ask.

"I'm still in the park. I can send you a pin."

"Stay there. I'm on my way," I say, even though I don't know where I'm going yet. "Have you called anyone else?" I send a silent prayer up to the Creator thanking him that Kade gave us all phones so we can get in touch with each other.

"I tried Becks first, but he's not picking up."

I swallow down the panic that something might have happened to him too, telling myself he probably just wasn't picking up because he was still upset about what he saw in the warehouse.

"Keep trying him. But call Talon first and tell him what happened."

"Aren't you with him?" Titus asks, confused.

I shake my head even though he can't see me. "Not right now, but I'm headed back to the warehouse. We'll both come meet you."

There's silence for a second and then Titus says, "What if they hurt her? I'll never forgive myself." His voice is broken. I've never heard Titus like this before.

"We're going to find her and get her back, just like we did Becks."

"Okay, just hurry."

"I will," I say, and then hang up without waiting for a response and break into a run, the wind burning my face, my boots pounding the pavement.

Because no matter what's happened between me and Talon—or Becks—this isn't about them anymore.

It's about getting Ensley back.

I didn't realize how far I'd wandered until it takes me over ten minutes at a dead sprint before the warehouse finally comes into view. I round the side of the building, breath ragged, legs burning, sweat clinging to me, and find Talon already outside, waiting.

The second he spots me, he pushes off the wall where he'd been leaning. I try to spit out what's happened between pants, but he waves me off and says, "I talked to Titus. Let's go."

I nod, and we head to a more populated area to find a taxi. My anxiety spikes when it takes longer than I'd like. I start wringing my hands, pacing the sidewalk while scanning for headlights, until Talon finally manages to flag one down.

The ride from Brooklyn to Central Park feels endless, stretched tight with tension neither of us bothers to name. We sit in heavy silence, the weight of what's waiting for us pressing in on every mile.

When the taxi finally rolls up to one of the park's entrances, I have the door open and I'm jumping out before the car comes to a complete stop. The driver yells at me, but I don't pay him any attention as I break into a run, forgoing the paved path and heading over grass and through trees, determined to get to Titus.

We have to find Ensley. Nothing else matters.

Talon catches up quickly and grabs my arm, forcing me to stop.

"Locklyn, stop. Look at yourself." His voice isn't angry, it's steady, but laced with an emotion that pulls me up short: concern.

I glance down and freeze.

Shadows are drifting toward me from all sides, curling off my skin in thin wisps. The air smells like smoke, and the grass beneath my feet is withering in patches, the tips browned as if scorched.

"I didn't even mean to," I murmur, breath catching in my throat.

"It's hard to control magic when emotions are involved," he says, his gaze locked on me. No judgment, just quiet understanding.

I nod, slowly, my pulse still racing, but now it's not from urgency.

It's fear.

Because no matter how hard I try to keep it in check, my magic keeps slipping loose. It's happened before, especially when I was angry, scared, desperate. I already burned Talon once. And this isn't some harmless trickle of energy. I'm carrying power that was never meant for one creature, let alone one human, to hold. Not like this. Not without consequences.

Talon steps in close enough that his presence anchors me. His hand lifts, slowly, deliberately, and cups the side of my face. His thumb brushes just beneath my eye, not to wipe away tears but to steady me.

"Hey," he says softly. "You're okay. You're still in control. Just breathe."

I do, because he asks me to. The quiet strength in his voice reaches through the panic clawing at my chest.

One breath in. One out.

The shadows unravel from around me, slithering back into the darkness where they belong, and the scent of smoke blows away with the next gust of air.

"See?" he murmurs. "You've got this."

I nod again, this time more sure of myself.

"Okay," I whisper. Every time Talon helps me rein in my magic, I feel a touch more in control. "Let's go find Titus."

WHEN WE FIND TITUS, he isn't alone. Imogen and Kade have beaten us there and are standing in a loose semi-circle around someone bound to a tree with thick vines and ivy. Titus' handiwork, probably. As we approach, I have to choke back a gasp when I lay eyes on Titus.

One of his eyes is swollen completely shut, his lip split and crusted with blood. His shirt hangs in tatters, splattered red and torn across his chest. Through one of the rips, I catch a glimpse of a deep gash still oozing blood down his ribs.

He looks wrecked.

And the worst part? Titus is one of the strongest among us. Ensley is a powerful fae as well, but she's not a trained fighter. Under normal circumstances I believe she could hold her own, but if they could do *this* to Titus, then what kind of shape is Ensley in?

I try to push the thought away, but it claws at the edges of my mind. Whatever happened here wasn't a scuffle. It was a message. And if they have Ensley, I'm terrified of what they might do to her now.

We're met with matching grim faces when we join them, and I know instantly there's something I don't know. Something bad.

"What's happened?" I ask, the words barely leaving my mouth before Titus answers.

"We know who has her," he says, his voice rough.

He nods toward the figure bound to a nearby tree. I follow his gaze and have to stifle another gasp. The guy is barely conscious, slumped forward against the vines holding him in place. I'm assuming he's a creature and not a human, because otherwise I think he would have died from his injuries already. His face is a ruin of blood and bruises. Both eyes are swollen shut, his nose clearly broken; his jaw is jutting to the side at an unnatural angle. Deep gashes crisscross his chest and arms, and what's left of his shirt is soaked in blood. His shoulder looks dislocated and one boot is missing. He looks like he got hit by a truck made of fists and claws.

Talon lets out a low whistle and raises his brows at Titus. "You look bad, but now that I see the other guy, it's clear you didn't lose the fight."

Titus doesn't smile. No one does. Because whatever the bound creature knows, it cost something brutal to get it.

"Who has her?" I ask, and Titus and the others share a look. I'm surprised when it's Imogen who finally answers.

"Kerrim," she says, and my entire body goes cold.

I should have suspected, but even so, the news hits me like a shockwave.

"Why? How?" I ask, searching for someone to make sense of this for me.

"He took her to get to you," Titus says, a touch of bitterness in his voice that makes me flinch.

Seeing my reaction, he sighs and runs a hand through his hair, tinting the white strands pink with either his or his victim's blood.

"Sorry," he mumbles.

But I don't blame him. Once again, it's my fault one of my friends is hurt. The guilt coils low in my stomach, thick and sharp, like it's trying to eat its way out.

No matter how many times I tell myself I didn't ask for this, that none of this was my choice, it always circles back to me.

Kerrim wants *me*. And those I care about are paying the price.

My resolve hardens. No matter what happens to me, I'm going to end this one way or another. If it's me he wants, then that's who he'll get.

"Let him go," I order Titus, and he stares at me like I've just suggested we hand over the keys to the kingdom.

"Hell no," he says flatly. "I'm not letting this slime just walk out of here."

I glance at the creature and think that it would be a miracle if he could walk anywhere right now. We may actually have to carry him out of here ourselves to get him back to Kerrim.

"I'm not letting him go, I'm baiting the trap," I say, and everyone goes still.

"They took Ensley to draw me out," I continue, my voice steady despite the ache tightening in my chest. "So let's give him what he wants. We release this guy, let him crawl back to Kerrim with a message that I'll turn myself over tomorrow. No tricks. No backup. Just me in exchange for Ensley."

Titus crosses his arms, jaw clenched. "You want to walk straight into his hands? You really think he's going to honor that kind of deal?"

"Hasn't this been the plan all along?" I ask and then cast a wary glance at the creature, not wanting to divulge any secrets in front of him.

"Don't worry. He's definitely out," Imogen confirms, which gives me the green light to speak freely.

"Just this morning we talked about drawing Kerrim out so I can get Shadow Striker away from him. This just moves the timeline up. I won't be walking straight into his hands. He'll be walking right into *mine*."

There's a beat of silence before Talon steps closer. His eyes search mine with an emotion that's dangerously close to fear.

"You're not seriously doing this alone."

"I won't be alone," I say. "Not really. He thinks he's playing me, but we'll set the terms, not him. We control the location, the timing. And we'll be ready."

Talon still doesn't look convinced. His jaw works as he tries to find the right words.

"It's not that I don't believe in you, Locklyn," he says finally, his voice low. "But this is fast. You haven't had enough time to learn how to use everything you've got. Facing Kerrim now, it's like stepping onto a battlefield with armor you haven't finished forging."

The words land in my chest like stones, but there's no doubt in his eyes. No disbelief. Only concern.

"I'm not saying you can't take him," he adds quickly. "I'm saying you shouldn't have to do it unprepared."

"I know," I say quietly. "But if we wait, he'll have more time to hurt her. And I can't live with that."

Kade grunts softly, arms folded as he leans against a nearby tree. "Sounds risky as hell."

"It is," I agree. "But it's the only shot we've got to get Ensley back before he breaks her. Or worse. Can you pull together the Order members this fast?"

"It doesn't look like you're giving me a choice," he says gruffly.

I look to Talon next. "Tomorrow, you take the kid gloves off. You'll have the day to teach me what I need to know to face Kerrim."

Talon exhales slowly, his expression tight as he studies me for a moment.

"One day's not enough," he says. "But I'll use every second of it." He steps closer, his gaze steady. "You listen. You push. And you don't hold back. Because I won't. Then when it counts, you'll know how to survive. Because I won't let you walk in blind."

I meet his gaze without flinching. "Just to be clear, I don't plan on dying tomorrow."

He nods once, like he's making a promise to himself as much as to me. "Just so we're clear, I don't plan on letting you."

With that settled, I look to Titus. He stares at the bound creature for a long second, then lets out a breath and gives a grudging nod. "Fine. But if he so much as blinks wrong, I'm ending him."

"He's barely blinking at all," I murmur. "But fair enough."

Talon lingers beside me as Titus uses his magic to loosen the binds around his captive. His gaze is shadowed as it meets mine.

"One day," he says. "Let's make it count."

Thirty-Three

KADE LEAVES to start rallying his forces for tomorrow's battle just after we release Kerrim's lacky with a message for his boss. It's not five minutes after we watch the bloodied creature stumble into the trees and out of sight that a frantic Becks barrels into the small clearing, breathless and wild-eyed. There's a sheen of sweat on his brow; his hair looks like he's run his hands through it a dozen times too many. His phone is clutched tight in one hand, screen still lit up with missed calls.

His gaze darts from face to face, desperate. "Where is she?" he asks, but I can see in his eyes that he's terrified of the answer.

"Kerrim has her," Titus answers.

Becks' face goes white. "We have to get her back."

"We will," I say, speaking up.

Becks angles in my direction, but he won't meet my eyes.

It hurts, but I can't blame him.

"If he uses that dagger on her . . ." he says, and the words hit like a punch to the gut.

I feel the blood drain from my face too.

It hadn't even crossed my mind. But he's right.

If Kerrim stabs Ensley with Shadow Striker, it won't just hurt her, it'll strip her magic.

Just like it did to Becks.

"We have a plan to lure him out to the park tomorrow rather than in a couple weeks. We sent a message back to him with one of his goons to—"

I don't get the rest of the plan out before Becks erupts.

"You had someone and you let him go?" he shouts, his furious gaze finally locking on me.

It's not a look I'm used to seeing from Becks, sharp and burning. It hits hard enough to make me instinctively step back.

"You could have made him talk. You could have found out where they're keeping her."

Becks takes an aggressive step toward me, and Talon shifts slightly so he's standing at my side, a clear warning without uttering a single word. Becks' nostrils flare.

"He didn't know where they were taking her," Titus says, speaking up. "Trust me, we got all the information out of him that we were going to."

I cringe inwardly, remembering the shape he was in. Bloodied, broken, barely conscious. Whatever Titus did to make him talk, it worked.

But I don't feel bad for the creature. They took my best friend just to get to me. He deserved every second of it.

"You could have been here to question him yourself if you'd answered your phone," Titus says, clearly annoyed.

Becks' gaze flicks to me, and a flash of guilt twists in my chest. "Yeah, well, I didn't know it was you that was calling."

"Then next time pick up and check," Titus snaps.

"Yeah," Becks says, the fire draining out of him all at once, leaving only raw pain behind.

No matter how he feels about me right now, we both love Ensley with everything we have. Ensley may not be my sister by blood, but she's my sister in every way that matters. If anyone understands what he's going through, it's me.

"Becks." I take a cautious step closer. "We're going to get her back. I swear."

He goes still, fists curling at his sides, but he doesn't look at me. "You swear, huh? I'm not sure how much your word means to me right now."

The words hit harder than I expect, carving straight through the guilt already tearing me up inside. But I can't argue. Not when he's right to hate me a little.

"Hey, watch it," Talon warns. "She's hurting too."

Becks finally lifts his head, his gaze bouncing between the two of us. Me, still trying to stand my ground, and Talon, unmoving at my side.

His jaw tics.

"Yeah," he mutters. "Looks like she's doing just fine."

"Okay, what is going on here?" Imogen asks, and I glance over to see her and Titus watching the three of us with sharp, suspicious eyes.

"You're acting like—" she cuts herself off, eyes suddenly widening.

And just like that, I know.

She's figured it out, or at least come close enough to the truth.

She crosses her arms. "I see. So this tension isn't about the missing sister, it's about who Locklyn kissed." A pause. "Priorities."

Titus' mouth drops open, and my face goes hot with embarrassment.

Becks turns away from all of us, but not before a glint of shame crosses his face.

My heart aches.

Ensley's abduction is more important than anything that's happened between us, but that doesn't mean he's not allowed to be affected by what I've done.

All I want is to go to him, to reach out, to say something that might make this less awful. But he won't let me close. Not now.

"You said that we're moving the plan up to tomorrow," Becks asks.

"Yes," Talon answers before I can. "Locklyn offered herself up in exchange for Ensley."

Becks' head snaps toward me. Despite the anger still lingering in his eyes, there's something else beneath it. Fear.

"Can you be ready that fast to face him?" he asks.

I lift a shoulder. "I don't have a choice."

I can see the conflict written all over his face. He wants his sister back, desperately, but he knows how dangerous this is going to be for me. Even if he wants to argue, to beg me not to, he also knows he's lost the right to tell me what to do.

Becks exhales through his nose, his mouth a hard line. "Then you better come back in one piece," he mutters.

It's not quite forgiveness, but it's a start.

"I intend to," I say.

Becks' gaze softens and he nods.

"Does Kade know about all this?" he asks Titus.

"Yeah," Titus says. "He's gone back to Order headquarters to rally his people and speed up their planning."

Becks nods again, more firmly this time. "Okay. I'll go and see how I can help."

I blink, caught off guard. "Seriously? You're going back there?" Even earlier today, the thought of stepping foot in the Order's headquarters again made his blood boil. "After everything they did to you?"

He shrugs, but there's a grim steadiness in his eyes now. "I'm not exactly overflowing with magical usefulness these days." A faint smile ghosts his lips, bitter but resigned. "If they've got a job for a guy without powers, I'll take it. Ensley's out there. I'm not sitting this out."

For a moment, none of us say anything. Even Titus seems surprised.

Imogen breaks the silence first. "Don't get too excited. They'll probably have you filing paperwork." But there's a glint of reluctant respect in her eyes.

Titus studies Becks for a long second, then gives a small, approving nod. "The Order could use someone with firsthand knowledge of Kerrim's tactics. Especially someone who's fought him before and isn't afraid to call them out on their crap."

Becks' mouth lifts in the ghost of a grin. "That I can do."

Talon, still at my side, adds, "They'll take one look at you and know you've got skin in the game."

Becks' gaze shifts to me, then back to Talon. "I do," is all he says.

With that, I watch him turn, ready to walk away, and a tight ache clenches in my chest. He only gets a handful of steps away before I'm calling his name and jogging to catch up.

He pauses, shoulders tense as I reach him.

"I know going back there isn't easy. So . . . just . . . thanks for not letting that stop you."

What I really want to say is *Thank you for still caring about me, even though you're hurting*. Because I know he's going back there as much for me as he is for his sister.

But I don't. I can't.

He dips his head slightly, like he's acknowledging the weight of it. "It's not about me," he says. "It's about getting her back, and doing what I can to protect the ones I love."

He meets my eyes then, and the look that passes between us sends a jolt straight through me. "That's all that matters."

His gaze lingers just a second too long before he turns and walks away.

I don't stop him. I just stand there, heart pounding, the weight of everything between us pressing down on me.

It's complicated. It's painful. And it's far from over.

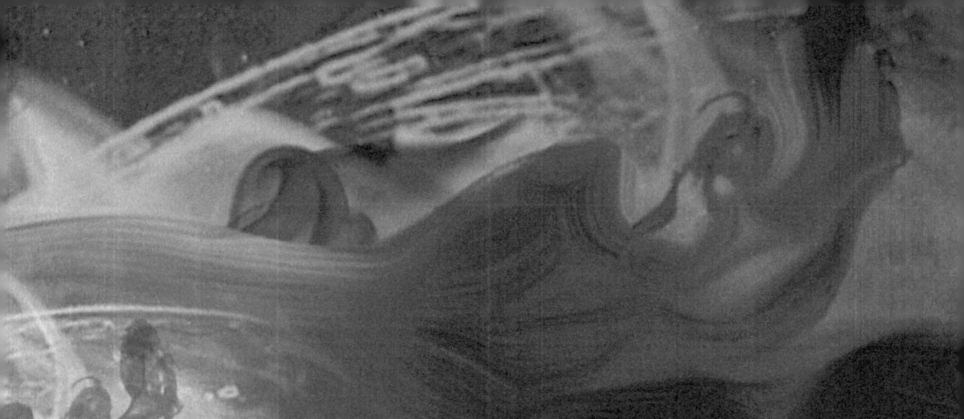

Thirty-Four

I SUGGEST GOING BACK to the warehouse to train, but Talon vetoes the idea, saying that as much as I need the practice, I need rest even more. I'll be no good to anyone tomorrow, whether it's for training or fighting, if I don't get some sleep.

With everything going on, I don't know how I'm supposed to sleep, but I relent.

Imogen plans to use her undercover status within Kerrim's ranks to try to dig up any information she can about Ensley. There's still a chance, however small, that if she figures out where they're keeping her, we could mount a rescue and revert to the original plan, giving me more time to prepare. It's a long shot, but it's something.

When we go to hail a cab back to the hotel, Titus hangs back, saying he wants to walk to blow off some steam and clear his head. The swelling around his eye is already going down thanks to his enhanced healing, and the gash on his ribs has stopped bleeding, but he still looks bad.

When I suggest that walking through the city in his condition might cause a scene, he gives me a look and says, "Trust me. Humans in this city have seen worse. No one will even blink."

I'm not sure that's true, but there's a haunted flicker in his eyes that makes me pause. A fraying around the edges, like he's just barely holding it together.

I sigh and say softly, "We'll see you later."

Talon and I don't speak on the short cab ride to the hotel, but everything that's happened between us hangs in the air, heavy, steady, and impossible to ignore. The silence continues when we arrive, but as we walk through the lobby, Talon places his hand on the small of my back. It's such a simple gesture but it calms me, reminding me I'm not alone, even with everything crashing down around us.

When we return to our adjoining rooms, I start toward the girls' side, but Talon catches my hand and gently tugs me toward him. He runs his hands up and down my arms, slow, deliberate strokes that leave a trail of goosebumps, zings of electricity chasing the path of his palms.

"Cold?" he asks, noticing my reaction.

I could lie to save myself the embarrassment, but I meet his gaze and slowly shake my head.

One side of his mouth lifts in a knowing half smile, but he doesn't press. He searches my eyes and asks quietly, "Are you okay?"

It's such a simple question but it cracks the fragile shell holding me together. My throat tightens, and I feel the sting behind my eyes. I shake my head again, this time more shaky, more honest. Words won't come.

Talon's hands still on my arms, then slide upward until they're cupping my face.

"Come here," he murmurs, drawing me into his chest like it's the most natural thing in the world.

I don't resist. I fold into him, the tension I didn't realize I'd been carrying unraveling in his arms.

"I won't tell you everything's going to be all right," he says honestly. "But I will promise to be there every step of the way. Just like I have been from the beginning. I won't let you face any of this alone."

His words pierce straight through me, not because he's telling me what I want to hear, but because he isn't. He's giving me raw honesty, and somehow that's more comforting than any pretty lie could ever be.

It reminds me that Talon has been there from the very start, even back in the first Chaos trial, when he saved me after Jules left me for dead in that underground cavern. Since that day, we've been saving each other.

I soak in the comfort he's offering, then lean back just enough to meet his eyes. I need him to see how serious I am about what I'm about to say.

I didn't lie when I told him he's been under my skin since the beginning. What's blossoming between us now started as a seed that was planted that first day, slowly growing ever since. I just didn't realize it until now.

"I want you to promise me something," I say softly.

Talon tilts his head as he gazes down on me. "What?"

I take a deep breath, not sure how he's going to react.

"I need you to promise that you'll do whatever it takes to protect Ensley and Becks tomorrow night, even if it means sacrificing me."

They're my family. If anyone should make it out alive, it's them, and everyone else who's risked so much to help.

Titus, Talon, even Imogen. If they all survive and make it home, then it's worth it.

Even if I don't.

"I'm prepared for whatever happens tomorrow," I add. "But I won't be able to focus if I'm worried about them."

Talon goes still. His shoulders tense; his eyes flash with a mix of anguish and restraint.

Slowly, he closes the space between us, resting his forehead against mine as he exhales a shaky breath, like I just asked him to tear out a piece of himself.

"I get that they're your world, but you need to understand," he says, leaning back to cup my face with one hand. "They may be your world . . . but you're mine. And because they matter to you, I'll do everything I can to protect them. Even if it means risking my own life. But I can't, and won't, promise to put their lives above yours."

I huff out a frustrated breath, already knowing this is as close to a promise as I'm going to get from him.

"Must you be so difficult?" I mutter, which earns me a crooked grin. "Well, at least promise you'll save yourself. That if things go bad, you'll get out."

"No can do, Freckles," he interrupts gently, his smile softening. "Just like you're wired to protect the ones you love, so am I. If you go down, I go down with you."

The breath catches in my throat. He didn't say the words, not exactly, but the meaning is clear.

That was an admission of love.

Talon's gaze drops to my mouth in a silent question. And Creator help me, I want to answer it. But a small voice in the back of my mind whispers caution, because if we start kissing again I'm not sure we'll stop. With everything looming ahead, and Becks' grief-filled face still looming in the forefront of my mind, I don't know if my heart can handle that tonight.

But I want him to. More than I should.

And yet . . . I don't.

He must see the conflict in my eyes, because instead of closing the space between us, he leans in and presses a chaste kiss to my forehead.

Even that simple, innocent touch sends my heart into overdrive, leaving me dizzy with everything I'm trying not to feel.

"Get some rest," he says and then his hands fall away from me as he takes a step back.

I miss his warmth instantly, and have to stop myself from swaying toward him. I have to steel myself. As much as I want to lean on Talon right now, I need to stand on my own two feet, because tomorrow, no matter what he or anyone else says, I'll be facing off against Kerrim on my own.

"You too," I say.

Turning away from him, I enter the empty room I should be sharing with Ensley and Imogen, and shut the door behind me.

I TOSS in bed for what has to be the tenth time, trying—and failing—to get comfortable enough to sleep. I knew shutting my brain off tonight would be a struggle, but with every minute that ticks by, my anxiety only climbs higher.

If I'm not sleeping, I should be practicing. And if I'm not practicing, I should be sleeping.

Instead, I'm doing neither, just lying here, wasting time I don't have.

Maybe a glass of water will help?

Who am I kidding? I don't think anything short of a partial lobotomy is going to help me fall asleep tonight, but I suppose I can still give the water a shot.

With a huff, I throw the covers off and stand. I'm padding my way to the bathroom when I notice a low glow coming from the guys' room.

Is Talon still awake? Maybe Titus is back.

I walk over to the connecting door and knock softly. No answer.

I should probably leave it at that, but I'm more awake than I should be, and definitely too curious, so I crack the door and peek inside. The room is dark except for the bathroom, where soft light spills out from the open doorway.

I'm about to close the door and resume my mission for water when something clatters onto the tile, followed by a sharp curse.

Talon.

I'm through the door and moving toward the bathroom before I can think better of it. When I reach the open doorway, I freeze, my brain momentarily glitching.

Talon stands there in low-slung joggers, twisting awkwardly to reach his lower back.

So. Much. Bronze. Skin.

So many muscles. So many ripples.

Am I drooling? I might be drooling.

I've seen Talon shirtless before, more than once, but now that I know how he tastes, my body reacts like someone turned the volume all the way up.

I should say something. Announce myself. Instead, I swipe beneath my mouth in case I actually am drooling, mildly impressed to find I'm not.

Talon sighs in frustration and straightens. Catching my reflection in the mirror, he turns, and that's when I see it.

The gashes across his ribs. The bullet wound on his side.

Still not fully healed.

I couldn't tell before, the way he was angled, but now it's obvious. He was trying to rewrap his wounds.

Seeing them clears the fog from my head, snapping everything into focus.

"Why aren't those healed yet?" I ask, my voice sharper than I mean it to be.

I think of how fast Titus recovered, his eye already improving just an hour after the fight. Talon's a matured creature. Wounds like those should be faint scars by now, if anything. It's almost as if he's healing at the rate a child would before coming into their magic. Or a human.

Taking a step forward, I take a better look at his wounds.

Thankfully, they're not life-threatening. But they're still raw. Too raw.

"You're supposed to be asleep," Talon says, rubbing the back of his neck, clearly uncomfortable.

"Right, like I could sleep at a time like this," I shoot back. "I'd need an elephant tranquilizer just to take the edge off. But don't change the subject." I gesture at his ribs and lower abdomen. "What's going on here?"

Talon exhales slowly. "It's not a big deal."

"The Komodo dragon bite, maybe I'd buy. But the bullet wound . . ." I cross my arms. He's lying, or at the very least, dodging, and I want to know why.

Talon meets my gaze for a long beat, then finally speaks.

"I didn't want to worry you." He leans back against the counter, bracing his hands on either side and making his biceps bulge in a way that is more distracting than I'm willing to admit.

I give my head a light shake and hope he doesn't notice.

"Something's been off since I got separated from Shadow Striker," he confesses. "My healing, it's slowed down. Not stopped, just . . . dulled."

His voice is steady, but I don't miss the tension in his jaw.

"You think it's the dagger," I say.

He nods. "It's a theory. I don't know for sure. But it's the only thing that makes sense."

"And you didn't think to mention this sooner?" I ask, trying not to sound hurt.

Talon gives me a small smile. "I didn't want to add more to your plate. You've got enough weighing on you."

He pushes off the counter and takes a step toward me, gaze softening. "But I'm okay. Really. It's really no more than a nuisance."

That's downplaying it and we both know it.

"You shouldn't be dealing with this alone," I murmur.

He shrugs one shoulder. "I'm not. Not anymore."

A moment passes. The weight between us shifts. Less tension, more understanding.

His eyes flick toward the connecting door. "You can't sleep?"

I shake my head.

He grins faintly. "Want me to try helping with that?"

"And how do you plan to do that?" I ask.

"By staying close. Sometimes it helps to not be alone with your thoughts."

"Staying close?" I ask with a raised eyebrow.

"Very close," he says with a wicked glint in his eye that threatens to distract me all over again.

I order my mind not to go to places it shouldn't. "You think getting into bed with me is going to help me fall asleep?"

He's delusional if he thinks that will work. Lying next to him in bed might take my mind off of some of tomorrow's trials, but that's only because being that close to him would make it impossible to think about anything else.

"No," he admits. "But I think being near someone who cares about you might help. Might quiet your mind."

He offers a soft smile, one laced with just enough vulnerability to make my chest ache. He gently tucks a piece of hair behind my ear, his fingers brushing the shell and sending a shiver down my spine.

"And honestly?" he adds with a quiet smile, "I'll take the excuse to hold you."

A tender warmth unfurls in my chest, melting me around the edges.

All the noise in my head, everything looming ahead, fades just a little. He's not offering promises he can't keep, or pretty lies to soothe me. Just this moment. Just him.

I swallow hard, my voice barely above a whisper.

"Okay." Swallowing to wet my suddenly dry throat, I point to his chest. "But you have to let me help you with that first."

"Deal."

I make Talon put on a shirt. I have willpower, but it seems to be stretched to its limit when it comes to him. And I was serious before. Now isn't the time for us to dive into something headfirst. There are too many unknowns still swirling around us.

I've finally admitted to myself that I have real feelings for Talon, but that may not be enough, and I don't want to do anything I'll regret later.

We return to my room and I get back into bed, sudden nerves making me hyperaware of every creak and rustle as I wait for Talon to join me.

Talon doesn't say anything at first. He just stands there for a few seconds, his figure hardly visible in the low light, before he crosses the room in a few quiet steps. He pulls back the covers on the far side of the bed and slides in beside me without hesitation, like he's done it a thousand times. Like this is where he's meant to be.

I shift to face him, my body still tense with everything I'm holding on to. But when his arm slips around my waist and draws me in—slow, unassuming, warm—I let myself go. Just a little.

He settles on his back and encourages me to rest my head on his shoulder. His body is solid and comforting against mine, the steady rhythm of his breathing centering me in a way I didn't know I needed.

"Is this okay?" he murmurs near my temple.

I nod into his chest, not trusting my voice. *More than okay.*

For a long time, neither of us speaks. But just like I feared, my thoughts start to drift from Ensley and Becks, to the dark cloud hanging over tomorrow, and finally to Talon and how I'm still conflicted about so many things I wish I wasn't.

And yet, beneath all that noise is one undeniable truth: I don't want to let this feeling go.

"Talon," I whisper, breaking the silence, "should we talk? About us, I mean."

"Shhh." His breath stirs the fine hairs at my temple, sending a soft shiver down my spine. "We will. When this is all over, there'll be time for that. But right now, this doesn't have to mean anything more than what it is. For now, it's okay to just be."

His words settle the storm inside me, give me permission to sink fully into his embrace without analyzing what it means or where it might lead. Just here. Just this.

He shifts slightly, then lifts his arm and begins rubbing slow, steady circles on my back, each one pulling me deeper into quiet, into calm.

We just lie there, wrapped in silence and each other. And maybe I don't fall asleep right away. But for the first time in hours, the storm in my mind settles. And eventually, sleep finds me.

Thirty-Five

CRUNCH.

An obnoxious noise yanks me from sleep, and when my eyes pop open I come face-to-face with Imogen. She's perched in a nearby armchair, legs casually propped on the edge of the bed, way too close to my face. A shiny red apple, already missing a bite, rests in her hand as she chews and stares at me like she's been waiting.

She swallows, then grins. "One day and you're already crawling into bed together. I'm impressed."

She takes another bite, somehow managing to grin around the chew.

"It's not what—" I start, but I'm cut off by a low groan from behind me.

Talon grumbles incoherently, then slings a bare arm around my waist and tugs me back against his chest.

Imogen raises a brow, smug. "You were saying?" she says, nodding at the arm currently wrapped around me like a vise.

I roll my eyes, more annoyed she's disturbed my peace than embarrassed.

That was the best sleep I've had since we entered the human world. All I want to do is soak in Talon's warmth and burrow back under the covers.

I'm about to tell her to shove off when the reason she was gone last night hits me.

Kerrim. Ensley.

She was supposed to try to find her.

Drowsiness vanishes, replaced by a spike of adrenaline. I bolt upright, Talon's arm slipping away as he startles awake beside me.

"Ensley?" I ask, and the grin slips from Imogen's face. She shakes her head, and it feels like a ball of lead drops into my stomach.

The bed dips as Talon slides out behind me.

"You tried, but it was always a long shot," he says, his voice rough with sleep.

I peek over my shoulder at him and immediately forget what I was going to say.

His dark hair is tousled, a little messy from sleep, and there's a faint crease on his cheek from the pillow. His eyes are still heavy-lidded, the stormy blue-gray softer in the morning light. Even half-awake, shirtless and stretching, he looks effortlessly lethal and unfairly good.

Wait, shirtless?

I quickly scan the bed and the floor.

Didn't I make him put on a shirt before getting in bed? Where did it go?

"We still have a solid plan in place," Talon says, and I give up on my search. Let's be honest. I can't be mad about a shirtless Talon.

"We'll get her back tonight and end this. Then we'll all go home." He says it with so much conviction, I almost believe it's true. He glances at me, then adds, "We should get going. Lots to do today."

"Understatement," I say, but nod in agreement.

He starts toward the adjoining door, but just before slipping through it, he turns back and gives me a slow once-over that has heat creeping up my neck.

"You look beautiful, by the way," he says.

The words hit me harder than I expect. I barely stop myself from smoothing my hair or pulling the blankets tighter. He says it so casually, like it's fact, not a compliment or a flirtation. Just something he needed me to know.

With that, he enters his room and shuts the door. Just before it closes, I catch a glimpse of Titus stepping out of the bathroom, a towel slung low around his hips. There's hardly a bruise left on his face, and the wound on his side is closed, already healed more than Talon's, even after nearly a week.

The reminder of Talon's slowed healing sobers me.

"You're good for him," Imogen says, breaking me out of my thoughts.

I turn to her, blinking in confusion.

Did Imogen really just say that? She's never hidden her disdain for me. Especially when it comes to her cousin.

"Don't look at me like that," she says, pushing out of the chair. "If you hurt him, I'm still going to break your face."

Ah. There she is.

She strolls toward the bathroom, announcing that I'm not allowed in until after her shower. But just before she shuts the door behind her, she pauses. "For real, though. Don't hurt him."

No sarcasm, no smirk, just honesty.

The door clicks shut, and the rush of running water fills the space.

I just sit there, staring at the bathroom door, unsure what to make of the last five minutes, or the strange ache settling in my chest. Because even if I don't mean to, sometimes I hurt the ones I care about.

I never meant to hurt Becks. And look how that turned out.

The last thing I want is to hurt Talon too. But what if I'm powerless to stop it?

"YOU'RE ready for the next phase," Talon says.

We've trained all morning, and boy, has he taken off the kid gloves. The moment we stepped into the warehouse, he shifted from attentive and supportive to strict and demanding. Even though it's exactly what I need—he's coaxed out three more hidden powers in just two hours—I think I might hate him just a little bit.

Then I remember how irresistibly kissable he looked right after waking up, and the look on his face when he told me I was beautiful this morning, and the negative emotions wither to dust.

"I'm scared to ask. What's the next phase?"

"There's still more magic in you we haven't touched yet," he says, crossing the space to stand in front of me. "But we've pulled out all the ones I think will be useful against Kerrim. Now we have to work on enhancing them."

I'm relieved we're done trying to dig for more magic. I didn't mind learning to manipulate faelight, or wind control, but we'd worked on compulsion, a power I honestly wish I didn't have. It's just as creepy and invasive to use on someone as it is to have it used against me.

"Enhancing them?" I ask, and he nods.

"But how?"

He reaches up, and for a second I think he's going to tuck my hair behind my ear or cradle my face, but his fingers find the curve of my neck. Then he gently lifts the chain of my necklace until the pendant is dangling in the air in front of me.

With everything that's happened, I'd almost forgotten about the lunacite pendant entirely.

"With this," he says, nodding toward the stone.

Immediately, I remember how it amplified Titus' powers back

when we were fleeing Grimspire Castle, and a shiver runs down my spine. I'm almost a little scared to use it.

"You already know it's a power amplifier," Talon explains. "Since your magic's coming easier now, if used properly, this will help you channel it more precisely. Stronger. Faster."

"Or blow something up," I mutter, trying to keep the unease out of my voice.

His mouth quirks. "We'll aim for stronger. Not explosive."

"I've been wearing it this whole time. Why hasn't it kicked in before now?"

"There has to be intention behind it," he explains. "The gem amplifies what you *choose* to channel, not just what's swirling inside you. Until now, you haven't tried to tap into it directly."

"So, like, do I have to be holding it? That's what Titus did."

Talon shakes his head and lets the pendant fall gently back against my chest.

"No, it's not about touch, it's about focus. The amplifier's already in contact with you. What matters now is intention. You have to reach for it, concentrate on your magic, and consciously draw power through the stone."

He steps back and moves behind me to give me space. "It's like opening a door from the inside. The gem won't do it for you, you have to want it."

I nod slowly, nerves churning in my stomach. I close my eyes, draw in a steady breath, and reach inward—past the noise, past the pressure—to the well of power I know is there.

I don't even touch the pendant. I don't have to. It's already against my skin, already humming like it's waiting.

I try to picture the power moving through it, like a lens sharpening a beam of light. Focusing, concentrating.

At first, nothing happens. Then—

A sharp crack snaps through the air nearby as I feel the shadows at the edge of the room ripple to life, slithering across the floor toward me like they've been summoned. My breath catches.

"Locklyn," Talon warns gently, "try to focus. Don't fight it, just direct it."

I try. I really do.

But the power pouring through me is like a firehose with no shutoff valve. The pendant grows warmer against my skin, glowing brighter, until—

BOOM.

A table ten feet away explodes in a cloud of splinters and dust, knocked clear across the room as a shockwave of faelight bursts out from me. One of the overhead lights sparks and dies.

Talon's there in an instant, wrapping his arms around me from behind, steadying me. "Hey. Breathe. You're okay. You're okay."

I clutch his forearm, chest heaving.

"That wasn't me," I whisper. "It was the pendant."

He shakes his head. "No. It was you. The pendant just revealed how much magic's in you now."

He turns me gently to face him, his expression serious but not afraid. "You have to learn to control it, or it'll control you. This is why we train."

After that initial explosion of power, I'm more cautious when drawing from the gem, learning to filter and direct the magic the way Talon explained. Titus and Imogen show up midday with all the weapons we brought with us through the portal and offer their help as well. Imogen, surprisingly, is full of useful tips, offering guidance with minimal sarcasm.

At one point, Talon pulls out the wavy-bladed dagger I'd insisted we leave behind, the one that looks like Shadow Striker, and shows me how to disarm someone wielding it. The demonstration is fast and jarring, and I quickly realize how critical that skill will be in the fight ahead.

By late afternoon, I'm finally starting to get the hang of it, or at least I think I am, and Talon calls it quits for the day, not wanting to drain me before tonight.

I know there's more to learn, more I could master with time.

But time is the one thing we've never had much of. My meeting with Kerrim is set for just after midnight, after the park closes to the public.

Throughout the day, we've received updates from the others. Kade and the Order have been working nonstop on plans to form a perimeter around the anticipated battle zone, partly to protect any humans who might accidentally stumble into the park after hours, and partly to keep our fight hidden from the public. Using both magic from some of their creature members, as well as brute force, they're determined to shield the city from the chaos to come.

The Order is also preparing for a confrontation with whatever forces Kerrim shows up with. Even though we told him to come alone and bring Ensley, no one believes he'll actually follow those terms. Just like we won't.

The heads of the different chapters, along with Becks, are supposed to arrive any minute now so we can review the plan one last time and make sure we're all on the same page.

As we wait, a knot begins to form in my stomach, the kind that tightens with every tick of the clock, every rustle of wind outside the warehouse. I try to sit still, to breathe through it, but the anticipation gnaws at me like a living thing.

Talon and Imogen are discussing strategy across the room, and Titus is running through a silent, fluid sequence with his twin blades, each movement precise and deadly, the controlled violence of it somehow making me more anxious, not less.

My knee bounces uncontrollably. I press my palm flat against it, trying to force the nerves into submission. But it's like my body knows what's coming, even if my mind keeps trying to play it cool.

We're so close now. Too close.

Every second that passes brings us nearer to midnight, nearer to Kerrim, nearer to whatever this night is going to become.

Footsteps crunch outside the warehouse, and I shoot to my feet before I even realize I've moved.

The door creaks open, and Becks steps inside.

He looks exhausted, his shoulders stiff, dark circles smudged beneath his eyes, making me wonder if he slept at all last night. But he's here. That alone makes the knot loosen inside my chest.

"Hey," he says when he spots me, his voice quieter than usual.

"Hey," I echo, unsure what else to say. There's so much between us, so much we've left unsaid, but tonight none of it seems to matter as much as what lies ahead.

He glances around the cavernous room. "Am I the first?"

I nod. "Yeah. Kade and the others should be here soon. I thought you'd be coming with them actually."

"I left the headquarters before them. I wanted a little time to think." He hesitates, then walks toward me, hands in his pockets. "Mind if we talk for a minute . . . before it all starts?"

"Yeah, I'd like that," I say, and mean it, even though I'm not even sure what I'm going to say to him. I don't know what I could say to make any of this easier or better, but at the least, I can give him the truth.

Becks walks out of the warehouse for privacy, and when I glance over my shoulder before following, I find Talon's gaze locked on me. I'm not looking for his permission. I know I don't need it. But there's still a subtle release of tension in my chest when he gives me a small nod. I think it's his way of saying he understands. It's one of the things I appreciate most about him. His quiet, unwavering faith in me.

After I shove through the door, I scan the area and find Becks sitting on the top of a rotting picnic table in a small area off to the side, probably once a break spot for employees back when this was a working warehouse.

I feel shy and a little awkward as I walk up to him. It's almost like being with a stranger, which is new. Over the years, Becks has been a lot to me, but never a stranger. Being around him, even when we fought, never felt like this, and I don't like it.

I don't know how to start, but thankfully, Becks speaks first.

"Whatever happens from here, and whatever's happened in the

past, I want you to know that I love you. I have for years. Probably from the first moment you punched that bully in the nose for making my sister cry, you've had me completely captivated. I wanted to be near you, even if it was just to be in your orbit, because to me you've always been the most brilliant, fierce, and impossible girl I've ever known."

My throat tightens. Why does he have to say something like that now? When everything is already so tangled?

I blink back the sudden sting in my eyes and fold my arms. Not because I'm angry, but because I'm trying to hold myself together. I'm still struggling to find my words, but Becks isn't done wrecking me yet.

He stands and walks toward me, stopping just within arm's reach. From this distance, I can see the sheen in his green eyes and know he's struggling just as much as I am. But he pushes through and says, "And it's not just that I love you—which I do, and will until the day I die—but that I'm *in love* with you. And I thought you were too. Help me understand," he pleads softly.

I take in a shaky breath, hoping it steadies me and buys me a few seconds, because how am I supposed to explain something to him that I don't understand myself?

Becks is perfect. He always saw the best in me, even when I was at my worst, never asked me to be anything more than I was, and made me feel safe in a world that rarely is. He knows me better than anyone, makes me laugh when I need it most, and held pieces of me together when I felt like I was falling apart. I was in love with him, and that love was strong. No one will ever be able to convince me otherwise. But even as much as he's been my safe harbor, I'm starting to wonder if we were meant to stay tethered forever. No matter how perfect he is . . . maybe we're just not perfect for each other.

"I don't know that I have the answers you're looking for," I confess, my voice barely above a whisper. "I love you too, Becks. I always will. You're a part of me that I'll never let go."

His eyes spark with hope. Until I pause.

"But," he prompts, his expression tightening like he's bracing for impact.

"Something's changed. Or maybe I've changed. I just don't know."

"Are you trying to say that you love me," he says slowly, each word dragging out like it physically hurts him to speak, "but you're not in love with me anymore?"

"No, that's not it," I say quickly, my heart lurching as I take a small step forward, hands twisting together. "I don't think that's completely true."

It would be easier to nod and let him believe that. To give him a clean break. But that would be a lie, and Becks deserves the truth, even if it hurts.

"It's not as simple as that," I admit, forcing myself to meet his gaze. "It's . . ."

"Talon," he finishes for me, the name a quiet exhale that seems to deflate him.

"I didn't lie to you before. At least, not intentionally. My feelings for Talon, they snuck up on me. And they're more powerful than I ever expected."

I see it hit him like a physical blow. His shoulders drop, and for a second he looks like he might shatter.

Becks exhales slowly, his gaze dropping to the ground for a long moment before he looks back up at me. The pain in his eyes is raw, but there's no malice there. Only love, steady and unwavering.

"I won't pretend this doesn't hurt," he says, his voice quiet but sure. "And I'm not going to tell you I'm okay with it, because I'm not. But I meant what I said, Locklyn. I love you. That doesn't go away overnight."

He takes a small step back, like he needs to give me space even if it's the last thing he wants.

"If this thing with Talon doesn't work out, if somewhere down the line you realize he wasn't the one after all—just know

I'm still here. I don't know if that makes me an idiot or just someone who's never stopped believing in us. But either way, I'll be waiting."

A lump rises in my throat. I take a slow step toward him, placing my hand lightly over his heart.

"Becks, I don't want that for you," I say softly, my voice thick. "I know how much it hurts to be on the other side of waiting. To be left wondering if someone's going to choose you. We lived that, remember? When we had to hide what we were because of your title. Because loving me wasn't fair to you, not really."

His jaw tightens, but he doesn't pull away.

"You deserve someone who chooses you without hesitation. Who doesn't make you wait or wonder or hurt. That's what I want for myself, and that's also what I want for you."

I blink fast, willing the sting in my eyes to fade.

"I will always love you, Becks. That's never going to change. But don't wait for me. Live your life. Be happy. You deserve that. You always have."

Becks lets out a long breath, his eyes searching mine like he's memorizing every detail. Then, with a half shrug and the kind of crooked smile that doesn't quite reach his eyes, he says, "I hear you. I do. But I've never been great at letting go of things that matter."

I open my mouth to argue, but he holds up a hand.

"I'm not saying I'll wait forever, Locklyn. Just . . . don't expect me to move on tomorrow. Not when there's still a chance. Not when I've spent years loving you." His lips twitch into a faint smile. "Besides, we've got to survive the next twenty-four hours first. If one of us gets turned into creature chow, this whole conversation's going to feel pretty pointless."

A surprised laugh escapes me, and some of the tightness in my chest eases.

He grins, softer now. "Go save the world. At least this one. I'll try to keep the dramatic rescues to a minimum this time."

Thirty-Six

WHEN WE RE-ENTER THE WAREHOUSE, I wouldn't say things are completely resolved with Becks, but I feel better knowing I haven't lost him. At least not fully. Becks is a part of me, and if I'd lost him—truly lost his friendship and presence in my life, which was a real possibility—it would have shattered me. Perhaps beyond repair. And although we have no guarantees about what comes next, at least we're not carrying the weight of unspoken words into the night ahead.

The moment I walk back through the door, I search for Talon, finding him in the far corner, seated beneath one of the flickering lights, sharpening a blade with slow, steady strokes. The rhythmic scrape of metal against stone ceases the moment his gaze finds mine. For a beat, neither of us moves. Then he sets the weapon down and quiet tenderness creeps into his eyes. I see the question there—*Are you okay?*—but he doesn't ask. He just stands and strides toward me.

Out of the corner of my eye, I catch Becks peel off and head toward Titus on the other side of the open room. Talon casts a brief look his way before meeting my eyes again. When he reaches me, his hand brushes lightly against mine in a barely-there touch, but it centers me more than anything else could.

"You good?" he murmurs, voice low.

I manage a smirk, though it wobbles at the edges. "Define good."

Talon huffs a quiet breath that's almost a laugh, but his thumb brushes mine again, silently reminding me I'm not alone in this.

Behind Talon, I catch Becks watching the two of us, but he quickly looks away when my gaze connects with his. Talon glances over his shoulder and then back at me, but he doesn't ask how it went with Becks. He's letting me decide what I want to share, and I appreciate that.

"It was a hard conversation, but we're all right. Or we will be, eventually," I say with a sad smile.

"You need to give yourself some grace. You don't have to make any big decisions right now. You'll have time for that later," he says, once again giving me the space I need without having to ask for it.

There's no guarantee I *will* have time, but even so, I'm not sure I'll need it.

I open my mouth to tell him that, but the moment is cut short when Kade and the leaders of the Order step through the warehouse doors. Kade heads straight for me, while the others make their way to the back meeting area where we gathered before. Tobias looks jumpy, his gaze scanning the space, no doubt searching for Imogen, as he follows the others. I can't help but get a little satisfaction at his discomfort.

"So," Kade says as he approaches, arms folding across his chest. His expression is all business. "You ready?"

A nervous laugh escapes before I can stop it, and Kade's brow tightens.

"She's ready," Talon answers before I can speak, his voice steady and sure.

It's not the full truth, but the confidence in his tone wraps around me like armor. And for now, that's enough.

"Good." Kade gives a sharp nod and then tips his head toward the back. "Let's go compare notes. It's time we took this bastard down."

THE MEETING with the Order leaders lasts a couple of hours. I listen closely, though I don't contribute much. Strategy isn't exactly my forte, and my role in this mission is straightforward: face off against Kerrim and do whatever it takes to get Shadow Striker back. Still, it's important I understand what everyone else will be doing, if only for my own peace of mind.

Becks and Titus have been tasked with getting Ensley away from Kerrim and to safety. Imogen and Talon are my direct backup, along with Kade and a few of his most trusted fighters. They'll be hidden near the open field where I'm supposed to meet Kerrim. The same place the portal from the creature world first opened on that fateful night.

The rest of the Order will focus on concealing the battle from the human world. Their first mandate is to protect humanity from supernatural threats, and in their minds that includes keeping the public unaware. If they're not managing illusions and containment, they'll be fighting whatever forces Kerrim brings with him.

The meeting breaks a few hours before midnight, final plans made, final words spoken. There's nothing left but the waiting.

Becks gives me a hug, holding me tightly and whispering in my ear that he believes in me, precious words I've been waiting to hear from him for so long, and now I wonder if they'll be the last I ever hear from him. He gives me a lingering look before leaving with Titus to collect their weapons and get into their positions in the park.

The warehouse empties out slowly after that, voices fading as everyone prepares in their own way for what's coming.

I linger near the table, my hands resting flat on the cool metal. My nerves buzz like static, and for a moment I close my eyes just to steady my breathing. When I open them again, Talon is still there, leaning against the far wall, arms folded, watching me like I'm the only thing in the room worth looking at.

When our eyes meet, he pushes off the wall and walks over.

"Come with me?" he says quietly.

I nod.

We step outside into the warm night air. The city hums in the distance. Distant traffic, a car alarm somewhere far off, the faint thump of bass from a rooftop party. But here, under the stretch of stars overhead, it's just us.

Talon leads me to a small unkempt park behind the warehouse. It's secluded, more paved than grassed, but the kind of place where the world feels like it pauses for just a little while. We find a grouping of trees and sit with our backs against the same trunk, shoulders brushing.

For a while, neither of us says anything. The silence isn't awkward. It's safe.

Then he reaches for my hand, his fingers brushing lightly over my knuckles before he laces them through mine. I let him. I need the warmth.

"You good?" he asks softly.

He's been asking me that a lot today, but I can't say that I mind.

"No," I whisper. "But I'm here."

He gives a slight nod, his thumb stroking gently along the side of my hand. "That's enough."

I tilt my head toward him, studying his profile in the half-light. His jaw is tight, his eyes full of things he isn't saying. For once, I don't press. I just lean my head against his shoulder and close my eyes.

He adjusts, resting his chin lightly on top of my head.

"I keep thinking about what happens after this," I say. "If there is an after."

"There is," he replies, steady and sure.

"How can you be so confident?"

"Because I have to be." He shifts slightly so he can look at me. "For you."

A fragile place inside me cracks open at those words.

"I'm not ready for this fight," I admit. "For everything I could lose."

He presses his forehead gently to mine. "Then don't think about the fight. Not yet. Just take this moment. Take me."

I blink hard, tears stinging at the edges of my eyes. "I don't want to go into this afraid."

"You won't," he promises. "You'll go in fierce. Because that's who you are, Freckles."

I nod, and he pulls me closer, wrapping an arm around my shoulders as I curl into him.

We sit there for what feels like both seconds and forever, wrapped in each other and the kind of quiet that doesn't need words. For this one moment, I'm not a weapon. I'm not a girl facing impossible odds. I'm just Locklyn. And he's just Talon.

And that's enough.

WHEN WE RETURN to the warehouse, I don't exactly feel peaceful, but as close to it as possible considering the circumstance. The only ones still here are Imogen, Kade, and his men. Ares is among them. He and another fae have been tasked with glamouring my backup team to keep them invisible so they can remain close without being seen.

As I enter, Ares gives me a small smile and a wave, but it's the look in his eyes that catches me, like he pities me, like he thinks I'm going to lose. I appreciate that he cares enough to look concerned at all, but the doubt in his eyes lands like a stone in my stomach.

I don't need pity. I need belief. I'm trying hard enough to hold on to my own.

"Time to go," Kade says with a grim look. We all go outside, where a set of black SUVs are waiting to take us to the edge of Central Park. The drive is silent, each of us lost in our own thoughts, our own fears. Talon sits beside me, close enough that our shoulders touch, but neither of us speaks. It's not until the vehicle slows near the 72nd Street entrance that he reaches over, quietly taking my hand in his.

We're dropped off near the edge of the park under the cover of darkness. A breeze stirs the leaves above us, and somewhere in the distance, a siren wails. The city keeps moving, oblivious to the storm building in its heart.

I'm supposed to go on my own from here, but Talon tells the others to hang back and that he's going to walk me a little farther. I'm surprised when no one argues with him.

I know there are Order members scattered all over this area, keeping humans away and doing what needs to be done to magically prep for later, but I don't see a single other soul as Talon and I walk through the trees together. The deeper we go, the more the noise of the city fades, replaced by the soft rustle of leaves and the chirp of insects. Eventually, we reach the edge of the tree line of the open field where I'm supposed to meet Kerrim.

This is as far as Talon can go.

I take a deep breath to ground myself, summoning the courage I need to take the next step. I remind myself of everything I've already overcome and all the ways I've proven my strength. I tell myself I can do this. Not because I'm magically juiced, but because I'm a fighter at my core. Always have been. Always will be. That's what will give me the edge over Kerrim. That's what's going to get me, and the ones I love and care about, out of this alive.

I take a step toward the open field, my boot catching the edge of a silver moonbeam, but before I can go any farther, Talon's hand clamps around mine. In one swift motion, he pulls me back into the shadows and spins me to face him, pressing me gently, but firmly, against the rough bark of a nearby tree.

I open my mouth to ask what's wrong, but the words never leave my lips.

Because his are already on mine.

He kisses me like the world might end tonight and this is the last chance he'll ever get. His hands slide up my sides; his mouth claims mine in deep, urgent strokes. There's nothing tentative about it. It's all heat and hunger, frustration and fear, need and knowing.

My fingers find the front of his shirt and then climb up his chest and wrap around his neck, pulling him closer until there's no space left between us. His tongue brushes mine, and I feel the air rush from my lungs like he's pulled it with that single touch.

When we finally break apart, we're both panting as we stare at each other with a mix of hunger and awe.

In the dim light, I catch something wild in his eyes, like shards of ice catching fire, splintering through the blue-gray.

"I needed to do that," he says, his voice hoarse and low. "For me."

That probably shouldn't make sense, but it does.

Reaching up, he brushes his thumb gently across my cheek, his eyes searching my face like he's trying to memorize every detail, every line, every breath.

"I love you," he says, and my heart stutters in my chest.

This isn't an implication or a half confession. It's real. Clear. Undeniable. And it makes something inside me bloom with joy.

A smile breaks across my face, wide and uncontrollable.

"I—" I start to say, but he silences me with another kiss. It's swift but sure, and it still leaves me breathless.

Kissing Talon is addictive, and something I desperately hope I get the opportunity to get used to.

When he pulls back, his voice is low, steady. "You can tell me after."

Will there even be an after? What if this is the only chance I'll ever get to tell him how I truly feel, and I let it slip by?

"There will be an after, I promise," he says, and the words are so in tune with my thoughts that I blink at him in surprise.

"Can you read minds?" I ask, half joking, with genuine curiosity. Maybe it's another hidden power I didn't know he had.

He chuckles softly, low and warm as he brushes a strand of hair behind my ear. Then he takes a step back, and with it, the warmth of his body leaves mine, making the space between us feel colder.

"It's just written all over your face," he says with a small smile.

I take in a breath, worry rising again. "But Talon . . . we don't know for sure what's going to happen out there."

His expression softens as he closes the distance between us again, reaching out to cradle my cheek. "You don't need to say it, because I already know, Freckles. I've just been waiting for you to figure it out. I want to wait to hear it from those beautiful lips when this is all behind us. When your head is clear and we can finally have the beginning we always should've had. No fear. No battles looming. Just us."

My throat tightens, and I nod, pressing my hand over his where it still rests on my cheek. I want that too.

He gives me one final look, intense and unwavering. Then slowly lets his hand fall away.

I square my shoulders, forcing my feet to move. "Okay. It's time."

"Come back to me," he orders, and I nod.

"I will."

The look he gives me is one of pride. One that gives me the extra boost I need, because I can tell Talon really does believe in me. Believes I'll defeat Kerrim and come back to him.

Talon steps back into the shadows, his presence still wrapped around me like a second skin as I turn and walk toward the open field.

The night air is cool, the grass damp beneath my boots as I cross into the clearing where everything changes.

Where it ends . . . or begins.

Thirty-Seven

I STEP into the center of the clearing, my feet barely making a sound against the damp earth. Trees stand sentinel on all sides, forming a wide, shadow-draped circle that feels more like an arena than a natural grove. Beyond the treetops, the tallest skyscrapers of Manhattan rise like silent watchers, their spires piercing the night sky with cold, indifferent grace.

The stillness here is oppressive. It's too still for Central Park. No rustle of wind. No distant hum of traffic. Just the pounding of my own heartbeat and the whisper of my boots in the grass.

I'm early. That was the plan: to arrive first, find my footing, and gather myself so that I'm ready when I face him.

But the silence doesn't last.

Without warning, the air shifts, charged with a pulse of magic that raises goosebumps along my arms and neck. My breath catches as a ripple distorts the air across from me. Then, like a nightmare stepping through a veil, Kerrim appears.

Not approaching. Not emerging. Just there, ten paces in front of me, his presence hitting like a cold gust of wind to the chest.

He looks the same. And yet . . . not.

The man I once knew is still there: sharply dressed, peppered hair slicked back, dark eyes behind dark-rimmed glasses. But something about him has shifted. His frame seems broader, as if the magic swelling inside him has reshaped him to better contain it. His skin carries an unnatural sheen, catching the moonlight in a way that makes him look almost otherworldly. And clenched in one hand, Shadow Striker.

I've known Kerrim for years. I trusted him. The man standing before me now feels like a stranger. A very dangerous one.

He was always power hungry, that much I knew. It's what drove him to steal Shadow Striker and bring it to the human world. But this? This feels like more than ambition. The madness in his eyes, the way he moves, the shift in his presence. I start to wonder if the old rumors about the dagger warping the mind of its wielder are true—the more power it gives, the more it takes in return.

A slow smile curves Kerrim's lips as he tilts his head, eyes glinting like cut glass in the moonlight.

"Well," he says, voice smooth and familiar; there's a razor's edge to it now that wasn't there before. "You always were the punctual one."

"Actually, you're early," I say, my tone flat, wary.

"Am I?" he replies, deceptively mild. His gaze sweeps over me, calm and calculated, as if he's already figured out the entire game and is simply waiting for me to realize it too. "Funny, I thought I was late to your little ambush."

My stomach tightens.

"Don't look so surprised," he continues, taking a measured step forward. "You think I didn't know what you were planning? That your little friends could sneak around undetected in my city?" He shakes his head. "No, Locklyn. I'm afraid they're already being handled."

A chill skitters down my spine, but I can't help the instinctive glance I cast toward the tree line where I know Talon is hidden.

"Oh, I wouldn't expect any help from there," Kerrim says, making a low *tsk*ing sound. "You see, I've been picking up some very powerful allies since I arrived in this world. And with Shadow Striker, I've developed some rather interesting magic."

He smiles, cold and triumphant. "Right now, all anyone sees is you, standing here alone, waiting for a confrontation to begin. But really, it'll be over before they even realize it's started."

I take a step back, conceding ground to keep distance between us. "Where's Ensley?" I ask, panic rising fast in my chest, sharp, urgent, impossible to hold back any longer.

"She's around," he says casually, lifting a hand to gesture toward the darkness beyond the clearing.

"You were supposed to bring her here."

"And you were supposed to come alone," he growls, his voice low and dangerous.

His grip tightens around Shadow Striker, and I don't miss the way his stance shifts, like he's ready to strike.

"Okay, fine. So we both broke the rules," I say quickly, trying to buy myself some time. At least long enough to figure out where he's keeping Ensley. "Just bring her here and we can move forward as planned."

He cocks his head in that birdlike way, a subtle reminder of the hawk shifter he is, but tonight there's a wildness under the surface. A feral wrongness that makes my insides twist.

"And why would I do that," he says, his voice silk over steel, "when I already have what I came here for? You."

A chill races down my spine, but I hold my ground, forcing myself not to flinch beneath his twisted smile. His eyes gleam with cold satisfaction as he takes a slow step forward, Shadow Striker in his grip.

"You still don't get it, do you?" he says, voice almost pitying. "Oh, Locklyn, don't you realize? You didn't come here to surrender . . . but to die."

Before I can form a response, the night splits open with a thunderous boom. A flash of blue light streaks across the sky. Not above the city, but within the magical dome the Order cast to shield the park, similar to the one that Kerrim placed over the ruins for the final Chaos trial. The barrier flares in reaction, its surface shimmering like heat waves on asphalt.

A split second later, a ripple of crackling magic rolls through the dome, slamming into the earth with a low, vibrating thrum that rattles in my bones. The ground quakes beneath my feet.

Whatever just exploded, it happened inside the barrier.

Inside the battlefield.

Another explosion, closer this time.

My breath catches.

Kerrim smiles, slow and satisfied, as the sky flares again with unnatural light.

"Ah," he says, almost lazily, "there it is."

He lifts his head slightly, listening as another detonation shakes the night air, this time laced with screams. Creature and human alike.

With a sickening sensation, I know exactly what's happened. The Order is under attack. And from the sound of it, they never saw it coming.

"Sounds like your little trap just snapped shut," he murmurs, gaze locked on me. "Only problem is, you're the one caught inside."

Even though I know he can't see me, I cast a glance in Talon's direction again, desperately wishing I could give the signal to let him and the others know I need backup. If he believes I'm still just standing in the field, waiting for Kerrim to arrive, he won't emerge from the tree line, not even if our allies are under attack elsewhere in the park.

It's what we agreed on. No interference unless I gave the signal. Or my life was in danger.

For the briefest moment, there's a shift in Kerrim's expression, muting the menace in his eyes and making him resemble the version of himself I once knew and trusted.

"I wish it didn't have to be this way," he says quietly, and for a moment I almost believe the emotion behind his words. "But as long as you're alive, the dagger won't truly be mine. Shadow Striker resists me because of you. You're its wielder, and until that bond is severed, it'll never give me everything I need."

His expression hardens once more, all warmth retreating like a shadow at sunrise.

"You were always strong, Locklyn. But strength won't save you now."

And without warning, he attacks.

Thirty-Eight

TALON

SOMETHING'S WRONG.

That much is clear from the attacks rattling the park, but it's more than that. A deeper disturbance is brewing.

A low hum beneath my skin, a gnawing pressure I can't shake.

I stand in the shadows of the trees, eyes locked on Locklyn as she stands in the clearing. I haven't let her out of my sight for even a second since she stepped away from me. Her shoulders are tense, her chin lifted in quiet defiance, but the way she holds herself—too rigid, too controlled—feels unnatural. Not like her.

She fidgets when she's nervous. Shifts her weight, cracks jokes under pressure, bites her lip when she's deep in thought. But this version of her . . . she's unnervingly calm. *Like someone playing the part of Locklyn instead of being her.*

If I know anything, I know Locklyn. Every breath, every flicker of emotion that flashes in her warm brown eyes. I've studied her in battle, in quiet moments, in the heat of conflict. And this . . . this isn't her.

Every instinct I've honed over my lifetime is telling me it's not right.

A bead of sweat rolls down my spine, cold and sharp. My pulse hammers in my ears, steady and relentless, as if my own body is trying to warn me of something I can't see.

I glance to the side. Imogen's standing nearby, arms crossed, her usual mask of cool calculation in place, but there's a furrow between her brows that wasn't there a few minutes ago. Kade, Ares, and the others are waiting too, coiled like predators ready to pounce, waiting for the signal.

Waiting for her.

The plan was simple. We don't move until Locklyn gives the signal. But standing here, every instinct in me is screaming that we've made a mistake. That *I* have.

The connection between us, whether forged through raw emotion or the tether created through Shadow Striker's magic that shouldn't exist but does, is pulling tight. A subtle ache in my chest like a rubber band being stretched too far.

I scan the tree line again, tension crawling down my spine. Still no sign of Kerrim, or Ensley, when it's clear his forces are already here, which is the biggest red flag of all.

He's late. Or early. Or already here. And whatever trap he's set, I fear she's already stepped into it.

Where the hell is he?

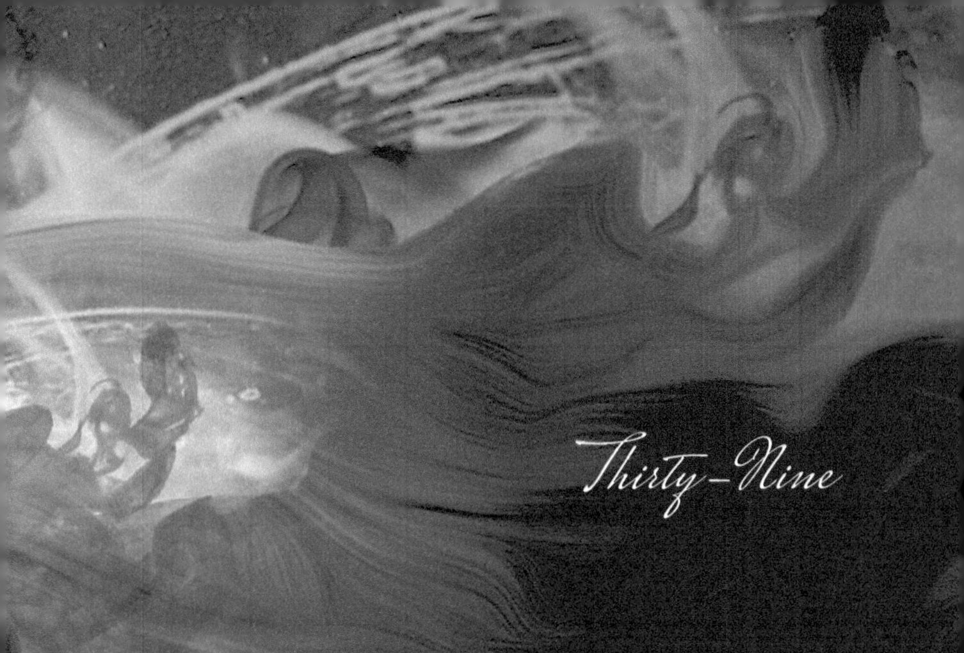

Thirty-Nine

I SHOULD HAVE BEEN PREPARED for Kerrim's attack, but I don't get my faelight shield up fast enough and take a searing bolt of magic straight to the ribs.

The impact knocks the wind from me and launches me through the air. I slam to the ground, skidding across dirt and leaves before coming to a jarring stop, every breath a struggle as pain radiates through my ribs.

Kerrim strides toward me and halts. His eyes narrow, glinting with sudden, sharp confusion.

"Well, well," he says slowly, as if tasting the realization on his tongue. "Magic?"

His gaze drops to my hands, still faintly glowing with residual faelight. "You're not supposed to have magic."

The shock is fleeting. His expression hardens. "Doesn't matter. You can light up like a star for all I care. The dagger won't be mine until you're out of the picture." He lifts Shadow Striker, its black blade humming with energy. "Let's not drag this out."

I force myself to my feet, breath ragged, every nerve on fire. My own magic crackles at my fingertips, unsteady but ready. Drawing on the amplification powers of my pendant like Talon taught me, I shove my hand out and send a spear of shadow straight at him. He dodges, but not fast enough. It clips his shoulder, spinning him half a step.

He recovers, and suddenly he's right in front of me, swinging the dagger in a downward arc. I throw up my shield just in time. The impact flares white-hot, and pain lances through my arms as I'm driven back.

"Impressive," he sneers, circling me like a predator. "But regardless of what magic you must have inherited from the former wielder, it won't be enough. I have more."

I stretch a hand to the side and the shadows nearby twitch, then surge. They slither across the ground like living tendrils, twisting into jagged shapes that rise and lash in a wide arc, carving deep grooves into the dirt at my feet. One coils toward Kerrim's boot before dissipating in a sharp crack of energy.

"You sure about that?" I ask, my voice low and steady.

Then I lunge.

Our magic collides midair, clashing torrents of power that explode between us with a thunderclap. The shockwave sends both of us flying in opposite directions.

I hit the ground hard, coughing, but scramble to my feet.

Kerrim is already on the move again, faster than I remember, stronger than I expected. I duck under a swipe of his blade and drive a burst of fire into his chest at close range. He grunts, stumbling, smoke curling off his jacket.

"You're better than I gave you credit for," he snarls, eyes gleaming. "But it won't save you."

We clash again—weapons, fists, magic—locked in a brutal rhythm. I can feel myself tiring, every attack slower, every dodge narrower. I don't even have an opportunity to try to disarm Kerrim, because I'm fighting for my life. Using this much magic is tiring me faster than I expected.

I'm holding my own. But just barely.

And he knows it.

He grins, the expression wild and sharp, and says, "Let's see how long you can last."

Forty
TALON

ANOTHER MAGICAL EXPLOSION shudders through the earth beneath my boots, shaking branches overhead. The containment dome the Order cast over the park keeps the battles veiled, but that much magic can't be fully muffled. New York has to be feeling these aftershocks. Probably writing them off as tremors. In this case, ignorance really is bliss.

But I can't afford ignorance.

Not with her out there.

Imogen shifts beside me, eyes narrowing on the field.

"She's just standing there," she mutters. "Not moving. Not reacting. That's not like her."

I nod once, fists clenched. "It's not her. Or . . . not entirely." As soon as the words leave my mouth, I know it's not just paranoia.

Her gaze cuts to mine, sharp with realization. "You think it's a glamour?"

"Or an illusion," I say, voice low. "Either way, something's wrong. That version of her isn't real."

My fists clench at my sides. We agreed, no one moves until we get the signal.

But this? This is Kerrim rewriting the rules.

Whatever game he's playing, she's already on the board.

A pulse surges through me. Sharp, cold, electric. Like my veins are filling with ice instead of blood. My breath hitches, and I swear the air around me cracks with the force of it. Frost forms at my feet, webbing across the damp earth in thin tendrils.

Imogen notices.

Her head jerks toward me, her expression morphing from suspicion to outright shock. "What on earth—?"

I can't answer. I'm too busy fighting to stay in control. My teeth clench hard enough my jaw aches, but the power inside me—my creature—surges to the surface, wild and unrestrained.

My vision sharpens, the world gleaming like ice in sunlight, every detail glittering with a deadly clarity.

It's never happened like this before. Not in all my years of suppressing what I am. But a wild instinct, a primal force, is howling that she needs me now.

I can't hold it back. I don't want to hold it back.

"Talon," Imogen hisses, taking a step back from the sudden chill radiating off me. "What are you doing?"

The frost creeps up the trees, spreading along bark and branches like the forest itself is freezing in place. My heart pounds hard against my ribs, the ache in my chest tightening unbearably.

"She's in trouble," I grind out, voice barely more than a growl.

Imogen's eyes narrow, scanning the field again. "She hasn't signaled."

"She can't," I snap, the words tearing from me. I take a step forward, my breath visible in the night air.

I don't wait for permission, or backup. I move. Fast, silent, barely a whisper on the wind as I break from cover and head for the clearing.

Frost blooms in my wake, trailing behind me in jagged, shimmering paths as my body transforms into its other form.

I'm coming, Freckles. Hold on.

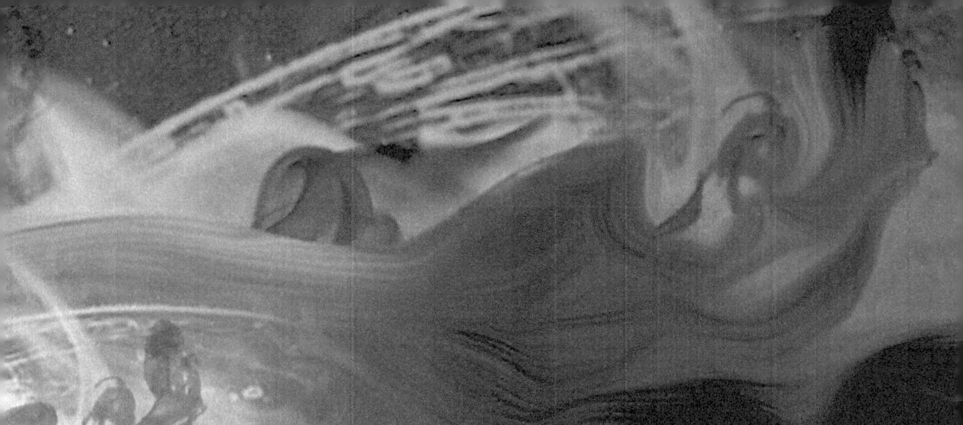

Forty-One

SWEAT SLICKS my hair to my face, running in rivulets down my back as I block another of Kerrim's relentless attacks. My arms tremble, nearly too weak to lift, let alone fend him off for much longer. Every muscle burns, screaming at me to stop, but I can't stop. I won't.

I'm losing. I'm going to lose.

And there's nothing I can do about it, because with every strike Kerrim seems to grow stronger, his magic crackling and pulsing brighter, while mine flickers like a dying flame, slipping through my grasp no matter how tightly I try to hold on to it or how much I pull on the power from the pendant stone.

Digging as deep as I can, I summon a shadow whip and crack it at him with the last of my strength. It snaps through the air, but the blow is so weak it barely grazes his side. He doesn't even flinch. Instead, Kerrim smiles a sharp, unhinged grin that twists my insides into knots.

He's not just doing this because he has to. He's going to enjoy burying Shadow Striker in my gut. Going to savor twisting the blade and watching the light drain from my eyes as he finally takes everything for himself.

Kerrim thrusts his hands forward, a blast of wind slamming

into me with bone-shattering force. My feet leave the ground as I'm flung backward, flailing through the air before I slam into the earth like a ragdoll, the impact knocking the air from my lungs.

A groan slips from me as I roll over, my side screaming in protest. Sharp, stabbing pain radiates through my ribs, stealing my breath, leaving me gasping, dizzy.

I try to rise. I have to rise. But my body refuses, my limbs dead weight. My magic lies dormant, hollow and unreachable, like it's slipped beyond my grasp.

I stare up at the sky, the moon haloed by the faint shimmer of the Order's containment dome, tears filling my eyes.

This is it. I'm going to die.

Both worlds—human and creature—are going to pay the price because I wasn't good enough. Wasn't strong enough.

A shiver racks through me, sharp and cold, as if the very thought is siphoning the last of my strength. My heart squeezes painfully, a hollow ache where hope should be.

I hope Becks, Ensley, and the others make it back without me. That they get home and stay safe, for as long as possible. And this mess I've dragged them into doesn't swallow them whole.

And Talon . . .

A single tear spills down the side of my face, cutting a hot path across my chilled skin.

I'll never get the chance to say what I should have said before I walked into this fight.

That I love him.

I catch a blur of movement out of the corner of my eye, Kerrim, I think, coming to finish me off.

My breath stutters. I squeeze my eyes shut, not ready to see the end coming, when a roar splits the night. Deep, guttural, ancient. The beastly cry rattles my bones, shaking loose every thought except one: danger.

A pulse of magic surges in the air, sharp and biting, like winter itself has descended on the park, and my eyes snap back open. The temperature plummets so fast my breath fogs in front of me, frost crackling in the grass as the air crystallizes.

A massive form bursts from the tree line in a blur of silver and white, a streak of frost spiraling in its wake. Wings unfurl—wide, powerful, and shimmering like fractured ice in the moonlight. Its scales are a swirling blend of silver, blue, and white that gleams like a storm trapped in crystal. A blast of freezing air explodes from its terrifying jaws, a shockwave of cold so intense the moisture in the air crackles into snowflakes.

Kerrim, caught in the blast, is hurled across the clearing, spinning wildly out of control over the frost-slick grass before slamming into a tree with a sickening thud.

The creature turns, chest heaving, breath curling out in shimmering plumes. He's *huge*, easily twice the size of any dragon I've ever heard of, let alone seen.

My heart stutters, frozen by fear and something else: recognition.

Then I see them.

Those eyes.

Blue-gray, sharp as shattered glass, familiar, and locked on me like I'm the only thing in the world that matters.

Impossible.

"Talon?" I breathe, my voice barely a whisper as I somehow manage to struggle to a sitting position.

The dragon—Talon—locks eyes with me, a promise burning in that feral gaze.

He's an ice dragon, the rarest of all shifters, a myth in the creature world, the last of which was said to have been hunted out of existence hundreds of years ago by the fire-breathing dragons because their power was so great they were seen as a threat to the rest of the clans.

But clearly he's no myth.

And he's here for me.

Frost blooms across the ground with every step he takes

toward me, the earth cracking beneath the weight of his claws. Every breath he takes exhales a ghostly mist, curling around him like a living thing.

A shudder runs through me, sharp and disorienting, as I stare up at him, at the impossible creature he's become. My pulse pounds in my ears, and for a moment the weight of what I'm seeing crushes everything else. My mind can't quite keep up. It's too much. Too impossible. Too . . . Talon.

The truth clicks into place, sharp and searing, leaving me breathless.

A hundred questions claw at the edges of my mind, but as I stare up at the impossible creature before me, his scales catching the moonlight like shards of glass and his breath curling in the air like a storm contained, it all makes sense.

The careful control. The restraint. The secrets and misdirection.

He's been hiding this his whole life. Not just from me, but from everyone.

Because being an ice dragon, a creature of legend, of power so rare it was hunted to extinction, means he's always been a target. A threat.

A secret that could cost him everything.

And now he's here. Not running from it, but becoming it.

For me.

I should be doing . . . something, I know I should, but all I can do is breathe, tremble, and stare as he lowers his massive head, those familiar blue-gray eyes locked on mine with a silent promise.

A slow, strangled sound escapes me, a half-sob, half-laugh, as my fingers twitch against the frost-dusted grass.

It's really Talon, and he just saved my life.

I struggle to my feet shakily, but still able to stand. Before I can say anything, movement explodes from the tree line.

Becks, bloodied and out of breath, bursts into the clearing, his voice hoarse and raw with desperation. "We found her! They have Ensley. We need help. Now!"

He catches sight of Talon, and for a second he falters. Even from a distance I see his breath hitch; a wild, stunned look flashes across his face as he stares up at the enormous dragon towering over me.

"You've gotta be kidding me," he mutters under his breath when he reaches us, disbelief warring with awe, but it's gone as quickly as it came, swallowed by urgency. "No time. They demolished the Order forces in minutes. Titus is holding them off, but he won't last much longer!" He wipes at blood streaking down his temple.

I hear more shouts and we snap our heads to the side to catch Imogen, Kade, Ares, and the others running at us from the direction Talon burst into the clearing, weapons drawn, their faces a mix of determination and awe.

Kerrim, I realize, is gone, having vanished into the trees to regroup. But there's no time to dwell on that now.

Before the others reach us, Talon's massive form stiffens, and with a low, guttural rumble that rattles the air, frost explodes outward in a shimmering burst, and in the blink of an eye he's standing in front of me, back in his usual form, chest heaving, dark hair tousled and damp with sweat. His eyes glint with residual power. Steam curls off his skin where the frost lingers.

It's as impressive as it is intimidating, but I've run out of time awing over Talon's creature magic.

Talon's gaze sweeps over me with a sharpness that steals my breath, checking for wounds and mentally cataloging each one he finds. He reaches out, his fingers brushing lightly over my shoulder, like he's assuring himself that I'm still standing.

"You okay?" he murmurs, voice low and rough, and it's not a question so much as a desperate need for confirmation.

A faint shimmer of cold trails wherever his hand touches me, but his touch is careful, like he's afraid of breaking me.

I nod, chest tight. “Yeah. I’m okay.” But we both know there’s no time to worry about me. Not when I’m still standing and Ensley’s life, and so much more, is hanging in the balance.

“Where is she?” I ask Becks just as the others rush up behind him.

Kade glances between Talon and the frost-slicked ground, his expression sharpening with cold calculation. “Would have been nice to know about this before the attack.”

“You’re telling me,” Imogen says, staring at her cousin like she’s never seen him before.

“Doesn’t matter right now,” Becks snaps, voice tight with urgency. “We have to get to Ensley.”

In short, clipped bursts, Becks relays what he knows. Titus is holding the line, fighting to keep Kerrim’s forces at bay while they hold Ensley hostage. There are too many of them. Powerful creatures who strike down anyone who gets too close. And the Order? They’re barely holding on. All over the park, our forces are being overwhelmed.

Kade doesn’t waste a second. He turns, voice sharp and commanding as he barks orders, sending Ares and the bulk of the Order to reinforce their outmatched fighters. Then, without hesitation, he faces us, his expression grim. “I’m coming with you. Let’s move.”

With a grateful nod, Becks starts back toward where he entered the clearing. When I go to follow, Talon grabs my hand, stopping me.

His gaze cuts to mine, sharp and urgent. “Do you have enough left to do this?” he asks, knowing that I’m waning but letting me make the decision.

I nod once, breath catching, my body aching but my resolve steel-strong.

For Ensley, I do.

“Okay, then. Let’s go get her back,” he says, his voice low and steady, and together we run.

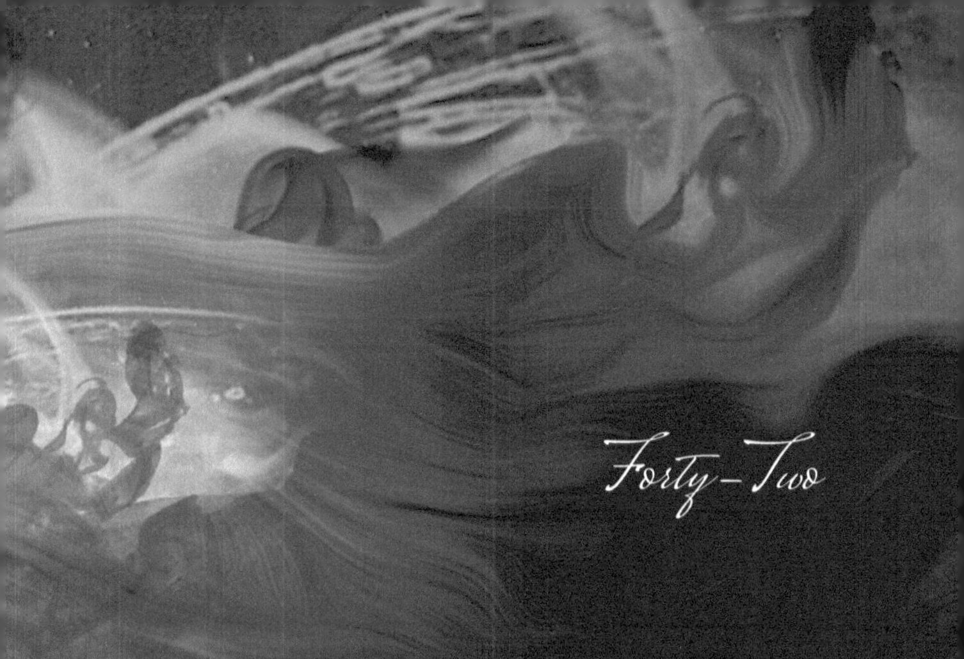

Forty-Two

WE DON'T WASTE another second. With Becks in the lead, we tear back into the trees, racing toward the zoo, where they're holding Ensley. The city's lights glint cold and distant beyond the dome, a reminder of the normal world we're fighting to protect. The sounds of battle rise with every step—lashing magic, the crack of weapons, the guttural cries of creatures and humans locked in a desperate fight for survival.

I try not to picture Titus, bloodied, exhausted, barely standing, still fighting to protect Ensley. But the image roots in my chest like a thorn, pushing me harder, faster.

My pulse hammers in my ears, my muscles burn like fire, but I don't slow down. I push until I'm gasping for air, running on fumes alone. The others outpace me, stretching the distance between us, and no matter how hard I try, I can't keep up.

Talon notices. Of course he does.

He hangs back, matching my slowing strides. His gaze cuts sideways, burning into mine, reading me like he always does. He doesn't say anything, until I stumble on a crack in the asphalt and nearly hit the ground.

His arm snaps out, catching me before I fall. The contact steadies me; his voice is firm as he stops me in my tracks.

"Breathe, Freckles. We need a second."

"I'm fine," I say, shaking my head, struggling to keep going and catch up to the others.

Talon's hand stays firm on my arm, sturdy and unyielding. His eyes narrow slightly, and I know what he's about to say before the words leave his mouth.

"Locklyn." His tone drops low, urgent but calm. "You're our secret weapon, remember? We can't afford for you to burn out before we even reach her."

I open my mouth to protest, but the truth of it steals my breath. I'm at the edge of my limits, and if I collapse, I'll be no help to anyone. Not to Ensley, not to Becks, not to Talon.

He glances up at the dome above, frustration tightening his jaw. "Not enough altitude. I can't fly us there. We'll have to run," he says, almost to himself.

His gaze returns to me, softer now, fierce and protective. "Let me help you."

Before I can argue, he bends over and sweeps me into his arms like it's the most natural thing in the world.

His strength is effortless, his body solid and warm against mine, even as the chill of his lingering frost magic clings to him. His breath brushes the top of my head as he mutters, "Hold on, Freckles. We'll get her back. We'll end this."

He takes off like a force of nature, and I press my face into his shoulder, clinging to the solid strength of him as I try to level out my breathing. The rush of air stings my cheek, whipping my hair back in tangled streams. Each long, powerful stride vibrates through me, a reminder of just how strong Talon is, of how much he's carrying. Not just me, but all of this.

Even without looking, I can feel us gaining on the others, their familiar footsteps merging with the noise up ahead.

The night has turned into a battlefield, a mess of colliding shouts, bursts of magic, and the sharp clash of metal. It presses in from every direction, but I force myself to tune it out, to focus inward and try to find my center. I grasp on to the threads of magic I know I have, except every time I reach for them, they slip through my fingers like water, leaving only a hollow ache behind.

That terrifies me more than anything.

As we near the zoo, the sounds shift. It's not just the chaos of battle anymore.

There are animal calls. Low, panicked grunts, the rhythmic thud of hooves, the sharp crack of breaking branches, and somewhere, a high-pitched, keening cry that twists my gut.

The battle rages around us, laced now with a savage energy thickening the madness we're already lost in.

Familiar voices break through the turmoil and I lift my head just as Talon slows, nearing a huddle of bodies surrounding a motionless form on the ground. I squirm in his arms and he lets me down. Becks glances up at me, his gaze haunted, and a chill runs through me even though I'm still overheated and coated in sweat.

I push forward, nudging Imogen to the side to get a clear look at what they're surrounding, and a gasp rips from my throat. Titus lies crumpled on the ground, his body twisted like a ragdoll tossed aside. Blood stains his skin in dark streaks, seeping into the shredded remains of his shirt. His breathing is shallow and ragged, each inhale a struggle that rattles in his chest like broken glass.

Bruises bloom across his face, deep and mottled, and one eye is swollen completely shut. A jagged gash splits across his cheek, the blood still gleaming in the low light. His lip is cracked, caked with dried blood, and his hands tremble where they clutch weakly at the dirt, as if sheer will alone is the only thing keeping him from slipping away.

His chest rises and falls in uneven jerks, each breath a battle. He looks utterly wrecked, barely holding on to consciousness. Yet there's a stubborn set to his jaw, a faint glint of defiance that lingers even in the midst of his collapse, because this is Titus, and he's too stubborn to let go that easily.

I twist to Kade. "Do you have a healer?"

He glances back at me with a look I've never seen on the strong, unflinching human before. It's not fear exactly, but it's close. "I do, but she'll be hard to locate in this bedlam. I'm not sure I'll be able to get to her in time. He's . . ." His gaze flicks down to Titus, and rather than finish his sentence, he shakes his head once, a grim finality in the motion.

I know what he's trying to say. That Titus' wounds are bad enough to be fatal. But I'm not ready to give up, and I won't let him give up either.

"Find her," I say, my voice sharp with command.

Kade draws a breath through his nose, then nods. As he turns to leave, I grab his shoulder. "Hurry."

"I will," he promises, and then he's gone.

I drop to the ground beside Titus, my hands hovering over his battered body because I'm terrified to touch him.

"We're sending for help. You're going to be okay," I try to assure him, though the words feel thin in the air.

His jaw works as if he's trying to form words, but they're too quiet to hear over the madness swirling around us. I lean in closer, and suddenly he grips my arm with a surprising strength, his fingers digging in like iron clamps.

"Leave me," he rasps, voice hoarse but urgent. "Save her."

I shake my head, heart racing. "We're not—"

"Now," he says, his grip tightening for emphasis. His eyes burn into mine, fierce and unrelenting.

I look up at the others—Imogen, Talon, and Becks—my pulse thundering in my ears, unsure what to do.

"I'll stay with him," Becks says, stepping forward with a look of fierce determination that makes my chest ache. It's not what I expected. He should be the first to charge in after his sister, but he's steady, calm. "Without my powers, I'm not much defense against those creatures, but I can do what I can for Titus until Kade gets back."

Reaching behind him, he pulls a gun from a holster I didn't realize he had under his shirt. He checks it with practiced hands, the cold click of metal echoing between us. I'm not sure how I feel about that.

"Go," he says firmly, his expression hard as steel.

I stand, my heart twisting, and before we leave, Becks catches my arm.

"Locklyn." His voice is low and tight, like he's forcing the words out before they slip away. "You've got this. Just promise me you'll get her back . . . and that you'll come back too." His gaze lingers, fierce and tender, refusing to let me go until I tell him I will.

"I swear to do everything I can to get her back," I say, knowing it's the only promise I can make right now.

He clears his throat, urgency snapping back into his tone as he nods toward the zoo. "They're holding her in the reptile house, last I saw. Titus was the only thing keeping them from dragging her deeper inside. There were at least four of them, big ones. Be careful."

I nod, pulse roaring in my ears, and turn to Talon and Imogen. No more hesitation. We have to move.

"This way," Imogen says, darting off.

She leads us toward what was once a security gate but now is a mangled heap of twisted metal, and without pause we enter the zoo.

Animal cries echo through the dark, making it nearly impossible to hear anything else. The noise and darkness are disorienting, but a map near the entrance helps guide us. We follow it, moving fast, heading straight for the reptile house.

My stomach tightens when we round a corner and spot a large yellow sign: Reptile House. The air feels heavier here, charged with magic. And danger.

We slip into the reptile house, the door creaking shut behind us. The noise from outside mutes like a switch has been flipped.

The animal cries, the distant sounds of battle, all of it dims to a strange, muffled hum, as if the building itself is holding its breath.

The air is thick and humid, heavy with the scent of damp stone and reptile musk. Every step echoes too loudly in the eerie quiet, and the low hum of the overhead lights buzzes like static.

We round a corner and I freeze.

There, at the far end of the room, above a massive open tank exhibit, is Ensley.

She hangs suspended in midair, held aloft by dark tendrils of shadow that weave and twist around her like serpents. The way they coil over her arms, her legs, her throat, it's like watching a nest of snakes writhe over her skin. My stomach lurches, bile rising in my throat.

Her head lolls to the side, hair draping down like a golden curtain, her arms hanging limp. Beneath her, the glassy surface of the water ripples, disturbed by the slow, sinuous movement of a massive snake.

An anaconda, I realize with a jolt.

Why does it have to be a snake?

The shadows slither lower, drawing her closer to the water.

I strain my senses, searching for Kerrim, expecting him to step from the shadows at any moment, but there's no sign of him. Four figures emerge from the shadows and I'm momentarily stunned by the damage Titus managed to inflict on them all alone. Blood stains their clothes, and they move with a stiffness that speaks of pain, but they're still standing. They're locked on to us, their eyes faintly glowing in the dim light.

Vampires.

I feel it instantly, the tug of their compulsion, like invisible threads pulling at my mind.

Whether it's their intent to kill us or just detain us, one thing is clear.

They aren't planning to let us leave.

Talon and I share a quick glance. He feels it too. But we've been training for this. Over the last two days we've worked on blocking compulsion, and though the pull tugs at the edges of my mind, I force it back.

Imogen, being a vampire herself, laughs—actually laughs—echoing sharp and bright in the cavernous space.

"Sorry, boys. If you want to take me down, you're going to have to do better than that."

Then she launches. A blur of speed and fangs, she collides with the nearest vampire in a snarl of teeth and fists. Talon isn't far behind, moving with lethal precision, ice crackling at his fingertips as he slams into the next one, sending the vampire sprawling across the floor. The other two converge, hissing, but Talon whirls on them, frost blooming at his feet, a blast of cold air erupting from his palms as he sweeps out his arm. One of the vampires is flung back into a glass enclosure, shattering it in an explosion of water and scales.

The room erupts into pandemonium.

I have no time to focus on them, because Ensley is slipping.

The shadows coil tighter around her, dropping her closer to the surface of the water. The anaconda stirs beneath her, its massive body rippling like liquid muscle.

"Hold on," I whisper, voice shaking as I rush closer.

My fingers tremble as I reach out, feeling for my magic. It's weak, flickering like a candle on the verge of snuffing out, but it's still there.

Come on, come on.

Ignoring the fight raging behind me, I extend my hand. The shadows are sluggish at first, reluctant, but then they surge forward, responding to my call. They meet the tendrils holding Ensley, tangling with them in a silent, writhing battle.

For a breathless second, it feels like they're going to snap back, like I'm too drained, too weak to fight them off.

No. Not her. Not now.

I push harder, teeth gritted, and reaching up with my free hand

I grasp the lunacite pendant in my fist, squeezing so tightly the gem is cutting into my palm. The magic inside me flares, searing through my veins like fire. With a sharp *crack*, the vampire's shadowy tendrils shatter apart, and Ensley drops—

I lunge forward, the shadows at my command forming a blanket underneath her. The effort nearly buckles my knees, but I hold on, guiding her over the glass partition, and then gently down to the floor in front of me, away from the water, away from the tank.

My breath comes in ragged gasps, the world tilting around me as I drop to my knees and pull Ensley to me.

Her eyes flutter, her skin pale and clammy. But she's breathing. She's alive.

"I've got you," I whisper, a tear slipping down my cheek as I cradle her against me. "I've got you."

A blur of motion has me looking up just as a body crashes into a glass enclosure across from us with a sickening crack. The impact shatters the tank, water gushing across the floor in a rush.

A massive reptile, maybe a monitor lizard or maybe a crocodile, slides free, gliding over the limp, unmoving body of one of the vampires as if they're nothing more than an obstacle in its path.

Talon and Imogen stand over the unconscious bodies of the remaining vampires, breathing hard but still on their feet. They high-five between pants.

"We have to get her somewhere safe," I call out, my voice shaky but urgent.

Talon and Imogen rush over to help. Talon gently eases Ensley from my arms, holding her carefully against his chest.

"You did good, Freckles," he murmurs, his eyes steady and reassuring. I want to believe him, but I'm too rattled to smile back.

"Let's find Becks and Titus," I say, forcing the words past the tight knot in my throat. "Then we get out of here."

Forty-Three

WE LEAVE Kerrim's vampires behind in the reptile house. I don't know if they're dead or alive, and honestly, I don't care. At this point, all I want is to get out of this zoo, and out of this park, with all my friends still breathing. This whole night was a disaster, but at least we have Ensley back. As far as our mission to get Shadow Striker back from Kerrim, that will have to wait. I worked as hard as I could to prepare, but Kerrim was stronger. I need more time. So whether this was a missed opportunity or not, I'm just grateful we're leaving with our lives, ready to fight another day.

Ensley comes to in Talon's arms around the time we exit the zoo. Her lashes flutter weakly, her breath shallow and ragged. By the time we reach the clearing where we left Becks and Titus, she's fully awake, struggling to lift her head and take in her surroundings.

"Easy," I whisper, brushing a damp strand of hair from her face. "You're safe."

Her eyes, dull with exhaustion but wide with panic, search frantically until they land on something in front of us, and then life sparks back into them. She jolts in Talon's arms, squirming to be let down.

I follow her line of sight and instantly know why: Titus.

He is still slumped on the ground, pale and barely moving, but now there's a figure crouched beside him, a woman with a halo of dark curls and a satchel of supplies, her glowing hands moving swiftly over his battered body. Kade stands nearby, issuing clipped orders to his remaining forces, but his sharp gaze turns to us as we approach.

Talon gently sets Ensley down and she stumbles toward Titus, going as far as to push past her shocked brother to fall to her knees at the broken fae's side.

The healer pauses just long enough to reassure her, "He's critical, but he's holding on. He'll make it."

Titus' eyes crack open, glassy but alive; a broken smile twists his bloodied lips. His fingers twitch, reaching for her. Ensley clasps his hand in both of hers, tears streaming down her face.

Becks crouches down beside his sister, pulling her into a fierce hug, his breath hitching.

"You're okay. Thank the Creator you're okay." His voice is raw, breaking on the words.

After a minute, he lets her go and stands. Turning to me, he pulls me in for a tight, almost breathless hug.

"Thank you for getting her back." His gaze shifts to Talon and Imogen, the gratitude plain in his eyes. "All of you, thank you."

Talon nods in acknowledgement, and Imogen shrugs like it was no big deal, but even in the low light I catch her cheeks reddening a little.

Kade takes a step toward us, his expression strained. "The fights around the park are breaking up. My teams are pulling back, just holding the barrier as long as they can to keep humans out. We need to leave. Now."

The healer presses a bandage over Titus' ribs, securing it tightly. "He's stable enough to move, but he'll need help."

Talon and Becks exchange a look, then crouch to lift Titus carefully between them. Ensley clutches one of Titus' hands, refusing to let go even as we move. Imogen falls into step beside me, her usual sharpness muted by the exhaustion in her eyes.

But we don't make it far.

A chilling ripple of power slices through the air. Sharp, electric, and unmistakable. The temperature drops, the ground vibrating beneath our feet. We freeze mid-step, the hair on the back of my neck rising.

Kerrim.

Before we can react, a blast of searing magic erupts from the darkness, slamming into the ground in front of us. The shockwave sends us sprawling, a blinding flash lighting up the night as the air crackles with raw energy.

This night's not over yet. Not even close.

I start to get to my feet when Talon's voice cuts through the commotion, fierce and ragged. "Stay down!" he shouts as a fiery ball streaks over our heads close enough that the heat singes the air and prickles across my skin, making me flinch as it slams into a tree behind us and explodes in a shower of embers.

"Locklyn!" Kerrim booms from somewhere in the darkness, echoing across the night and sinking like a stone in the pit of my stomach. "Come face me so we can end this. I promise not to harm your friends. I'll even let them return to their world when this is over. You have my word."

Lying flat on my belly, I exchange a glance with Talon. His eyes are sharp, unyielding. He doesn't believe Kerrim any more than I do. But it doesn't change the fact that I still have to face him.

I let Becks go up against Kerrim before, and look what happened. He was stranded in the human world, stripped of his creature magic. I won't let something like that happen again. I won't let someone else fight my battle. Shadow Striker is bonded to me. If anyone has a shot at taking it back from that monster, it's me.

Breaking eye contact with Talon, I look at Becks. His face is tight with concentration, scanning the shadows for any sign of Kerrim.

"Becks," I call softly. His head snaps toward me, his eyes wide. "Get Titus and Ensley out of here."

He bares his teeth in a grimace, shaking his head hard. "No. I'm staying. I can help you."

"I'm not asking because you're weak," I say firmly, holding his gaze. "I'm asking because they need you. If they stay, they die. I know you can protect them. I *need* you to protect them."

A trace of frustration slips across his face, familiar and gutting. I know that look. I know what it's like to feel like the weakest link, the one without magic, the one who's always just a step behind. But I'm asking him to protect those I love, because if there's anyone who will fight with everything they have to keep Ensley and Titus safe, it's him.

Another streak of fire tears through the night, hissing past just inches above our heads.

"Move!" Talon barks, his voice sharp, cutting through the mayhem like a blade.

We scramble to our feet, instinct driving us toward the cover of the trees. There's so many of us to conceal. Not far from us, Kade with the healer and his fighters are running for cover as well.

Becks slings an arm under Titus, who's barely conscious, while Talon grabs his other side to help support his weight. Imogen shadows them, sharp and fluid, scanning for the next threat.

We hide behind a grouping of trees. The cover is flimsy and won't last for long, especially with fireballs being hurled at us.

"Becks," I plead. "You have to go."

For a heartbeat, he hesitates, torn between staying and going. Then Ensley appears, nudging Talon out of the way and slipping her arm under Titus' other shoulder. Tears stream down her face.

Becks locks eyes with me, a raw, desperate intensity behind his gaze. "You better come back to me. I'm not ready to lose you again," he says, his voice hoarse.

With one last lingering look, he nods to his sister and then they vanish into the darkness, Titus barely upright between them.

Another fireball streaks past, slamming into a tree with a crack and a burst of flame. One of Kade's men cries out—a searing, guttural scream that pierces my ears—and collapses, smoke rising from his back. The healer dives toward him, already working to stabilize him as Kade curses under his breath, scanning for more threats.

"Kade!" I shout over the madness. "Hold the line here! I'll handle Kerrim."

He starts to argue, but I shake my head fiercely. "I have to do this. Keep the others safe."

I whirl around, trying to center myself, trying to find that flicker of power inside me, but . . . it's gone. A hollow echo, a dead weight in my chest. Not even the pendant causes it to spark to life.

Panic rises like a wave, sharp and suffocating.

"Locklyn." Talon's voice comes from behind me, steady and low, like an anchor in the storm. I turn to him, wide-eyed, breath ragged.

"I don't have any more in me," I whisper, voice breaking. "I can't fight him."

Talon reaches for me, cupping my face in his hands. His touch is cool, grounding. "You can. We're connected. Draw from me."

"But—"

"Do it," he orders, his voice rough, urgent.

I close my eyes, focusing on him. Focusing on me. And there it is, a pulse of magic, silver and gold threads shimmering between us, flaring bright as they weave through my veins. The power rushes in like a flood, sharp and sweet, and I gasp as it ignites my skin.

"Talon!" comes Imogen's alarmed voice. "What are you doing? You know what might—"

He cuts her off with a sharp look. "It's fine."

"What's wrong?" I ask, glancing between the two of them as

the threads connecting Talon and me glow brighter, pulsing like a living thing.

"Nothing," Talon says, but when I glance at Imogen, she looks away, a deep scowl tightening her face.

"Am I hurting you?" I ask, my concern spiking.

"No," Talon murmurs, his thumb brushing gently across my cheek. His voice is tight, strained. "But I won't be able to shift or use any of my magic if you're pulling from me."

I nod, swallowing hard. Maybe that's why Imogen is so on edge.

"I can do this," I say, because I have to.

"You can," Talon agrees, his gaze steady and fierce. "Focus on keeping a shield up. Get close, then strike. If you need more magic, draw from me. I have plenty."

"Okay." But a prickle of unease skitters down my spine. A ripple of wrongness. I don't know what it is, or why, and I don't have time to figure it out.

I raise my faelight shield just as a gust of wind, too strong and sudden to be anything but magical, slams into the trees, branches cracking and leaves swirling in a frenzied dance. My hair whips wildly around me as the world trembles.

Kerrim's voice rings out from the shadows, cold and arrogant. "Locklyn, I'm tired of waiting. I'm coming for you, and I'll end anyone who stands in my way."

No.

I can't let him make the first move. If I wait, he'll target Talon, Imogen, and everybody else within striking distance.

With one last look at Talon for courage, I force myself to break from cover, sprinting toward where I think Kerrim is lurking. The problem is, the darkness feels thicker than before, a suffocating blanket swallowing the clearing. I can't see him.

There's a flash of motion to my left, then a blinding bolt of faelight streaks toward me, aimed at my heart. I throw up my faelight shield just in time, the blast ricocheting off the barrier with a crackling snap that leaves my ears ringing.

I know where the attack came from, but I still don't see him. Shadows swirl in the air in front of me and I realize he's using them to conceal himself, twisting the darkness into a weapon, cloaking his presence.

I grit my teeth and reach for Talon's magic, pulling hard, feeling the threads between us blaze brighter, hotter. The surge of power floods me, igniting my core, and I shove it outward in a blast of light. The shadows recoil, splintering like smoke under a sudden gust.

And there he is.

Kerrim stands in the open, face twisted in a sneer, Shadow Striker gripped tightly in his fist, surrounded by a pulsating black mist that I've never seen before.

Our eyes lock, and without hesitation, I charge.

Kerrim doesn't come at me. He waits for me to reach him before lashing out with his magic. A dark bolt of electricity erupts from his hand, shooting toward me like a dagger, but I anticipated the attack and dodge to the side, not letting it slow down my momentum. Within two more quick strides I'm in his face, and rather than attacking with magic as he probably expects, I strike with what I know. A sharp punch to the gut.

Kerrim may have the magical advantage, but I've trained nearly my whole life in hand-to-hand combat. He doesn't know how to block or absorb the hit, so he staggers back, losing his footing, barely catching himself before falling. Still hunched over, he tries to lift his hand to launch another attack, but I'm already there, slamming my knee into his face before he can recover.

His head snaps back, his glasses flying off, a cut opening above his brow. Blood spills down his face. A quick jab to his nose sends more gushing out, and he finally collapses, landing hard on his side.

I'm mid-swing with a kick aimed for his gut when he throws

out his hand and a blast of wind slams into me. The force sends me flying backward. I hit the ground hard, the impact rattling my bones and driving the air from my lungs.

I cough, struggling for breath as pain blooms through my ribs.

We scramble to our feet, both of us bruised and battered, both of us fueled by a savage will to survive.

Kerrim's eyes flash with rage, madness, and something feral. For a split second, I swear they glint red in the dim light.

Diving at each other, we clash again. Magic and fists, light and shadow. My training gives me an edge, at first—ducking, weaving, landing blows that knock him off balance.

But it's not enough.

With Shadow Striker in his grasp, Kerrim is relentless, his power growing with every strike. Even with Talon's magic flooding through me, I can feel myself slipping, my body slowing.

Kerrim drives me back, each blow heavier than the last, his magic crackling hotter, stronger, my strength draining with every clash. My hands tremble. My lungs burn. My arms scream from the strain.

This might be it, my mind whispers. The end.

No.

I won't give up. Not now. Not ever.

But the truth is, I can't win like this. One-on-one against Kerrim and Shadow Striker, I'm outmatched. Out-magicked. Too drained.

Every second we fight, he gets stronger, and I lose more ground.

I search desperately for a weakness, a flaw in his technique I can exploit. But there's nothing. Every time he sends a wave of power at me, I stagger, closer to collapse. Every slash with the blade, he gets closer to cutting me. Closer to victory.

In the midst of everything, a memory bursts through the fog of battle. Talon's voice in my parents' shop, the day he told me the legend of Shadow Striker and the first Vampire King. The one who ruled through terror. The one who couldn't be killed by brute force, no matter how many tried.

"The one caveat of Shadow Striker was that if anyone willingly sacrificed themselves for the wielder, the power he or she had gathered would be stripped from them."

Sacrifice.

Not everything Talon told me that day was the complete truth. Some were half lies and misdirection, but I know in my heart sacrifice is the key.

It wasn't brute strength that defeated the Vampire King. It was the love of the one who gave her life for him.

It wasn't about being stronger, faster, more magically powerful. It was about being willing to lose everything for someone else.

I'm not sure how it works or why, but I'm suddenly sure that's the dagger's weakness.

And my only hope.

My heart clenches as the truth settles deep inside me. I don't love Kerrim, but I would give my life to save those I love. That has to be enough.

I barely have time to process the thought as Kerrim drives the blade toward me, aiming low, a vicious strike meant for my gut.

I have time to twist out of the way, but I don't, even as my instincts scream at me to dodge, to run. Instead, I root myself in place.

Someone shouts my name. Talon, his voice raw with terror.

I glance up, and there he is, sprinting toward me. The silver-and-gold threads connecting us flare like wildfire, leading him to me. His face is twisted in a look of horror, a silent plea in his eyes.

He thinks I've given up.

He couldn't be more wrong.

I hold his gaze, hoping he understands, praying he forgives me.

And then it happens.

A white-hot explosion of pain tears through my gut as Shadow Striker sinks deep. My breath catches in my throat. It feels like fire and ice colliding inside me, a searing agony that radiates through every inch of my body.

My muscles lock, my vision dims. It's not just my body the blade has sliced into, but my magic as well. I feel it being ripped away, drained like water through a sieve. It's as if Kerrim is tearing my soul out through the blade.

A triumphant grin spreads across his bloodied face as he wrenches the dagger free. My knees buckle, and I collapse backward, but strong arms catch me, lower me gently to the grass.

Talon.

His hands cradle my face, trembling as he leans over me, his breath ragged, his eyes wild with desperation.

"Freckles," he chokes out, voice breaking. "What have you done?"

Forty-Four

TALON APPLIES pressure to my wound, trying to stop the blood, and a scream tears from my throat because it feels like a blade stabbing me all over again.

"Hold on, Freckles. Hold on. It's okay. Imogen's going to get a healer."

Imogen? Was she here? I didn't see her. But my vision is as fuzzy as my brain.

"You're going to make it," he says, but when I look into his eyes, I see something there I've never seen in Talon before.

Fear.

Behind him, I catch sight of Kerrim lifting Shadow Striker into the air. He watches my fresh blood slide down the blade, dripping from the tip.

"Finally," he murmurs, his own blood staining his skin as a wide, maniacal smile splits his face. He looks like a predator savoring his victory as he watches each red drop fall to the ground.

Talon ignores him, his full focus on me. He keeps the pressure on my wound, whispering that I'm going to be fine, even though we both know it's a lie.

With what little strength I have left, I lift my hand, fingers trembling as I trail them over Talon's cheekbone. His eyes lock on to mine, the depth of his pain shining back at me.

"Had to," I whisper. "A sacrifice. It was the only way."

Talon shakes his head, clearly not understanding.

"The Vampire King's love. Only a sacrifice can counteract the blade's dark magic."

His eyes widen with sudden sharp understanding, but before he can say anything, Kerrim's panicked voice breaks through the night, sharp and raw.

"What? No. No!"

A silent gasp leaves my lips as black mist erupts from Shadow Striker. It curls through the air like smoke, only thicker, darker, until it surrounds Kerrim, wrapping around him like writhing tentacles.

He stumbles, swiping at the mist in a panic, but it clings to him, seeping under his skin, sinking into his flesh. His screams tear through the night, raw and desperate, as he tries to bat it away, but it's no use. The mist pulses, drawing tighter around him, almost as if it's feeding off his life force. His body convulses, spasming in place. His frantic cries turn to gurgles, then ragged gasps, before they're gone altogether.

Kerrim collapses to the ground, motionless.

Before the shock of it can fully register, a deafening boom shakes the clearing. A pulse of power erupts from Shadow Striker, still clutched in Kerrim's lifeless hand.

The blade glows red-hot, then cracks appear before it shatters in a burst of black smoke that spirals upward, twisting and writhing like a living thing. The air vibrates with a terrible, almost feral energy.

It feels . . . ancient. Dangerous. Wrong.

For a second, I think I hear a deep, guttural rumble, like a distant roar carried on the wind. Then the smoke vanishes, unraveling into the night like a shadow melting into deeper darkness.

In the sudden, breathless quiet, I catch sight of something crumpled on the ground near Kerrim's body.

A figure.

Pale, gaunt, motionless.

His body is skeletal, his eyes sunken; he's barely breathing, if he's breathing at all.

A rustle of footsteps breaks the eerie stillness, followed by urgent voices. Imogen, Kade, and the healer, her bag already swinging from her shoulder, burst through the tree line in front of us, breathless and wide-eyed, as if they've only just caught up with the aftermath.

"Locklyn!" Imogen's voice is sharp with alarm as she spots me lying in Talon's arms.

She skids to a halt, but it's the healer who moves first, dropping to her knees beside us, already pulling supplies from her bag.

Kade follows, his gaze sweeping over the area, taking in Kerrim's lifeless form, the shattered remnants of Shadow Striker, and the unknown figure crumpled on the ground.

"Who on earth is that?" he mutters, but there's no time for answers.

"Help her!" Talon snaps, voice tight, as the healer moves to press gauze against my wound, sending another spike of excruciating pain through me as she works with practiced speed to stem the bleeding.

I catch Imogen's gaze dart nervously toward the figure lying near Kerrim as Kade turns to stand guard, tense as if ready for whatever this new threat might bring. For now, the crumpled figure is ignored, though none of us can shake the wrongness that clings to the air. It's like the night itself is holding its breath, waiting for something to shift.

I feel myself slipping away. My eyelids grow heavy, and a gentle force tugs at me, promising peace as it drags me under.

"Don't you dare," Talon orders, shaking me.

My eyes snap open, but even so, the edges of my vision start to darken.

"You're not going anywhere," he says, his voice rough, his face tight with worry.

Above me, I catch the look the healer gives him.

"What is it?" Talon asks.

She hesitates. "I can try to use my magic to save her life, but I don't know if she's strong enough to endure the healing process."

"She is." Talon's face hardens, his words sharp. "She's the strongest creature I've ever met. This won't break her."

But that's the problem, isn't it? Because I'm not actually a creature. I'm *human*. And I know with certainty that my magic is gone. Not depleted or I just can't reach it, there's an empty void inside where it used to be. Maybe I should care about that, but I don't. In fact, I'm glad. It was never meant to be part of me.

I was enough on my own, and if I'm going to die tonight, I want to do it as myself.

A shadow moves at the edge of my fading vision, and then Becks is there, breathless and wide-eyed.

"I felt it," he says, voice raw. "My magic came back to me in a rush, and I knew that she'd defeated him, but, what happened?" His face crumples, torn between relief and panic as he takes in my condition.

"She sacrificed herself," Talon explains, and then turns back to the healer. "You have to do it now. We don't have any more time."

The healer nods, her face tight with focus. She places her hands over my wound, and a silvery light kindles between her hands. It's faint, but I can feel it. The weak spark of her magic trying to knit torn flesh back together, but it's not enough. My body is too fragile, too drained to respond.

The healer's breath shudders, her voice barely a whisper. "She's too weak. I can't—"

"Yes, you can," Talon growls, his voice low and fierce. His tone softens, urgent and raw. "I'll give her the strength she needs."

He reaches for me, but Imogen grabs his wrist before he can touch me, her eyes wide with alarm. "Talon, don't!" she hisses, panic bleeding into every word. "You've been lucky so far, but if you give her any more, it could kill you."

What?

I don't understand what's happening. Their voices feel like they're coming from far away, the edges of their words blurring and slipping.

Talon jerks out of Imogen's grip, his expression hard as ice. "We don't know that."

"Yes we do!" Imogen snaps. "You've been feeding her your magic. More than I realized before today. More than you should have. If you push this, you're risking your life. You're—"

"I know what I'm doing!" Talon roars, and for a second even Imogen recoils from the intensity in his voice.

He looks down at me, his jaw tight, breath ragged. His hand trembles as he hovers it next to my face, his voice quieter but no less determined. "If it takes my life to save hers, then so be it."

Laying his hand against my cheek, I feel his icy magic surge into me, sharp and cold, like plunging into a frozen river. It's startling at first, an ache that shudders through my chest, leaving frost blooming across my skin.

The silver and gold threads that connect us spark to life, igniting like thin lines of lightning, crackling in the air between us. They pulse in time with my faltering heartbeat, weaving brighter and stronger, wrapping around me like a cocoon.

I gasp, breath catching in my throat as the threads tighten, infusing me with Talon's magic. It's not just cold, there's a familiar warmth beneath it, steady and strong, like a quiet fire buried in the frost.

Talon looks to the side and says, "Try it now," speaking to the healer, who leans over me again, her magic lighting up her palms as she presses them against my wound.

Almost immediately the ache in my chest starts to ease, the pressure in my head lifting just enough that my vision sharpens at the edges. But Talon shudders, his breath hitching, a flicker of strain tightening his face as the magic drains from him and flows into me.

"Talon," I rasp, barely a whisper, but his eyes stay on mine, fierce and unyielding.

"Stay with me, Freckles," he murmurs, voice low and ragged. "Just stay."

As the healer works, I feel life start to return to me, slow and steady, like a spark catching flame. Strength seeps back into my limbs, my awareness sharpening, the fog in my mind thinning as if a heavy veil is being slowly lifted.

My breath comes easier. My heart beats stronger.

But as the seconds pass, the small relief I feel is overshadowed by the subtle, creeping dread that all is not well.

My gaze drifts to Talon and my pulse lurches.

The color is draining from his face, leaving his skin pale beneath its usual golden tan. His breath rasps, shallow and uneven, his jaw clenched so tightly the muscle flexes under his skin. A faint shimmer of sweat beads across his forehead, and there's a tremor in his hands, small but unmistakable.

Then I feel it. That uncontrollable pull.

The silver and gold tendrils that appeared back in the creature world when I accidently bonded to the dagger, and that have appeared so many times since, now they *sting*, like they're cutting into him. I can feel his magic flowing into me, too much, too fast, like a dam bursting all at once.

I remember the way he coughed at my feet as he lay dying under the ruins after the last Chaos trial. His skin pale, his breath ragged, the way the magic drained from him and into me. How he asked me to get him through the portal before it was too late.

It's the same wrongness I felt before. The same tightening in my chest, the same panic clawing at my throat as I watched him collapse that night, powerless to stop it.

No. Not again.

"Talon," I whisper, my voice cracking, but he doesn't meet my gaze. His shoulders hunch, tense and trembling, his breathing grows harsher, and I know he's trying to hold himself together, but I *feel* it.

He's slipping. He's pouring too much of himself into me.

And it's killing him.

A surge of strength born of panic, love, and sheer determination pulses through me and I lurch upright, forcing the healer to pause. There's still a sharp ache in my gut where Shadow Striker cut into me, but I know without looking that the wound isn't bleeding anymore.

I may not be fully healed, but it's enough. It has to be. Talon can't give me any more.

I grab his face in both hands, tilting it toward mine. His breath hitches. His blue-gray eyes strained, rimmed in silver, pass over my face as he assures himself I'm well before dropping down to my lips, then back to my eyes.

"Stop," I whisper, desperate, my thumb brushing over his cheekbone.

Then I kiss him. Hard. Fierce. Like I can pour all my thanks, all my hope, all my everything into him and somehow save us both.

For a breathless moment, it's just us, his lips moving against mine, his hands braced on my waist like he's the only thing keeping me from breaking apart entirely.

I pull back, gasping, my forehead resting against his.

"I'm fine. I'm okay, I'm alive," I repeat over and over again, knowing he needs that reassurance.

A shudder runs through him as his hands move up my arms to cup my face as the torrent of magic he's trying to force into me ceases.

He leans back, gaze sweeping over me like he's desperate to memorize every detail, every breath, every trace of life in my eyes.

His chest heaves. "I almost lost you," he whispers, the words raw and frayed as they spill out. His thumb brushes gently over my cheek. A silent promise that he won't let it happen again.

"But you didn't," I murmur.

A flutter of motion at the edge of my vision draws my attention, reminding me we're not alone.

I catch Becks' gaze first. His face is a mix of relief and sadness as he stares down at me in Talon's arms, and my heart pinches. I never want to hurt him, but I know seeing me with Talon will always sting.

Beside him, Imogen stands with her arms crossed and a scowl on her face, reminding me of her concern and warnings for Talon. I glance back at him, still kneeling beside me. He looks drained, pale, and exhausted, but his gaze is steady, and the tension in his shoulders eases just enough for me to believe he'll be okay.

Kade and the healer are there too. I thank her softly, and she gives me a quick nod of acknowledgement before saying she needs to check on the others. Kade thanks her as well, then she's gone.

I push up to my feet with Talon's help, feeling the lingering ache in my body but grateful for the strength to stand just as Ensley and Titus come hobbling toward us, slow but steady. Titus still looks rough, but he can move with Ensley's support, giving me hope that with time he'll recover.

When they reach us, Ensley glances at me, her face weary and tight. "Is it over?" she asks.

I glance around, taking it all in. The crumpled body of Kerrim lying motionless nearby, the shattered remnants of Shadow Striker lying in the grass, gleaming faintly in the moonlight, and the strange, skeletal figure still slumped on the ground, barely breathing.

"I . . . I think so," I say, my voice raw.

Becks follows my gaze to the prone figure. "Who is that?" he asks.

I swallow hard, the memory of the black smoke pouring out of Shadow Striker flashing in my mind.

"After Kerrim died the blade cracked, then shattered. There was an explosion of black smoke and, it felt wrong. Like it had been trapped in the blade," I say, feeling a little silly voicing something so out there. "And then he appeared." I nod toward the figure. "I don't know who he is."

Imogen's eyes narrow, her posture tense as she takes a step closer, scrutinizing the gaunt, pale figure. "That's no ordinary creature." Her gaze sharpens, a glint of realization flashing in her eyes. "If I had to guess, that's the Vampire King. The first one. Shadow Striker's first wielder."

A stunned silence settles over the group, broken only by the distant shouts of the retreating Order forces.

"Is that even possible?" I ask. "He would be over two thousand years old."

Kade looks thoughtful. "No one ever knew what happened to the first Vampire King. He was never seen after his love sacrificed herself. The assumption was that he went off on his own in his grief, but what if he's been somehow trapped in that blade ever since then?"

The thought of that sends a cold chill through me. To have been trapped for that long . . . a mind would break under those conditions. Even the strongest one.

"Tonight's been long enough. We can take him back to headquarters and get answers later," Kade says.

There's a round of nods of agreement. Kade asks Becks to help him get the figure upright, but before they even reach him, Talon staggers beside me, a low groan tearing from his throat. His grip on my arm slips and I spin toward him in alarm. The silver and gold threads flare back to life, weaving through the air between us, and a sharp, gut-wrenching ache twists in my chest.

"Talon!" I cry, catching him as he collapses to his knees. His skin is pale, almost ashen; his breath comes in ragged gasps.

The threads shimmer and pulse, and I know in my gut what's happening.

"No. No, no, no," I whisper, panic surging as I drop to my knees beside him.

My hands shake as I reach for him, but I don't know how to stop it. It's starting all over again, just like the first time the dagger bonded to me, just like I feared when I was being healed. I'm stealing his life away.

The others rush forward, but I barely hear them over the roar of blood in my ears. All I can see is Talon slipping away right in front of me.

"Quick!" Imogen snaps. "Find all the pieces of the dagger."

"What? Why?" I ask, my head snapping toward her as she digs through the grass, searching for Shadow Striker's shards.

Becks and Kade join her without asking why, and together they start gathering the sharp pieces. Even Ensley helps Titus to the ground and starts looking.

"We need to use it to create a portal and get you back to the creature world," she says without looking up.

Talon shudders in my arms, a low groan escaping him. When I look down, his skin has gone gray and clammy. His breathing is ragged, his body trembling so hard I can barely hold him.

"I knew this would happen," Imogen snaps. "I *told* him."

"Told him what?" I yell back, terrified as I feel Talon slipping away in my arms.

She pauses, glancing at me with a gaze full of fury. "You're still tethered from when you first bonded with the blade. Separating Talon from the blade is what saved his life before, but there was always a risk that coming here, with you, would reopen that connection. It's been killing him slowly since the moment he arrived in this world. Saving your life sped it up and may have just sealed his fate."

I shake my head in denial. No. That can't be true. I don't want to believe it.

"But the blade is destroyed," I say, still not understanding.

"But the connection between you two *isn't*. The magic is still trying to complete the transfer. Every time your magic connected, it was a risk to his life. The only way to stop it is to sever the connection between you."

"How are we going to do that?" I ask, desperate.

"Shadow Striker created a portal here. You're going to use what's left of it to open a portal home. And then you're going to go there, and Talon is going to stay here."

"What? No," I say, shaking my head, struggling to grasp everything she's saying, not wanting to believe that in order to save his life I have to leave him.

That can't be the only way. It's too cruel. We just found each other. I can't lose him now.

"There has to be another way to sever the connection."

Imogen starts to respond, but then cuts herself off. Pressing her lips together, she shakes her head. "There's not," she says, but the flash of hesitation in her eyes makes me doubt her.

"What is it?"

She shakes her head again. "There may be another way to sever the connection, but we don't have time to figure it out. Talon may only have minutes left. Right now, if you want to save him, this is the only way."

My heart feels like it's being shredded. I'd do anything to save Talon, including leaving him forever, but the thought of that is almost too painful to consider. But I can't just let him die.

"Freckles," Talon says, his voice weak and hollow.

I look down at him, my vision blurred with unshed tears.

"It's going to be okay," he assures me, and I know that's a lie.

If I have to leave him, or he dies, it will never be okay again.

"You'll have your family and friends. And you'll have him," he says, nodding over to where Becks is collecting pieces of Shadow Striker.

I shake my head, too wrecked to even voice my denial.

I don't want Becks, not like I used to. I want *him*.

Talon lifts a shaky hand and gently brushes my hair behind my ear, his fingers grazing the shell in the way he always does, bringing a fresh ache to my chest.

"You still have feelings for him. Don't deny it."

I open my mouth to do just that, but he's right. Becks is still in my heart. I've loved him for so long, it's confusing to separate romantic love from the deep care and affection I have for him. In truth, regardless of what happens in the future, Becks will probably always be a part of me.

But what I have with Talon is different. Deeper. It blows past the first-love layer of my heart, burrowing down into the center of my soul and rooting there. My love for him, and his for me, started as a seed that bloomed, branching out through every part of me until there was no space left for anyone else.

"It's good," Talon says, his voice thin but certain. "If we can't be together, I want to know that you have someone. A partner who cares and loves you as much as I do."

"If it's not you, it's not anyone," I say, the words broken through sobs.

Talon just smiles, as if to say I think that now but he knows it will change.

He's wrong. It won't.

Even though Becks was my first love, Talon was supposed to be my forever love. It's not the same. Becks can't just be a stand-in for Talon. That's not fair to him, or me, or any of us.

"Get up," Imogen orders, and when I look up at her, she's holding a bundle of Shadow Striker shards in some sort of cloth someone must have ripped from their shirt.

"You have to do this now or it's going to be too late."

I shake my head. "I don't know how to open a portal. I didn't even really do anything before. It just happened. I don't have any magic anymore."

"You have to at least try," she says.

Talon cups the side of my face, his hand trembling, and I snap my gaze back to him. "I believe in you, Freckles. You can do this. And this might help." He hands me the tamalite ring that had been on his finger.

As I take it, the threads shimmer faintly between us, pulsing like they're waiting.

With a deep, shuddering breath, I close the ring in my fist. Letting go of Talon, I rise to my feet, legs shaking beneath me. As I accept the cloth bundle of shards from Imogen, dropping the ring in with them, an unexpected warmth spreads through my palms, as if the remnants of the blade still hum with energy. I can feel Talon's gaze on me, a silent tether pulling me back to him.

I close my eyes, focusing on the weight of the shards in my hands, the echoes of power they still hold.

The threads pulse brighter between Talon and me, and I let myself feel the connection. Not the magic, but the love, the bond we forged together. I think about home, the creature world I grew up in; my parents who are there; our apartment above our shop; Pete's gym that's practically a second home. I think about the times I spent with Ensley and Becks at Sloan's drinking milkshakes and laughing. I think about how desperate I am to get back.

"Please," I whisper. To whom or what, I'm not exactly sure. I've never thought much about the Creator before, but if demons forged this cursed blade, then maybe there is a force out there with greater power who can help me now, because I know I can't do this on my own.

Suddenly, the atmosphere shifts, crackling like static, and when I open my eyes a faint glow appears at the edges of the shards. The space in front of me ripples with heat and energy, while the ground trembles beneath my feet.

"Come on," I whisper. "Come on."

The air distorts; a crack splits open in the ripples before me, leaving what looks like a rip in the air—shimmering, unstable, but real.

A portal.

Different than the one that appeared before, but that's clearly what it is.

"Go!" Imogen snaps, her voice cutting through the hum of the magic.

She doesn't wait for anyone to argue, grabbing Titus' arm to help him up. Ensley quickly moves in, supporting him as they make their way toward the shimmering tear.

Before crossing through, Titus lifts his head, catching Talon's gaze. His face is pale, battered, bloodied, but there's fire in his eyes as he rasps, "You're a good creature, Talon. Don't let anyone tell you otherwise."

Talon gives him a sharp nod, but the gratitude in his eyes says more than words could.

Ensley's sad gaze lingers on Talon, her voice soft but full of meaning. "Thank you. For everything you've done for us. And for getting my brother back."

Then, with Titus leaning heavily on her, they step through the portal and vanish.

"Becks, Locklyn, let's go," Imogen says, waving us over. "I'll stay behind and—"

"No," Talon says, struggling to sit up. The movement looks like it costs him. "You're all going," he says, his voice firmer than it should be considering how weak he is. "Take the shards and him." He gestures toward the figure on the ground that's been all but forgotten since Talon collapsed. "Neither of them belongs in this world. Bring them back to the Society. They'll know what to do."

With her lips pressed into a tight line, Imogen hesitates for only a second before nodding. Bending down, she hefts the figure to his feet and all but drags him toward the portal. She glances back once before stepping through.

"I love you," she says to her cousin, her face fierce.

Talon nods back. "And I you. Live well."

With shining eyes, she walks through the portal and disappears.

I know I have to leave. If I don't, and soon, Talon will die. But with my eyes locked on his, I can't make my feet move.

Talon's gaze shifts over my shoulder and connects with something. "Becks," he says, asking for help, then strong hands grab me from behind.

"It's time," Becks says softly, his familiar heat seeping into me, yet doing nothing to warm me. "We have to go."

I shake my head, my world shattering around me.

I can't.

But I have to.

"Promise to protect her," Talon says to Becks.

"I won't have to," Becks answers. "We both know she can take care of herself. But I promise to be there if she ever needs me."

A weak smile crosses Talon's face. "Now you're getting it."

Becks pulls me back a step, and panic tears through me. Talon is still so weak, and we're just leaving him here.

I snap my gaze to Kade, who stands a bit off to the side. I don't know him well, but after everything that's happened, I trust him. I trust his word, and I at least need to know that when I'm gone, someone will look out for Talon.

"You'll make sure he's okay?" I plead with the Order leader.

His dark eyes soften, and he gives a firm nod. "You don't need to worry. He's one of us now."

With that, my tears only fall harder.

"Thank you. For what you've done for us, for this world," Kade says, even as Becks all but drags me toward the portal behind us. "For your sacrifice. It won't be forgotten."

I glance behind me and see we're mere feet from the portal. Two more steps and I'll be separated from Talon forever.

"Wait! Wait!" I scream, right before Becks forces me through.

He pauses, and I lock eyes with Talon, pouring everything I feel for him and everything I am into the next words.

"I love you," I say, knowing it's the last and truest thing I will ever say to him.

A smile splits his face as a single tear runs down his cheek.

"I know," he says. "I always have."

And then Becks pulls me through the portal.

Forty-Five

TALON / SIX MONTHS LATER

I'D LIKE to say the hollow ache in my chest gets a little better every day, but that would be a lie, and I don't lie to myself anymore, just everyone else. I must be getting good at it, because I no longer have to endure the concerned glances from Kade or Ares like I did in the first few months after she left. After Locklyn and the others returned to their world, my world—and I was left here.

My strength may have returned the moment she disappeared through that portal, but she took a part of me, a part of my soul, with her, a piece I'll never get back, leaving behind an emptiness I'm only now learning how to hide.

If there was ever any question about whether or not someone could live with half a soul, I now know they can. Because that's what I do every day.

But even if I can't be with her, knowing she's out there, somewhere, alive and well, living out her life . . . that's enough. Or at least, it will have to be, because that's all I'll ever get.

Do I have regrets? No . . . and yes.

I knew the risks before we ever stepped foot in the human world. Locklyn and my situation with Shadow Striker was unprecedented. Nothing like it had ever happened before, at least not in the Society's history. But based on what we knew about the dagger, Imogen and I suspected there was a very real possibility that if I went to the human world with Locklyn, what Shadow Striker had started the moment she bonded with the dagger would eventually be completed.

Every time I shared my magic with her, I knew I was gambling with my life. And I'd do it all over again, because for her, I'd risk everything without a second thought.

So no, I don't regret going with her to this different world, even though now I'm trapped in it. I don't regret sharing my magic and teaching her how to use it, because she needed that power to protect herself. I don't regret a single moment we spent together.

What I do regret is that we didn't have more time.

I'm a greedy bastard, because with her I wanted it all.

Every moment. Every touch. Every experience.

I wanted a lifetime.

But that will never be, so now I have to learn to live the rest of my life with only the memories we made, because for me, she's it. There will never be another. There isn't room inside my icy heart for anyone else.

Even a world away, she fills it completely, consuming every part of me.

Even though the thought of her in another's arms feels like a hot iron searing through my chest, I hope she loves again. I want that for her. She loved before me, deeply, so I'm hopeful there's room in her heart for someone else, because I don't want her to live like I am.

A shell. A half life, because the other half is missing.

A hand waves in front of my face, shaking me back to the present. "Yo, earth to Talon," Violet says, her mouth twisted into a sardonic grin. "Where did you just go?"

I give my head a light shake and refocus on the world around me, plastering on what I hope is a lighthearted smile.

"Nowhere," I say, and pick up a fry and pop it in my mouth, not really tasting it.

I'm at an all-night diner with some fellow Order members, including Violet, who asked to be reassigned to the NYC Order after the battle in Central Park. Grabbing a bite at three a.m., after our night shift is over, has become somewhat of a ritual of ours.

When my friends returned after Kerrim was defeated and the remains of Shadow Striker were brought back to the creature world, I decided to join the NYC Order under Kade's command. Protecting the world from things they shouldn't know about is just who I am, what I was raised to be. He tried to elevate me to second-in-command, but I turned him down, knowing I wasn't ready to take on something like that.

Kerrim is gone, but there are still repercussions from the unrest he stirred up in the small creature community in the short time he was here. Factions of creatures are no longer content to stay hidden in the human world like they have for two millennia.

I can't help but feel it's only a matter of time before the truth is revealed.

Central Park was a mess after that night. And although the Order was able to keep the barrier up throughout the battle, shielding the humans from the truth of what transpired in the park that fateful night, there was no hiding the evidence after. The park looked like a warzone, and the humans scrambled for an explanation, eventually settling on believing it was just a mass vandalization by some unknown group.

The whole park has been closed since that night, something that's never happened in Central Park's history, and the city hasn't even given a date for it to reopen.

Violet takes a long sip from her wide straw. "Mmm. I'm telling you," she says, closing her eyes to savor the lingering flavor in her mouth. "This chocolate milkshake is the best in New York. No, strike that. It's the best *ever*. Period."

My heart twists. I didn't pick this place. It's nowhere near an exact replica of Sloan's back in Everton, the diner where I first laid eyes on Locklyn, but there are enough similarities to taunt me every time we come. The vinyl booths. The sticky menus. The bold "World's Best Chocolate Milkshake" scrawled in chalk above the bar.

At first, I didn't mind coming here. It reminded me of Locklyn, and I was desperate to hold on to any part of her I could, even if it was only a memory. I could see her in my mind's eye, sitting in a booth, laughing with her friends. I remembered the way her gaze locked on to mine for the first time, full of curiosity . . . before it turned into a glare.

Now every visit feels like exposure therapy. Painful and relentless. I'm not sure how much longer I can take it.

I force a lighthearted chuckle at Violet's comment, but it comes out sounding strangled, even to my own ears. Colton and Mike barely notice, still locked in a heated debate over whether the Yankees or the Mets have the better chance of making the World Series, but Violet doesn't miss it. She sets her milkshake down, her playful smirk fading as concern shadows her gaze from across the booth from me.

"You okay?" she asks.

I shrug. "Yeah. Yeah, of course. It's just an off night. Nothing to worry about." I push the fries away, knowing I don't have the stomach for them anymore. "I think I'm going to take off. I'm beat."

She nods, but her frown deepens. As I slide out of the booth and turn, she catches my hand.

"Hey, Talon." Her voice is quiet, searching. "If something's wrong, if you're not okay, you can tell me. You know that, right?"

I've been hanging out with Violet because even though they barely met, she knew Locklyn, and for some reason that is comforting to me. She's also just a good person and has been a good friend over the months. But there are parts of myself I'm not willing to share, and this is one.

I slide my hand out of hers and dig deep. "I'm good," I lie. "Just need to get some extra sleep. I'll catch you tomorrow. I want to check out that warehouse in the Bronx where those two bodies were found. The circumstances around those deaths feels creature-related to me."

She nods, and it looks like she's about to speak again, but then her gaze catches on something behind me and her eyes widen. Her mouth opens and closes a few times; she can't seem to get words out.

I glance over my shoulder to see what has her so thunderstruck and my heart stops beating.

There's a girl standing outside the diner, a leather jacket cropped at her waist, jeans hugging her legs. Her head dips as she studies a small piece of paper in her hands.

I blink a few times, not trusting my own eyes.

This city is big enough that there are humans of all shapes and sizes running around. I've been fooled before, thinking I caught a glimpse of her, even knowing it was impossible. Just last week, I scared a poor girl half out of her mind chasing her through Chinatown, convinced it was Locklyn, only to find out it wasn't.

I know in my mind she can't be here, but my heart isn't convinced. It keeps conjuring her.

The girl glances up at the diner's glowing neon sign, her face angled just enough for me to catch the slope of her nose, the curve of her neck, the light brown, almost amber eyes.

And then the freckles, those adorable kissable freckles scattered across the bridge of her nose like tiny constellations waiting to be traced.

I'm moving before I even know I've made the decision to do so.

As I weave through the tables to the door, someone pushes their chair back in front of me and I vault over them, eliciting a round of gasps from nearby tables for being able to do a feat humans probably shouldn't be able to.

I'm usually good about tamping down my reflexes in public, which are heightened and stronger than a regular human's, but right now I don't care who sees me. I'm one second away from blasting anyone else who gets in my way with ice.

I haven't taken my eyes off Locklyn since I spotted her, too afraid she'll disappear if I so much as blink. She's pacing back and forth outside the diner, looking like she's talking to herself as I reach the entrance and swing the front door open. It slams against the brick wall beside the frame, rattling the glass and drawing a gasp from Locklyn, who startles at the sudden noise.

There's no magic involved, but it still feels like I take a direct shot of faelight to the chest when her gaze snaps up and connects with mine.

The shock on her face only lasts an instant before I hear my name tumble from her lips. Barely a whisper, but it's the sweetest thing I've heard in six months.

After my mad dash through the diner, my feet seem sealed to the ground as my eyes greedily drink her in.

Her hair's longer than I remember, thick auburn tendrils falling around her shoulders to her lower back, and there's a stunned, almost disbelieving look in her eyes that makes my chest feel too tight. I'd almost forgotten the exact color and bow of her lips that always made me want to taste them. Or the fine arch of her brows, and the faint flush that colors her cheeks when she's caught off guard.

My memory didn't do her justice. Nothing ever could.

As I stare at her, her hands fidget, gripping the edges of her jacket one moment, then shoving them in her pockets the next, like she can't quite figure out where to put the nerves.

"How are you here?" I ask, still frozen by the indecision of whether to sweep her into my arms or demand answers.

She lifts the delicate chain around her neck and holds out the pendant dangling from it. The lunacite, of course. She left with it, so she could have used it to get back. But how is she here without killing me?

"The tether?" I ask, my voice cracking with confusion.

Why am I still talking? Who cares how she's here or even if being here is killing me?

Seeing her now, I'd trade a lifetime for just a few more minutes with her. I don't want to waste another second on the *hows* or *whys*. I only want to hold her, to savor this impossible moment.

She opens her mouth to answer but I'm already moving, closing the distance between us in a heartbeat. My hands find her hips and I lift her, carrying her around the corner of the restaurant in a blur too fast for human eyes.

I press her gently against the brick wall, my gaze devouring every detail of her face before finally settling on the soft curve of her mouth.

"The tether between us, we figured out—"

"Later," I cut in, my voice rough. "That can wait. But this can't."

My mouth is on hers, coaxing, claiming, until she melts against me and responds in kind, like no time has passed at all.

Her lips part beneath mine, a soft, shuddering breath catching in her throat as her hands clutch the fabric of my shirt. It's everything I remember. Everything I've missed. Yet it feels new and raw, like a wound just starting to heal.

I pull her closer, clutching her against me as if I can fuse us back together, erase the months we spent apart, and make this moment stretch into forever. My heart pounds so hard it feels like it might break free from my chest, and I swear I can feel her pulse racing to match mine.

For a heartbeat, we're all tangled breath and lips and the desperate crush of bodies. My hands slide up her sides, rememorizing every curve, every line. She's warm and real and alive beneath my fingertips and I want this moment to last for eternity.

Then she pulls back, gasping, her eyes shining too brightly, like she's on the verge of tears.

"Talon," she whispers, her voice breaking on my name. "I wasn't sure I'd ever—"

I shake my head, cupping her face in my hands, brushing my thumbs over her cheeks. "Don't. Don't say it. You're here now."

For now, that's enough.

I lower my forehead to hers, our breaths mingling, hearts pounding in the same rhythm. I know there are questions that still need answers, but they don't matter. Not now, not when she's in my arms again, where she's always belonged.

"Freckles," I murmur, voice barely audible. The word tastes like hope and regret and everything I've been starving for.

Her fingers tremble as they brush against my jaw. "I missed you," she breathes.

I smile faintly, though my chest feels like it's caving in. "You have no idea."

And then, because I can't help myself, I kiss her again. Soft, slow, a promise stitched into every movement. I don't know how much time we have, but I'll steal every second I can.

It's a long while before I'm able to summon the willpower to pull away. As much as it kills me, I step back, forcing a sliver of space between us so I can hear what she has to say.

With her standing there, lips swollen, hair mussed from where I ran my fingers through it . . . I almost cave. Especially as she stares back at me, half stunned, half flustered, looking both adorable and impossibly sexy. A combination on her that I've never been able to resist.

Even now, I wonder if I'll need to close my eyes just to concentrate on what she's saying.

I can't stop myself from brushing the hair behind her ear, letting my fingers trace the delicate slope of her lobe.

A shudder runs through her, and I feel it, too, like a current sparking between us.

"How?" is all I can manage, but she knows exactly what I'm asking.

"Imogen," she answers softly, then takes a shaky breath, like she's trying—and failing, like I am—to slow her heart rate.

I lift an eyebrow, not having expected that answer.

"Imogen?" I repeat, and she nods.

"She found another way to sever the tether between us. The method took a while to track down, a lot of boring research, and there were some unusual ingredients we had to gather to make it work, but it did. At least I think it did, because I'm here." A nervous laugh slips out of her. "And you're still alive."

I huff out a half laugh with her. "I'm very glad about that."

"Me too," she says with a smile that dulls a moment later. "You need to know, I couldn't have done it without your mother's help," she adds quietly, her gaze watching me carefully, as if bracing for my reaction.

My mother?

The mention of her sends a sharp pain through my chest. When I fled Grimspire with Locklyn and the others, I knew it would probably be the last time I ever saw my mother. I'd come to terms with that, but hearing her brought up now hits me harder than I expected.

I love my family, but in their eyes—and in mine until Locklyn stormed into my life—the mission of the Society always came first. Before friends. Before family. Before love.

I never would have believed my mother would lift a finger to help Locklyn, an outsider who was never meant to know our secrets. My chest tightens with a quiet kind of gratitude, knowing I was wrong.

"She also granted me permission to go through a gate closer to New York City this time," Locklyn says softly.

I shake my head, stunned, speechless.

Her expression dims, just a flicker, like there's something she doesn't want to tell me. But then I watch her gather the courage, like she always does, and she presses on.

"Even though Shadow Striker is in pieces, it still holds some lingering power. We don't know if it's safe for you, or rather, for us, to be in the same world as what's left of the blade."

I nod, understanding what she's not saying outright. That I can never return to the creature world. Not while the remnants of Shadow Striker still exist.

There's a pinch of sadness at that thought, but not as much as I would have expected. Perhaps the human world has grown on me over these past few months?

Maybe, but I suspect the real reason is that it's not really the creature world I've been longing for.

It's her.

And now that she's here, standing in front of me, real and solid, I don't seem to care as much about the world and the life I left behind.

Her tongue slides over her bottom lip, wetting it, probably without even realizing it. That small, familiar gesture nearly snaps my control. I miraculously manage to hold on, because I have to know. How long do I get? How many minutes, hours, days do I have to squeeze in a lifetime's worth of moments before we're parted again?

"When do you go back?" I ask, the words rough, bracing myself for the answer I don't want to hear.

Her head tilts slightly, confusion crossing her face.

"To the creature world," I clarify. And because I can't stand not touching her, I cradle her face in my hands. "How long do I have with you?"

Understanding lights in her eyes, and she places her hand over mine, her touch grounding me, assuring me she's really there and not some figment of my imagination that's going to disappear when I blink.

"I'm not going back," she says quietly, her gaze moving between my eyes.

The words hit me like a shockwave, and I reel back, stunned.

"But your parents. Your friends. Becks. They're all back in the creature world."

"They are. And I love my parents and my friends. But they

understand my decision. They support me." She draws a breath, her eyes steady, her voice stronger. "I never really belonged in the creature world to begin with. I belong here. With you."

Her words hit me and sink deep into my soul, warming those icy places that froze over the moment she disappeared through that portal.

"So, you're staying . . . for good?" I ask, almost tentatively. I need to hear it again to believe it.

A wide, radiant smile spreads across her face, her eyes lighting up, color blooming in her cheeks, turning her from achingly beautiful to breathtakingly stunning.

She nods. "I love you. And I'm here for good."

I lean down and press my forehead against hers, overwhelmed.

"I love you too, Freckles."

The words are rough and raw in my throat, and almost lost before she wraps her arms around my neck and pulls me in for another kiss.

This one isn't born of desperation or fear that it might be our last. It's born of joy and hope for the future. The future we'll finally get to have together. And the passion we'll have a lifetime to explore.

Epilogue

LOCKLYN / ONE YEAR LATER

A YEAR.

It's been a whole year since I left everything behind. My friends, my family, the creature world, and chose to stay here, in the human world, with Talon.

It's been the best decision of my life.

Well, the second-best decision, after the one we made not quite a month ago: getting married.

It was right after a late-night patrol when we stumbled upon a human couple being attacked by vampires. We fought the vampires off, but they ultimately got away. One of the humans almost didn't make it, but after we got them to safety, Talon turned to me and asked me to marry him.

I was completely taken off guard, but he told me that life was too short to put anything on pause. He didn't want to waste another minute where I wasn't *his* in every sense of the word.

I know I'm young, and marriage is a big step, but there wasn't a single part of me that disagreed with him.

So I said, "Yes," and a day later we were married.

It was rash and impulsive, born out of the need we both felt to be connected in every way possible.

Simply put, it was us. And it was perfect. I haven't regretted a single moment since I said, "I do."

If I have any regrets, it's that I didn't do it sooner, because I quickly learned how much I loved living with Talon and having twenty-four-seven access to him, and *all* the perks that come with it.

Now we live in a cozy loft tucked high in an old brick building in downtown New York. It's nothing fancy. Creaky floors, an old radiator that rattles, and a fire escape that's seen better days. But it's ours.

The space feels like home in a way no other place ever could. It's cluttered with books, half-empty mugs, and the scent of Talon's coffee in the mornings. It's filled with laughter, shared secrets, and a love that neither of us ever saw coming.

And sure, we've had our challenges. Missing friends and loved ones and adjusting to human life after everything we've been through hasn't exactly been easy, but we've made it work. Together.

Which is why mornings like this, lazy, quiet, wrapped in sheets and each other, feel like stolen treasures.

Talon's warm body is pressed against mine, his arm heavy around my waist, the steady rise and fall of his chest lulling me into that hazy, half-asleep state where time doesn't exist. His breath brushes my temple and I smile, content and full in a way I never thought possible.

At least, until someone starts banging on the front door like the world's about to end.

I groan and burrow deeper into the blankets. Talon mutters a curse under his breath, his voice thick with sleep.

"I'll tell whoever it is to sod off," he says, and then gives me a kiss on the nose and rolls out of bed, the cool morning air making me shiver in his absence.

I chuckle, feeling sorry for whoever's on the other side of the door. They're about to come face-to-face with a very grumpy ice dragon.

As Talon pads across the floor in his bare feet, I slip from the bed and head to the kitchen. Now that I'm up, I know I won't be able to fall back asleep. I might as well make myself a cup of coffee.

Before Talon even reaches the door, whoever is on the other side starts banging again, louder this time.

"I swear to the Creator," I hear my husband grumble, "I'm going to turn whoever interrupted our morning into a giant ice sculpture if they don't—"

His words cut off abruptly, and the sudden silence makes my skin prickle.

When I don't hear anything else, I pop my head around the corner, curiosity and unease tangling in my gut.

Talon stands in front of the open door, his body tense, posture rigid. It immediately puts me on edge.

Something's wrong.

"Talon, who's—?" My own words freeze in my throat as Talon steps aside, revealing the person who had been pounding on our door.

The empty coffee mug slips from my fingers, crashing to the floor and shattering on impact. I hardly notice.

It's been a year, and in that time my best friend has changed. His hair is longer, falling in loose waves around his face. A faint stubble dusts his jaw, accentuating the sharper angles that have erased the last traces of boyishness.

But even with the changes, I would never mistake him for anyone else.

"Becks," I whisper, my heart hammering in my chest.

He stares at me, and I wouldn't call the look in his eyes hard, exactly, but it's not soft or welcoming either.

"Can I come in?" he asks, his gaze cutting to Talon.

Talon steps aside without a word, letting him in.

I watch Becks standing almost awkwardly in our loft, a strange mixture of familiarity and disbelief tugging at my chest.

My mind whirls as I try to piece together how he's here—in the human world. When I left the creature world, there was no other known lunacite capable of opening a gate. But he must have found a way, somehow, because he's standing not ten feet away from me.

"Hey, Lock," he says, dipping his head a little, a small half smile tugging at his lips. One that makes my heart ache.

Without thinking, I leap over the shattered ceramic at my feet and crash into him, wrapping my arms around his middle in a hug so tight I can feel the steady thrum of his heartbeat beneath my cheek.

He catches me easily, his arms winding around my back, absorbing the full weight of my body without hesitation. The familiar warmth of his skin, that signature fire-dragon heat, sinks into me, a reminder of home and the comfort I didn't know I'd missed until now.

"Okay, okay," he says on a chuckle, the gentle rumble of it wrapping around me like a blanket. "Squeeze any tighter and you're going to crack a rib."

"Good thing you're a fast healer, then," I reply with a grin, though I force myself to loosen my grip and step back.

When I glance up at him, the lighthearted curve of his mouth fades, and something tightens in my chest. The shift in his expression to serious and determined sends a pit of dread curling in my stomach.

"We need to talk," he says, his gaze darting briefly to Talon as if to make it clear this isn't just for me, but for both of us.

I nod, swallowing down the nerves tightening my throat, and gesture to the small seating area off to the side. Talon settles next to me on the loveseat, a silent wall of support at my side, while Becks lowers himself into the armchair across from us.

Talon reaches for my hand and rests it on his knee, giving it a light squeeze. A subtle reminder. *I'm here. I've got you.*

I don't know what Becks is about to say, but the weight in his eyes tells me this is just the beginning. His gaze drops to our clasped hands, lingering on the gold band on my left ring finger, before flicking back up to my face. His expression is utterly unreadable in a way that makes my heart ache.

Becks never used to hide his feelings from me. But that was then. Things are different now, and as much as I hate it, I have to accept it. The most important thing right now is that it's clear he's here for a reason, and we need to know what that is.

"What are you doing here?" I ask. I almost add, *How are you here?* but the look on his face tells me the *how* isn't the most important question right now.

Becks takes a slow, steadying breath before he says, "We have a problem."

I glance at Talon beside me, and he squeezes my hand again.

"What's wrong?" I ask.

"That's just it," Becks says. "We were wrong. About the prophecy. About you." His gaze holds mine. "About a lot of things."

"What do you mean?" Talon asks, his voice sharp as he leans forward.

Becks' gaze shifts to Talon, then back to me. "The prophecy wasn't about Kerrim like we thought. It was about the demon."

A cold prickle races down my spine. My pulse stutters.

"What demon?" I ask, my stomach dropping like a stone.

"The one who created Shadow Striker," Becks answers. "We didn't know it, but the demon had been trapped in the dagger, along with the Vampire King, since Lucian defeated it two millennia ago. That is, until the night you went up against Kerrim. Your sacrifice, your blood, it released both of them from their prison. The Vampire King . . . and the demon he made a bargain with all that time ago."

I gasp as the memory crashes back—the black smoke erupting from Shadow Striker, the way it twisted and spiraled into the night, leaving behind an oppressive, dark energy that seeped into my bones.

"How do you know all this?" Talon asks, his tone clipped, as I struggle to catch my breath.

Becks hesitates, a flash of emotion crosses his face, guilt maybe, or something else, before he wipes it away. "The Vampire King told me," he says.

"He's talking?" I ask, my voice tight with disbelief.

When we brought the Vampire King's emaciated body back to the creature world, he was barely clinging to life. The Society took custody of him, but in the months I spent searching for a way to sever the tether between Talon and me before leaving the creature world, he hadn't improved much. He was half comatose most of the time, and when he did speak, it was nonsense at best. Whatever power he'd once held, years trapped in the dagger had stripped it away. The last time I saw him, he'd been a shell of the creature he once was.

Becks nods, running a hand through his hair. A familiar tell when he's nervous.

"That, and more," he says.

I lean forward, dread coiling tight in my chest. "What else is it?"

Becks draws in a breath, and the words he says next hit like a wrecking ball.

"The demon isn't just free, it's hunting for the one mentioned in the prophecy."

Talon's grip tightens on my hand, the air around us dropping a few degrees as his protective instincts flare to life.

But Becks isn't finished. The next words he speaks change everything.

"And that's not you. The demon's looking for your sister. It's looking for your twin."

Please Write a Review

REVIEW.KINGDOMOFCHAOSBOOK.COM

Dear friend,

Thank you for reading! If you enjoyed this book, please take a few moments to rate and review it so that others might decide to read my books. Thank you!

~Julie

http://Review.KingdomOfChaosBook.com

Read the epic conclusion in:

BOOK THREE

QUEEN OF CHAOS

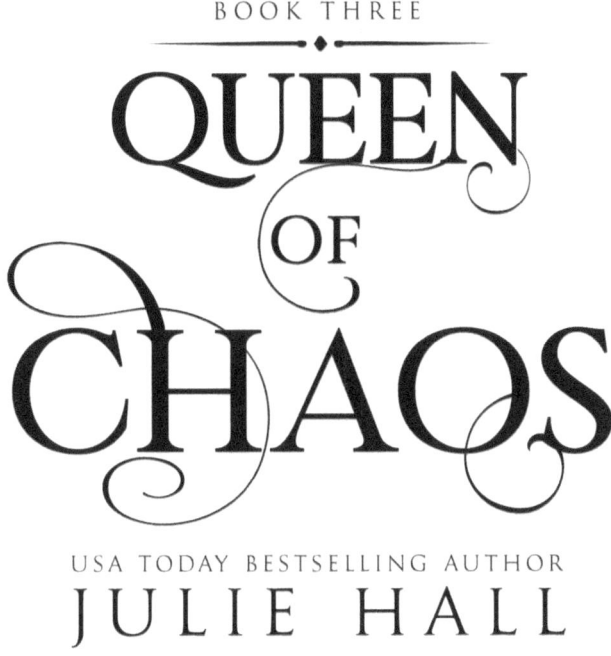

USA TODAY BESTSELLING AUTHOR

JULIE HALL

www.QueenOfChaosBook.com

Acknowledgments

Every book is its own kind of chaos, and *Kingdom of Chaos* was no exception. I am endlessly grateful to the people who helped me turn this whirlwind of ideas into the story you now hold in your hands, whether you are reading the ebook, paperback, hardcover, audiobook, or a limited deluxe edition.

First, to my husband, Lucas. Thank you not only for your constant love and encouragement, but for rolling up your sleeves and tackling the wild ride of creating a deluxe edition right beside me. From brainstorming and late-night packaging marathons to troubleshooting problems I did not even have the brain space to solve, you have been my partner through it all. This story and the many beautiful formats it lives in would not exist without your patience, creativity, and sheer determination.

To my incredible PAs, Kelly and Heidi. Kelly, thank you for your years of support and for laying such a strong foundation for me to build on. Heidi, thank you for stepping in with so much heart and energy. I am so excited for what is ahead with you by my side.

To my editorial dream team: Lee, your sharp insights and steady guidance push me to be a better writer with every draft. Janelle and Priscila, thank you for combing through pages with such care and precision, catching all the little things that make the story shine brighter.

To my agents, Flavia and Meire at Bookcase Literary Agency, thank you for believing in me and this story, and for championing my work with such dedication. I am so grateful to have you both in my corner.

The visual magic of this series belongs to so many talented artists. Irene, Damián, Sasha, Nadia, Maya, Koti, Vivxor, and Grace you have once again brought characters and scenes to life in breathtaking ways. To Maria and K.D., thank you for another stunning cover that I am proud to showcase.

To my Chaos Crew, you made spreading the word about this release fun, exciting, and so much less overwhelming. Thank you for your passion, your hype, and for shouting about this book louder than I ever could on my own. And to all my readers, thank you for your support, your excitement, and for embracing this series so wholeheartedly. I am both humbled and overjoyed by the way *Creatures of Chaos* was received. I also owe you an apology for the cliffhanger I left you with in that book. Thank you for coming back for more.

Finally, to my children, both furry and otherwise, Ashtyn, Coco, and Moose, thank you for your love, your chaos, and the daily reminders of what really matters. You make life infinitely brighter.

The Author

JULIE HALL

Julie Hall is a *USA Today* bestselling, multiple award-winning author. Before diving into the world of publishing, she was a publicist and marketer for Sony, Summit Entertainment, Paramount, The Weinstein Company, and the National Geographic Channel.

Now, she crafts addictive action-packed fantasy stories that leave readers with epic book hangovers. Julie's books have been translated to four languages and won or were finalists in over 20 national and international awards.

Julie currently lives in Colorado with her four favorite people–her husband, daughter, and two fur babies.

Website:
JulieHallAuthor.com

Join the Fan Club:
facebook.com/groups/juliehall

Get exclusive updates by email:
JulieHallAuthor.com/newsletter

Let's Connect:

amazon.com/author/julieghall
facebook.com/JulieHallAuthor
instagram.com/Julie.Hall.Author
tiktok.com/@juliehallauthor
goodreads.com/JulieHallAuthor
youtube.com/JulieHallAuthor

Get Updates

JOIN MY EMAIL NEWSLETTER

Join my email newsletter and you'll be notified of new books, get exclusive bonus scenes, sneak peeks, ridiculous videos, and you'll be eligible for special giveaways. Occasionally, you will see puppies. 🐶

JulieHallAuthor.com/newsletter

I respect your privacy. No spam.

Unsubscribe anytime. 🩶

The Fan Club
ON FACEBOOK

If you love my books, I invite you to get involved by joining my fan club. You'll get exclusive sneak peeks before anyone else, private giveaways, and sometimes I even give out free puppies (#joking-notjoking).

You'll get to know other passionate readers like you, and you'll get to know me better too! It'll be fun!

facebook.com/groups/juliehall

See you in there!
~ Julie

Books by Julie Hall

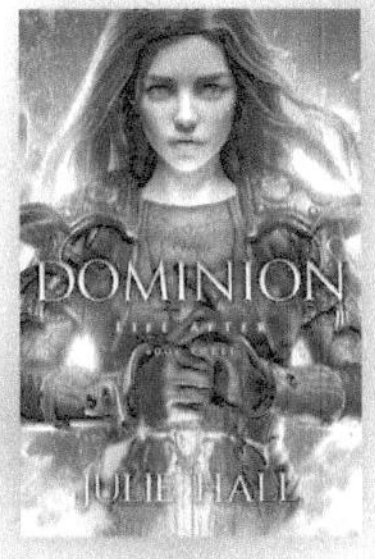

www.JulieHallAuthor.com

Audiobooks

AUDIO.JULIEHALLAUTHOR.COM

Julie's books are also available as audiobooks!

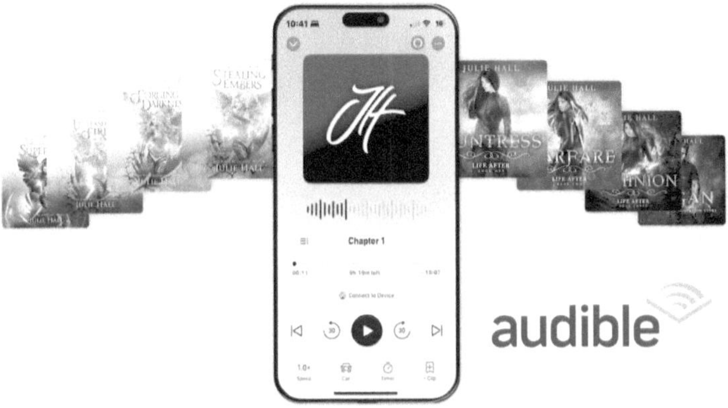

www.ingramcontent.com/pod-product-compliance
Lightning Source LLC
Chambersburg PA
CBHW021725190726
48289CB00008B/2696